RANDOM HOUSE · NEW YORK

christmas
THE NEW

christmas at THE NEW YORKER

stories, poems, humor, and art

FROM THE EDITORS OF **THE NEW YORKER**

FOREWORD BY **JOHN UPDIKE**

All rights reserved under International and Pan-American Copyright Conventions.
Published in the United States by Random House, an imprint of The Random
House Publishing Group, a division of Random House, Inc., New York, and
simultaneously in Canada by Random House of Canada Limited, Toronto.

RANDOM HOUSE and colophon are registered trademarks of Random House, Inc.

All the pieces in this collection were originally published in *The New Yorker*.
The publication date of each piece is given at the end of the piece.

LIBRARY OF CONGRESS CATALOGING-IN-PUBLICATION DATA
Christmas at The New Yorker : stories, poems, humor, and art.
    p.   cm.
  ISBN 1-4000-6140-7
    1. Christmas—Literary collections.   2. Christmas—New York (State)—
New York.   3. New York (N.Y.)—Literary collections.   4. American literature—
20th century.   5. Christmas in art.   I. New Yorker (New York, N.Y. : 1925)
PS509.C56C517   2004
810.8'0334—dc21   2003046931

Printed in the United States of America on acid-free paper

Random House website address: www.atrandom.com

987654321

FIRST EDITION

BOOK DESIGN BY CASEY HAMPTON

CONTENTS

and Talk of the Town by Russell Maloney, Harold Ross, Charles Noble
Constance Feeley, Robert A. Simon, and E. J. Kahn, Jr.

christmas carols

drawings

FOREWORD

JOHN UPDIKE

New York City is the capital of the American Christmas. The Puritan settlements to the north banned the holiday as Popish and pagan; and so it was, descended from the ancient Roman solstitial Saturnalia. But mercantile, diverse Nieuw Amsterdam—not just Dutch fur traders but French-speaking Protestant Walloons; arrivals from Ireland, Spain, Portugal, and Poland; African slaves, twenty-three Sephardic Jews (as of 1654); a Danish sea-captain, Jonas Bronck, whose plantation, known as the Broncks, gave its name to a borough; and, in the alarmed words of Peter Stuyvesant's adviser the Calvinist minister Johannes Megapolensis, "Papists, Mennonites, and Lutherans among the Dutch"—celebrated two separate winter occasions with gift-giving. St. Nicholas Day, on December 6th, involved Santa Claus and goodies left in good children's wooden shoes; New Year's Day was the traditional Dutch day for adult presents and ceremonial calls.

When the English took over, in 1664, they brought with them an Anglican toleration of customs frowned upon by the stricter Reformed churches. St. Nicholas survived the eighteenth century and by the early nineteenth his day had merged with the English Christmas. In 1823, a New Yorker, the Bible scholar Clement Clarke Moore (who also donated the land for the General Theological Seminary of the Episcopal Church), published the poem, beginning "'Twas the night before Christmas," that gave Christmas its American mythos. The most famous American short story about the holiday, O. Henry's "The Gift of the Magi," was composed by an adopted New Yorker and concerns two humble, striving, big-hearted members of the city's then population of four million; it appeared in the New York *World* in 1905, and in the author's 1906 collection "The Four Million." The best-known American Christmas movie, "Miracle on 34th Street" (1947), takes place in and around Macy's, and was partly shot on location.

In the Yuletide season, which now begins before Halloween and extends through many a worried January review of consumer shopping performance, Manhattan becomes one big bauble—a towering mass of glowing boxes, a cascade of elaborate window displays, an island gaily tied with ribbons called, north-south, avenues and, east-west, streets. The Empire State Building glows red and green; St. Patrick's Cathedral gazes toward Rockefeller Center's giant Christmas tree while rubbing its left shoulder against Saks Fifth Avenue, one of the enduring venues of spectacular Christmas windows. Throughout America, Main Street has run to the suburbs and hidden in the malls, but New York still wears Christmas on its sleeve. Here Salvation Army bell-ringers still tend charity's tripodded pot and chestnuts roast on street vendors' grills. Here Santa Claus sports, behind his white beard, many a subarctic complexion.

So it is no wonder that *The New Yorker,* a publication devoted since 1925 to the gala spirit of its eponymous metropolis, has generously partaken, year after year, of Christmas cheer. The writer of this preface, when a boy, intimately associated the magazine with the season, since his list for Santa usually included one of the *New Yorker* cartoon anthologies that, in the early decades of the magazine's existence, Doubleday and Random House and Simon & Schuster regularly offered book buyers. The glossy paper of these droll and sophisticated albums gathered sheen from the snow (or hopes of snow) outside the living-room windows; the scent of the fresh binding glue mingled with the resin of the family Christmas tree; the elegance of the drawings glittered like the paper star topping the tree. Those big slim volumes, either devoted to an individual cartoonist—Arno, Addams, Cobean, Robert Day, George Price, Carl Rose—or culled from a few years of the magazine's run, endure on my shelves, sixty years later, as still-precious remembrances of otherwise irrecoverable Christmases past.

But the book in your hands contains more than cartoons. It samples *The New Yorker*'s breadth of offerings—covers, fiction, poetry, humor, reminiscence, Talk of the Town, even spot drawings and newsbreaks—as it basked in the Christmas glow from 1925 (Rea Irvin, showing a maharaja receiving an elaborately presented necktie) to 2002 (Roz Chast, showing Santa being nagged by his elves). The editors have sifted assiduously, retrieving the tiniest bright bit of tinsel along with paper chains, cranberry festoons, papiermâché angels, and hand-painted glass balls the size of emu eggs. Here you will find James Thurber rewriting Clement Moore's poem in the voice of Hemingway (1927); S. J. Perelman putting Santa's workshop onstage in the manner of Clifford Odets (1936); William Cox redoing "The Gift of the Magi" for hippies (1967); Max Hill remembering a not totally unmerry Christmas in a Japanese prison (1942); and Alice Munro evoking, even more fondly, a season of girlhood spent gutting Christmas turkeys in Ontario (1980). Here are poems by Karl Shapiro and Phyllis McGinley, Adrienne Rich and Ogden Nash, James Dickey and Calvin Trillin and others, in mood reverent or ir-, in form rhymed or un-, in import pro-Christmas or anti-. "Greetings, Friends!," of which four rollicking examples are included, is, of course, the annual seasonal salute, in rhymed couplets of festive breeziness, that *The New Yorker* has traditionally addressed to its friends and some celebrities of the day; the first was composed by Frank Sullivan in 1932 and his last in 1974; from 1976 until recently the custom has been carried on, in kindred metrics and jubilo, by Roger Angell.

Younger readers who know the opening paragraphs of The Talk of the Town, once called Notes and Comment, only as political editorials of a pondered weight, should be aware that this section began and long continued as a grab bag of humorous oddments, a short-winded gallimaufry of mild, resolutely apolitical jests and grimaces. It was, above all, E. B. White who broadened and deepened the department; no one has ever been better at infusing a light, even facetious tone with graver notes from the inner man and the larger world. His Notes and Comment of Christmas, 1944, is a wartime threnody; dozens of battles and thousands of deaths are wrapped into a central conceit, the conquered terrains of global war as Christmas presents to us, the American people. The Norman coast, Saipan, Guam, Leghorn, the Alban Hills, a forest south of Aachen, and many other hard-won territories come "not wrapped as gifts (there was no time to wrap them), but you will find them under the lighted tree with the other presents."

The magazine's covers ring the first chime and get our holiday juices flowing. Butlers, those anachronistic representatives of well-financed domestic order, figure in some of the most memorable—in 1940, Helen E. Hokinson's servitor lends a dignified finger to his harried mistress's ribbontying; that same December, Robert Day's man, in white hair and muffler, smartly brings a blazing plum pudding to an English bomb shelter; eight years later, Peter Arno's monumental old retainer ignites *his* plum-pudding brandy with a cigarette lighter. Santas—Santa being dressed by his valet, Santa punching a time clock, Santa sitting alone and rueful in a cafeteria or sitting sleek and dapper at a corporation desk where the Naughty stack towers above the Nice—recur, forming a jigsaw puzzle here and a dog's uncomfortable costume there and, in a subway car, a veritable mob of masquerading misfits, caught red-suited by George Price's scratchy pen. Curiously, this was Price's only cover, though his raffish cartoons were legion; two other prolific artists, Ralph Barton and Edward Gorey, also seized the occasion of Christmas for their solo *New Yorker* covers. Whereas Charles Addams, both as cover artist and as cartoonist, couldn't get enough of the holiday, unveiling a sinister side to it usually suppressed.

Suicides, notoriously, rise in the Christmas season; its call for rejoicing and universal good will stresses the human psyche in ways faithfully recorded by the seismograph of fiction. "Christmas is a kids' gag," one of John McNulty's barflies tells another in a vignette of 1944. For the characters in Sally Benson's "Spirit of Christmas" and Peter De Vries's "Flesh and the Devil," the holiday stirs up romantic sparks and marital awkwardness. For those in Emily Hahn's "No Santa Claus" and Richard Ford's "Crèche," the celebrative muddle borders on the noir. Frank O'Connor's "Christmas Morning" ends with this grim realization by the young hero: "I knew there was no Santa Claus flying over the rooftops with his reindeer and his red coat—there was only my mother trying to scrape together a few pence from the housekeeping money that my father gave her. I knew that he was mean and common and a drunkard, and that she had been relying on me to study and rescue her from the misery which threatened to engulf her." With the writer's inimitable hyperbole, John Cheever's "Christmas Is a Sad Season for the Poor" proposes that the city's lower echelons, beginning with elevator operators, are overwhelmed by a surfeit of gifts, rich and poor all "bound, one to another, in licentious benevolence." Licentious benevolence!

Christmas light can be a cruel light. But in William Maxwell's "Homecoming" and Vladimir Nabokov's "Christmas" it shines in two death-scarred households, as an electrical connection is mended and an old cocoon gives birth. Ken Kesey and H. L. Mencken see a measure of cheer brought to Skid Row. In Patrick Chamoiseau's Martinique, a cherished pig becomes gifts for many; in J. F. Powers' Minnesota, a peripatetic priest finds "Christmas as it was celebrated nowadays still pretty much to his liking" and compares the season's agile, hard-breathing merchants to the tumbler who performed acrobatics as an offering to Our Lady; in the Pennsylvania of John O'Hara and Linda Grace Hoyer, poetry and memory shed grace on a rather obligatory social whirl. To get through the year's shortest, darkest days, we grasp at straws. The holiday offers little resistance to the secular; its hustle blends, in New York, with the all-year hustle. There is something in the Christmas story for everyone—the baby in the manger for innocents, the sheep and the oxen for animal lovers, Joseph for natural bystanders, the Magi for diversity and high fashion, the Star for astrophysicists. The whole panorama sprouted from rather few Biblical verses: the Virgin Birth and the wise men appear in Matthew, the Annunciation and the shepherds and angels and the manger in Luke. If crèches, haloes, and bended knees have been phased out of department-store windows, that still leaves Frosty the Snowman and Rudolph the Red-Nosed Reindeer, Tiny Tim and sleigh riders from Knickerbocker days, with top hats and ermine muffs. The tree with pagan roots continues to accept grafts.

The prose and poetry and art assembled here range widely in setting and tone, but for this sentimental reader it kept coming home to an older, gentler, more credulous New York, a pre-Lever House city of brick and granite, a pre-television city that lived for parties, a city where a wreath on an apartment door and a tree in a brownstone window came and went as naturally as jonquils in the spring and yellow ginkgo leaves in the fall. The oldest poem here reports from 1926:

> When bankers quote the Golden Rule,
>   And visitors enjoyment seek,
> And lads and maids are home from school,
>   New York's engulfed in Christmas week.

A city, in short, *drenched* in Christmas, which is the way I think of New York in December, and the way it exists—rejoice!—in these pages.

the spirit of
GIVING

MORE OF A SURPRISE

SALLY BENSON

Just after Thanksgiving Day every year, Jim and Rhoda Huston made out their Christmas lists. The lists were for each other and were nicely balanced, combining a feeling for the practical with Yuletide abandon. For instance, one of the items on Mrs. Huston's list might be "Pigskin gloves—size 6½," a good, sensible suggestion, but it would be followed by a bit of frivolity, such as "Bath salts—something spicy."

Some years ago, Mr. Huston had made the grave mistake of picking out things from Rhoda's list that he thought she really needed and he had lived to regret it. It was the Christmas she had dutifully supplied the three pairs of pajamas, no buttons, that he had asked for but had also added six boxes of tobacco from Dunhill's so that he could blend his own pipe mixture. Since then she had hammered away at the idea that while it was lovely to get the presents one needed, it was even lovelier to be surprised with some foolish little thing. Jim Huston tried to explain that if Christmas presents were to be surprises, there wasn't much use in their making out lists, but he couldn't get Rhoda to understand. "I'd rather be surprised than anything," she told him. "And it's a perfectly simple thing to be able to do to anybody. Just let yourself go."

This year, the advertising firm Jim Huston worked for gave all its employees a bonus, and when his bonus check was sent in to him early in December and he saw that it was for six hundred dollars, he was going to telephone Rhoda right away about it when a thought struck him, and he decided that he would spend the whole amount on one staggering Christmas present for her. He took the list she had made for him out of his pocket and read it. She had written, "Set of dishes—service for four—Altman's—$5.95—plenty good enough. Barbizon slips—peach—size 36. Lipstick—*your* choice. Bath towels—like the ones we have. A scarf—something *gay*. 6 small glasses—the kind for tomato juice. Heart-shaped sachet—smallest size. Bath soap—*luxurious*. Bridge-table cover—maroon. Breakfast tray, if not too much—I *long* for one. Sweater—pullover—better get size 38, as apt to run small."

He looked at the bonus check and, taking Rhoda's list he tore it into fine pieces. Then he rang for Miss Thompson, his secretary, told her that he would not be back at the office until three, and, putting on his hat and coat, started out. For a while he wandered up Fifth Avenue, stopping to stare at the displays in the store windows. It was the sight of a fur coat in Gunther's window that made him realize that he had heard Rhoda complain about her nutria coat, which she had worn every winter for the last ten years, and he walked bravely in. An hour later, somewhat staggered at the price of furs, he paid most of his bonus check for a soft, pretty squirrel coat.

"I'll pick it up the Saturday before Christmas," he told the salesgirl. "I don't want it delivered. It's a surprise."

"And a wonderful one," she said.

His face lit up and he began to smile. "I just had an idea," he said. "You haven't an old fur of some sort around here, have you? I mean, it would be pretty funny if I got an old piece of fur, something like an old neckpiece, and had that wrapped up, wouldn't it? Then she'd think that's what she was getting and then I'd spring the coat on her later. I mean, fool her, sort of."

"I see," the girl said. "I'm afraid we haven't anything. You might try a thrift shop. They have second-hand furs."

When Jim went back to his office, he carried with him a slightly worn white rabbit-fur square, for which he had paid fifteen dollars. He showed it to Miss Thompson, explaining the joke to her and laughing uproariously. "And I want you," he said, "to wrap it up. Do a job on it. Make it look like something. You know, something I'd taken pains about."

He smiled every time he thought about it the rest of the afternoon, and when he went home that night, he was ready for the buildup. He assumed a gloomy air, and, during dinner, he mentioned the fact that the bonus he'd sort of counted on hadn't materialized. "We're not getting one," he said.

"Isn't that mean!" Rhoda said.

He sighed. "Worse than that," he said. "I was counting on it for your Christmas. I've bought a lot more War Bonds than I could afford. You'll have a pretty slim Christmas, I'm afraid."

"Oh, that's all right," Rhoda said. "Of course, I always sort of save ahead for your Christmas. I always *know* what I have to spend ahead of time."

"That's what I should have done," he said contritely.

"The things on my list won't amount to much," Rhoda said.

"I was going to surprise you this year, though," he said.

"And I'm sure you will," she said brightly.

~~~

In the days that followed, Rhoda was more than helpful with small, extra suggestions. She told Jim that nothing made her feel as gay as a pretty plant on Christmas Day—a colorful one. She mentioned the fact that small, Shocking-pink makeup cases could be had for as little as one dollar. She had seen, she said, some enchanting ashtrays, trimmed with gold dots, that were

"Come in, come in, whoever you are."

seventy-four cents. "I don't know when I've run across so many darling little things, things I'd never think of buying for myself, and for practically nothing, if a person takes the time to *shop* for them," she said.

Every time she mentioned Christmas, Jim let himself appear to be sunk in gloom. As the holiday approached, she began to watch him to see if he brought in any packages when he came home at night, and she made a great point of telling him to keep out of the hall closet, where she had hidden the few things she had bought for him. On the Saturday before Christmas, he brought the fur coat home and left it with the superintendent of the building, who promised to keep it in a safe place. Jim then went happily up to his apartment, carrying the white rabbit-fur square, which was wrapped magnificently.

He set the package down on the hall table and kissed Rhoda, who pretended that she hadn't even noticed that he had a package. And later in the evening, she said, "Do you know, darling, that I was just sitting here wishing that I hadn't bought you just a lot of *stuff*. I was wishing I'd just put all my efforts on *one* thing. Something you really wanted. I think we've always made a mistake in getting too many small things and never anything really important."

Jim thought he could never keep his face straight.

Christmas Eve, Rhoda carried six packages from the hall closet and arranged them under the tree with the presents from his family and hers. Jim took the elegant parcel that Miss Thompson had wrapped and, sighing, laid it with the others. "Doesn't look like much, does it?" he asked.

"Darling," she answered, "I'm sure it's lovely."

That night Rhoda couldn't go to sleep. She lay awake in the dark trying to imagine what Jim had bought her. It was not jewelry, she decided, because it was too big. She found it hard to convince herself that if Jim had bought her only one thing, it must be something really handsome. For one thing, he didn't act as though he were satisfied with it himself, and, thinking about him, she reached over and touched him protectively on the shoulder.

~~~

Rhoda was embarrassed for Jim Christmas morning. Usually they came out about even on their gifts, and it had been their custom to take turns opening their presents, starting off with the inconsequential ones and saving the best ones until the last. This day, as she handed him package after package, she had to sit there, falsely gay, while he unwrapped the things she had bought him. She tried to make it less obvious by opening some of the things she had received from her family, but she was glad when they got to the last presents—the monogrammed briefcase she had bought him and the gift he handed her. She waited until he had admired the briefcase, and then she sat, his present to her in her lap.

"I never saw anything so beautifully wrapped," she said.

"Go on and open it," Jim said.

She turned it over, patting at the large red satin bow. "Really, darling," she said, "I just like to sit here and look at the outside of it. It's so *pretty.*"

"I hope you'll like it," Jim said. "But I'm afraid . . ."

"Of course I'll like it," she said.

"Well, open it," he repeated.

Reluctantly, she untied the bow and, taking the ribbon off, she smoothed it, wound it into a ball, and laid it carefully on the table. "I'm going to save that lovely ribbon," she said. "And I'm going to save the lovely paper, too."

She folded the paper and set it on the table with the ribbon. She read the card, "Merry Christmas to my best girl."

Then she opened the box. For a moment she had no idea what it was, and she held the fur square in her hands, torn with emotion. "I must be brave," she thought, and she remembered all sorts of things like the women of Russia and England and that there was a war on and that Jim had not got his bonus. She glanced quickly at Jim and saw that his face looked red, as though it were burning, and, so that he need never feel a sense of shame, she gave a cry of delight.

"Jim!" she said. She got up and threw her arms around him, kissing him again and again. "Jim! It's enchanting!"

"It's to wear around your neck," he said.

"Of course it's to wear around my neck!" She ran toward the mirror that hung over the fireplace and tucked the bit of fur around her throat. It was bulky and had a gray look.

"There!" she exclaimed triumphantly. "Did you ever see anything so sweet? I can wear it in the evening under my evening wrap, and I can wear it, well, just with anything!"

Jim stared at her. Her face glowed with excitement and happiness. She gave the fur a little pull and it somehow settled into place. He spoke slowly. "Do you like it?"

"*Like* it!" she repeated. "I *adore* it. It's so *smart!* There's nothing smarter than a touch of white. You couldn't have given me anything I loved as much. Not if you'd thought a million years!"

"Look," he said. "You don't really like it, do you?"

"Darling," she cried, "I love it! Summer ermine! And in a square! Not one of those dull stoles! Just a darling little square, and not *too* little but with the most *utter* elegance!"

"I didn't think you'd like it," he said. "I thought you'd be disappointed."

She turned away from the mirror and almost danced toward him. "Jim," she said, "how could you think that? Do you want to know what I think, what I truly think? Well, I think it's the nicest and most personal thing you ever thought of giving me. Wait until I telephone Mother!"

"She won't think it's so hot," Jim said.

"Oh, she won't, won't she?" Rhoda asked. "Just wait!"

Holding the fur around her neck lovingly, she picked up the telephone and dialled her mother's number. Jim sat staring at her. Rhoda, he thought, wasn't putting on any act. Remembering how childish she had been about hinting for inexpensive presents, he was sure she wasn't just putting on an act. He sat listening, appalled, as she talked to her mother.

"And you know how most men get big, gobby things," he heard her say. "Well, darling, you should see this charming little thing. It's without doubt the smartest idea I ever heard of. I never would have thought of it, but Jim did."

She talked a long time to her mother and her adjectives were all superlatives. Jim wanted to get up from the chair, he wanted to go down and get her fur coat, her really wonderful present, from the superintendent, but he couldn't move.

When she finished talking to her mother, she came over and sat on the arm of his chair and put her arm around his shoulders. "Darling," she said. "My *clever* darling."

"Why, Rhoda," he said, "that thing's just rabbit."

"Rabbit!" she said. "Summer ermine! Darling, that isn't the point. The point is that I love it. It's so—well, it's not vulgar or anything. It's just *right.*"

Jim got up suddenly and went out, while she looked after him uncomprehendingly. He came back in a few minutes, carrying a large package, and laid it on her lap. He took the fur square from her neck and threw it on the table with a savage gesture.

"What is it?" she asked. "What's this?"

"Open it," he said angrily. "Just open it, that's all I ask."

He cut the string from the parcel with his pocketknife and helped her take the paper off. She opened the box and stared at the coat.

"Well," he said. "What do you think of it?"

"A fur coat," she said. "A fur coat."

He stood back uneasily and looked down at her. "Well," he said, "what do you think of it? Can't you say something."

"A fur coat," she said. "It's *nice.*" 1944

"I've been thinking. This year, instead of giving everything away,
why don't we charge a little something?"

SCHOOLBOY

SALLY BENSON

By eight o'clock in the morning, the boys in Room 1-B had almost finished trimming the Christmas tree they had bought for Mr. Parsons. Every master in St. Benedict's School, in the East Eighties, had his own tree, and although it was an established custom and not a surprise at all, the boys made a practice of hiding the trees on the roof and getting to school as early as six in the morning on the last day before the holidays, so as to have the trees set up and trimmed before the masters arrived. This year, Cecil Warren had been in charge of the Tree Fund and the Decoration Fund for 1-B, not because he was popular but because it was generally agreed that he was very good at getting money out of people. He was ruthless about it. He didn't even mind mentioning money, although the other boys at St. Benedict's understood that money was something to be mentioned carelessly, if at all. He came right out and called it money, or cash, or dough, and the way he said it made the other boys feel uncomfortable. It was like calling a boy by his first name. St. Benedict's boys were never called by their first names.

Warren had set about collecting the money in a businesslike manner. He had made an alphabetical list of the boys' names and, by dunning them, had collected a dollar from every boy in the class, a total of fifteen dollars. His method had been painful, but it was generally agreed that the result was nothing short of magnificent, as the 1-B tree was the largest and most expensive one to be carried down from the roof that morning. In fact, it was so much handsomer than the other trees that Lockwood and Brewster even wondered if it wasn't too fine. Lockwood and Brewster were the committee in charge of buying the tree and the decorations. Lockwood had flawless taste, and Brewster was strong enough to carry the tree up the four flights to the roof, carry it down again to the classroom, and set it up on the stand in the corner by the blackboard. Its branches sagging under the weight of ornaments, tinsel, and lights, the tree seemed—to Lockwood, at least—a trifle ostentatious. He stepped back and looked at it. "Well, there it is," he said. "You don't think it's too . . ."

"I know what you mean," Brewster said quickly. "I was sort of thinking the same thing myself."

"Precisely," Lockwood said. "It doesn't seem quite—well, you know—to have Mr. Parsons have a larger tree than Captain Foster." Captain Foster was the headmaster.

"Of course, it's Mr. Parsons' first Christmas here, and that might sort of explain it away," Brewster said.

Lockwood looked pained. "The very reason," he said, "*not* to make anything special of it. I mean to say it must be rather grim for him anyway."

Warren, who had not helped with the decorating, laughed. "It's his first Christmas all right," he said. "Maybe it'll be his last. Could be."

Lockwood and Brewster turned and stared at him coldly. "All right, Warren," Lockwood said quietly. "You did a good job and we're duly grateful, but you've said enough."

"Could be," Warren repeated stubbornly. "Could be that he'd go back to jolly old England." He fumbled in his coat pocket and brought out a small black book, which he opened. "And by the way, Lockwood, you owe me fifty cents for comic sheets."

Earlier in the year, Warren had cornered the comic-sheet market at St. Benedict's. He bought the Sunday papers every week and then rented the comic sheets from them to the boys to read, at five cents each.

Lockwood took two quarters from his pocket and tossed them on Mr. Parsons' desk. Warren picked them up deliberately, checked the amount off in his black book, and spoke. "Pope—" he began.

"If you have any more *business* to attend to," Lockwood said, "will you mind putting it off until later?" His voice was finely sarcastic and Brewster glanced at him admiringly.

"And now," Lockwood went on, "we'd better get on with the presents."

The boys rushed toward the coatroom and came out again carrying packages, which they placed on Mr. Parsons' desk. The room looked bright and cheerful, with the red, white, and green packages covering the brown desk blotter. There were wreaths at the three windows, and the blackboard was covered with sprays of holly and a Santa Claus drawn with colored chalk.

Warren walked to his desk and began arranging the stamps in his collection. He had a fine collection, with duplicates which he sold or traded. His desk was in the front of the room, and when a boy was sent to the blackboard to write, Warren would hold out his hand, palm up, with a stamp in it, to show it. He would hold his hand low, so that Mr. Parsons couldn't see him. Now he pretended not to see that the other boys were getting ready to walk to chapel. He sat still as they filed out, and then he got up and went over to Mr. Parsons' desk. He took his present for the master from his pocket and laid it on top of a large package wrapped in red-and-gold paper and tied with wide green ribbon. Then he ran out of the room.

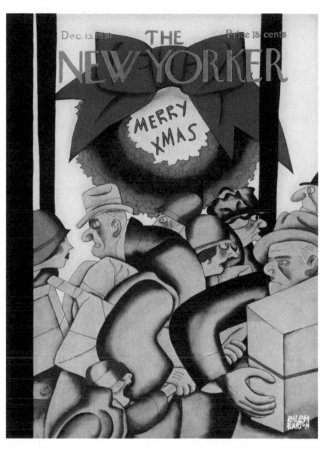

~~~

Chapel was at eight-thirty, and it was held in the large hall on the first floor. Captain Foster was seated in the center of the platform, with Mr. Gaines and Mr. Martin, who had been at the school the longest, seated on either side of him. Mr. Parsons sat at one end of the row. He was a thin man in his early thirties, and his hair, his skin, and his tweed suit were the color of dust. He wore a sprig of holly in his buttonhole, and as his class filed in, he smiled down at them. The 1-A boys and the 1-B boys sat in the front rows, as they were the class that would graduate in the spring, and they sat quietly and didn't fidget in their seats, as the younger boys did.

Captain Foster waited until all the boys were settled, and then he nodded to Mr. Howard, who taught music and played the organ, and the school rose to sing the St. Benedict's Christmas hymn. The boys' voices were high and clear.

"Christmas is nighing. Hark!" they sang.

Mr. Parsons sang with them. He had learned the hymn the night before. The hymn, Captain Foster had explained to him, was, like the St. Benedict's school song, "very dear to us all," and by that Mr. Parsons understood that he was supposed to learn it by heart. It was not a very good

CHRISTMAS RUSH

Dropping in at the main Post Office to see how business was a week before the deadline for soldiers' Christmas presents, we found the staff in a light perspiration. The man who took us around, a Mr. Gillen, said that since September 15th they had handled some four million parcels with APO addresses and that the last-minute rush was sure to be something fierce. Many of the temporary helpers are high-school students, who are of no great help in a Christmas log jam. "We have spiral parcel chutes in the building, and the kids keep running up to the fifth floor and sliding down," Mr. Gillen told us wearily. The real worry at the Post Office, though, is improperly wrapped or addressed parcels. Improperly wrapped par-cels are handled by the "reconstruction department," which has now been built up to fifty men working three overlapping shifts of twelve hours a day. Between them they do what they can for the day's intake of flimsy parcels, which averages about eight thousand.

If a package has merely softened up enroute, it's just a matter of cutting off the address, rewrapping the contents in brown paper, and pasting the address on the new package. An experienced man can handle twenty such packages an hour. A really insoluble problem is the gummed address label of the "To —— From ——" type. Some people just don't use enough spit, the label drops off, and the anonymous package winds up six months later at a public auction. "There's going to be some mighty disappointed guys this Christmas," Gillen predicted. In general, the wrapping jobs done by the stores are good, Gillen told us. He had a word of special commendation for Schrafft's. "Can't *budge*

hymn, but as he stood on the platform singing it, looking down at his boys, Mr. Parsons almost felt at home. His shoulders relaxed and the color came to his face. "Upon this holy night," he sang. And then, as the hymn ended, he bowed his head for the Lord's Prayer. With his head bowed, he could see where his sleeve was frayed, and he thought that he must do something about a new suit. It was quite all right to look comfortably shabby, but his suit was a step beyond that, and once he knew where he stood, he would feel justified in getting a few things for himself. Not that he hadn't understood Captain Foster's point when he explained that it was a question of getting the boys to like you, getting their confidence. In a school like St. Benedict's, you had to get the boys to like you, because boys had a way of complaining to their parents, and if the parents weren't satisfied—well, there was no school. "Of course," Captain Foster had said, "we can only give up to a point. But we do have to see eye to eye with the boys and their parents up to that point."

their packages," he said. The Post Office gets a good many lunches in smashed shoe boxes, which would have been contraband anyhow under the rules for mailing food. Most of them are mailed by people with R.F.D. addresses and no sense of geography. Naïve addresses are not uncommon. We peeped over one postal man's shoulder and found that he was puzzling over a box of candy addressed to "Richard F——, Infantry, U.S. Army. Overseas." "By the time I go off work, I'm wondering just what goes on in people's heads," he muttered to us.

A good many packages simply disintegrate, and it's impossible ever to tell which article goes in which package, let alone where the packages were intended to go. The contents of such packages are piled in crates and are sold at auction unless they are claimed within six months by the senders. In one salvage crate, we saw chewing gum, a bologna sausage, soap, an electric shaver, tobacco and cigarettes, and bath powder. We remarked that it all resulted in rather a heady aroma, and one of the wrappers said we should of been there yesterday. "We had four fried chickens," he said. "From San Francisco." Judging by the smashed packages, there's a good deal of contraband going overseas—beer, wine, whiskey, and lighter fluid, all expressly banned. Most of the booze is spilled even before it gets to the post office. "We had a broken bottle of imported Scotch here yesterday," a wrapper told us. "I could of wept." That day's prize package, so to speak, was one which, when opened for rewrapping, was found to contain a wristwatch, a Colt .45, and a box of chocolate-covered cherries.

—ROSANN SMITH, WILLIAM KINKEAD,
AND RUSSELL MALONEY, 1943

Mr. Parsons lifted his head at the end of the Lord's Prayer and sat down with the others as Captain Foster began to address the school. He wondered if he had tried to see eye to eye with Warren when reporting Warren's stamp dealings and the little matter of the comic sections to Captain Foster. Not that he minded the boys' trading things—it was a natural thing to do—but there was something about the way Warren did it. He looked down and his eyes found Warren. Warren was staring at Captain Foster, and suddenly Mr. Parsons heard what Captain Foster was saying.

". . . and a certain boy who has been trading in stamps and has managed to get a monopoly on comic strips, which he peddles during school hours . . ." Captain Foster said.

It was all Mr. Parsons could do to keep from interrupting Captain Foster to tell him that it was a matter of no consequence and that he'd mentioned it to him only to ask his advice, certainly not to have it dragged out in front of the whole school. He looked back at Warren to see how he was taking it, and he saw that Warren was smiling a little, and suddenly Warren's eyes met his in a way that made him uneasy. He was glad when Captain Foster left Warren and went on to the matter of water pistols and the unsportsmanlike behavior of some of the boys during a football game.

When the school rose once more, to sing the St. Benedict's Alma Mater, Mr. Parsons relaxed again. He was glad he had not told Captain Foster about the loaded dice Warren had made in manual-training class, and when the exercises were over, he stopped to say a word to Captain Foster about the boy.

"Captain Foster," he said, "I'm glad you didn't mention the boy's name."

"We never do," Captain Foster said. "We merely bring such matters up, lay them on the board, and start off the new year with a clean slate."

"I see," Mr. Parsons said. "I'm sure the boy means no harm. He's a clever boy, does well in his studies, and I don't think I should have mentioned it at all if he hadn't proved himself to be so distracting to the rest of the class. There's nothing wrong with the boy." He swallowed, and his hand went up to the sprig of holly in his buttonhole. After all, he thought, it is Christmas. "The fact is," he went on, "I like the boy." Then he nodded brightly to Captain Foster and hurried out of the hall.

Mr. Parsons almost bounded up the flight of stairs that led to his own classroom, and when he opened the door and saw the tree shining with lights

"When I jerk twice, pull as hard as you can."

and saw the boys, who were waiting for him expectantly, he called out to them, "Merry Christmas! Merry Christmas!"

He walked toward them as they stood grouped around his desk, nervously waiting for him to open his packages. "Merry Christmas, sir," they said.

He looked down at his desk, and the sight of the packages tied with bright ribbons warmed him. "Well, what's this?" he asked.

"Christmas, sir," Lockwood said.

"It *looks* like Christmas," Mr. Parsons said. "Even to the fine tree. I think I'll have to take that tree home with me."

"Why not?" Brewster said. "I'll help you carry it."

The boys laughed appreciatively. "Open your presents, sir," Pope said.

Mr. Parsons reached for a package, carefully untied the ribbon, and opened it. It was a bottle of whiskey from Brewster, and the boys screamed with laughter. Mr. Parsons read the label and held the bottle up to the light. "Too bad to waste it," he said, "so I suppose I'll have to drink a little of it— *later.*"

He picked up another package and opened it. "A cigarette lighter," he called out. "From Pope!"

He pressed on the lighter and it worked, and the boys cheered. Mr. Parsons looked down at the table and picked up an envelope. Inside the envelope was a card. "From Warren," Mr. Parsons read, and, feeling inside the envelope, his fingers felt a smaller envelope. As he felt it, he knew what was in it. He took it out and slipped it into his pocket.

"What is it, sir?" Brewster asked.

Mr. Parsons' hand held the envelope in his pocket. It was the small kind that people hand to doormen and janitors.

"It's money," Warren said. "Five dollars."

The boys glanced uneasily at one another and the room grew still. Someone jostled the tree and needles fell to the bare floor with a dry, cold sound. Mr. Parsons looked at Warren, and he knew that the boys were waiting for him to help them out. He took the envelope from his pocket, opened it, and held the five dollars so that they all could see it, and then he laid it with the other presents on the desk. When he spoke, his voice was without expression. "Thank you very much, old man," he said.

1946

CHRISTMAS MORNING

FRANK O'CONNOR

We were living up Blarney Lane, in Cork, at the time, in one of the little whitewashed cottages at the top, on the edge of the open country. It was a tiny house—a kitchen with two little bedrooms off it—and the kitchen door opened to the street. There were only the four of us—my parents, my brother Sonny, and myself. I suppose, at the time I'm speaking of, Sonny was six or seven and I was two years older. I never really liked that kid. He was the mother's pet; a proper little Mummy's darling, always racing after her to tell her what mischief I was up to. I really believe it was to spite me that he was so smart at his books. In a queer sort of way, he seemed to know that that was what the mother valued most, and you might say he spelled his way into her favor. "Mummy," he'd say, "will I call Larry in for his t-e-a?" Or "Mummy, the k-e-t-e-l is boiling." And, of course, if he made a mistake, the mother would correct him, and next time he'd have it right and get stuffed up with conceit. "Mummy," he'd say, "aren't I a good speller?" We could all be good spellers if we went on like that. Mind you, it wasn't that I was stupid, or anything of the kind, but somehow I was restless and I could never fix my mind on the one thing for long. I'd do the lessons for the year before or the lessons for the next year—anything except the ones I should be doing. And in the evenings I loved to get out to the Dempseys, the kids who lived in the house opposite and were the leaders of all the blackguarding that went on in the road. Not that I was a rough child, either. It was just that I liked excitement, and I never could see what it was in schooling attracted the mother.

"I declare to goodness, Larry," she said once, catching me with my cap in my hand, "you ought to be ashamed of yourself, with your baby brother better than you at reading."

"Ah, I'll do it when I come back," I said.

"The dear knows what'll become of you," she said. "If you'd only mind your lessons, you might be something worth while—an engineer or a clerk."

"'Tis all right, Mummy," Sonny said. "*I'll* be a clerk."

"I'm going to be a soldier," I said.

"God help us!" my mother said. "I'm afraid that's all you'll ever be fit for."
Sometimes, I used to think she was just a shade simple. As if a fellow could
be anything better than a soldier!

And then it began to draw on to Christmas, with the days getting shorter
and, coming on to dusk, the crowds getting bigger in the streets, and I began
to think of all the things I might get from Santa Claus. The Dempseys said
there was no Santa Claus and that it was only what your mother and father
gave you, but the Dempseys were a rough class of children and you wouldn't
expect Santa Claus to come to them anyway. I was scouting round for whatever information I could pick up about it from the mother. I wasn't much
good at writing, but it struck me that if a letter would do any good, I
wouldn't mind having a shot at one.

"Ah, I don't know will he come at all this year," my mother said with a
distracted air. "He has enough to do looking after good little boys that mind
their lessons, without bothering about the others."

"He only comes to good spellers, Mummy," Sonny said. "Isn't that right?"

"He comes to any little child that does his best," my mother said firmly,
"whether they're good spellers or not."

Well, from then on I tried to do my best. God knows, I tried. It was
hardly my fault if my teacher, Flogger Dawley, gave us sums we couldn't do,
within four days of the holidays, and I had to play hooky with Peter
Dempsey. It wasn't for the pleasure of it. December is no month for playing

hooky, and most of our time was spent sheltering from the rain in a store on the quays. The only mistake we made was imagining that we could keep it up until the holidays without being noticed. Of course, Flogger Dawley noticed and sent home to know what was keeping me. When I came home the third day, my mother gave me a look she had never given me before and said, "Your dinner is there." She was too full to talk. When I tried to explain to her, she only said, "Ah, you have no word." It wasn't the fact that I'd been playing hooky so much as all the lies I'd told her. For two days, she didn't open her mouth to me, and still I couldn't see what attraction schooling had for her or why she wouldn't let me grow up like anybody else.

That evening, Sonny stood at the front door with his hands in his trousers pockets, shouting to the other kids so that he could be heard all over the road, "Larry isn't allowed to go out. He played hooky with Peter Dempsey. Me mother isn't talking to him." And at night, when we were in our bed, he kept at me. "Santa Claus isn't bringing you anything this year."

"He is," I said.

"No," Sonny said.

"Why isn't he?"

"Because you played hooky with Dempsey," Sonny said. "I wouldn't play with them Dempsey fellows. They're no class. They had the bobbies up at the house."

"And how would Santa Claus know that I played hooky with Dempsey?" I asked.

"He'd know," Sonny said. "Mummy would tell him."

"And how could Mummy tell him and he up at the North Pole? Poor Ireland, she's rearing them still! 'Tis easy seen you're only a baby," I said.

"I'm not a baby," Sonny said, "and I can spell better than you, and Santa Claus won't bring you anything."

"You'll see whether he will or not," said I, letting on to be quite confident about it. But in my own heart I wasn't confident at all. You could never tell what powers those superhuman chaps would have of knowing what you were up to. And I had a bad conscience about skipping school. I had never seen the mother like that before.

~~~

I decided there was really only one thing for me to do, and that was see Santa Claus and have a talk with him myself. Being a man, he'd probably understand that a fellow wouldn't want to spend his whole life over old books, as the mother wanted me to. I was a good-looking kid, and when I liked, I had a way with me. I had only to smile nicely at one old gent on the Mall to get a penny off him, and I felt sure if only I could get Santa Claus alone, I could explain it all to his satisfaction and maybe get round him to give me something really worth while, like a model railway. I started practicing staying awake at night, counting five hundred and then a thousand and trying to hear first eleven and then midnight from the clock tower in Shandon. I felt sure Santa Claus would appear by midnight on Christmas Eve, seeing that he'd be coming from the north and would have the whole of the south side of town to do before morning. In some ways, I was quite an enterprising and farsighted kid. The only trouble was the things I was enterprising about.

I was so wrapped up in those plans of mine that I never noticed what a hard time my mother was having of it. Sonny and I used to go downtown with her, and while she was in the grocery shop, we stood outside the toyshop in the North Main Street, arguing about what we'd like for Christmas.

At noon the day before Christmas, my father came home to dinner and handed my mother some money. She stood looking at it doubtfully and her face went white.

"Well?" he said, getting angry. "What's wrong with that?"

"What's wrong with it?" she asked. "On Christmas Eve?"

"Why?" he said, sticking his hands in his trousers pockets and thrusting his head forward with an ugly scowl. "Do you think I get more because 'tis Christmas Eve?"

"Lord God!" she said, and raised her hand to her cheek. "Not a bit of cake in the house, nor a candle, nor anything!"

"All right!" he shouted. "How much will buy the cake?"

"Ah, for pity's sake!" she cried. "Will you give me the money and not argue with me in front of the children? Do you think I'm going to leave them with nothing on the one day of the year?"

"Bad luck to you and your children!" he said. "Am I to be slaving from one year's end to another just for you to be throwing my money away on toys? There!" He threw two silver coins on the table. "That's all you're going to get, so you can make the best of it," he said, as he went out the door.

"I suppose the publicans will get the rest," she called after him.

In the afternoon, she went downtown, but she didn't take us with her. She came back with several parcels, and in one of them was the big red Christmas candle. We waited for my father to come home to his tea, but he didn't, so we had our own and a slice of cake for each of us, and then my mother put Sonny on the kitchen chair with the holy-water stoup before the window by him, so that he could sprinkle the candle, and after that he lit it, and she said, "The Light of Heaven to our Souls." I could see she was upset because my father wasn't there. When Sonny and I hung up our stockings at either side of the bed in our room and got into bed, he was still out.

Then began the hardest couple of hours I ever put in. I don't think I was ever so sleepy, but I knew if I went to sleep, my chances were done, so I kept myself awake by making speeches to say to Santa when he came. The speeches were different, according to the sort of chap he turned out to be. When I had said them all, I nudged Sonny and tried to get him to wake up and keep me company, but he lay like the dead and neither moved nor opened his eyes. I knew by the light under the kitchen door that my mother hadn't gone to bed.

Eleven struck from Shandon, and shortly afterward I heard the latch of the front door raised very softly, but it was only my father coming home.

"Hullo, little girl," he said in an oily tone, and then he began to giggle. "What is keeping you up so late?"

"Do you want your supper?" my mother asked in a low voice.

"Ah, no, I had a bit of pig's cheek in Daneen's on my way home," he replied. "My goodness, is it as late as that? If I knew that, I'd have strolled up to the North Chapel for Midnight Mass. I'd like to hear the 'Adeste' again. That's a hymn I'm very fond of, a most touching hymn." And he began to sing falsetto, as if he were a ladies' choir:

> *Adeste, fideles,*
> *Solus domus dagos . . .*

My father was very fond of Latin hymns, particularly when he had a drop in, but he could never get the words right. He just made them up as he went along, and for some reason which I could never understand, that drove my mother into a fury. This night she said, "Oh, you disgust me," and closed the bedroom door behind her.

My father gave a low, pleased laugh. Then I heard him strike a match to light his pipe, and for a couple of minutes he puffed it noisily, and then the light under the door dimmed and went out. From the dark kitchen, I suddenly heard his falsetto voice quavering emotionally:

> *Dixi medearum*
> *Tutum tonum tantum,*
> *Venite, adoremus . . .*

I knew that the chorus bit of it was the only thing he had right, but in a queer sort of way it lulled me to sleep, as if I were listening to choirs of angels singing.

~~~

I woke, coming on to dawn, with the feeling that something shocking had happened. The whole house was still, and our little room looking out on the foot and a half of back yard was pitch-dark. It was only when you looked at the tiny square of window that you could see that all the purple was gone out of the sky. I jumped out of bed and felt my stocking, and I knew at once that the worst had happened. Santa Claus had come while I was asleep, and had gone away with an altogether false impression of me, because all he had left me was a book like a reading book folded up, a pen and pencil, and a tuppenny bag of sweets. For a while, I was too stunned by the catastrophe to be able to think of anything else. Then I began to wonder what that foxy boy, Sonny, had got. I went to his side of the bed and examined his stocking.

For all his spelling and sucking up, Sonny hadn't done much better, because apart from a bag of sweets about the same size as my own, all Santa had left him was a gun, one that fired a cork, and you could get it in any toyshop for sixpence. All the same, it was a gun, and a gun was better than an old book, any day of the week. The Dempseys had a gang, and the gang fought the Strawberry Lane kids and never let them play ball on our road. That gun, it struck me, would be quite useful to me in a lot of ways, while it would be lost on Sonny, who wouldn't be let play with the gang, even if he wanted to.

Then I got the inspiration, as it seemed to me, direct from Heaven. Suppose I took the gun and gave Sonny the book! He was fond of spelling, and a studious child like him could learn a lot of spelling out of a big book like mine. Sonny hadn't seen Santa any more than I had, and what he didn't know wouldn't trouble him. I wasn't doing the least harm to anyone; in fact, I was doing him a genuine good turn, if only he knew it. So I put the book, pen, and pencil into Sonny's stocking and the gun into my own, and then I got back into bed again and fell fast asleep. As I say, in those days I had quite a lot of initiative.

It was Sonny who waked me, shaking me like mad to tell me that Santa Claus had come and look what he'd brought me—a gun! I let on to be very surprised and rather disappointed, and I made him show me the book and told him it was much better than what Santa had brought me. As I knew, that child was prepared to believe anything, and within a few minutes he wanted to rush in to the mother to show her what he'd got. That was my bad moment. After the way she had carried on the previous time, I didn't like telling her the lie, though I had the satisfaction of knowing that the only person who could contradict me was at that particular moment somewhere by the North Pole. The thought gave me confidence, and Sonny and myself stormed in to the bedroom and wakened my father and mother, shouting at the top of our voices, "Oh, look! Look what Santa Claus brought!"

My mother opened her eyes and smiled, and then, as she saw the gun in my hand, her face changed suddenly. It was just as it had been the day I had come home from playing hooky, when she said, "You have no word."

"Larry," she said, "where did you get that?"

"Santa Claus left it in my stocking, Mummy," I said, and tried to look hurt.

"You stole it from that poor child's stocking while he was asleep," my mother said. "Larry, Larry, how could you be so mean?"

"Whisht, whisht, whisht!" said my father testily. "'Tis Christmas morning."

"Ah!" she cried, turning to him. "'Tis easy it comes to you. Do you think I want my son to grow up a thief and a liar?"

"Ah, what thief, woman?" he said. He was as cross if you interrupted him

in his rare moods of benevolence as in his commoner ones, of meanness, and this one was exacerbated by the feeling of guilt for the previous evening. "Can't you let the child alone? Here, Larry," he said, putting out his hand to the little table by the bed. "Here's sixpence for you and another for Sonny. Don't lose it, now."

I looked at my mother and saw the horror still in her eyes, and at that moment I understood everything. I burst into tears, threw the popgun on the floor by the bed, and rushed out by the front door. It was before a soul on the road was awake. I ran up the lane behind the house into the field, and threw myself on my face and hands in the wet grass as the sun was rising.

In some queer way, I understood all the things that had been hidden from me before. I knew there was no Santa Claus flying over the rooftops with his reindeer and his red coat—there was only my mother trying to scrape together a few pence from the housekeeping money that my father gave her. I knew that he was mean and common and a drunkard, and that she had been relying on me to study and rescue her from the misery which threatened to engulf her. And I knew that the horror in her eyes was the fear that, like him, I was turning out a liar, a thief, and a drunkard.

After that morning, I think my childhood was at an end.

1946

WHERE CHRISTMAS ENDS

For some time, we have suspected that Christmas in New York is principally a north-south phenomenon; that is, it runs in mighty parallel rivers up and down the central avenues but often trickles away to nothing in the shallow irrigation ditches of the cross streets. The other day, we thought to put our theory to the test. First, we had to locate the center of Christmas in New York. We debated whether to head north, toward the great Norway spruce of Rockefeller Center, with its Currier & Ives prospect of skaters, or to head south, toward the gossamer, tree-shaped web of electric-light bulbs clinging to the front of Lord & Taylor. The latter seemed more crassly commercial, and hence more truly in the spirit of things, so south we went, past the giant mailbox in front of the Public Library, past the marble lions (who look more and more, by the way, as if they were melting; are they really made of ice cream?), past a siren bookstore window stuffed with Larousse Encyclopedias—past all this to the entrance of Lord & Taylor. Here, surely, Christmas reigned supreme; it reigned in the leaden hearts, killing shoes, and ravaged faces of female shoppers, it reigned in the tweeting throbble-o of the apple-cheeked apprentice policeman's whistle, it reigned in the empurpled lids of the mannequins who sleepwalked through a window world of plastic icicles and porcelain borzoi hounds. We had reached Camp 1.

We turned west, along the south side of Thirty-eighth Street. For the first hundred paces, Christmas held its own, in the stolidly professional side windows of Franklin Simon. Chrysanthemums of gold paper and three little boys in snug winter wear smiled glossily from windows framed in sprigs of ersatz evergreen. We next struck the Antoinette Beauty Salon, at No. 18 West Thirty-eighth Street. Looking beyond the window, we saw two long rows of silver eggs, from each of which was hatching a woman's face wearing a mask of boredom. *In* the window was a lone cardboard candle flanking a Christmas-tree-shaped sign that read, "Prettiest Gift of All—the Gift of Beauty—Prices to Suit Your Convenience!" To clinch her point, Antoinette also displayed photographs of smiling ladies wearing hairdos christened Heart of Gold, French Mood, Angellite, Enchantress, and On the Town. The photographs looked a bit crinkled and brown, perhaps from being under the dryer too long.

On the town, we advanced, to No. 20, the Tall Apparel Shops. Here hung gold balls on hairy ropes so thickly strung that the dresses in the window were not so much seen as glimpsed through the interstices. Also in the window was a small tree spiral-wound with gold ornaments and sprayed with glistening snow. We looked carefully to see if, under the artificial snow, the tree was artificial, too. It was. The stream of Christmas was still running strong, though by now the policeman's whistle on Fifth Avenue had a remote twang, like sleigh bells in the next valley.

Next door, Yule began to thin and grow wan. No. 22 was shared by the Commodore Stationery Company and Paul's Coffee Shop. The first window was dominated by a vortical tumble of paper bearing such legends as "RUBBER STAMPS MADE TO ORDER," "Family Budget Book No. 54-395," and "Mutual Adjustable Hand Punches—'What a Punch!' " Diligent searching, however, revealed, at last, a bit of crimped tinfoil at the base of a paper pyramid of Norcross cards, on one of which white kittens bordered the rather vague and unconvincing message "To All of You Lots of Christmas Wishes." Next door, Paul didn't wish us lots of anything. Rather, his window carried the image of the Christmas tree to a kind of terminal degradation. Two trylons of painted green cardboard dusted with iridescent confetti and closely set foil flowers made a weary, battered stab at seasonal cheer, while a sign between them bleakly promised:

Served to your order
CHEF'S
Special Luncheon
also
Cold *Crispy* Salads
99¢.

We pressed on, daunted. No. 26, the Embassy Beauty Salon, was desultory indeed. The decorator of its two windows had thrown down a handful of green discs the size of subway tokens, tossed some strings of fake pine over an elephant plant and a pot of ivy, and called it a day. In fairness, there was also the one attempt at religious imagery that we saw during the trek. But what was the religion? Zoroastrianism crossed with starlet worship? Its cardboard idol showed the top half of a young woman's face: she had green eyes, white skin, and black hair, and in her hair were set five tall white candles, vigorously flaming. We searched for a clue to this exotic and ominous iconography, and found none. "Eyebrows and Lashes Tinted 1.25," one sign said. "Superfluous Hair Removed Permanently by Electrolysis," said another. We were near the end of the line.

Next door, at No. 28, Louis Weinberg Associates, Inc. (Silks, Velvets, Ribbons, Novelties, Felts, Straws), had filled its windows with pastel-colored unblocked hat forms and what looked like yards of fine-spun taffy. In all this feathery color there seemed to be no gesture toward Christmas until we spotted a little bouquet, lying as if cast down by a wistful child, of small red objects. Whatever it was made of, its colors were red and green, and we took it to be a gesture, though an ambiguous one, toward holly and ivy.

Next door, even ambiguity ceased. Fred Frankel & Sons, Inc. (Stones, Pearls, Trimmings), offered to the pedestrian "the first truly permanent window display, demonstrating the applied artistry of diamond-cutting in nine crystal-clear illustrated steps." And it was an interesting display, if not *truly* permanent; the first of the nine steps, illustrating either lopping, faceting, or brilliandeering, had toppled over and lay on its side in the dust. Also, there were scattered about glass diamonds the size of children's tops and necklaces of pearls so large that if they were real, the oysters must have outweighed sea turtles. But in all this there lay not a hint of Christmas, and, as if to emphasize the point, in the next window, on the other side of the doorway, there was nothing—no diamonds, no pearls, no sprigs of mistletoe, no papier-mâché fireplaces, no cotton snow, no season's greetings, nothing. The trickle of Christmas had sunk into the sand. Soot drifted onto our notebook; a bitter wind riffled the gutter chaff. It might have been March. We were a third of the way down the block, and had come, from Fifth Avenue, just a hundred and sixty-seven paces.

—JOHN UPDIKE, 1961

CHRISTMAS IS A SAD SEASON FOR THE POOR

JOHN CHEEVER

Christmas is a sad season. The phrase came to Charlie an instant after the alarm clock had waked him, and named for him an amorphous depression that had troubled him all the previous evening. The sky outside his window was black. He sat up in bed and pulled the light chain that hung in front of his nose. Christmas is a very sad day of the year, he thought. Of all the millions of people in New York, I am practically the only one who has to get up in the cold black of 6 A.M. on Christmas Day in the morning; I am practically the only one.

He dressed, and when he went downstairs from the top floor of the rooming house in which he lived, the only sounds he heard were the coarse sounds of sleep; the only lights burning were lights that had been forgotten. Charlie ate some breakfast in an all-night lunchwagon and took an Elevated train uptown. From Third Avenue, he walked over to Park. Park Avenue was dark. House after house put into the shine of the street lights a wall of black windows. Millions and millions were sleeping, and this general loss of consciousness generated an impression of abandonment, as if this were the fall of the city, the end of time. He opened the iron-and-glass doors of the apartment building where he had been working for six months as an elevator operator, and went through the elegant lobby to a locker room at the back. He put on a striped vest with brass buttons, a false ascot, a pair of pants with a light-blue stripe on the seam, and a coat. The night elevator man was dozing on the little bench in the car. Charlie woke him. The night elevator man told him thickly that the day doorman had been taken sick and wouldn't be in that day. With the doorman sick, Charlie wouldn't have any relief for lunch, and a lot of people would expect him to whistle for cabs.

~~~

Charlie had been on duty a few minutes when 14 rang—a Mrs. Hewing, who, he happened to know, was kind of immoral. Mrs. Hewing hadn't been to bed yet, and she got into the elevator wearing a long dress under her fur coat. She was followed by her two funny-looking dogs. He took her down and watched her go out into the dark and take her dogs to the curb. She was outside for only a few minutes. Then she came in and he took her up to 14 again. When she got off the elevator, she said, "Merry Christmas, Charlie."

"Well, it isn't much of a holiday for me, Mrs. Hewing," he said. "I think Christmas is a very sad season of the year. It isn't that people around here ain't generous—I mean I got plenty of tips—but, you see, I live alone in a furnished room and I don't have any family or anything, and Christmas isn't much of a holiday for me."

"I'm sorry, Charlie," Mrs. Hewing said. "I don't have any family myself. It is kind of sad when you're alone, isn't it?" She called her dogs and followed them into her apartment. He went down.

It was quiet then, and Charlie lighted a cigarette. The heating plant in the basement encompassed the building at that hour in a regular and profound vibration, and the sullen noises of arriving steam heat began to resound, first in the lobby and then to reverberate up through all the sixteen stories, but this was a mechanical awakening, and it didn't lighten his loneliness or his petulance. The black air outside the glass doors had begun to turn blue, but the blue light seemed to have no source; it appeared in the middle of the air. It was a tearful light, and as it picked out the empty street and the long file of Christmas trees, he wanted to cry. Then a cab drove up, and the Walsers got out, drunk and dressed in evening clothes, and he took them up to their penthouse. The Walsers got him to brooding about the difference between his life in a furnished room and the lives of the people overhead. It was terrible.

Then the early churchgoers began to ring, but there were only three of these that morning. A few more went off to church at eight o'clock, but the majority of the building remained unconscious, although the smell of bacon and coffee had begun to drift into the elevator shaft.

At a little after nine, a nursemaid came down with a child. Both the nursemaid and the child had a deep tan and had just returned, he knew, from Bermuda. He had never been to Bermuda. He, Charlie, was a prisoner, confined eight hours a day to a six-by-eight elevator cage, which was confined, in turn, to a sixteen-story shaft. In one building or another, he had made his living as an elevator operator for ten years. He estimated the average trip at about an eighth of a mile, and when he thought of the thousands of miles he had travelled, when he thought that he might have driven the car through the mists above the Caribbean and set it down on some coral beach in Bermuda, he held the narrowness of his travels against his passengers, as if it were not the nature of the elevator but the pressure of their lives that confined him, as if they had clipped his wings.

He was thinking about this when the DePauls, on 9, rang. They wished him a merry Christmas.

"Well, it's nice of you to think of me," he said as they descended, "but it isn't much of a holiday for me. Christmas is a sad season when you're poor. I live alone in a furnished room. I don't have any family."

"Who do you have dinner with, Charlie?" Mrs. DePaul asked.

"I don't have any Christmas dinner," Charlie said. "I just get a sandwich."

"Oh, Charlie!" Mrs. DePaul was a stout woman with an impulsive heart, and Charlie's plaint struck at her holiday mood as if she had been caught in a cloudburst. "I do wish we could share our Christmas dinner with you, you know," she said. "I come from Vermont, you know, and when I was a child, you know, we always used to have a great many people at our table. The mailman, you know, and the schoolteacher, and just anybody who didn't have any

family of their own, you know, and I wish we could share our dinner with you the way we used to, you know, and I don't see any reason why we can't. We can't have you at the table, you know, because you couldn't leave the elevator—could you?—but just as soon as Mr. DePaul has carved the goose, I'll give you a ring, and I'll arrange a tray for you, you know, and I want you to come up and at least share our Christmas dinner."

Charlie thanked them, and their generosity surprised him, but he wondered if, with the arrival of friends and relatives, they wouldn't forget their offer.

Then old Mrs. Gadshill rang, and when she wished him a merry Christmas, he hung his head.

"It isn't much of a holiday for me, Mrs. Gadshill," he said. "Christmas is a sad season if you're poor. You see, I don't have any family. I live alone in a furnished room."

"I don't have any family either, Charlie," Mrs. Gadshill said. She spoke with a pointed lack of petulance, but her grace was forced. "That is, I don't have any children with me today. I have three children and seven grandchildren, but none of them can see their way to coming East for Christmas with me. Of course, I understand their problems. I know that it's difficult to travel with children during the holidays, although I always seemed to manage it when I was their age, but people feel differently, and we mustn't condemn them for the things we can't understand. But I know how you feel, Charlie. I haven't any family either. I'm just as lonely as you."

Mrs. Gadshill's speech didn't move him. Maybe she was lonely, but she had a ten-room apartment and three servants and bucks and bucks and diamonds and diamonds, and there were plenty of poor kids in the slums who would be happy at a chance at the food her cook threw away. Then he thought about poor kids. He sat down on a chair in the lobby and thought about them.

They got the worst of it. Beginning in the fall, there was all this excitement about Christmas and how it was a day for them. After Thanksgiving, they couldn't miss it. It was fixed so they couldn't miss it. The wreaths and decorations everywhere, and bells ringing, and trees in the park, and Santa Clauses on every corner, and pictures in the magazines and newspapers and on every wall and window in the city told them that if they were good, they would get what they wanted. Even if they couldn't read, they couldn't miss it. They couldn't miss it even if they were blind. It got into the air the poor kids inhaled. Every time they took a walk, they'd see all the expensive toys in the store windows, and they'd write letters to Santa Claus, and their mothers and fathers would promise to mail them, and after the kids had gone to sleep, they'd burn the letters in the stove. And when it came Christmas morning, how could you explain it, how could you tell them that Santa Claus only visited the rich, that he didn't know about the good? How could you face them when all you had to give them was a balloon or a lollipop?

On the way home from work a few nights earlier, Charlie had seen a woman and a little girl going down Fifty-ninth Street. The little girl was crying. He guessed she was crying, he knew she was crying, because she'd

"Just how do you propose to pay for this giveaway?"

seen all the things in the toy-store windows and couldn't understand why none of them were for her. Her mother did housework, he guessed, or maybe was a waitress, and he saw them going back to a room like his, with green walls and no heat, on Christmas Eve, to eat a can of soup. And he saw the little girl hang up her ragged stocking and fall asleep, and he saw the mother looking through her purse for something to put into the stocking— This reverie was interrupted by a bell on 11. He went up, and Mr. and Mrs. Fuller were waiting. When they wished him a merry Christmas, he said, "Well, it isn't much of a holiday for me, Mrs. Fuller. Christmas is a sad season when you're poor."

"Do you have any children, Charlie?" Mrs. Fuller asked.

"Four living," he said. "Two in the grave." The majesty of his lie overwhelmed him. "Mrs. Leary's a cripple," he added.

"How sad, Charlie," Mrs. Fuller said. She started out of the elevator when it reached the lobby, and then she turned. "I want to give your children some presents, Charlie," she said. "Mr. Fuller and I are going to pay a call now, but when we come back, I want to give you some things for your children."

He thanked her. Then the bell rang on 4, and he went up to get the Westons.

"It isn't much of a holiday for me," he told them when they wished him a merry Christmas. "Christmas is a sad season when you're poor. You see, I live alone in a furnished room."

"Poor Charlie," Mrs. Weston said. "I know just how you feel. During the war, when Mr. Weston was away, I was all alone at Christmas. I didn't have any Christmas dinner or a tree or anything. I just scrambled myself some eggs and sat there and cried." Mr. Weston, who had gone into the lobby, called impatiently to his wife. "I know just how you feel, Charlie," Mrs. Weston said.

~~~

By noon, the climate in the elevator shaft had changed from bacon and coffee to poultry and game, and the house, like an enormous and complex homestead, was absorbed in the preparations for a domestic feast. The children and their nursemaids had all returned from the Park. Grandmothers and aunts were arriving in limousines. Most of the people who came through the lobby were carrying packages wrapped in colored paper, and were wearing their best furs and new clothes. Charlie continued to complain to most of the tenants when they wished him a merry Christmas, changing his story from the lonely bachelor to the poor father, and back again, as his mood changed, but this outpouring of melancholy, and the sympathy it aroused, didn't make him feel any better.

At half past one, 9 rang, and when he went up, Mr. DePaul was standing in the door of their apartment holding a cocktail shaker and a glass. "Here's a little Christmas cheer, Charlie," he said, and he poured Charlie a drink. Then a maid appeared with a tray of covered dishes, and Mrs. DePaul came out of the living room. "Merry Christmas, Charlie," she said. "I had Mr. DePaul carve the goose early, so that you could have some, you know. I didn't want to put the dessert on the tray, because I was afraid it would melt, you know, so when we have our dessert, we'll call you."

"And what is Christmas without presents?" Mr. DePaul said, and he brought a large, flat box from the hall and laid it on top of the covered dishes.

"You people make it seem like a real Christmas to me," Charlie said. Tears started into his eyes. "Thank you, thank you."

"Merry Christmas! Merry Christmas!" they called, and they watched him carry his dinner and his present into the elevator. He took the tray and the box into the locker room when he got down. On the tray, there was a soup, some kind of creamed fish, and a serving of goose. The bell rang again, but before he answered it, he tore open the DePauls' box and saw that it held a dressing gown. Their generosity and their cocktail had begun to work on his brain, and he went jubilantly up to 12. Mrs. Gadshill's maid was standing in the door with a tray, and Mrs. Gadshill stood behind her. "Merry Christmas, Charlie!" she said. He thanked her, and tears came into his eyes again. On the way down, he drank off the glass of sherry on Mrs. Gadshill's tray. Mrs. Gadshill's contribution was a mixed grill. He ate the lamb chop with his fingers. The bell was ringing again, and he wiped his face with a paper towel and went up to 11. "Merry Christmas, Charlie," Mrs. Fuller said, and she was standing in the door with her arms full of packages wrapped in silver paper, just like a picture in an advertisement, and Mr. Fuller was beside her with an arm around her, and they both looked as if they were going to cry. "Here are some things I want you to take home to your children," Mrs. Fuller said. "And here's something for Mrs. Leary and here's something for you. And if you want to take these things out to the elevator, we'll have your dinner ready for you in a minute." He carried the things into the elevator and came back for the tray. "Merry Christmas, Charlie!" both of the Fullers called after him as he closed the door. He took their dinner and their presents into the locker room and tore open the box that was marked for him. There was an alligator wallet in it, with Mr. Fuller's initials in the corner. Their dinner was also goose, and he ate a piece of the meat with his fingers and was washing it down with a cocktail when the bell rang. He went up again. This time it was the Westons.

"Merry Christmas, Charlie!" they said, and they gave him a cup of eggnog, a turkey dinner, and a present. Their gift was also a dressing gown. Then 7 rang, and when he went up, there was another dinner and some more toys. Then 14 rang, and when he went up, Mrs. Hewing was standing in the hall, in a kind of negligee, holding a pair of riding boots in one hand and some neckties in the other. She had been crying and drink-

ing. "Merry Christmas, Charlie," she said tenderly. "I wanted to give you something, and I've been thinking about you all morning, and I've been all over the apartment, and these are the only things I could find that a man might want. These are the only things that Mr. Brewer left. I don't suppose you'd have any use for the riding boots, but wouldn't you like the neckties?" Charlie took the neckties and thanked her and hurried back to the car, for the elevator bell had rung three times.

~~~

By three o'clock, Charlie had fourteen dinners spread on the table and the floor of the locker room, and the bell kept ringing. Just as he started to eat one, he would have to go up and get another, and he was in the middle of the Parsons' roast beef when he had to go up and get the DePauls' dessert. He kept the door of the locker room closed, for he sensed that the quality of charity is exclusive and that his friends would have been disappointed to find that they were not the only ones to try to lessen his loneliness. There were goose, turkey, chicken, pheasant, grouse, and pigeon. There were trout and salmon, creamed scallops and oysters, lobster, crabmeat, whitebait, and clams. There were plum puddings, mince pies, mousses, puddles of melted ice cream, layer cakes, *Torten*, éclairs, and two slices of Bavarian cream. He had dressing gowns, neckties, cuff links, socks, and handkerchiefs, and one of the tenants had asked for his neck size and then given him three green shirts. There were a glass teapot filled, the label said, with jasmine honey, four bottles of aftershave lotion, some alabaster bookends, and a dozen steak knives. The avalanche of charity he had precipitated filled the locker room and made him hesitant, now and then, as if he had touched some wellspring in the female heart that would bury him alive in food and dressing gowns. He had made almost no headway on the food, for all the servings were preternaturally large, as if loneliness had been counted on to generate in him a brutish appetite. Nor had he opened any of the presents that had been given to him for his imaginary children, but he had drunk everything they sent down, and around him were the dregs of Martinis, Manhattans, Old-Fashioneds, champagne-and-raspberry-shrub cocktails, eggnogs, Bronxes, and Side Cars.

His face was blazing. He loved the world, and the world loved him. When he thought back over his life, it appeared to him in a rich and wonderful light, full of astonishing experiences and unusual friends. He thought that his job as an elevator operator—cruising up and down through hundreds of feet of perilous space—demanded the nerve and the intellect of a birdman. All the constraints of his life—the green walls of his room and the months of unemployment—dissolved. No one was ringing, but he got into the elevator and shot it at full speed up to the penthouse and down again, up and down, to test his wonderful mastery of space.

A bell rang on 12 while he was cruising, and he stopped in his flight long enough to pick up Mrs. Gadshill. As the car started to fall, he took his hands off the controls in a paroxysm of joy and shouted, "Strap on your safety belt, Mrs. Gadshill! We're going to make a loop-the-loop!" Mrs. Gadshill shrieked. Then, for some reason, she sat down on the floor of the elevator. Why was her face so pale, he wondered; why was she sitting on the floor? She shrieked again. He grounded the car gently, and cleverly, he thought, and opened the door. "I'm sorry if I scared you, Mrs. Gadshill," he said meekly. "I was only fooling." She shrieked again. Then she ran out into the lobby, screaming for the superintendent.

~~~

The superintendent fired Charlie and took over the elevator himself. The news that he was out of work stung Charlie for a minute. It was his first contact with human meanness that day. He sat down in the locker room and gnawed on a drumstick. His drinks were beginning to let him down, and while it had not reached him yet, he felt a miserable soberness in the offing. The excess of food and presents around him began to make him feel guilty and unworthy. He regretted bitterly the lie he had told about his children.

He was a single man with simple needs. He had abused the goodness of the people upstairs. He was unworthy.

Then up through this drunken train of thought surged the sharp figure of his landlady and her three skinny children. He thought of them sitting in their basement room. The cheer of Christmas had passed them by. This image got him to his feet. The realization that he was in a position to give, that he could bring happiness easily to someone else, sobered him. He took a big burlap sack, which was used for collecting waste, and began to stuff it, first with his presents and then with the presents for his imaginary children. He worked with the haste of a man whose train is approaching the station, for he could hardly wait to see those long faces light up when he came in the door. He changed his clothes, and, fired by a wonderful and unfamiliar sense of power, he slung his bag over his shoulder like a regular Santa Claus, went out the back way, and took a taxi to the lower East Side.

The landlady and her children had just finished off a turkey, which had been sent to them by the local Democratic Club, and they were stuffed and uncomfortable when Charlie began pounding on the door, shouting "Merry Christmas!" He dragged the bag in after him and dumped the presents for the children onto the floor. There were dolls and musical toys, blocks, sewing kits, an Indian suit, and a loom, and it appeared to him that, as he had hoped, his arrival in the basement dispelled its gloom. When half the presents had been opened, he gave the landlady a bathrobe and went upstairs to look over the things he had been given for himself.

〰

Now, the landlady's children had already received so many presents by the time Charlie arrived that they were confused with receiving, and it was only the landlady's intuitive grasp of the nature of charity that made her allow the children to open some of the presents while Charlie was still in the room, but as soon as he had gone, she stood between the children and the presents that were still unopened. "Now, you kids have had enough already," she said. "You kids have got your share. Just look at the things you got there. Why, you ain't even played with the half of them. Mary Anne, you ain't even looked at that doll the Fire Department give you. Now, a nice thing to do would be to take all this stuff that's left over to those poor people on Hudson Street—them Deckkers. They ain't got nothing." A beatific light came into her face when she realized that she could give, that she could bring cheer, that she could put a healing finger on a case needier than hers, and—like Mrs. DePaul and Mrs. Weston, like Charlie himself and like Mrs. Deckker, when Mrs. Deckker was to think, subsequently, of the poor Shannons—first love, then charity, and then a sense of power drove her. "Now, you kids help me get all this stuff together. Hurry, hurry, hurry," she said, for it was dark then, and she knew that we are bound, one to another, in licentious benevolence for only a single day, and that day was nearly over. She was tired, but she couldn't rest, she couldn't rest.

1949

"Now, there's a guy who's ruined Christmas for every other man in the neighborhood."

THE MAGI HANGUP

WILLIAM COX

One thousand eight hundred and seventy dollars. That was all. And seven hundred of it in nickels. Nickels saved one and two at a time by spreading his sandwiches with mayonnaise that wasn't "real," by the purchase of Levi's brutally stamped "seconds," by fuelling his hopped-up Yamaha with low-test regular, and by oh so many pride-deflating devices that Clarence wondered if he could ever again hold his head high in any but the shabbiest of coffee-houses. Nine times he counted the money. One thousand eight hundred and seventy dollars. Not a dollar more. And tomorrow—Christmas!

Clarence glanced over at his wife's guitar, started to reach for it, then stopped. Surely this was the time to sing "The No Bread Blues." But just as surely this was *not* the time. Playing it would not increase the one thousand eight hundred and seventy dollars by a single sou. Now its thin notes would only add to his pain. And this was the Christmas when Clarence had so wanted to get something special—really special—for Clarissa. His Clarissa. Oh, the weeks that had gone into thinking of something suitable—something truly worthy of the honor of being owned by his wife of just three months! It had been a simple wed-in in Central Park. Under a spreading chestnut tree—the date, September 24th; the weather, perfect. Everything according to plan except for the untimely falling of first one soot-exhausted chestnut then another. With unwavering resolution, he pushed the thought aside.

As he paced the floor, Clarence caught his reflection in the mirror. He stopped and ran a comb through his hair—the magnificently full head of hair that fell just below his shoulders, rippling and shining like a waterfall of pure, luminous gold. Glorying in the reflection, Clarence grimaced only slightly as he recalled the scene that had taken place last week between himself and the university's beetle-browed dean. Clarence had refused to be shorn, and the dean had retaliated by "expunging" him—that was the way he'd put it—from the senior class, "until such time as you choose to return to classes looking like a recognizably normal, well-trimmed American male."

Now Clarence bravely turned to other matters, but not before a few tears had fallen to his sandalled feet.

Clarence's hair, however, was but one of the two possessions in which he and his wife took fierce pride. The other was Clarissa's twelve-string supersonic double-cutaway guitar—perfect except for its embarrassingly bourgeois, unelectrified state. But it would remain an embarrassment only until that time when Clarence could earn the amount needed for the crowd-exciting two-channel amp, with 90-watt peak, patented baffle, crossover network, and master control, they had seen in the window of a music supply store on St. Marks Place. The price was two thousand dollars, federal and city taxes included. And here it was, the day before Christmas, and Clarence had but one thousand eight hundred and seventy dollars toward Clarissa's guitar-electrification project. A hundred and thirty clams short!

Earlier that day, Clarence had gone to the store and promised to pay twice the amount he was short before the fifteenth of January if only the proprietor would let him take the amplifier now. But the man knew Clarence and refused. It was payment in full or no dice.

And then it dawned on Clarence. Why hadn't he thought of it before? Hadn't he seen an advertisement in the *East Village Other* for the Greater Precision Instruments Corp.? Yes, he remembered now. "Wanted—fine hair for use in delicate industrial instruments," it read.

On went his Hindu bead collar. On went his sleeveless denim vest. On went his boots. A bit of hair jelly on his hair, then a quick spray of Command, and Clarence was on his way. Whistling his favorite fifteenth-century madrigal, he hurried down the street. A light, delicate snow was transforming the parking meters into a veritable wonderland. He quickened his step. The solution was so perfect for Clarissa that the sacrifice could be borne. With short hair, he might have to return to class, but at least Clarissa would be able to play along with her records of the Screaming Ends, and that rich, happily hippy sound would not only liberate his sensibilities but might also help him with his evening studies.

Clarence stopped whistling when he came to the door of the Greater Precision Instruments factory. He paused for a moment in the wet street, feeling the familiar, luxuriant weight on his neck and ears. Then he took a deep breath, entered the building, and carefully shook the snow from his hair. "Hair purchases?" he said to the receptionist in a steady voice. "I want to sell my hair."

The receptionist looked up, then caught her breath sharply. "Oh, no," she gasped. "Not *your* hair."

"It's my wife," said Clarence resolutely. "Something for my wife."

Tears came to the girl's eyes. "Your need must be very great," she whispered. "You are a brave man."

"It is Christmas," said Clarence simply.

~~~

The snow felt cold on Clarence's crew-cut head, but he hardly noticed it. The highly prized amplifier was now his, and would shortly be Clarissa's. Outside their pad, he silently hid the bulky parcel in the hall, then opened the door and stepped inside. "Hi, baby!" he called. "It's me."

Clarissa quickly ran some white lipstick across her lips and, still carrying the leek she was peeling, danced toward him from the sink. But on seeing Clarence she let out a gasp and stared as if he were something she had discarded in Scarsdale.

The smile on Clarence's face disappeared. "Clarissa!" he said. "Don't look at me that way."

Clarissa shook her head from side to side, as if telling herself that what she saw wasn't true. "*They!*" she cried bitterly. "They've got this big authority game going, and like you sold out to them."

"I sold my hair," he said, "but I didn't sell out, baby." He hesitated momentarily, groping for the rest of his answer. "Like I sold it because they were buying. And I needed the bills to get you—"

Clarissa threw the leek to the floor. "If it was better phrased," she shouted, "I'd call it liberal rhetoric!" Apparently startled at the sound of her own voice, she lowered it slightly. "But pretty soon you'll start wearing socks. And like the next thing, I'll be washing them, and before long . . . before long you'll end up going back to school, back where the girls are the ones with long hair." She began sputtering, searching for words. "And then, then . . . then what'll happen to our heightened catharsis of experience?"

Clarence envied her way with words, her uncompromising ideals. He could see that this was not the time to reason with Clarissa. Maybe tomorrow. He'd think of it tomorrow—on Christmas Day. "Let's wish each other a merry Christmas," he said softly. "A very merry Christmas." It was a little like Tiny Tim's speech, and Clarence hoped it would work in an apartment full of posters of the Grateful Dead. Remembering the beautiful amplifier, he went to the hall and retrieved the parcel. In a moment he had it open. The chrome, glistening like Christmas-tree lights, reflected her tear-filled eyes.

Clarissa smiled briefly, but then the smile vanished. "I sold it," she said. "Like just this afternoon I sold it. Sold it so you could get a tutor and graduate with your hair on. But now you don't need a tutor, and you don't need me."

Clarence put his arms around his sobbing wife. "I don't want no tutor," he said. "But I do want you. And we can take that money and buy back your guitar."

"Take the money and buy back your hair!" shouted Clarissa as she pushed Clarence away and ran to the window. Sullenly, she stared out at the snow, which was now falling more heavily.

Clarence joined her at the window, but the arm he tried to put around her shoulder was quickly brushed away. He glanced across the street at the snow-laden Psychedelicatessen sign, then down at the wet pavement below. "It's turning to slush," he said. "Everything's turning to slush."

1967

PARENTAL ADVISORY

DANIEL MENAKER

For the few people not familiar with the idea behind the Domestic Rider to Parkinson's Law—children expand to fill the space allotted to them and also a great deal of the space not allotted to them—a brief, selective inventory of the contents of the "public" areas of our apartment (entrance hall, dining room, living room) will demonstrate it nicely: Plastic bag filled with cheap Walkmans, dead batteries, and Gordian earphone cords. Pieces of paper on the floor, including an old birthday-party list on a page torn off an Amoxil Chewable notepad and a drawing done by Elizabeth, my eight-year-old daughter, of an Asian-looking smile face with a third, Caucasian eye in the middle of its forehead and mucus dripping from its nose. A pair of navy-blue Stride Rite party shoes. Small clay figure resembling Mr. Bill, the victim of "Saturday Night Live"'s sadistic Sluggo. Similar figure of a woman in a chair, whom I think of as Dame Edith Sitwell. A drawing done by my eleven-year-old son of a nightmare version of a subway station. A wedge of wood that my daughter painted green and red, with black pips, to resemble a slice of watermelon. Lionel XR Speed Machine bicycle with two flat tires. A two-foot-long Medusa's coiffure of plastic lanyard under a chair. A pair of Reebok Blacktop sneakers. Advanced Dungeons & Dragons Players' Handbook. And so forth.

The Domestic Rider will surely prove to govern not only real space but electronic space. In fact, around our cyber-household it already does. I bought a PowerBook a few weeks ago and, the other day, when I turned it on I noticed that a new icon had floated down onto its desktop. Its title was "Willy's Folder," and in it I found one document called "The Moron Gang"

and another called "Wish." Yeah, I opened them. (Hey, it's my PowerBook!) "The Moron Gang" turned out to be a short story, abandoned, at least for the time being, after a few pages; and this is "Wish," a docket-in-progress of Christmas desiderata (reprinted with the permission of the author):

WISH LIST

Music

1. Beastie Boys: Ill Communication
2. Offspring: Smash
3. Nirvana: Bleach
4. Nirvana: Nevermind
5. Janes Addiction: Ritual de lo Habitual

Clothing

1. Princess Mary flannel
2. muted Dress Stewart flannel
3. pair of faded denim jeans
4. pair of saddle jeans
5. pair of stonewashed denim jeans
6. pair of double black jeans
7. Green Day Dookie Bombs T-shirt
8. Nirvana in Utero T-shirt
9. Pearl Jam Flame Picture T-shirt
10. Soundgarden Black Hole Sun T-shirt
11. Barney eating kids T-shirt
12. Parental Advisory Explicit Lyrics T-shirt

Necklaces, Rings

1. Nirvana necklace
2. Soundgarden necklace
3. skull rings
4. claw holding crystel necklace
5. wizard necklace
6. anarcy necklace

Exspense Things

1. black leather 8 eyelet pair of doc martians
2. Sony disc man

For all their found-poetry quality, and despite my having watched the Grammys with Willy last fall, some of the bytes that "Wish" took out of my PowerBook are Klingon to me, but even so they clearly illustrate another article of the universal Code of Parenthood: children grow up five years for every five minutes their parents aren't looking. Skull ring? Not for that molarless tyke my wife just now put down for a nap. Jane's Addiction? Not for that towhead who yesterday was afraid of the Cookie Monster. And so on. I could have sworn I saw him teetering into his room Pampers-clad and with oatmeal adorning his head this morning, and yet here he is at 7 P.M. going out to a dance wearing (single?) black jeans held up around the tops of his thighs by what means I have no idea, and a dab of mousse in his hair.

So it wasn't truly surprising to learn that a kid's eminent domain extends beyond real estate and into RAM. What did arrest me was the extreme force with which Willy's wish list applied the law of They Grow Up Too Fast, and it made me understand that my children's childhood, like a lot of other things around here, will remain, for me, unfinished. That's the law, too, of course: you have to let your children go before you're ready to. And that is why childhood is poignant even when it's not. I will someday, too soon, fatten my laptop's trash can with Willy's file folder and put Elizabeth's Stride Rites away for good, but Christmas is around the first corner, so wish away, the two of you—all of a sudden you're old enough to know a soft touch when you see one.   1994

CHRISTMAS CARDS

JOHN UPDIKE

How strange it is—gut-wrenchingly strange—to realize that your parents, in a snapshot taken by memory, are younger not only than you now but than your own children. If I was seven or eight on a certain Christmas that I remember, my father would have been thirty-nine or forty, and my mother thirty-five or six. A couple of kids, really, living in her parents' house with their only child, in a Depression that war's excitement and mounting public debt hadn't yet lifted. The taste of Christmas in the little Pennsylvania town of Shillington—one of the more penetrating in my life's bolted meals—was compounded of chocolate-flavored piety, as sweetly standardized as Hershey's Kisses, and a tart, refreshed awareness of where one stood on the socioeconomic scale.

Since at that latitude white Christmases were a rarity, the proper atmosphere had to be created within the front parlor: an evergreen tree more or less richly laden with decorations brought down from the attic; beneath the tree a "Christmas yard," a miniature landscape of cotton snow and mirror ponds and encircling railroad tracks; a heap of wrapped presents, which at my age of seven or eight had not yet quite shed the possibility, like a glaze, that an omniscient, fast-moving Santa Claus had personally deposited them. Though we had the tree, our neighbors' trees were in my impression bushier, pressing against the ceiling and crowding the front windows, and more sumptuously hung with reflective balls, colored lights, and glittering tinsel. We didn't bother with tinsel; my mother, I believe, found it vulgar and messy. Though we had the yard, with a lovable blue Lionel train—engine, coal car, and two or three passenger cars, going around and around in tooting obedience to a cubic black transformer—friends of mine, or friends of theirs, had entire basements dedicated to mountainous, suburbanized mazes of tracks, switchoffs, tunnels, and toy stations. Our yard had a single tunnel, through a papier-mâché mountain whose snowy crest was approached up green-sprayed sides diagonally dented by what I understood to be sheep paths. Our pond was square, and any illusion of landscape fomented by the toy cows and cottages on its cotton banks clashed with the reality of my own huge, freckled face looking up from it when I peeked in. Though we had the presents, they seemed less numerous and luxurious than presents bestowed up and down Philadelphia Avenue, in houses externally more modest than ours.

On the Christmas that I painfully remember, one of the presents was a double deck of playing cards in a pretty box, whose gray surface had a fuzzy texture, and whose paper drawer was pulled out by a silken tab. I had unwrapped the box and had assumed that

Is there a professional friend or associate for whom it is always difficult to select a suitable nonpersonal Christmas gift? Here's one suggestion that will answer the problem for you—give him a copy of the 20 Year Index to Sewage Works Journal.

—*Adv. in the Sewage Works Journal*

It's as good as done.

1951

it was for me until my father's voice, which was almost never raised to me in disapproval or correction, gently floated down from above with the suggestion that the cards were a present from him to my mother. This made sense: one of her habits—the most alarming habit she had, indeed—was to play solitaire at night at the dining table, under the stained-glass chandelier. "The weary gambler," she would intone theatrically, "stakes her all," as she doggedly laid out the cards in their rows. Now her voice descended to me, saying that the cards were for all of us to share; and it was true, we did play cards, three-handed pinochle, and the box said "PINOCHLE" on it. Nevertheless, I was humiliated, as deeply as only a child can be, to be caught trying to appropriate her present. At the same time, I thought that if there had been more presents I would not have made such a mistake. And I was afflicted by the paltriness of this present from my father to his wife. At least, I am afflicted now, or have been the hundreds or thousands of times I have remembered this incident. The something pathetic about our Christmases, the something that strived and failed to live up to Shillington's Noël ideal, was bared; a pang went through me that dyed the moment indelibly.

Some elemental, mournful triangle seems sketched: my grandparents, those distant, grave, friendly adjuncts, are absent from the room as I remember it. My parents are above me, the presents shorn of wrapping are around me, the three-rail Lionel tracks are by my knees, the tree with its resiny scent presses close. I have no memory of what I did receive that Christmas—the wooden skis, perhaps, with leather-strap bindings that never held, or a shiny children's classic that would stay unread. I feel, for a moment, the triangle flip: through the little velvety box of cards I see my parents in their poverty, their useless gentility, their unspoken plight of homelessness, their clinging to each other through such tokens, and through me. I become in my memory their parent, looking down and precociously grieving for them.

Captured in this recollection, I want to look out the window for relief, at the vacant lot next to our house, at the row houses opposite. If there was no white Christmas, there was at least a public Christmas, a free ten-o'clock cartoon show at the Shillington movie theatre, followed by a throng of us children lining up at the town hall to receive a box of chocolates from the hands of Sam Reich, the fat one of the three town policemen. I remember eating these chocolates, trying to avoid the ones with cherries at their centers, while walking up Philadelphia Avenue with the other children as they noisily boasted of their presents—I seeming to be, as one sometimes is in a dream, tongue-tied.

1997

the FEAST

A FINE TURKEY DINNER

BRENDAN GILL

Father Hagerty sat at his desk in the bay window of the rectory parlor stacking, in precarious piles, the nickels and dimes of the annual Christmas collection. This little hoard had been gathered at Mass the previous Sunday in order to buy, according to parish custom, a fine turkey dinner for the rectory household—Father Hagerty; his curate, Father Cain; and his housekeeper, Mrs. Katharine O'Degnan Malone. Father Hagerty added coin to coin in mixed discouragement and hope. After setting aside four dollars for the dinner, he planned to turn over the rest of the collection to a fund he had fostered in secret for several years. Sooner or later he would have the means to buy a new Saint Anthony to stand by the sacristy door. The plaster fingers of the present Saint Anthony, who was twelve years old, were beginning to chip.

Father Hagerty had placed his desk in the bay window twenty years before. He called it his lighthouse, since from it, as he worked on parish records and reports—he had long ago given up preparing sermons—he could keep an eye on the doings of the town. Barnardsville's Main Street ran directly in front of the rectory. Across the street stood Dodd's garage, where everyone gathered in the early morning to discuss the temperature, a various topic in a town built among the hills; and just beyond the church stood O'Connor's general store, where everyone gathered in the early evening to discuss the temperature again and to make a pattern of the long, lazy day. Now, as he totted up his sums, Father Hagerty watched his parishioners walking home from work. It was impossible, with the dusk falling, to make out faces, but he nodded to everyone and everyone nodded in return. Father Hagerty supposed that a few of those to whom he nodded were Protestants, but even they, in this town, made good friends.

From the racket of pots and dishes in the kitchen, Father Hagerty guessed it was time he washed his hands. He had, after all these years, given up telling time by the clock. Mrs. Malone woke him as she entered the house at seven every morning. He got up to the sound of the kettle's being set on the stove to boil. He shaved to the sound of places being laid for Father Cain and him on the naked dining-room table. It was like that all day. Now it could hardly be earlier than six, for at that hour Mrs. Malone reached the noisy climax of her preparations for supper. Father Hagerty swept the neat piles of coins into a heap in the middle of the desk.

The collection totalled twelve dollars and twenty-five cents. Eight dollars and twenty-five cents of that amount could be hidden in Father Hagerty's fund. The Saint Anthony on whom he had his eye, pictured in color in a catalogue in the bottom drawer of the desk, was priced at one hundred and ten dollars, plus the cost of shipping. Five more years, Father Hagerty figured, should find him at his goal. He nodded with satisfaction. As he got up from the desk, he caught sight of young Father Cain on the path outside. Father Hagerty shook his head. His new curate worried him; the boy was too thin. He stepped into the hall to meet him as he opened the front door. Father Cain's lips were blue with cold.

"No muffler?" Father Hagerty asked severely.

"I didn't know how cold it was, Father."

"Coldest town in Connecticut. I told you that when the Bishop sent you up here this fall."

"I'm sorry, Father." Father Cain had been ordained in June. He still felt humble in front of other priests and stared at them in wonder when they bowed to him and called him Father.

"How's Mrs. O'Donaghue?"

Father Cain tried to smile. "She's like all the rest. She wants you, of course. She knows you don't think she's very sick if you only send me."

"Don't let that worry you. She'll be up and in the thick of it Christmas morning, now she's had a priest to talk to."

Father Cain said, "You can feel Christmas! The whole town's excited about it. Everybody's got a tree and lights on it and the kids all say 'Hello, Father' to me very carefully and you can see the cars coming back from Hartford and Waterbury full of packages." His eyes widened. "It's really here."

Father Hagerty studied the banister of the stairs. "This is your first Christmas away from home, isn't it? There's always a first one, you know."

Father Cain kept smiling. "Yes, Father."

"I've been thinking," Father Hagerty said. "Why shouldn't you go home? It's only forty miles. You can take my Ford. No reason for staying here. I won't hear of anything else."

The boy shook his head. His lips were still a little blue. "I want to stay. I want to say my first Christmas Mass here."

Father Hagerty climbed the stairs, resting his weight heavily on each step. "We're having a fine turkey dinner. Mrs. Malone always gives

us a real old-fashioned Christmas, with all the trimmings." He looked down on Father Cain from the second floor. "I hope we have snow, too. It always makes it seem more like Christmas to me. Do you think we will?"

"Feels like it, Father," the boy said.

~~~

Father Cain offered Mass at nine o'clock on Christmas morning, Father Hagerty at eleven. Everyone said "Merry Christmas, Father" to Father Cain as he stood in the back of the church after each Mass. From twelve until one, Father Hagerty and he sat in the parlor and waited for Mrs. Malone to call them into the dining room. There was hardly anything to talk about. Father Cain's family had sent him, by mail, a sweater, some books, and a pair of skis, of which he felt ashamed. Father Hagerty's sister had knitted him woollen socks. "She always makes them too big in the heel," Father Hagerty had said. "I've got twenty pairs of them up in the drawer. She's a good girl." Father Hagerty had given Father Cain a pipe and Father Cain had given Father Hagerty a box of cigars. They were embarrassed by the similarity of their gifts. It seemed easier to say nothing about them.

"All right, Father," Mrs. Malone said finally. She stood in the doorway in a clean apron, wiping her clean hands. "The bird looks like leather. You ought to give Tim Bowen a piece of your mind."

"You always say that, Mrs. Malone. It wouldn't seem natural to sit down at the table if you didn't."

The dining room faced north, toward the green spruce woods that bordered the town. In spite of the four candles making a square of light on the table, the room was dark. Father Hagerty sat down, folded his hands, and recited, "Bless us, O Lord, and these Thy gifts which of Thy bounty we are about to receive. Through Christ our Lord. Amen." Then he sipped his tomato juice. "It didn't snow," he said.

Father Cain shook his head. "No. Most Christmases, I guess, it doesn't." He spoke hurriedly, ignoring his tomato juice. "I remember I got a Flexible Flyer for Christmas once and there wasn't any snow. I wanted to take it out and try it on the bare ground. I couldn't wait."

Father Hagerty looked at the boy. "You can't, when you're a kid."

"We always buy a tree the first day they come in. Mom and Dad and all of us go down and pick out the biggest one we can find. Then, on Christmas Eve, we set it up in the hall by the stairs, where there's room for it, no matter how high it is. Sometimes we get one so high we have to go up on the second floor to put the star on its top."

"That's a real tree."

"You should see it. Then, about midnight, everybody goes up to his room and gets the presents he's bought, all wrapped up in green and red paper, and brings them down and puts them under the tree. Everyone has a special pile. We always try to see who has the biggest pile, but they're usually just about the same. We've caught Mom sneaking extra presents into any pile that looks a little smaller than the rest."

Mrs. Malone entered and removed the tomato-juice glasses. She frowned at the talkative Father Cain but said nothing. Then she carried the turkey to the table, a thin brown turkey on a mended porcelain platter.

Father Hagerty rubbed his chin. "It does look a little small," he said.

"What did I tell you?" Mrs. Malone demanded. "That Tim Bowen!"

"And the next morning," Father Cain said, "Christmas morning, we all get up in the dark and go down and open our presents."

"Thirty-eight cents a pound for meat like that," said Mrs. Malone.

"Which do you prefer, dark meat or light?" asked Father Hagerty.

Father Cain swallowed. "I'm sorry," he said. He got up and walked carefully from the room. Father Hagerty and Mrs. Malone turned to follow the sound of his feet on the stairs. As the door of his bedroom closed behind him, Mrs. Malone sucked in her breath. "They're all the same. Next year he'll tuck it in fast enough."

Father Hagerty cut off a leg of the turkey with some difficulty and put it on his plate. "He doesn't know that now," he said. He was thinking he might just as well have added the cost of the turkey to his secret fund. He might have brought Saint Anthony a half year nearer the faded pedestal in the church. The meat was tough, all right.

1939

STARE DECISIS

H. L. MENCKEN

Despite all the snorting against them in works of divinity, it has always been my experience that infidels—or freethinkers, as they usually prefer to call themselves—are a generally estimable class of men, with strong overtones of the benevolent and even of the sentimental. This was certainly true, for example, of Leopold Bortsch, *Totsäufer** for the Scharnhorst Brewery, in Baltimore, forty-five years ago, whose story I have told, alas only piecemeal, in various previous communications to the press. If you want a bird's-eye view of his character, you can do no better than turn to the famous specifications for an ideal bishop in I Timothy III, 2–6. So far as I know, no bishop now in practice on earth meets those specifications precisely, and more than one whom I could mention falls short of them by miles, but Leopold qualified under at least eleven of the sixteen counts, and under some of them he really shone.

He was extremely liberal (at least with the brewery's money), he had only one wife (a natural blonde weighing a hundred and eighty-five pounds) and treated her with great humanity, he was (I quote the text) "no striker . . . not a brawler," and he was preëminently "vigilant, sober, of good behavior, given to hospitality, apt to teach." Not once in the days I knew and admired him, *c.* 1900, did he ever show anything remotely resembling a bellicose and rowdy spirit, not even against the primeval Prohibitionists of the age, the Lutheran pastors who so often plastered him from the pulpit, or the saloon-keepers who refused to lay in Scharnhorst beer. He was a sincere friend to the orphans, the aged, all blind and one-legged men, ruined girls, opium fiends, Chinamen, oyster dredgers, ex-convicts, the more respectable sort of colored people, and all the other oppressed and unfortunate classes of the time, and he slipped them, first and last, many a substantial piece of money.

Nor was he the only Baltimore infidel of those days who thus shamed the

---

*A *Totsäufer* (literally, dead-drinker) is a brewery's customers' man. One of his most important duties is to carry on in a wild and inconsolable manner at the funerals of saloonkeepers.

churchly. Indeed, the name of one of his buddies, Fred Ammermeyer, jumps into my memory at once. Fred and Leopold, I gathered, had serious dogmatic differences, for there are as many variations in doctrine between infidels as between Christians, but the essential benignity of both men kept them on amicable terms, and they often coöperated in good works. The only noticeable difference between them was that Fred usually tried to sneak a little propaganda into his operations—a dodge that the more scrupulous Leopold was careful to avoid. Thus, when a call went out for Bibles for the paupers lodged in Bayview, the Baltimore almshouse, Fred responded under an assumed name with a gross that had to be scrapped at once, for he had marked all the more antinomian passages with a red, indelible pencil—for example, Proverbs VII, 18–19; John VII, 7; I Timothy V, 23; and the account of David's dealing with Uriah in II Samuel XI. Again, he once hired Charlie Metcalfe, a small-time candy manufacturer, to prepare a special pack of chocolate drops for orphans and ruined girls, with a deceptive portrait of Admiral Dewey on the cover and a print of Bob Ingersoll's harangue over his brother's remains at the bottom of each box. Fred had this subversive exequium reprinted many times, and distributed at least two hundred and fifty thousand copies in Baltimore between 1895 and 1900. There were some Sunday-school scholars who received, by one device or another, at least a dozen. As for the clergy of the town, he sent each and every one of them a copy of Paine's "Age of Reason" three or four times a year—always disguised as a special-delivery or registered letter marked "Urgent." Finally, he employed seedy rabble rousers to mount soap boxes at downtown street corners on Saturday nights and there bombard the assembled loafers, peddlers, and cops with speeches which began seductively as excoriations of the Interests and then proceeded inch by inch to horrifying proofs that there was no hell.

~~~

But in the masterpiece of Fred Ammermeyer's benevolent career there was no such attempt at direct missionarying; indeed, his main idea when he conceived it was to hold up to scorn and contumely, by the force of mere contrast, the crude missionarying of his theological opponents. This idea seized him one evening when he dropped into the Central Police Station to pass the time of day with an old friend, a police lieutenant who was then the only known freethinker on the Baltimore force. Christmas was approaching and the lieutenant was in an unhappy and rebellious frame of mind—not because he objected to its orgies as such, or because he sought to deny Christians its beautiful consolations, but simply and solely because he always had the job of keeping order at the annual free dinner given by the massed missions of the town to the derelicts of the waterfront and that duty compelled him to listen politely to a long string of pious exhortations, many of them from persons he knew to be whited sepulchres.

"Why in hell," he observed impatiently, "do all them goddam hypocrites keep the poor bums waiting for two, three hours while they get off their goddam whimwham? Here is a hall full of men who ain't had nothing to speak of to eat for maybe three, four days, and yet they have to set there smelling the turkey and the coffee while ten, fifteen Sunday-school superintendents and W.C.T.U. sisters sing hymns to them and holler against booze. I tell you, Mr. Ammermeyer, it ain't human. More than once I have saw a whole row of them poor bums pass out in faints, and had to send them away in the wagon. And then, when the chow is circulated at last, and they begin fighting for the turkey bones, they ain't hardly got the stuff down before the superintendents and the sisters begin calling on them to stand up and confess whatever skulduggery they have done in the past, whether they really done it or not, *with us cops standing all around.* And every man Jack of them knows that if they don't lay it on plenty thick there won't be no encore of the giblets and stuffing, and two times out of three there ain't no encore anyhow, for them psalm singers are the stingiest outfit outside hell and never give a starving bum enough solid feed to last him until Christmas Monday. And not a damned drop to drink! Nothing but coffee—and without no milk! I tell you, Mr. Ammermeyer, it makes a man's blood boil."

Fred's duly boiled, and to immediate effect. By noon the next day he had rented the largest hall on the waterfront and sent word to the newspapers that arrangements for a Christmas party for bums to end all Christmas parties for bums were under way. His plan for it was extremely simple. The first obligation of hospitality, he announced somewhat prissily, was to find out precisely what one's guests wanted, and the second was to give it to them with a free and even reckless hand. As for what his proposed guests wanted, he had no shade of doubt, for he was a man of worldly experience and he had also, of course, the advice of his friend the lieutenant, a recognized expert in the psychology of the abandoned.

First and foremost, they wanted as much malt liquor as they would buy themselves if they had the means to buy it. Second, they wanted a dinner that went on in rhythmic waves, all day and all night, until the hungriest and hollowest bum was reduced to breathing with not more than one cylinder of one lung. Third, they wanted not a mere sufficiency but a riotous superfluity of the best five-cent cigars on sale on the Baltimore wharves. Fourth, they wanted continuous entertainment, both theatrical and musical, of a sort in consonance with their natural tastes and their station in life. Fifth and last, they wanted complete freedom from evangelical harassment of whatever sort, before, during, and after the secular ceremonies.

On this last point, Fred laid special stress, and every city editor in Baltimore had to hear him expound it in person. I was one of those city editors, and I well recall his great earnestness, amounting almost to moral indignation. It was an unendurable outrage, he argued, to invite a poor man to a free meal and then make him wait for it while he was battered with criticism of his ways, however well intended. And it was an even greater outrage to call upon him to stand up in public and confess to all the false steps of what may have been a long and much troubled life. Fred was determined, he said, to give a party that would be devoid of all the blemishes of the similar parties staged by the Salvation Army, the mission helpers, and other such nefarious outfits. If it cost him his last cent, he would give the bums of Baltimore massive and unforgettable proof that philanthropy was by no means a monopoly of gospel sharks—that its highest development, in truth, was to be found among freethinkers.

It might have cost him his last cent if he had gone it alone, for he was by no means a man of wealth, but his announcement had hardly got out before he was swamped with offers of help. Leopold Bortsch pledged twenty-five barrels of Scharnhorst beer and every other *Totsäufer* in Baltimore rushed up to match him. The Baltimore agents of the Pennsylvania two-fer factories fought for the privilege of contributing the cigars. The poultry dealers of Lexington, Fells Point, and Cross Street markets threw in barrel after barrel of dressed turkeys, some of them in very fair condition. The members of the boss bakers' association, not a few of them freethinkers themselves, promised all the bread, none more than two days old, that all the bums of the Chesapeake littoral could eat, and the public-relations counsel of the Celery Trust, the Cranberry Trust, the Sauerkraut Trust, and a dozen other such cartels and combinations leaped at the chance to serve.

If Fred had to fork up cash for any part of the chow, it must have been for the pepper and salt alone. Even the ketchup was contributed by social-minded members of the Maryland canners' association, and with it they threw in a dozen cases of dill pickles, chowchow, mustard, and mincemeat. But the rent of the hall had to be paid, and not only paid but paid in advance, for the owner thereof was a Methodist deacon, and there were many other expenses of considerable size—for example, for the entertainment, the music, the waiters and bartenders, and the mistletoe and immortelles which decorated the hall. Fred, if he had desired, might have got the free services of whole herds of amateur musicians and elocutionists, but he swept them aside disdainfully, for he was determined to give his guests a strictly professional show. The fact that a burlesque company starved out in the Deep South was currently stranded in Baltimore helped him here, for its members were glad to take an engagement at an inside rate, but the musicians' union, as usual, refused to let art or philanthropy shake its principles, and Fred had to pay six of its members the then prevailing scale of four dollars for their first eight hours of work and fifty cents an hour for overtime. He got, of course, some contributions in cash from rich freethinkers, but when the smoke cleared away at last and he totted up his books, he found that the party had set him back more than a hundred and seventy-five dollars.

~~~

Admission to the party was by card only, and the guests were selected with a critical and bilious eye by the police lieutenant. No bum who had ever been known to do any honest work—even such light work as sweeping out a saloon—was on the list. By Fred's express and oft-repeated command it was made up wholly of men completely lost to human decency, in whose favor nothing whatsoever could be said. The doors opened at 11 A.M. of Christmas Day, and the first canto of the dinner began instantly. There were none of the usual preliminaries—no opening prayer, no singing of a hymn, no remarks by Fred himself, not even a fanfare by the band. The bums simply shuffled and shoved their way to the tables and simultaneously the waiters and sommeliers poured in with the chow and the malt. For half an hour no sound was heard save the rattle of crockery, the chomp-chomp of mastication, and the grateful grunts and "Oh, boy!"s of the assembled underprivileged.

Then the cigars were passed round (not one but half a dozen to every man), the band cut loose with the tonic chord of G major, and the burlesque company plunged into Act I, Sc. 1 of "Krausmeyer's Alley." There were in those days, as old-timers will recall, no less than five standard versions of this classic, ranging in refinement all the way from one so tony that it might have been put on at the Union Theological Seminary down to one so rowdy that it was fit only for audiences of policemen, bums, newspaper reporters, and medical students. This last was called the Cincinnati version, because Cincinnati was then the only great American city whose mores tolerated it. Fred gave instructions that it was to be played *à outrance* and *con fuoco,* with no salvo of slapsticks, however brutal, omitted, and no *double entendre,* however daring. Let the boys have it, he instructed the chief comedian, Larry Snodgrass, straight in the eye and direct from the wood. They were poor men and full of sorrow, and he wanted to give them, on at least one red-letter day, a horse doctor's dose of the kind of humor they really liked.

In that remote era the girls of the company could add but little to the exhilarating grossness of the performance, for the strip tease was not yet invented and even the shimmy was still only nascent, but they did the best they could with the muscle dancing launched by Little Egypt at the Chicago World's Fair, and that best was not to be sneezed at, for they were all in hearty sympathy with Fred's agenda, and furthermore, they cherished the usual hope of stage folk that Charles Frohman or Abe Erlanger might be in the audience. Fred had demanded that they all appear in red tights, but there were not enough red tights in hand to outfit more than half of them, so Larry Snodgrass conceived the bold idea of sending on the rest with bare legs. It was a revolutionary indelicacy, and for a startled moment or two the police lieutenant wondered whether he was not bound by his Hippocratic oath to raid the show, but when he saw the whole audience leap up and break into cheers, his dubieties vanished, and five minutes later he was roaring himself when Larry and the other comedians began paddling the girls' cabooses with slapsticks.

I have seen many a magnificent performance of "Krausmeyer's Alley" in my time, including a Byzantine version called "Krausmeyer's Dispensary," staged by the students at the Johns Hopkins Medical School, but never have I seen a better one. Larry and his colleagues simply gave their all. Wherever, on ordinary occasions, there would have been a laugh, they evoked a roar, and where there would have been roars they produced something akin to asphyxia and apoplexy. Even the members of the musicians' union were forced more than once to lay down their fiddles and cornets and bust into laughter. In fact, they enjoyed the show so vastly that when the comedians retired for breath and the girls came out to sing "Sweet Rosie O'Grady" or "I've Been Workin' on the Railroad," the accompaniment was full of all the outlaw *glissandi* and *sforzandi* that we now associate with jazz.

The show continued at high tempo until 2 P.M., when Fred shut it down to give his guests a chance to eat the second canto of their dinner. It was a duplicate of the first in every detail, with second and third helpings of turkey, sauerkraut, mashed potatoes, and celery for everyone who called for them, and a pitcher of beer in front of each guest. The boys ground away at it for an hour, and then lit fresh cigars and leaned back comfortably for the second part of the show. It was still basically "Krausmeyer's Alley," but it was a "Krausmeyer's Alley" adorned and bedizened with reminiscences of every other burlesque-show curtain raiser and afterpiece in the repertory. It went on and on for four solid hours, with Larry and his pals bending themselves to their utmost exertions, and the girls shaking their legs in almost frantic abandon. At the end of an hour the members of the musicians' union demanded a cut-in on the beer and got it, and immediately afterward the sommeliers began passing pitchers to the performers on the stage. Meanwhile, the pitchers on the tables of the guests were kept replenished, cigars were passed round at short intervals, and the waiters came in with pretzels, potato chips, celery, radishes, and chipped beef to stay the stomachs of those accustomed to the free-lunch way of life.

At 7 P.M. precisely, Fred gave the signal for a hiatus in the entertainment, and the waiters rushed in with the third canto of the dinner. The supply of roast turkey, though it had been enormous, was beginning to show signs of wear by this time, but Fred had in reserve twenty hams and forty pork shoulders, the contribution of George Wienefeldter, president of the Wienefeldter Bros. & Schmidt Sanitary Packing Co., Inc. Also, he had a mine of reserve sauerkraut hidden down under the stage, and soon it was in free and copious circulation and the guests were taking heroic hacks at it. This time they finished in three-quarters of an hour, but Fred filled the time until 8 P.M. by ordering a seventh-inning stretch and by having the police lieutenant go to the stage and assure all hands that any bona-fide participant found on the streets, at the conclusion of the exercises, with his transmission jammed would not be clubbed and jugged, as was the Baltimore custom at the time, but returned to the hall to sleep it off on the floor. This announcement made a favorable impression, and the brethren settled down for the resumption of the show in a very pleasant mood. Larry and his associates were pretty well fagged out by now, for the sort of acting demanded by the burlesque profession is very fatiguing, but you'd never have guessed it by watching them work.

At ten the show stopped again, and there began what Fred described as a *Bierabend,* that is, a beer evening. Extra pitchers were put on every table, more cigars were handed about, and the waiters spread a substantial lunch of

"Merry Christmas, folks. And I want to say I couldn't be president of this great company without the support of each and every one of you, or people very much like you."

rye bread, rat-trap cheese, ham, bologna, potato salad, liver pudding, and *Blutwurst*. Fred announced from the stage that the performers needed a rest and would not be called upon again until twelve o'clock, when a midnight show would begin, but that in the interval any guest or guests with a tendency to song might step up and show his or their stuff. No less than a dozen volunteers at once went forward, but Fred had the happy thought of beginning with a quartet, and so all save the first four were asked to wait. The four laid their heads together, the band played the vamp of "Sweet Adeline," and they were off. It was not such singing as one hears from the Harvard Glee Club or the Bach Choir at Bethlehem, Pennsylvania, but it was at least as good as the barbershop stuff that hillbillies now emit over the radio. The other guests applauded politely, and the quartet, operating briskly under malt and hop power, proceeded to "Don't You Hear Dem Bells?" and "Aunt Dinah's Quilting Party." Then the four singers had a nose-to-nose palaver and the first tenor proceeded somewhat shakily to a conference with Otto Strauss, the leader of the orchestra.

From where I sat, at the back of the hall, beside Fred, I could see Otto shake his head, but the tenor persisted in whatever he was saying, and after a moment Otto shrugged resignedly and the members of the quartet again took their stances. Fred leaned forward eagerly, curious to hear what their next selection would be. He found out at once. It was "Are You Ready for the

"For the last time, get the hell back to Toyland!"

Judgment Day?," the prime favorite of the period in all the sailors' bethels, helping-up missions, Salvation Army bum traps, and other such joints along the waterfront. Fred's horror and amazement and sense of insult were so vast that he was completely speechless, and all I heard out of him while the singing went on was a series of sepulchral groans. The man was plainly suffering cruelly, but what could I do? What, indeed, could anyone do? For the quartet had barely got halfway through the first stanza of the composition before the whole audience joined in. And it joined in with even heartier enthusiasm when the boys on the stage proceeded to "Showers of Blessings," the No. 2 favorite of all seasoned mission stiffs, and then to "Throw Out the Lifeline," and then to "Where Shall We Spend Eternity?," and then to "Wash Me, and I Shall Be Whiter Than Snow."

~~~

Halfway along in this orgy of hymnody, the police lieutenant took Fred by the arm and led him out into the cold, stinging, corpse-reviving air of a Baltimore winter night. The bums, at this stage, were beating time on the tables with their beer glasses and tears were trickling down their noses. Otto and his band knew none of the hymns, so their accompaniment became sketchier and sketchier, and presently they shut down altogether. By this time the members of the quartet began to be winded, and soon there was a halt. In the ensuing silence there arose a quavering, boozy, sclerotic voice from the floor. "Friends," it began, "I just want to tell you what these good people have done for me—how their prayers have saved a sinner who seemed past all redemption. Friends, I had a good mother, and I was brought up under the influence of the Word. But in my young manhood my sainted mother was called to heaven, my poor father took to rum and opium, and I was led by the devil into the hands of wicked men—yes, and wicked women, too. Oh, what a shameful story I have to tell! It would shock you to hear it, even if I told you only half of it. I let myself be . . ."

I waited for no more, but slunk into the night. Fred and the police lieutenant had both vanished, and I didn't see Fred again for a week. But the next day I encountered the lieutenant on the street, and he hailed me sadly. "Well," he said, "what could you expect from them bums? It was the force of habit, that's what it was. They have been eating mission handouts so long they can't help it. Whenever they smell coffee, they begin to confess. Think of all that good food wasted! And all that beer! And all them cigars!"

1944

THE TURKEY SEASON

ALICE MUNRO

When I was fourteen I got a job at the Turkey Barn for the Christmas season. I was still too young to get a job working in a store or as a part-time waitress; I was also too nervous.

I was a turkey gutter. The other people who worked at the Turkey Barn were Lily and Marjorie and Gladys, who were also gutters; Irene and Henry, who were pluckers; Herb Abbott, the foreman, who superintended the whole operation and filled in wherever he was needed. Morgan Elliott was the owner and boss. He and his son, Morgy, did the killing.

Morgy I knew from school. I thought him stupid and despicable and was uneasy about having to consider him in a new and possibly superior guise, as the boss's son. But his father treated him so roughly, yelling and swearing at him, that he seemed no more than the lowest of the workers. The other person related to the boss was Gladys. She was his sister, and in her case there did seem to be some privilege of position. She worked slowly and went home if she was not feeling well, and was not friendly to Lily and Marjorie, although she was, a little, to me. She had come back to live with Morgan and his family after working for many years in Toronto, in a bank. This was not the sort of job she was used to. Lily and Marjorie, talking about her when she wasn't there, said she had had a nervous breakdown. They said Morgan made her work in the Turkey Barn to pay for her keep. They also said, with no worry about the contradiction, that she had taken the job because she was after a man, and that the man was Herb Abbott.

All I could see when I closed my eyes, the first few nights after working there, was turkeys. I saw them hanging upside down, plucked and stiffened, pale and cold, with the heads and necks limp, the eyes and nostrils clotted with dark blood; the remaining bits of feathers—those dark and bloody, too—seemed to form a crown. I saw them not with aversion but with a sense of endless work to be done.

Herb Abbott showed me what to do. You put the turkey down on the table and cut its head off with a cleaver. Then you took the loose skin around the neck and stripped it back to reveal the crop, nestled in the cleft between the gullet and the windpipe.

"Feel the gravel," said Herb encouragingly. He made me close my fingers around the crop. Then he showed me how to work my hand down behind it to cut it out, and the gullet and windpipe as well. He used shears to cut the vertebrae.

"Scrunch, scrunch," he said soothingly. "Now, put your hand in."

I did. It was deathly cold in there, in the turkey's dark insides.

"Watch out for bone splinters."

Working cautiously in the dark, I had to pull the connecting tissues loose.

"Ups-a-daisy." Herb turned the bird over and flexed each leg. "Knees up, Mother Brown. Now." He took a heavy knife and placed it directly on the knee knuckle joints and cut off the shank.

"Have a look at the worms."

Pearly-white strings, pulled out of the shank, were creeping about on their own.

"That's just the tendons shrinking. Now comes the nice part!"

He slit the bird at its bottom end, letting out a rotten smell.

"Are you educated?"

I did not know what to say.

"What's that smell?"

"Hydrogen sulfide."

"Educated," said Herb, sighing. "All right. Work your fingers around and get the guts loose. Easy. Easy. Keep your fingers together. Keep the palm inwards. Feel the ribs with the back of your hand. Feel the guts fit into your palm. Feel that? Keep going. Break the strings—as many as you can. Keep going. Feel a hard lump? That's the gizzard. Feel a soft lump? That's the heart. O.K.? O.K. Get your fingers around the gizzard. Easy. Start pulling this way. That's right. That's right. Start to pull her out."

It was not easy at all. I wasn't even sure what I had was the gizzard. My hand was full of cold pulp.

"Pull," he said, and I brought out a glistening, liverish mass.

"Got it. There's the lights. You know what they are. Lungs. There's the heart. There's the gizzard. There's the gall. Now, you don't ever want to break that gall inside or it will taste the entire turkey." Tactfully, he scraped out what I had missed, including the testicles, which were like a pair of white grapes.

"Nice pair of earrings," Herb said.

Herb Abbott was a tall, firm, plump man. His hair was dark and thin, combed straight back from a widow's peak, and his eyes seemed to be slightly slanted, so that he looked like a pale Chinese or like pictures of the Devil, except that he was smooth-faced and benign. Whatever he did around the Turkey Barn—gutting, as he was now, or loading the truck, or hanging the carcasses—was done with efficient, economical movements, quickly and buoyantly. "Notice about Herb—he always walks like he had a boat moving underneath him," Marjorie said, and it was true. Herb worked on the lake boats, during the season, as a cook. Then he worked for Morgan until after Christmas. The rest of the time he helped around the poolroom, making hamburgers, sweeping up, stopping fights before they got started. That was where he lived; he had a room above the poolroom on the main street.

Christmas day to the Hubbards also means an oaken yule log in the fireplace, presents and a meal of Christ's favorite foods, including roast beef and German chocolate cake.

—Daily Iowan

Oh?

1968

In all the operations at the Turkey Barn it seemed to be Herb who had the efficiency and honor of the business continually on his mind; it was he who kept everything under control. Seeing him in the yard talking to Morgan, who was a thick, short man, red in the face, an unpredictable bully, you would be sure that it was Herb who was the boss and Morgan the hired help. But it was not so.

If I had not had Herb to show me, I don't think I could have learned turkey gutting at all. I was clumsy with my hands and had been shamed for it so often that the least show of impatience on the part of the person instructing me could have brought on a dithering paralysis. I could not stand to be watched by anybody but Herb. Particularly, I couldn't stand to be watched by Lily and Marjorie, two middle-aged sisters, who were very fast and thorough and competitive gutters. They sang at their work and talked abusively and intimately to the turkey carcasses.

"Don't you nick me, you old bugger!"

"Aren't you the old crap factory!"

I had never heard women talk like that.

Gladys was not a fast gutter, though she must have been thorough; Herb would have talked to her otherwise. She never sang and certainly she never swore. I thought her rather old, though she was not as old as Lily and Marjorie; she must have been over thirty. She seemed offended by everything that went on and had the air of keeping plenty of bitter judgments to herself. I never tried to talk to her, but she spoke to me one day in the cold little washroom off the gutting shed. She was putting pancake makeup on her face. The color of the makeup was so distinct from the color of her skin that it was as if she were slapping orange paint over a whitewashed, bumpy wall.

She asked me if my hair was naturally curly.

I said yes.

"You don't have to get a permanent?"

"No."

"You're lucky. I have to do mine up every night. The chemicals in my system won't allow me to get a permanent."

There are different ways women have of talking about their looks. Some women make it clear that what they do to keep themselves up is for the sake of sex, for men. Others, like Gladys, make the job out to be a kind of housekeeping, whose very difficulties they pride themselves on. Gladys was genteel. I could see her in the bank, in a navy-blue dress with the kind of detachable white collar you can wash at night. She would be grumpy and correct.

Another time, she spoke to me about her periods, which were profuse and painful. She wanted to know about mine. There was an uneasy, prudish, agitated expression on her face. I was saved by Irene, who was using the toilet and called out, "Do like me, and you'll be rid of all your problems for a while." Irene was only a few years older than I was, but she was recently—tardily—married, and heavily pregnant.

Gladys ignored her, running cold water on her hands. The hands of all of us were red and sore-looking from the work. "I can't use that soap. If I use it, I break out in a rash," Gladys said. "If I bring my own soap in here, I can't afford to have other people using it, because I pay a lot for it—it's a special anti-allergy soap."

I think the idea that Lily and Marjorie promoted—that Gladys was after Herb Abbott—sprang from their belief that single people ought to be teased and embarrassed whenever possible, and from their interest in Herb, which led to the feeling that somebody ought to be after him. They wondered about him. What they wondered was: How can a man want so little? No wife, no family, no house. The details of his daily life, the small preferences, were of interest. Where had he been brought up? (Here and there and all over.) How far had he gone in school? (Far enough.) Where was his girlfriend? (Never tell.) Did he drink coffee or tea if he got the choice? (Coffee.)

When they talked about Gladys's being after him they must have really wanted to talk about sex—what he wanted and what he got. They must have felt a voluptuous curiosity about him, as I did. He aroused this feeling by being circumspect and not making the jokes some men did, and at the same time by not being squeamish or gentlemanly. Some men, showing me the testicles from the turkey, would have acted as if the very existence of testicles were somehow a bad joke on me, something a girl could be taunted about; another sort of man would have been embarrassed and would have thought he had to protect me from embarrassment. A man who didn't seem to feel one way or the other was an oddity—as much to older women, probably, as to me. But what was so welcome a comfort to me may have been disturbing to them. They wanted to jolt him. They even wanted Gladys to jolt him, if she could.

There wasn't any idea then—at least in Logan, Ontario, in the late forties—about homosexuality's going beyond very narrow confines. Women, certainly, believed in its rarity and in definite boundaries. There were homosexuals in town, and we knew who they were: an elegant, light-voiced, wavy-haired paperhanger who called himself an interior decorator; the minister's widow's fat, spoiled only son, who went so far as to enter baking contests and had crocheted a tablecloth; a hypochondriacal church organist and music teacher who kept the choir and his pupils in line with screaming tantrums. Once the label was fixed, there was a good deal of tolerance for these people, and their talents for decorating, for crocheting, and for music were appreciated—especially by women. "The poor fellow," they said. "He doesn't do any harm." They really seemed to believe—the women did—that it was the penchant for baking or music that was the determining factor, and that it was the activity that made the man what he was, not any other detours he might take, or wish to take. A wish to play the violin would be taken as more a deviation from manliness than would a wish to shun women. Indeed, the idea was that any manly man would wish to shun women but most of them were caught off guard, and for good.

I don't want to go into the question of whether Herb was homosexual or not, because the definition is of no use to me. I think that probably he was, but maybe he was not. (Even considering what happened later, I think that.) He is not a puzzle so arbitrarily solved.

~~~

The other plucker, who worked with Irene, was Henry Streets, a neighbor of ours. There was nothing remarkable about him except that he was eighty-six years old and still, as he said of himself, a devil for work. He had whiskey in his thermos, and drank it from time to time through the day. It was Henry who had said to me, in our kitchen, "You ought to get yourself a job at the Turkey Barn. They need another gutter." Then my father said at once, "Not her, Henry. She's got ten thumbs," and Henry said he was just joking—it was dirty work. But I was already determined to try it—I had a great need to be successful in a job like this. I was almost in the condition of a grownup person who is ashamed of never having learned to read, so much did I feel my ineptness at manual work. Work, to everybody I knew, meant doing things I was no good at doing, and work was what people prided themselves on and measured each other by. (It goes without saying that the things I was good at, like schoolwork, were suspect or held in plain contempt.) So it was a surprise and then a triumph for me not to get fired, and to be able to turn out clean turkeys at a rate that was not disgraceful. I don't know if I really understood how much Herb Abbott was responsible for this, but he would sometimes say, "Good girl," or pat my waist and say, "You're getting to be a good gutter—you'll go a long ways in the world," and when I felt his quick, kind touch through the heavy sweater and bloody smock I wore, I felt my face glow and I wanted to lean back against him as he stood behind me. I wanted to rest my head against his wide, fleshy shoulder. When I went to sleep at night, lying on my side, I would rub my cheek against the pillow and think of that as Herb's shoulder.

I was interested in how he talked to Gladys, how he looked at her or noticed her. This interest was not jealousy. I think I wanted something to happen with them. I quivered in curious expectation, as Lily and Marjorie did. We all wanted to see the flicker of sexuality in him, hear it in his voice, not because we thought it would make him seem more like other men but because we knew that with him it would be entirely different. He was kinder and more patient than most women, and as stern and remote, in some ways, as any man. We wanted to see how he could be moved.

If Gladys wanted this, too, she didn't give any signs of it. It is impossible for me to tell with women like her whether they are as thick and deadly as they seem, not wanting anything much but opportunities for irritation and contempt, or if they are all choked up with gloomy fires and useless passions.

Marjorie and Lily talked about marriage. They did not have much good to say about it, in spite of their feeling that it was a state nobody should be allowed to stay out of. Marjorie said that shortly after her marriage she had gone into the woodshed with the intention of swallowing Paris green.

"I'd have done it," she said. "But the man came along in the grocery truck and I had to go out and buy the groceries. This was when we lived on the farm."

Her husband was cruel to her in those days, but later he suffered an accident—he rolled the tractor and was so badly hurt he would be an invalid all his life. They moved to town, and Marjorie was the boss now.

"He starts to sulk the other night and say he don't want his supper. Well, I just picked up his wrist and held it. He was scared I was going to twist his arm. He could see I'd do it. So I say, 'You *what?*' And he says, 'I'll eat it.'"

They talked about their father. He was a man of the old school. He had a noose in the woodshed (not the Paris-green woodshed—this would be an earlier one, on another farm), and when they got on his nerves he used to line them up and threaten to hang them. Lily, who was the younger, would shake till she fell down. This same father had arranged to marry Marjorie off to a crony of his when she was just sixteen. That was the husband who had driven her to the Paris green. Their father did it because he wanted to be sure she wouldn't get into trouble.

"Hot blood," Lily said.

I was horrified, and asked, "Why didn't you run away?"

"His word was law," Marjorie said.

They said that was what was the matter with kids nowadays—it was the kids that ruled the roost. A father's word should be law. They brought up their own kids strictly, and none had turned out bad yet. When Marjorie's son wet the bed she threatened to cut off his dingy with the butcher knife. That cured him.

They said ninety per cent of the young girls nowadays drank, and swore, and took it lying down. They did not have daughters, but if they did and caught them at anything like that they would beat them raw. Irene, they said, used to go to the hockey games with her ski pants slit and nothing under them, for convenience in the snowdrifts afterward. Terrible.

I wanted to point out some contradictions. Marjorie and Lily themselves drank and swore, and what was so wonderful about the strong will of a father who would insure you a lifetime of unhappiness? (What I did not see was that Marjorie and Lily were not unhappy altogether—could not be, because of their sense of consequence, their pride and style.) I could be enraged then at the lack of logic in most adults' talk—the way they held to their pronouncements no matter what evidence might be presented to them. How could these

women's hands be so gifted, so delicate and clever—for I knew they would be as good at dozens of other jobs as they were at gutting; they would be good at quilting and darning and painting and papering and kneading dough and setting out seedlings—and their thinking so slapdash, clumsy, infuriating?

Lily said she never let her husband come near her if he had been drinking. Marjorie said since the time she nearly died with a hemorrhage she never let her husband come near her, period. Lily said quickly that it was only when he'd been drinking that he tried anything. I could see that it was a matter of pride not to let your husband come near you, but I couldn't quite believe that "come near" meant "have sex." The idea of Marjorie and Lily being sought out for such purposes seemed grotesque. They had bad teeth, their stomachs sagged, their faces were dull and spotty. I decided to take "come near" literally.

~~~

The two weeks before Christmas were a frantic time at the Turkey Barn. I began to go in for an hour before school as well as after school and on weekends. In the morning, when I walked to work, the street lights would still be on and the morning stars shining. There was the Turkey Barn, on the edge of a white field, with a row of big pine trees behind it, and always, no matter how cold and still it was, these trees were lifting their branches and sighing and straining. It seems unlikely that on my way to the Turkey Barn, for an hour of gutting turkeys, I should have experienced such a sense of promise and at the same time of perfect, impenetrable mystery in the universe, but I did. Herb had something to do with that, and so did the cold snap—the series of hard, clear mornings. The truth is, such feelings weren't hard to come by then. I would get them but not know how they were to be connected with anything in real life.

One morning at the Turkey Barn there was a new gutter. This was a boy eighteen or nineteen years old, a stranger named Brian. It seemed he was a relative, or perhaps just a friend, of Herb Abbott's. He was staying with Herb. He had worked on a lake boat last summer. He said he had got sick of it, though, and quit.

Language at the Turkey Barn was coarse and free, but in telling us this Brian used an expression that is commonplace today but was not so then. It seemed not careless but flaunting, mixing insult and provocation. Perhaps it was his general style that made it seem so. He had amazing good looks: taffy hair, bright-blue eyes, ruddy skin, well-shaped body—the sort of good looks nobody disagrees about for a moment. But a single, relentless notion had got such a hold on him that he could not keep from turning all his assets into parody. His mouth was wet-looking and slightly open most of the time, his eyes were half shut, his expression a hopeful leer, his movements indolent, exaggerated, inviting. Perhaps if he had been put on a stage with a microphone and a guitar and let grunt and howl and wriggle and excite, he would have seemed a true celebrant. Lacking a stage, he was unconvincing. After a while he seemed just like somebody with a bad case of hiccups—his insistent sexuality was that monotonous and meaningless.

If he had toned down a bit, Marjorie and Lily would probably have enjoyed him. They could have kept up a game of telling him to shut his filthy mouth and keep his hands to himself. As it was, they said they were sick of him, and meant it. Once, Marjorie took up her gutting knife. "Keep your distance," she said. "I mean from me and my sister and that kid."

She did not tell him to keep his distance from Gladys, because Gladys wasn't there at the time and Marjorie would probably not have felt like protecting her anyway. But it was Gladys Brian particularly liked to bother. She would throw down her knife and go into the washroom and stay there ten minutes and come out with a stony face. She didn't say she was sick anymore and go home, the way she used to. Marjorie said Morgan was mad at Gladys for sponging and she couldn't get away with it any longer.

Gladys said to me, "I can't stand that kind of thing. I can't stand people mentioning that kind of thing and that kind of—gestures. It makes me sick to my stomach."

I believed her. She was terribly white. But why, in that case, did she not complain to Morgan? Perhaps relations between them were too uneasy, perhaps she could not bring herself to repeat or describe such things. Why did none of us complain—if not to Morgan, at least to Herb? I never thought of it. Brian seemed just something to put up with, like the freezing cold in the gutting shed and the smell of blood and waste. When Marjorie and Lily did threaten to complain, it was about Brian's laziness.

He was not a good gutter. He said his hands were too big. So Herb took him off gutting, told him he was to sweep and clean up, make packages of giblets, and help load the truck. This meant that he did not have to be in any one place or doing any one job at a given time, so much of the time he did nothing. He would start sweeping up, leave that and mop the tables, leave that and have a cigarette, lounge against the table bothering us until Herb called him to help load. Herb was very busy now and spent a lot of time making deliveries, so it was possible he did not know the extent of Brian's idleness.

"I don't know why Herb don't fire you," Marjorie said. "I guess the answer is he don't want you hanging around sponging on him, with no place to go."

"I know where to go," said Brian.

"Keep your sloppy mouth shut," said Marjorie. "I pity Herb. Getting saddled."

~~~

On the last school day before Christmas we got out early in the afternoon. I went home and changed my clothes and came into work at about three o'clock. Nobody was working. Everybody was in the gutting shed, where Morgan Elliott was swinging a cleaver over the gutting table and yelling. I couldn't make out what the yelling was about, and thought someone must have made a terrible mistake in his work; perhaps it had been me. Then I saw Brian on the other side of the table, looking very sulky and mean, and standing well back. The sexual leer was not altogether gone from his face, but it was flattened out and mixed with a look of impotent bad temper and some fear. That's it, I thought; Brian is getting fired for being so sloppy and lazy. Even when I made out Morgan saying "pervert" and "filthy" and "maniac," I still thought that that was what was happening. Marjorie and Lily, and even brassy Irene, were standing around with downcast, rather pious looks, such as children get when somebody is suffering a terrible bawling out at school. Only old Henry seemed able to keep a cautious grin on his face. Gladys was not to be seen. Herb was standing closer to Morgan than anybody else. He was not interfering but was keeping an eye on the cleaver. Morgy was blubbering, though he didn't seem to be in any immediate danger.

Morgan was yelling at Brian to get out. "And out of this town—I mean it—and don't you wait till tomorrow if you still want your arse in one piece! Out!," he shouted, and the cleaver swung dramatically towards the door. Brian started in that direction but, whether he meant to or not, he made a swaggering, taunting motion of the buttocks. This made Morgan break into a roar and run after him, swinging the cleaver in a stagy way. Brian ran, and Morgan ran after him, and Irene screamed and grabbed her stomach. Morgan was too heavy to run any distance and probably could not have thrown the cleaver very far, either. Herb watched from the doorway. Soon Morgan came back and flung the cleaver down on the table.

"All back to work! No more gawking around here! You don't get paid for gawking! What are you getting under way at?" he said, with a hard look at Irene.

"Nothing," Irene said meekly.

"If you're getting under way get out of here."

"I'm not."

"All right, then!"

We got to work. Herb took off his blood-smeared smock and put on his jacket and went off, probably to see that Brian got ready to go on the suppertime bus. He did not say a word. Morgan and his son went out to the yard, and Irene and Henry went back to the adjoining shed, where they did the plucking, working knee-deep in the feathers Brian was supposed to keep swept up.

"Where's Gladys?" I said softly.

"Recuperating," said Marjorie. She, too, spoke in a quieter voice than usual, and "recuperating" was not the sort of word she and Lily normally used. It was a word to be used about Gladys, with a mocking intent.

They didn't want to talk about what had happened, because they were afraid Morgan might come in and catch them at it and fire them. Good workers as they were, they were afraid of that. Besides, they hadn't seen anything. They must have been annoyed that they hadn't. All I ever found out was that Brian had either done something or shown something to Gladys as she came out of the washroom and she had started screaming and having hysterics.

Now she'll likely be laid up with another nervous breakdown, they said. And he'll be on his way out of town. And good riddance, they said, to both of them.

~~~

I have a picture of the Turkey Barn crew taken on Christmas Eve. It was taken with a flash camera that was someone's Christmas extravagance. I think it was Irene's. But Herb Abbott must have been the one who took the picture. He was the one who could be trusted to know or to learn immediately how to manage anything new, and flash cameras were fairly new at the time. The picture was taken about ten o'clock on Christmas Eve, after Herb and Morgy had come back from making the last delivery and we had washed off the gutting table and swept and mopped the cement floor. We had taken off our bloody smocks and heavy sweaters and gone into the little room called the lunchroom, where there was a table and a heater. We still wore our working clothes: overalls and shirts. The men wore caps and the women kerchiefs, tied in the wartime style. I am stout and cheerful and comradely in the picture, transformed into someone I don't ever remember being or pretending to be. I look years older than fourteen. Irene is the only one who has taken off her kerchief, freeing her long red hair. She peers out from it with a meek, sluttish, inviting look, which would match her reputation but is not like any look of hers I remember. Yes, it must have been her camera; she is posing for it, with that look, more deliberately than anyone else is. Marjorie and Lily are smiling, true to form, but their smiles are sour and reckless.

With their hair hidden, and such figures as they have bundled up, they look like a couple of tough and jovial but testy workmen. Their kerchiefs look misplaced; caps would be better. Henry is in high spirits, glad to be part of the work force, grinning and looking twenty years younger than his age. Then Morgy, with his hangdog look, not trusting the occasion's bounty, and Morgan very flushed and bosslike and satisfied. He has just given each of us our bonus turkey. Each of these turkeys has a leg or a wing missing, or a malformation of some kind, so none of them are salable at the full price. But Morgan has been at pains to tell us that you often get the best meat off the gimpy ones, and he has shown us that he's taking one home himself.

We are all holding mugs or large, thick china cups, which contain not the usual tea but rye whiskey. Morgan and Henry have been drinking since suppertime. Marjorie and Lily say they only want a little, and only take it at all because it's Christmas Eve and they are dead on their feet. Irene says she's dead on her feet as well but that doesn't mean she only wants a little. Herb has poured quite generously not just for her but for Lily and Marjorie, too, and they do not object. He has measured mine and Morgy's out together, very stingily, and poured in Coca-Cola. This is the first drink I have ever had, and as a result I will believe for years that rye-and-Coca-Cola is a standard sort of drink and will always ask for it, until I notice that few other people drink it and that it makes me sick. I didn't get sick that Christmas Eve, though; Herb had not given me enough. Except for an odd taste, and my own feeling of consequence, it was like drinking Coca-Cola.

I don't need Herb in the picture to remember what he looked like. That is, if he looked like himself, as he did all the time at the Turkey Barn and the few times I saw him on the street—as he did all the times in my life when I saw him except one.

The time he looked somewhat unlike himself was when Morgan was cursing out Brian and, later, when Brian had run off down the road. What was this different look? I've tried to remember, because I studied it hard at the time. It wasn't much different. His face looked softer and heavier then, and if you had to describe the expression on it you would have to say it was an expression of shame. But what would he be ashamed of? Ashamed of Brian, for the way he had behaved? Surely that would be late in the day; when had Brian ever behaved otherwise? Ashamed of Morgan, for carrying on so ferociously and theatrically? Or of himself, because he was famous for nipping fights and displays of this sort in the bud and hadn't been able to do it here? Would he be ashamed that he hadn't stood up for Brian? Would he have expected himself to do that, to stand up for Brian?

All this was what I wondered at the time. Later, when I knew more, at least about sex, I decided that Brian was Herb's lover, and that Gladys really was trying to get attention from Herb, and that that was why Brian had humiliated her—with or without Herb's connivance and consent. Isn't it true that people like Herb—dignified, secretive, honorable people—will often choose somebody like Brian, will waste their helpless love on some vicious, silly person who is not even evil, or a monster, but just some importunate nuisance? I decided that Herb, with all his gentleness and carefulness, was avenging himself on us all—not just on Gladys but on us all—with Brian, and that what he was feeling when I studied his face must have been a savage and gleeful scorn. But embarrassment as well—embarrassment for Brian and for himself and for Gladys, and to some degree for all of us. Shame for all of us—that is what I thought then.

Later still, I backed off from this explanation. I got to a stage of backing off from the things I couldn't really know. It's enough for me now just to think of Herb's face with that peculiar, stricken look; to think of Brian monkeying in the shade of Herb's dignity; to think of my own mystified concentration on Herb, my need to catch him out, if I could ever get the chance, and then move in and stay close to him. How attractive, how delectable the prospect of intimacy is with the very person who will never grant it. I can still feel the pull of a man like that, of his promising and refusing. I would still like to know things. Never mind facts. Never mind theories, either.

When I finished my drink I wanted to say something to Herb. I stood beside him and waited for a moment when he was not listening to or talking with anyone else and when the increasingly rowdy conversation of the others would cover what I had to say.

"I'm sorry your friend had to go away."

"That's all right."

Herb spoke kindly and with amusement, and so shut me off from any further right to look at or speak about his life. He knew what I was up to. He must have known it before, with lots of women. He knew how to deal with it.

Lily had a little more whiskey in her mug and told how she and her best girlfriend (dead now, of liver trouble) had dressed up as men one time and gone into the men's side of the beer parlor, the side where it said "Men Only," because they wanted to see what it was like. They sat in a corner drinking beer and keeping their eyes and ears open, and nobody looked twice or thought a thing about them, but soon a problem arose.

"Where were we going to go? If we went around to the other side and anybody seen us going into the ladies', they would scream bloody murder. And if we went into the men's somebody'd be sure to notice we didn't do it the right way. Meanwhile the beer was going through us like a bugger!"

"What you don't do when you're young!" Marjorie said.

Several people gave me and Morgy advice. They told us to enjoy ourselves while we could. They told us to stay out of trouble. They said they had all been young once. Herb said we were a good crew and had done a good job but he didn't want to get in bad with any of the women's husbands by keeping them there too late. Marjorie and Lily expressed indifference to their husbands, but Irene announced that she loved hers and that it was not true that he had been dragged back from Detroit to marry her, no matter what people said. Henry said it was a good life if you didn't weaken. Morgan said he wished us all the most sincere Merry Christmas.

When we came out of the Turkey Barn it was snowing. Lily said it was like a Christmas card, and so it was, with the snow whirling around the street lights in town and around the colored lights people had put up outside their doorways. Morgan was giving Henry and Irene a ride home in the truck, acknowledging age and pregnancy and Christmas. Morgy took a shortcut through the field, and Herb walked off by himself, head down and hands in his pockets, rolling slightly, as if he were on the deck of a lake boat. Marjorie and Lily linked arms with me as if we were old comrades.

"Let's sing," Lily said. "What'll we sing?"

" 'We Three Kings'?" said Marjorie. " 'We Three Turkey Gutters'?"

" 'I'm Dreaming of a White Christmas.' "

"Why dream? You got it!"

So we sang.   1980

MY EX-HUSBAND AND THE FISH DINNER

JOAN ACOCELLA

My ex-husband didn't care much for Christmas. What he loved was the night before Christmas. He was one of those Italian-Americans who in the wake of the civil-rights movement got deeply into their ethnic roots. So did others in his family, and consequently we spent a lot of time at what I recall as eighteen-hour cousins' parties, where they would all pass around Grandma's immigration papers and talk about the time Uncle Angelo got kicked by the mule. My son and I, when we had to go to these affairs, used to stow magazines in the glove compartment, and every few hours or so we would sneak out to the car for a little rest.

Around this time, too, my husband decided to Italianize our Christmas. The people in his grandparents' generation had followed the old-country custom of eating their feast not on December 25th, but the night before. And it wasn't turkey; it was a nine-course fish dinner. (December 24th was a fast day—no meat. Nine courses of fish was their way of fasting.) My in-laws, by way of assimilating, had switched over to turkey. This now seemed to my husband a hideous betrayal. We were going back to the old way, he declared. So the next December 24th, and every December 24th after that, we had a dinner that could kill an army.

Many of his recipes came out of Marcella Hazan's excellent cookbooks, but he had his problems with Marcella Hazan. Number one, she was a Northern Italian, which in his mind, as in the minds of most of the descendants of the largely Southern Italian people who immigrated to this country at the turn of the century, meant snob, cake-eater—Protestant, even. (Anna Magnani, as these people will point out to you, was not a Northern Italian.) Number two, Marcella Hazan tried to *demystify* Italian cooking, turn it over to non-Italians. In America, anyone can be President, and in Marcella Hazan anyone can make minestrone.

This worried my husband. Pretty soon, he figured, you'd have Basques, Northumbrians, British Columbians making Italian dinners. He preferred cookbooks that kept a few veils on. A favorite of his was Ada Boni's "Talisman Italian Cook Book," which you used to be able to get by sending in four dollars and ninety-five cents with a coupon from the Ronzoni box. Ada Boni called for things like "1 large can Italian tomatoes." How large? Only an Italian would know. Best of all, he would have liked a cookbook that said, "Take a handful of chopped meat, add some parsley, throw it in the *scolabast*. . . ." That would keep the Northumbrians out of the kitchen.

"See here, Pottsman! That happens to be <u>my</u> secretary!"

The menu of his Christmas Eve feast changed from year to year, but certain items remained constant. For the appetizer course, he always served *mozzarella in carrozza,* because everyone loved it. For the salad course, he always had Ada Boni's shrimp-and-potato salad, because I loved it. And he always made marinated eel, because he liked to drive everyone crazy with it.

He had a weakness for food machismo—that is, he prided himself on eating what you wouldn't. Tripe was nothing to him; he ate necks, tails, toes. One of the things he loved best was when we were out to dinner with friends and someone confessed an unwillingness to eat certain animal parts. Then he would tell the story of how the biggest treat in his grandfather's house was *capuzzell,* or sheep's head. They would take this head, roast it, and hoist it out onto a platter. Then Grandpa would crack it open. ("Stop! Stop!" we're all yelling at my husband by now. But there was no stopping him.) Grandpa would crack it open and then stick in the spoon and scoop out ("No! Please!")—Grandpa would scoop out the brains onto everyone's plate. The people who were really lucky got the ("No, Nick! Don't tell us!")—the people who were lucky got the eyeballs. The story thus triumphantly finished, our dinner companions would look down glassy-eyed at their plates, push them away, and order a drink. And my husband, glowing with happiness and ethnic pride, would pick up his fork and dig into whatever was in front of him—ears, probably.

That's why he liked the marinated eel. Right around the fourth course of the Christmas Eve feast, he would produce it: a big dead snake in a bowl of yellow oil. "No!" we would scream. "Take it away! Eat it in the kitchen!" And, beaming with joy, he would maneuver the thing onto his plate, eat it by himself, and look at us pityingly.

The rest was magnificent, though: mussel soup, spaghetti with scallops, baccala with olives, bass stuffed with vegetables. This year, he'll probably be cooking it again, for a tableful of cousins. I can see them now, happily lifting their forks. "Wait!" he says, and runs back to the kitchen for the eel.

1995

WINTER IN MARTINIQUE

PATRICK CHAMOISEAU

When I was a child, in Martinique, my mother, Ma Ninotte, kept pigs. They were little cochons-planches, fattened all year long and destined for the Christmas feast—a singsong time, filled with sausages, chops, pâtés, stews, and roasts. The pigs were fed on leftovers, green bananas, useless words, nicknames; they scarfed up the seasonal fruit peels, and we children lavished a kindly tenderness on them. Sometimes they escaped from the kitchen, which had become a pig park, and dashed into the streets of Fort-de-France. We could always catch them in less than an hour. In Fort-de-France, everyone knew how to corner a pig, and the countrywomen were able to stop them by calling out a single old word. Everyone knew, too, that a family's survival often depended on the skinniest, slightest little pig.

All pigs were different—some were more engaging or mischievous than others—and my brothers and sisters and I didn't love all of them equally. In our shared memory, though, there was Matador. He arrived a bag of rattling bones and turned into a charming monster who laughed at the world with the eyes of an old man. He loved chocolate, soup, loving scratches, and Creole songs. And he became huge. When he escaped into the city, he was like a rolling boulder. One kindly fellow who sought to corner him found himself driven into a pole. Others were dispatched into gutters. When Ma Ninotte, followed by her brat pack, caught up, one of Matador's victims asked her, "Tell us, Ma'am, what seventh species of animal is this, if you please?" Another said, "He's a sower of sores, a liver boiler, a rheumatism starter, a filth-maker, and, if you don't mind my saying so, Mrs. So-and-So, an ill-bred bastard of a beast." We finally rounded up Matador on the banks of the Pointe Simon, opposite the white man's warehouses, where he had stopped to suck down unceremoniously the scrumptious emanations of a salted-meat barrel.

As December approached, a parade of snivelling delegations implored Ma Ninotte to excuse Matador. Ma Ninotte responded, with a feigned rage (for she loved Matador as much as we did), "Tianmay soti en zèbe, muven"—"Get away from my feet, you brats."

A dog dressed as a man was the killer—a certain Marcel. He seemed to exist only as Christmas approached, when he became a pig slaughterer. We had become so attached to Matador that when the fellow appeared we greeted him with cries of hatred. He had brought no implements; he had come, as he did every year, to agree on a price, a day, and a time. He arrived by day, in his white visiting shirt. As usual, he called up from the first step, "Ma Ninotte, how'd the pig do this year?"

Then began a long wait, the most terrible of our childhood. December arrived, with its winds, cold drafts, swollen noses, upset stomachs, fitful coughs, and old flus. We remained vigilant. We counted the knives and the tubs, but Ma Ninotte seemed to be preparing a pigless Christmas. She tended to the peels of her orange liqueur. She prettied her salted ham, her conserves, the other delicacies she had accumulated in her cupboard while awaiting the days of joy. But we never heard her promise anyone even the smallest chop. The air was trimmed with scents from cake ovens and the steam of fricassees. We saw her buy neither the peppers nor the sack of onions nor the coarse salt nor the herbs that announced the evil Saturday of the fattened pig.

Marcel must have worked in the middle of the night, because he was long gone when we awoke and found no Matador but just a whitish, bloody mass, which Ma Ninotte then cut up with her broad-bladed knife and distributed in newspaper as gifts to the other families in our building, and to the doctor who cured us, to the pharmacist who gave her medicines, to the Syrian shopkeepers who helped her out of jams. The rest was for her, in the form of cured meats, roasts, chops, the pig's head, and sausages, which we had neither the stomach nor the heart to eat.

I have no memory of the pigs who succeeded Matador. Suffering is a harsh vaccine: it must have prepared us not to get too attached to Christmas pigs.

(Translated, from the French, by Carol Volk)

1997

K. KRINGLE,
esq.

A VISIT FROM SAINT NICHOLAS
(IN THE ERNEST HEMINGWAY MANNER)

JAMES THURBER

It was the night before Christmas. The house was very quiet. No creatures were stirring in the house. There weren't even any mice stirring. The stockings had been hung carefully by the chimney. The children hoped that Saint Nicholas would come and fill them.

The children were in their beds. Their beds were in the room next to ours. Mamma and I were in our beds. Mamma wore a kerchief. I had my cap on. I could hear the children moving. We didn't move. We wanted the children to think we were asleep.

"Father," the children said.

There was no answer. He's there, all right, they thought.

"Father," they said, and banged on their beds.

"What do you want?" I asked.

"We have visions of sugarplums," the children said.

"Go to sleep," said mamma.

"We can't sleep," said the children. They stopped talking, but I could hear them moving. They made sounds.

"Can you sleep?" asked the children.

"No," I said.

"You ought to sleep."

"I know. I ought to sleep."

"Can we have some sugarplums?"

"You can't have any sugarplums," said mamma.

Dec. 14, 1935   THE   Price 15 cents

NEW YORKER

"We just asked you."

There was a long silence. I could hear the children moving again.

"Is Saint Nicholas asleep?" asked the children.

"No," mamma said. "Be quiet."

"What the hell would he be asleep tonight for?" I asked.

"He might be," the children said.

"He isn't," I said.

"Let's try to sleep," said mamma.

The house became quiet once more. I could hear the rustling noises the children made when they moved in their beds.

Out on the lawn a clatter arose. I got out of bed and went to the window. I opened the shutters; then I threw up the sash. The moon shone on the snow. The moon gave the lustre of mid-day to objects in the snow. There was a miniature sleigh in the snow, and eight tiny reindeer. A little man was driving them. He was lively and quick. He whistled and shouted at the reindeer and called them by their names. Their names were Dasher, Dancer, Prancer, Vixen, Comet, Cupid, Donder, and Blitzen.

He told them to dash away to the top of the porch, and then he told them to dash away to the top of the wall. They did. The sleigh was full of toys.

"Who is it?" mamma asked.

"Some guy," I said. "A little guy."

I pulled my head in out of the window and listened. I heard the reindeer on the roof. I could hear their hoofs pawing and prancing on the roof. "Shut the window," said mamma. I stood still and listened.

"What do you hear?"

"Reindeer," I said. I shut the window and walked about. It was cold. Mamma sat up in the bed and looked at me.

"How would they get on the roof?" mamma asked.

"They fly."

"Get into bed. You'll catch cold."

Mamma lay down in bed. I didn't get into bed. I kept walking around.

"What do you mean, they fly?" asked mamma.

"Just fly is all."

Mamma turned away toward the wall. She didn't say anything.

I went out into the room where the chimney was. The little man came down the chimney and stepped into the room. He was dressed all in fur. His clothes were covered with ashes and soot from the chimney. On his back was a pack like a peddler's pack. There were toys in it. His cheeks and nose were red and he had dimples. His eyes twinkled. His mouth was little, like a bow, and his beard was very white. Between his teeth was a stumpy pipe. The smoke from the pipe encircled his head in a wreath. He laughed and his belly shook. It shook like a bowl of red jelly. I laughed. He winked his eye, then he gave a twist to his head. He didn't say anything.

He turned to the chimney and filled the stockings and turned away from the chimney. Laying his finger aside his nose, he gave a nod. Then he went up the chimney. I went to the chimney and looked up. I saw him get into his sleigh. He whistled at his team and the team flew away. The team flew as lightly as thistledown. The driver called out, "Merry Christmas and good night." I went back to bed.

"What was it?" asked mamma. "Saint Nicholas?" She smiled.

"Yeah," I said.

She sighed and turned in the bed.

"I saw him," I said.

"Sure."

"I did see him."

"Sure you saw him." She turned farther toward the wall.

"Father," said the children.

"There you go," mamma said. "You and your flying reindeer."

"Go to sleep," I said.

"Can we see Saint Nicholas when he comes?" the children asked.

"You got to be asleep," I said. "You got to be asleep when he comes. You can't see him unless you're unconscious."

"Father knows," mamma said.

I pulled the covers over my mouth. It was warm under the covers. As I went to sleep I wondered if mamma was right.

1927

THE GREAT SANTA SHOOT-OUT AT THE MALL

WAITING FOR SANTY: A CHRISTMAS PLAYLET

(WITH A BOW TO MR. CLIFFORD ODETS)

S. J. PERELMAN

Scene: The sweatshop of S. Claus, a manufacturer of children's toys, on North Pole Street. Time: The night before Christmas.

At rise, seven gnomes, Rankin, Panken, Rivkin, Riskin, Ruskin, Briskin, and Praskin, are discovered working furiously to fill orders piling up at stage right. The whir of lathes, the hum of motors, and the hiss of drying lacquer are so deafening that at times the dialogue cannot be heard, which is very vexing if you vex easily. (Note: The parts of Rankin, Panken, Rivkin, Riskin, Ruskin, Briskin, and Praskin are interchangeable, and may be secured directly from your dealer or the factory.)

~~~

RISKIN (*filing a Meccano girder, bitterly*)—A parasite, a leech, a blood-sucker—altogether a five-star no goodnick! Starvation wages we get so he can ride around in a red team with reindeers!

RUSKIN (*jeering*)—Hey, Karl Marx, whyn'tcha hire a hall?

RISKIN (*sneering*)—Scab! Stool pigeon! Company spy! (*They tangle and rain blows on each other. While waiting for these to dry, each returns to his respective task.*)

BRISKIN (*sadly, to Panken*)—All day long I'm painting "Snow Queen" on these Flexible Flyers and my little Irving lays in a cold tenement with the gout.

PANKEN—You said before it was the mumps.

BRISKIN (*with a fatalistic shrug*)—The mumps—the gout—go argue with City Hall.

PANKEN (*kindly, passing him a bowl*)—Here, take a piece fruit.

BRISKIN (*chewing*)—It ain't bad, for wax fruit.

PANKEN (*with pride*)—I painted it myself.

BRISKIN (*rejecting the fruit*)—Ptoo! Slave psychology!

RIVKIN (*suddenly, half to himself, half to the Party*)—I got a belly full of stars, baby. You make me feel like I swallowed a Roman candle.

PRASKIN (*curiously*)—What's wrong with the kid?

RISKIN—What's wrong with all of us? The system! Two years he and Claus's daughter's been making goo-goo eyes behind the old man's back.

PRASKIN—So what?

RISKIN (*scornfully*)—So what? Economic determinism! What do you think the kid's name is—J. Pierpont Rivkin? He ain't even got for a bottle Dr. Brown's Celery Tonic. I tell you, it's like gall in my mouth two young people shouldn't have a room where they could make great music.

RANKIN (*warningly*)—Shhh! Here she comes now! (*Stella Claus enters, carrying a portable gramophone. She and Rivkin embrace, place a record on the turntable, and begin a very slow waltz, unmindful that the gramophone is playing "Cohen on the Telephone."*)

STELLA (*dreamily*)—Love me, sugar?

RIVKIN—I can't sleep, I can't eat, that's how I love you. You're a double malted with two scoops of whipped cream; you're the moon rising over Mosholu Parkway; you're a two weeks' vacation at Camp Nitgedaiget! I'd pull down the Chrysler Building to make a bobbie pin for your hair!

STELLA—I've got a stomach full of anguish. Oh, Rivvy, what'll we do?

PANKEN (*sympathetically*)—Here, try a piece of fruit.

RIVKIN (*fiercely*)—Wax fruit—that's been my whole life! Imitations! Substitutes! Well, I'm through! Stella, tonight I'm telling your old man. He can't play mumblety-peg with two human beings! (*The tinkle of sleigh bells is heard offstage, followed by a voice shouting, "Whoa, Dasher! Whoa, Dancer!" A moment later S. Claus enters in a gust of mock snow. He is a pompous bourgeois of sixty-five who affects a white beard and a false air of benevolence. But tonight the ruddy color is missing from his cheeks, his step falters, and he moves heavily. The gnomes hastily replace the marzipan they have been filching.*)

STELLA (*anxiously*)—Papa! What did the specialist say?

CLAUS (*brokenly*)—The biggest professor in the country . . . the best cardiac man that money could buy. . . . I tell you I was like a wild man.

STELLA—Pull yourself together, Sam!

CLAUS—It's no use. Adhesions, diabetes, sleeping sickness, decalcomania—oh, my God! I got to cut out climbing in chimneys, he says—me, Sanford Claus, the biggest toy concern in the world!

STELLA (*soothingly*)—After all, it's only one man's opinion.

CLAUS—No, no, he cooked my goose. I'm like a broken uke after a Yosian picnic. Rivkin!

RIVKIN—Yes, Sam.

CLAUS—My boy, I had my eye on you for a long time. You and Stella thought you were too foxy for an old man, didn't you? Well, let bygones be bygones. Stella, do you love this gnome?

STELLA (*simply*)—He's the whole stage show at the Music Hall, Papa; he's Toscanini conducting Beethoven's Fifth; he's—

CLAUS (*curtly*)—Enough already. Take him. From now on he's a partner in the firm. (*As all exclaim, Claus holds up his hand for silence.*) And tonight he can take my route and make the deliveries. It's the least I could do for my own flesh and blood. (*As the happy couple kiss, Claus wipes away a suspicious moisture and turns to the other gnomes.*) Boys, do you know what day tomorrow is?

GNOMES (*crowding around expectantly*)—Christmas!

CLAUS—Correct. When you look in your envelopes tonight, you'll find a little present from me—a forty-percent pay cut. And the first one who opens his trap—gets this. (*As he holds up a tear-gas bomb and beams at them, the gnomes utter cries of joy, join hands, and dance around him shouting exultantly. All except Riskin and Briskin, that is, who exchange a quick glance and go underground.*)

1936

"I'd like to see old Ho-Ho-Ho try to assemble one of these damn toys."

NO SANTA CLAUS

EMILY HAHN

Mrs. Flynn was surprised to find herself caught fast in a social bottleneck several days before Christmas. It was not typical of her and it was not her fault, but it happened, nevertheless. She had arranged everything admirably and conscientiously around her three-year-old daughter's program for the holidays. Mrs. Flynn ordinarily didn't go in for social engagements; she devoted herself to Barbara and the apartment, and waited for Mr. Flynn, now Captain Flynn, to come home from Japan. In fact, in that holiday week, she didn't even go to Barbara's nursery-school party at ten o'clock one morning, but that was scarcely to be counted as a sacrifice. Reluctant to brave, so early in the day, the rigors of dark, horribly seasonable snowy weather, she sent Mamie, the cook, as deputy. Mamie came back alone—the children were to spend a last full day at school as usual—with a disquieting report on Barbara's behavior.

"You didn't miss much of a celebration, and that's a fact, Madam," she said. "They sang a couple of carols around the tree, and then Santa Claus come in to give out the toys, and Barbara, she cried fit to bust."

"Good gracious!" said Mrs. Flynn. "What on earth made her do that?"

"Just plain scared, I guess," said Mamie cheerfully. "You ought to take her around the big stores more, maybe, and let her talk to Santa Claus."

"I won't take the child into those crowds."

"Oh, well, she'd forgotten all about it in five seconds," said Mamie. "And, Madam, can I take my afternoon today?"

In spite of experience, Mrs. Flynn put up a feeble struggle. "Mamie, you know perfectly well," she said, "that I asked you distinctly, last Sunday, which day you would want, and you said tomorrow. I do think you might have made up your mind before now. It isn't as if I usually went out, and now I've accepted two Christmas parties for today. What am I to do about Barbara if you're not home?"

"Well, let's forget about it," said Mamie. But there was that in her tone which brought Mrs. Flynn to heel.

"Oh, well, go ahead," she said. "I can take Barbara along with me to Mrs. Tracy's, I suppose. They'll just have to understand, that's all. And I can easily beg off the evening party. It's a buffet supper."

"No need for that," said Mamie. "Once Barbara's in bed you can leave her with a sitter, can't you? That Mrs. Soper you had before for the theatre—she'll come, most likely. You go to your supper and stop worrying."

Mrs. Flynn was thinking aloud. "I don't suppose Leonora would really mind if I bring her for cocktails—"

"Of course not," said Mamie heartily. "Dress the child up and she looks a perfect doll. They'll love her."

~~~

That afternoon Mrs. Flynn, pushing an empty baby carriage ahead of her, arrived at the nursery school breathless and late, her yellow hair still pinned in damp ringlets after a hasty shampoo. Barbara romped out the door like a puppy and shoved a small wooden auto at her mother, crying, "Look! Look! Santa Claus gave it to me."

Tactlessly, thoughtlessly, Mrs. Flynn said, "So you cried when you saw Santa. Why, darling?"

"I did cry," said Barbara cheerfully. "But it was the janitor, Santa Claus was. He showed me under his face, it was the janitor. Why was it, Mummy?"

"He was helping out the real Santa Claus," said Mrs. Flynn. She tucked the carriage robe carefully around her daughter's plump legs and started to wheel the buggy homeward. The wind blowing down Madison Avenue was chilling. It searched out and pounced on the moisture in Mrs. Flynn's hair and struck to the bones of her fingers, too lightly covered in cotton gloves.

"Does Santa Claus want to come to me?" asked Barbara. "Does he, Mummy?"

"Oh, yes," said Mrs. Flynn, but in her heart she could not contemplate the icy, airy midnight voyage, the jingling, frosty reindeer, without a sympathetic chilly shudder. "He loves to come out," she continued mechanically, pushing the carriage. "Think what fun it is to ride in a sleigh and to slip down the chimney while Barbara sleeps, to fill her stocking."

"Will he fill my stocking?"

"You bet he will." At the corner the wind attacked them fiercely.

"Why? Why, Mummy?" asked Barbara.

"Why what, sweetheart?"

"Why does Santa Claus want to fill my stocking? Why does he?"

The snow, stirred into filthy slush in the gutters, impeded the stiff wooden wheels of the Victory carriage. It was easiest, Mrs. Flynn discovered, to tip the whole thing back on the rear wheels and just bump along. Her fingers sent sharp, shooting pains up her arms, and the cruel wind was freshening.

"Good Lord, I thought you'd gone to lunch!"

"Why, Mummy?"

"Oh, Barbara!" snapped Mrs. Flynn. "Stop saying 'Why'!"

The child was startled and aggrieved, and her lower lip shoved out ominously. "Are you mad, Mummy? Don't be mad."

"Mummy's not mad, sweets. Mummy's fingers are cold and it hurts, and that makes Mummy cross."

"Why does it make Mummy cross?"

"Oh, Barbara, *please.*"

Once Mrs. Flynn got home, with the lights on and her fingers chafed and comforted, she felt better. She saw herself flatteringly in the mirror, her childish nose, even more youthful than usual with its reddened tip, and her hair growing dry and fluffy between the pins. Some Christmas parcels had been delivered; they made a colorful little heap on the hall table. "For me? For me?" Barbara asked, dancing in her rubbers.

"No, darling, for Mummy. Your things will come with Santa Claus on Christmas, in his sack." Turning the parcels over, Mrs. Flynn was reminded of a snippy salesgirl in Saks' toy department. "You're letting your little girl believe in all that Santa Claus stuff?" she had asked. Mrs. Flynn had retorted, ruffling like an embattled canary, "Why shouldn't we tell them pleasant lies sometimes, instead of unpleasant ones?" Now she wondered if she were right. If only Ed had been here to talk things over with, such trivial decisions would be easy. She seemed to be getting the whole family into a mess of small, euphoric deceits. Lies about Ed himself, for instance. Had she been wise to begin those? Every week she read to Barbara a letter from Daddy, loving but quite imaginary. Ed would never think of writing letters to a baby. And the presents, the dolls and books and stuffed animals which she told Barbara that Daddy had sent from Japan—how could she expect Ed to live up to that reputation afterward? He wasn't the type. He didn't think about those things. Of course, as his mother always said, he was really soft-hearted, but . . . An icy hand squeezed Mrs. Flynn's heart. *Was* Ed really soft-hearted? It was the first time she had ever wondered. She went hastily into Barbara's room.

Mamie, probably conscience-stricken, had laid out Barbara's party clothes very neatly on the cot. With brisk efficiency, Mrs. Flynn scrubbed the child's face and hands, changed her clothes, and then put on her own party dress, the black one with the sequins. Leonora always noticed what she wore and scolded her if there was any sign of slackness. "You have to be careful," Leonora had said once. "You could so easily look like a down-at-the-heels chorine, like all you little blondes."

~~~

Excited by the adventure of being out after dark, Barbara chattered unceasingly all the way to the party. She and her mother walked hand in hand through the snow, the two little blondes. They were late and Leonora's rooms were full of people and of a pleasant, spicy smell from the Christmas tree that glittered bravely in the dining room. There were a few uniforms, ladies of all ages, a contingent from Harlem, and a hired butler with canapés on a tray, but there were no other children.

"You don't mind Barbara, do you?" asked Mrs. Flynn at the door. "If you do, we'll go straight home and I'll understand perfectly. But I simply couldn't leave her alone, and Mamie wanted to go out, and—"

Certainly Leonora didn't mind. She was busy and distrait persuading somebody to stop playing the piano so that somebody else could sing carols, and Mrs. Flynn wandered away, the chronically unsociable Barbara clinging to her skirt. They found a soft sofa and a plate of sandwiches, and then a boyish Army lieutenant came over and talked to them. He had wings on his uniform and Leonora had called him Bobby. Mrs. Flynn decided wistfully that at his age she had probably been a freshman in college.

"How about taking a closeup gander at this Christmas tree, kid? Want to?" he asked the baby. Without argument, surprisingly, Barbara clambered off the sofa, took the lieutenant's hand, and trotted away with him. For the next hour Mrs. Flynn enjoyed herself. Once, when she looked around for her child, she saw her sitting on the floor under the tree, completely happy with Bobby, and obviously he was equally happy with her. They were drinking together; Barbara had milk, Bobby an Old-Fashioned. "I'm racing you," Barbara was saying, holding up her glass. Poor little tyke, Mrs. Flynn thought. She never sees any men.

~~~

"Home? All right, pumpkin, I guess we can go now," said Mrs. Flynn at seven o'clock to her clamoring daughter. They made their way slowly through the increasing crowd, Barbara clinging stubbornly to the lieutenant, whose flushed face and rich breath testified to numerous Old-Fashioneds. Thus they all three emerged together on Park Avenue.

"You come, too," said Barbara shrilly, overexcited by the lateness and tugging at the lieutenant's gloved hand. "You come home with Mummy and me."

Bobby raised his fine-drawn brows. "How about Mummy having dinner with me?" he asked.

Mrs. Flynn took her married status seriously and with a certain amount of old-fashioned decorum. She didn't believe in going out alone with men.

"I can't," she said. "I can't leave Barbara by herself in the house. Thanks just the same."

"There are women, aren't there?" Bobby asked. "What do you call 'em, seaters or sitters or something?"

"Mrs. Soper," said Barbara brightly. "Mrs. Soper's a sitter and she's coming tonight when Mummy goes out."

Over Barbara's red-capped head Bobby looked reproachfully at Mrs. Flynn. Somehow, by this time, they were all walking chummily down the street hand in hand, Barbara in the middle.

"Well, yes," Mrs. Flynn said, embarrassed, and angry with her daughter. "I've got to go to a party—that's true. It's a big one with a buffet supper. I suppose you could come along if you want. But surely you have something better to do?" She resolved to introduce this boy, if he should accept, as a

"That's funny. For some reason, I always thought of him as a liberal."

MYSTERY SANTA

It having been sharply suggested that we have steadily ignored Santa Claus in these columns since 1930 and that we'd better mend our ways, we swing quickly into line with a few words about Captain X, in some ways the greatest of New York Santas. The Captain is at present serving his third season at Altman's. Previously he was three seasons at Lord & Taylor's, and by now he's pretty much of a celebrity among the children.

The funny thing is that nobody knows much about this Santa. Unlike most of the others, he's not an actor by profession, willing to talk about himself to the first inquirer. Nobody even knows his name. He was really a captain, it's been established—a British one in the Boer War. He looks very military when he arrives in the morning: clean-cut and erect, always dressed in rugged British-looking tweeds. It's also known that he lives somewhere in Greenwich Village, and that during the non-Xmas season he's a writer, making a fairly good living by turning out "confession" stories for the pulp magazines under noms de plume. He won't divulge these names, either. Every once in a while some associate at the store asks him, "What's your name?" "My name is Santa Claus, and I live at the North Pole," the Captain always replies. That's all he'll say.

Captain X's performance as Santa Claus is a good deal more varied than those of his rivals. He doesn't just sit in a sleigh all day, as some of them do, but does all sorts of things: stages an entrance through a chimney three times a day, cuts out paper reindeer, cares for Prancer's reindeer baby in a little bassinet he keeps beside him, and calls up everybody in "Mother Goose" on the telephone. This year

long-lost nephew from California, but she did not say so aloud. Perhaps he would refuse to go to the party and make everything easy. Meanwhile, it was cozy, walking along like this, with Barbara and Bobby, the kids. It was nice.

"We could get away afterward and go dancing," said Bobby. Lightly he swung Barbara across a snowdrift. "There you are," he said, putting her down gently. "You and those bells on your mittens. Some mittens. . . . She's cute, all right."

"Her father is in Japan," Mrs. Flynn said.

Bobby walked along silently until they reached the apartment.

"Where were you most of the time?" she asked, digging in her purse for the door key. As always, when she was with these uniformed, thin-faced youngsters, she felt apologetic for the smug safety that had been hers. She felt guilty of contentment.

"The Pacific." He mumbled his words a little. "Sometimes I wonder if I'm he also calls up Jack Frost and says, "No, no, no! We don't want Grade B snow, we want Grade A snow." The children eat it up. Another of the Captain's ideas, which we suspect is based on a grudge against the Telephone Company, is to tell the children to call him up when they get home. "Call me at Iceland 0000," he says, "and don't let the operator tell you there's no such number." He's made plenty of trouble that way.

The Captain is paid a good deal more than the forty-five dollars or so which seems to be the usual weekly wage for department-store Santas, and under the NRA he's listed as a "professional," not as a "clerk," the way some Santas are. The people at Altman's admit he's an artist, but they wish he weren't so temperamental. Weeks before the Santa Claus season begins, he brings in duplicate lists of the props he'll need for his work, and distrib- utes them among the various departments. He's terribly particular about his costume— insists upon having two wigs and two sets of whiskers, so he can always have one set clean and freshly curled, and demands a specially soft pillow for his stuffing. (All department-store Santas use pillows for stuffing, we hear, except Lord & Taylor's present incumbent, who's temperamental too, and insists on a whalebone abdominal frame.) Captain X doesn't mix with the clerks in the toy department at all. In the evening he changes quietly into his tweeds and glides away, toward Greenwich Village.

—WILLIAM SHAWN, FRANCIS STEEGMULLER, AND HAROLD ROSS, 1934

glad it's over. I'd like to be back there right now." They looked together at the dark sky.

"Right now," sang Barbara, "right now, right now."

Mrs. Soper, the baby sitter, was waiting in the hallway, glum and philosophical, as usual. Mrs. Flynn set her to preparing Barbara's supper, then moved around the apartment running bath water, picking up small garments and hanging them up, putting out bottles and glasses. She was uneasy, afraid that Bobby expected more of the evening than he was going to get if he stayed with her. How could she make that clear to him? His quiet behavior rebuked her for being evil-minded. Barbara sat on his lap and listened raptly while he read to her, leaning against him with half-closed eyes.

Nobody could have looked at Bobby now and continued to feel uneasy. A warm, innocent excitement pervaded the room. Mrs. Flynn, tying on her best apron, felt sentimental twinges at seeing Barbara in a man's arms and then laughed bitterly at herself. Ed was not the daddy to read page after page about the brownies to his little girl. It was no use hoping he would turn into that sort of man, either.

Then Bobby looked up at Mrs. Flynn and his blue gaze bypassed the maternal smile in her eyes. He looked straight into her mind, she told herself, panic-stricken. He spoke harmlessly enough, though.

"The infant here has just about passed out. How's for us getting under way?"

"Oh, we can't go yet. She's got to take her bath. I've got to put her to sleep—"

"What about the old lady?"

"That won't work. Barbara expects me to put her to sleep. Look here," Mrs. Flynn said desperately, "can't we call this off? You'll be awfully bored at my friend's party. There's still time to go back to Leonora's. There's lots of time."

He shook his head. "I won't be bored with you." Deliberately, ardently, he said it, still staring into her mind through her eyes. "I'll wait till you've put the kid to sleep," he added. Mrs. Flynn took Barbara to the bathroom. Bobby was possibly ten years younger than herself, she thought in confusion. Why wouldn't he give her an opening and let her make the situation clear?

After they came out of the bathroom, Mrs. Soper carried in the baby's tray. Her expressionless face only added to Mrs. Flynn's unhappy state. Was the baby sitter getting ideas? "There you are, Barbara," said Mrs. Soper, putting the supper down on the small table. "Now eat it all up like a good girl, because Santa Claus is watching you."

"No he isn't. Is he, Mummy?" Barbara turned her face up toward Mrs. Flynn appealingly. "Is Santa Claus here in this house right now?"

"Well, *I* don't see him," Mrs. Flynn said, temporizing.

"But is he coming?"

"Sure he's coming." Bobby, who was standing at the other side of the table, pouring out a stiff drink, spoke up. "He's got to bring your toys. What did you ask him for, honey?"

Barbara, eating porridge, made no answer.

"She's sort of funny about Santa Claus," said her mother. "She won't talk about the stuff he brings."

Bobby dropped to his knees beside the child's chair. "That so? What's the matter, honey, don't you want anything for Christmas?"

"No," said Barbara, eating porridge.

"But wouldn't you like a nice doll?"

"Yes." She nodded vigorously and spilled porridge on her bib. "I want Mummy to buy me a doll and a dog and a boat, like at school."

"But don't ask Mummy. This is Christmas, when Santa brings everything. Ask Santa Claus," said Bobby. Barbara said nothing. Mrs. Soper served her with chopped fruit, then shuffled from the room. Immediately Bobby stood up and away from the chair, seized Mrs. Flynn's hand, and gripped it firmly while he leaned over and looked deep into her eyes.

"I don't care about anything," he said in low, tense tones, "but this. I mean drinking, and beautiful women like you. See?"

"Oh, dear. Bobby, don't." Mrs. Flynn felt her face growing red and her heart beating ridiculously hard. "No, no, you'll have to understand—"

Barbara hammered on the table with her spoon, and the two adults jumped. Bobby sauntered away a step or two and lit a cigarette. He seemed quite sure of himself, quite collected. Mrs. Flynn wasn't either sure or collected. It's all wrong, she was thinking. We petted them and spoiled them and now we treat them like problems. And they *are* problems. Last year this child was a hero, a saviour—now he's a potential enemy of society, perhaps a permanent misfit. As soon as he's demobilized it'll begin. Without the war he's just another nuisance.

"Enough!" Barbara cried. "Mummy, I've had enough. I want bed."

"Wait here while I see to this," Mrs. Flynn said to Bobby, her voice dry and curt.

He nodded and grinned like a cheerful conspirator. "Don't be too long, will you?" He kissed Barbara.

Mrs. Flynn, sternly bidding her pulse to quiet down, carried the child in to bed. Mrs. Soper knew the routine. She would now wash up in the kitchen and wait there until Barbara was quiet so she could begin to sit, officially, at so much per hour. Mrs. Flynn forgot her pulse. She closed the bedroom door behind her, turned down the covers on the baby's cot, lit the night lamp and doused the others, took Barbara into the bathroom; it was all as familiar as sunset. But tonight, for some reason, Barbara hung back instead of running to bed.

"Mummy," she said, "will Santa Claus come now?"

"Gracious, no, pet. Not for three days more. He only comes on Christmas Eve. I told you that, darling. On Christmas Eve my Barbara hangs her stocking right up there on the mantel. That big red stocking we used last year. Do you remember? And Santa Claus will come down the chimney."

Barbara's eyes, large and sombre, were fixed on the fireplace. "Why?"

"Why? Why, to fill your stocking with presents, pumpkin."

"Why?"

"Why what? Because he's Santa Claus! Come on, pet. Bed."

Barbara still lingered, plucking at a button on her small pajama coat. "How does Santa Claus come?" she asked in a tiny voice. "How does he, Mummy?"

"He comes in a sleigh." Mrs. Flynn exerted all her patience. "I *told* you a dozen times. A sleigh is a big sled with bells on it. You know, 'Jingle Bells.' Reindeer pull the sleigh through the sky, and they come down to our roof and Santa comes down the chimney with toys for Barbara Flynn, for my good little girl. Come on, darling." She picked up the child and kissed her soft, fragrant cheek. "Come to bed, sweetheart."

Then Barbara cried out passionately, "I don't want!" She threw her arms around her mother's neck, gripping her in a frenzy. "I don't want him!"

"But darling!" In alarm, Mrs. Flynn felt the small heart pounding, the delicate cage of ribs pushing in and out with the baby's rapid breath. "What is it, dearest? What don't you want?"

"That old man!" cried Barbara. "Santa Claus. I don't want him, Mummy. I don't, Mummy."

"You don't want Santa Claus to come?"

"No!" It was a defiant wail.

"But, darling, don't you want toys or anything?"

"No! No! I don't want him."

"But, sweetheart, Santa Claus is *nice*. He's a nice old man. He only wants Barbara to be happy. He wants to give her things."

"I don't want him. Tell him not to come. Tell that old man, Mummy."

Mrs. Flynn stood there, the child clinging to her neck. She glanced around wildly and saw the telephone. "All right, Barbara," she said. "Listen now; listen to Mummy." She sat down at the telephone and settled Barbara firmly in her lap, then pretended to dial a number, holding down the plunger. "Hello," she said after an adequate pause. "Is this the North Pole? Is this Santa Claus? . . . How are you, Santa? This is Barbara's mother. Santa, Barbara and I have been talking it over and we've decided that we would rather not have you come to see us this Christmas. Yes, that's what I said. Thanks just the same, Santa. Goodbye."

A faint shadow of pleasure crossed Barbara's face as she listened, holding her breath. Her body relaxed. Obediently, wordlessly, as her mother hung up the receiver, she crawled into bed. Then she turned her head on the pillow and whispered, "Hold me."

In the half-light, Mrs. Flynn gathered her, sheet and blanket and all, into the ceremonial, traditional good-night hug. Her eyes closed, Barbara whispered, "No Santa Claus!"

"Absolutely," said Mrs. Flynn. She whispered, too. "No Santa Claus."

Barbara sighed and slept.

~~~

Mrs. Flynn's hat was on, her face was made up. She had changed her slippers and put on her coat. Tiptoeing, she left the bedroom and closed the door gently. Her thoughts buzzed back and forth between past and future—the

"Good grief! He thinks he is Santa Claus!"

scene just finished with Barbara, funny, pathetic baby, and the scene there would be with Bobby. And he was a pathetic baby, too.

How could she turn him away without being terribly ungracious, without hurting him. I'm tired, she thought plaintively, I'm too tired to go out with a hero, and dance and drink and listen. I'm too tired to pay Society's debt to our boys all by myself. Through the door into the kitchen she saw Mrs. Soper fulfilling her contract, rocking in the rocking chair while she waited for the company to get out of the living room. Mrs. Soper, sitting.

Mrs. Flynn, still thinking desperately, unhappily, went into the living room. Bobby was stretched full length on the sofa, asleep. A half-filled glass balanced uncertainly on the carpet near his dangling hand. He slept not like a drunken man but like a tired boy. His face was terribly pale.

Mrs. Flynn reached over and patted his near shoulder. "Bobby," she said, "wake up."

Bobby slept. Mrs. Flynn took hold of his shoulder, intending to give him a firm shake, the way she woke Barbara in the mornings. Then all of a sudden, with a burst of relief, she saw her way out. It was miraculous the way it had happened.

Mrs. Flynn turned and went into the kitchen. "I'm just going out, Mrs. Soper," she said, "and that boy has fallen into such a nice, deep sleep that I don't like to wake him up. Just let him go on sleeping for a while, will you? Of course, if it goes on more than an hour more, you'd better call him."

"Yes, Ma'am. You want me to tell him something?"

"No," said Mrs. Flynn happily, "not a thing. I'm going to a party, but it isn't a party he would be interested in. Just tell him I didn't want to wake him up."

"Sure, Ma'am. It would be a pity."

"That's what I thought."

She paused at the front door and looked again at Bobby, asleep. He was young, yes, but not too young to learn that there is no Santa Claus. The rest of us know it, she thought. Why shouldn't he?

As she closed the door she decided that, with a bit of luck, she could come home to an unencumbered apartment not too long after midnight. It was simply extraordinary, the relief she felt. Like Barbara's nursery-school janitor, perhaps, when he took off that false face and could breathe again.

1945

SKID-ROW SANTA

KEN KESEY

At the finale of the Christmas show last year in Eugene, Oregon, I came out as a skid-row Santa, complete with rubber nose, plastic sack full of beer cans, and a pint of peppermint schnapps to fortify the holiday spirit. I also borrowed my wife Faye's blue egg bucket and labelled it "Homeless." I'd jangle the cans like a bagful of aluminum sleigh bells while I worked the main-floor aisle seats: "Hey, come on, buddy. Put something in the bucket, for Chrissakes. Don't you know it's Christmastime? Hey, that's better. God bless you. You're beautiful."

I ended up with only about seventy-five bucks. Not much of a take for a full house at a Christmas show. But even seventy-five bucks was a wad too big to pocket.

So after I got out of my red suit and rubber snoot I drove off to seek a worthy recipient. I spotted a likely assortment of candidates in the 7-Eleven parking lot, corner of Sixth and Blair. I swung in and held the bucket out the window.

"All right. Who's the hardest-luck case in this lot?"

The candidates looked me over and edged away—all but one guy, pony-tailed and slope-shouldered, his chin tucked down in the collar of a canvas camouflage jacket. "I got a streak of hard luck runs all the way back to Jersey," he said. "What about it?"

"I'm on a mission from St. Nicholas," I told him. "And if you are, in fact, the least fortunate of the lot"—in the spirit of the season, I refrained from saying "biggest loser"—"then this could be your lucky night."

"Right," he said. "You're some kind of Holy Roller? Where's the string? What's the hustle?"

"No string, no catch, no hustle. I'm giving. You're getting. Get it?"

He did. He took the money and ran, taking Faye's egg bucket into the bargain. The last I saw of him, he was scurrying away, looking for a hole.

Since then, I've wondered about him. Did that little windfall make any difference? Did he rent a cheap room? Get a bath? A companion? Every time I found myself passing through one of Eugene's hard-luck harbors, I kept half an eye peeled for the sight of a long tail of black hair draggling down the back of a camouflage jacket. Last week, a year later to the day, I made a sighting.

I was in town with Faye and our daughter, getting in some Christmas shopping before we rendezvoused with my mom for supper. We'd done a couple of hours in the malls, and I was shopped out. I announced that I wanted to make some private purchases, and slipped off into the rainy cold—alone. I was headed for the liquor store on Eighth, thinking the spirit could use a little fortification.

But the trusty peppermint wasn't powerful enough. These home-town streets are just too strange, too vacant, too sad. Corner of Sixth at Olive: empty. The great Darigold Creamery that my dad built up from a little Eugene farmer's coöperative: bulldozed down. I ducked my head and kept walking in the rain.

The street in my memory was the clearer path anyway: John Warren's Hardware over there, where you could buy blasting powder across the counter; the Corral Novelty Shop,

where you could buy itching powder; the Heilig Theatre, with its all-the-way-across-the-street arch, flashing what we all took to be the Norwegian word for "hello," so big it could be read all the way from the windows of the arriving trains: "Heilig, Heilig, Heilig." All gone.

When I reached the city center, I noticed that the thing people had finally given up trying to call a fountain was newly disguised with pine boughs and potted plants. But to no avail. It still looked like the remnants of a bombed-out French cathedral. Then, when the rain eased up, I was surprised to discover that the ruins were not quite deserted: I saw a loose black braid hanging down the back of a camouflage jacket. That seemed right. He was in the old fountain's basin, bent in a concealing crouch at one of the potted pines.

I came up from behind and clapped my hand on his shoulder. "Whatcha doin', Hard Luck? Counting another bucket of money?"

He wheeled around and had my wrist clamped in a bone-breaking grasp

". . . flying low over housetops, landing on a roof, illegal entry into a residence via chimney, operating a sleigh without a license, keeping wild reindeer confined in harness, and creating a disturbance with loud laughter."

before I could finish the word. I saw then that this wasn't a chinless street rat standing down in the basin after all. This was a block-jawed American Indian built like two fireplugs, sitting in a wheelchair.

"Ouch! Man! Let go! I thought you were somebody else!"

He eased the hold, but kept the wrist. I told him about last year's long-hair and the matching jacket.

He listened, studying my eyes. "O.K. Sorry about the twist. I was taking a leak. You surprised me. Let's get out of the rain and see what kind of medicine you've got sticking out of your pocket."

We retired under some scaffolding. He was less than enthusiastic about my choice of pocket medicine. "I'd rather drink something like Southern Comfort if I have to choose a sugar drink," he said. But we passed the pint back and forth and watched the rain.

He leaned to spit and a folded Army blanket slipped out of his lap. His legs were as gone as the main gut of my poor home town.

He was a part-time fillet man from the Pike Place Market, up in Seattle, on his way to spend Christmas with family on "the res," outside of Albuquerque. His bus was laid up for a couple of hours: "I think they're getting the Greyhound spayed before she gets to California."

When the pint was about three-quarters gone, I screwed on the lid and held it out. "I gotta meet the women. Go ahead and keep it."

"Ah, I guess not," hc said.

"You're pretty choosy for a thirsty man, aren't you? What would be your best druthers?"

"To have the money and make my own choice."

I reached for my wallet. "I think I got a couple of bucks."

"And a quarter? If I had two bucks and a quarter, I could get a pint of Ten High. With four and change I'd go on to a fair-to-middlin' fifth. Cream of Kentucky."

I hesitated. Was I being hustled? "O.K. Let's see what we've got." I emptied the wallet and pockets onto his blanket. He added a few coins and counted the collection.

"Nine seventy-five. If I come up with another two dollars, I can get a bottle of Bushmill's Irish. Think I can panhandle two dollars between here and the liquor store?"

"Without a doubt," I assured him. "With both panhandles tied behind your back."

SANTA'S HELPERS

We shook hands goodbye and headed off in our separate directions, strolling and rolling through the rain. At the restaurant, my mother wanted to know what I was thinking about that gave me such a goofy grin.

"I was just thinking, if beggars can't be choosers, then it must follow that choosers, by definition, are not beggars."

This year for the Christmas show, Santa's got himself a classier outfit and wrangled some holiday helpers out of the high-school choir, God bless 'em. And we're gonna work all the aisles. Come on out here you helpers, come on out. Get down there and panhandle! And you guys in the audience start passing your money to the aisles here. This is no time to nickel-and-dime, for Chrissakes! It's Christmastime.

1997

THE TWELVE TERRORS OF CHRISTMAS

JOHN UPDIKE

1. SANTA: THE MAN. Loose-fitting nylon beard, fake optical twinkle, cheap red suit, funny rummy smell when you sit on his lap. If he's such a big shot, why is he drawing unemployment for eleven months of the year? Something scary and off key about him, like one of those Stephen King clowns.

2. SANTA: THE CONCEPT. Why would anybody halfway normal want to live at the North Pole on a bunch of shifting ice flocs? Or stay up all night flying around the sky distributing presents to children of doubtful deservingness? There is a point where altruism becomes sick. Or else a sinister coverup for an international scam. A man of no plausible address, with no apparent source for his considerable wealth, comes down the chimney after midnight while decent, law-abiding citizens are snug in their beds—is this not, at the least, cause for alarm?

3. SANTA'S HELPERS. Again, what is really going on? Why do these purported elves submit to sweatshop conditions in what must be one of the gloomiest climates in the world, unless they are getting something out of it at our expense? Underclass masochism one day, bloody rebellion the next. The rat-a-tat-tat of tiny hammers may be just the beginning.

4. O TANNENBAUM. Suppose it topples over under its weight of explosive baubles? Suppose it harbors wood-borers that will migrate to the furniture? There is something ghastly about a tree—its look of many-limbed paralysis, its shaggy and conscienceless aplomb—encountered in the open, let alone in the living room. At night, you can hear it rustling and drinking water out of the bucket.

5. TINY REINDEER. Hooves that cut through roof shingles like linoleum knives. Antlers like a hundred dead branches. Unstable flight pattern suggesting "dry leaves that before the wild hurricane fly." Fur possibly laden with disease-bearing ticks.

6. ELECTROCUTION. It's not just the frayed strings of lights anymore, or the corroded transformer of the plucky little Lionel. It's all those battery

packs, those electronic games, those built-in dictionaries, those robots asizzle with artificial intelligence. Even the tinsel tingles.

7. THE CAROLS. They boom and chime from the vaulted ceilings of supermarkets and discount stores, and yet the spirits keep sinking. Have our hearts grown so terribly heavy since childhood? What has happened to us? Why don't they ever play our favorites? What *were* our favorites? Tum-de-tum-tum, angels on high, something something, sky.

8. THE SPECIALS. Was Charlie Brown's voice always so plaintive and grating? Did Bing Crosby always have that little potbelly, and walk with his toes out? Wasn't that Danny Kaye / Fred Astaire / Jimmy Stewart / Grinch a card? Is Vera-Ellen still alive? Isn't there something else on, like wrestling or "Easter Parade"?

9. FEAR OF NOT GIVING ENOUGH. Leads to dizziness in shopping malls, foot fractures on speeded-up escalators, thumb and wrist sprain in the course of package manipulation, eye and facial injuries in carton-crowded buses, and fluttering sensations of disorientation and imminent impoverishment.

10. FEAR OF NOT RECEIVING ENOUGH. Leads to anxious scanning of U.P.S. deliveries and to identity crisis on Christmas morning, as the piles of rumpled wrapping paper and emptied boxes mount higher around every chair but your own. Three dull neckties and a pair of flannel-lined work gloves—is this really how they see you?

11. FEAR OF RETURNS. The embarrassments, the unseemly haggling. The lost receipts. The allegations of damaged goods. The humiliating descent into mercantilism's boiler room.

12. THE DARK. How early it comes now! How creepy and green in the gills everybody looks, scrabbling along in drab winter wraps by the phosphorous light of department-store windows full of Styrofoam snow, mock-ups of a factitious 1890, and beige mannequins posed with a false jauntiness in plaid bathrobes. Is this Hell or just an upturn in consumer confidence?

1992

family MATTERS

CHRISTMAS POEM

JOHN O'HARA

Billy Warden had dinner with his father and mother and sister. "I suppose this is the last we'll see of you this vacation," said his father.

"Oh, I'll be in and out to change my shirt," said Billy.

"My, we're quick on the repartee," said Barbara Warden. "The gay young sophomore."

"What are *you,* Bobby dear? A drunken junior?" said Billy.

"Now, I don't think that was called for," said their mother.

"Decidedly *un*-called for," said their father. "What *are* your plans?"

"Well, I was hoping I could borrow the chariot," said Billy.

"Yes, we anticipated that," said his father. "What I meant was, are you planning to go away anywhere? Out of town?"

"Well, that depends. There's a dance in Reading on the twenty-seventh I'd like to go to, and I've been invited to go skiing in Montrose."

"Skiing? Can you ski?" said his mother.

"All Dartmouth boys ski, or pretend they can," said his sister.

"Isn't that dangerous? I suppose if you were a Canadian, but I've never known anyone to go skiing around here. I thought they had to have those big—I don't know—scaffolds, I guess you'd call them."

"You do, for jumping, Mother. But skiing isn't all jumping," said Billy.

"Oh, it isn't? I've only seen it done in the newsreels. I never really saw the point of it, although I suppose if you did it well it would be the same sensation as flying. I often dream about flying."

"I haven't done much jumping," said Billy.

"Then I take it you'll want to borrow the car on the twenty-seventh, and what about this trip to Montrose?" said his father.

"I don't exactly know where Montrose is," said Mrs. Warden.

"It's up beyond Scranton," said her husband. "That would mean taking the car overnight. I'm just trying to arrange some kind of a schedule. Your mother and I've been invited to one or two things, but I imagine we can ask our friends to take us there and bring us back. However, we only have the one car, and Bobby's entitled to her share."

"Of course she is. Of course I more or less counted on her to, uh, to spend most of her time in Mr. Roger Taylor's Dort."

"It isn't a Dort. It's a brand-new Marmon, something I doubt you'll ever be able to afford."

"Something I doubt Roger'd ever be able to afford if it took any brains to afford one. So he got rid of the old Dort, did he?"

"He never had a Dort, and you know it," said Barbara.

"Must we be so disagreeable, the first night home?" said Mrs. Warden. "I know there's no meanness in it, but it doesn't *sound* nice."

"When would you be going to Montrose?" said Mr. Warden. "What date?"

"Well, if I go it would be a sort of a houseparty," said Billy.

"In other words, not just overnight?" said his father. "Very well, suppose you tell us how many nights?"

"I'm invited for the twenty-eighth, twenty-ninth, and thirtieth," said Billy. "That would get me back in time to go to the Assembly on New Year's Eve."

"What that amounts to, you realize, is having possession of the car from the twenty-seventh to the thirtieth or thirty-first," said his father.

"Yes, I realize that," said Billy.

"Do you still want it, to keep the car that long, all for yourself?" said his father.

"Well, I didn't have it much last summer, when I was working. And I saved you a lot of money on repairs. I ground the valves, cleaned the sparkplugs. A lot of things I did. I oiled and greased it myself."

"Yes, I have to admit you do your share of that," said his father. "But if you keep the car that long, out of town, it just means we are without a car for four days, at the least."

There was a silence.

"I really won't need the car very much after Christmas," said Barbara. "After I've done my shopping and delivered my presents."

"Thank you," said Billy.

"Well, of course not driving myself, I never use it," said Mrs. Warden.

"That puts it up to me," said Mr. Warden. "If I were Roger Taylor's father I'd give you two nice big Marmons for Christmas, but I'm not Mr. Taylor. Not by about seven hundred thousand dollars, from what I hear. Is there anyone else from around here that's going to Montrose?"

"No."

"Then it isn't one of your Dartmouth friends?" said Mr. Warden. "Who will you be visiting?"

"It's a girl named Henrietta Cooper. She goes to Russell Sage. I met her at Dartmouth, but that's all. I mean, she has no other connection with it."

"Russell Sage," said his mother. "We know somebody that has a daughter

there. I know who it was. That couple we met at the Blakes'. Remember, the Blakes entertained for them last winter? The husband was with one of the big electrical companies."

"General Electric, in Schenectady," said Mr. Warden. "Montrose ought to be on the Lehigh Valley, or the Lackawanna, if I'm not mistaken."

"The train connections are very poor," said Billy. "If I don't go by car, Henrietta's going to meet me in Scranton, but heck, I don't want to ask her to do that. I'd rather not go if I have to take the train."

"Well, I guess we can get along without the car for that long. But your mother and I are positively going to have to have it New Year's Eve. We're going to the Assembly, too."

"Thank you very much," said Billy.

"It does seem strange. Reading one night, and then the next day you're off in the opposite direction. You'd better make sure the chains are in good condition. Going over those mountains this time of year."

"A houseparty. Now what will you do on a houseparty in Montrose? Besides ski, that is?" said Mrs. Warden. "It sounds like a big house, to accommodate a lot of young people."

"I guess it probably is," said Billy. "I know they have quite a few horses. Henny rides in the Horse Show at Madison Square Garden."

"Oh, my. Then they must be very well-to-do," said his mother. "I always wanted to ride when I was a girl. To me there's nothing prettier than a young woman in a black riding habit, riding sidesaddle. Something so elegant about it."

"I wouldn't think she rode sidesaddle, but maybe she does," said Billy.

"Did you say you wanted to use the car tonight, too?" said his father.

"If nobody else is going to," said Billy.

"Barbara?" said Mr. Warden.

"No. Roger is calling for me at nine o'clock," said Barbara. "But I would like it tomorrow, all day if possible. I have a ton of shopping to do."

"I *still* haven't finished wrapping all *my* presents," said Mrs. Warden.

"I haven't even *bought* half of mine," said Barbara.

"You shouldn't leave everything to the last minute," said her mother. "I bought most of mine at sales, as far back as last January. Things are much cheaper after Christmas."

"Well, I guess I'm off to the races," said Billy. "Dad, could you spare a little cash?"

"How much?" said Mr. Warden.

"Well—ten bucks?"

"I'll take it off your Christmas present," said Mr. Warden.

"Oh, no, don't do that? I have ten dollars if you'll reach me my purse. It's on the sideboard," said Mrs. Warden.

"You must be flush," said Mr. Warden.

"Well, no, but I don't like to see you take it off Billy's Christmas present. That's as bad as opening presents ahead of time," said Mrs. Warden.

"Which certain people in this house do every year," said Barbara.

"Who could she possibly mean?" said Billy. "I opened one present, because it came from Brooks Brothers and I thought it might be something I could wear right away."

"And was it?" said his mother.

"Yes. Some socks. These I have on, as a matter of fact," said Billy. "They're a little big, but they'll shrink."

"Very snappy," said Barbara.

"Yes, and I don't know who they came from. There was no card."

"I'll tell you who they were from. They were from me," said Barbara.

"They were? Well, thanks. Just what I wanted," said Billy.

"Just what you asked me for, last summer," said Barbara.

"Did I? I guess I did. Thank you for remembering. Well, good night, all. Don't wait up. I'll be home before breakfast."

They muttered their good nights and he left. He wanted to—almost wanted to—stay; to tell his father that he did not want a Marmon for Christmas, which would have been a falsehood; to tell his mother he loved her in spite of her being a nitwit; to talk to Bobby about Roger Taylor, who was not good enough for her. But this was his first night home and he had his friends to see. Bobby had Roger, his father and mother had each other; thus far he had no one. But it did not detract from his feeling for his family that he now preferred the livelier company of his friends. *They* all had families, too, and *they* would be at the drugstore tonight. You didn't come home just to see the members of your family. As far as that goes, you got a Christmas vacation to celebrate the birth of the Christ child, but except for a few Catholics, who would go anywhere near a church? And besides, he could not talk to his family en masse. He would like to have a talk with his father, a talk with his sister, and he would enjoy a half hour of his mother's prattling. Those conversations would be personal if there were only two present, but with more than two present everyone had to get his say in and nobody said anything much. Oh, what was the use of making a lot of excuses? What was wrong with wanting to see your friends?

The starter in the Dodge seemed to be whining "No . . . no . . . no . . ." before the engine caught. It reminded him of a girl, a girl who protested every bit of the way, and she was not just an imaginary girl. She was the girl he would telephone as soon as he got to the drugstore, and he probably would be too late, thanks to the conversation with his family. Irma Hipple, her name was. She lived up the hill in back of the Court House. The boys from the best families in town made a beeline for Irma as soon as they got home from school. A great many lies had been told about Irma, and the worst liars were the boys who claimed nothing but looked wise. Someone must have gotten all the way with Irma sometime, but Billy did not know who. It simply stood to reason that a girl who allowed so many boys to neck the hell out of her had delivered the goods sometime. She was twenty-one or two and already she was beginning to lose her prettiness, probably because she could hold her liquor as well as any boy, and better than some. In her way she was a terrible snob. "That Roger Taylor got soaked to the gills," she would say. "That Teddy Choate thinks he's a cave man," or "I'm never going out with that Doctor Boyd again. Imagine a doctor snapping his cookies in the Stagecoach bar." Irma probably delivered the goods to the older men. Someone who went to Penn had seen her at the L'Aiglon supper club in Philadelphia with George W. Josling, who was manager of one of the new stockbrokerage branches in town. There was a story around town that she had bitten Jerome Kuhn, the optometrist, who was old enough to be her father. It was hard to say what was true about Irma and what wasn't. She was a saleswoman in one of the department stores; she lived with her older sister and their father, who had one leg and was a crossing watchman for the Pennsy; she was always well dressed; she was pretty and full of pep. That much was true about her, and it was certainly true that she attracted men of all ages.

The telephone booth in the drugstore was occupied, and two or three boys were queued up beside it. Billy Warden shook hands with his friends and with Russell Covington, the head soda jerk. He ordered a lemon phosphate and lit a cigarette and kept an eye on the telephone booth. The door of the booth buckled open and out came Teddy Choate, nodding. "All set," he said to someone. "Everything is copacetic. I'm fixed up with Irma. She thinks she can get Patsy Lurio for you."

Billy Warden wanted to hit him.

"Hello there, Billy. When'd you get in?" said Teddy.

"Hello, Teddy. I got in on the two-eighteen," said Billy.

"I hear you're going to be at Henny Cooper's houseparty," said Teddy.

"Jesus, you're a busybody. How did you hear that?"

"From Henny, naturally. Christ, I've known her since we were five years old. She invited me, but I have to go to these parties in New York."

"Funny, she told me she didn't know anybody in Gibbsville," said Billy.

"She's a congenital liar. Everybody knows that. I saw her Friday in New York. She was at a tea dance I went to. You ever been to that place in Montrose?"

"No."

"Daddy! Daddy! American planes bombed a key rail depot near Hanoi and knocked out a power station today in a record number of strikes for the third consecutive day!"

"They've got everything there. A six-car garage. Swimming pool. Four-hole golf course, but they have the tees arranged so you can play nine holes. God knows how many horses. The old boy made his money in railroad stocks, and he sure did spend it up there. Very hard to get to know, Mr. Cooper. But he was in Dad's class at New Haven and we've known the Coopers since the Year One. I guess it was really Henny's grandfather that made the first big pile. Yes, Darius L. Cooper. You come across his name in American-history courses. I suppose he was an old crook. But Henny's father is altogether different. Very conservative. You won't see much of him at the houseparty, if he's there at all. They have an apartment at the Plaza, just the right size, their own furniture. I've been there many times, too."

"Then you do know them?" said Billy.

"Goodness, haven't I been telling you? We've known the Cooper family since the Year *One,*" said Teddy. "Well, you have to excuse me. I have to whisper something to Russ Covington. Delicate matter. Got a date with Irma."

"You're excused," said Billy. He finished his phosphate and joined a group at the curbstone.

"What say, boy? I'll give you fifty to forty," said Andy Phillips.

"For how much?" said Billy.

"A dollar?"

"You're on," said Billy. They went down the block and upstairs to the poolroom. All the tables were busy save one, which was covered with black oilcloth. "What about the end table?" said Billy.

"Saving it," said Phil, the houseman. "Getting up a crap game."

"How soon?"

"Right away. You want to get in?"

"I don't know. I guess so. What do you think, Andy?"

"I'd rather shoot pool," said Andy.

"You're gonna have a hell of a wait for a table," said Phil. "There's one, two, three, four—four Harrigan games going. And the first table just started shooting a hundred points for a fifty-dollar bet. You're not gonna hurry *them.*"

"Let's go someplace else," said Andy.

"They'll all be crowded tonight. I think I'll get in the crap game," said Billy.

Phil removed the cover from the idle pool table and turned on the overhead lights, and immediately half a dozen young men gathered around it. "Who has the dice?" someone asked.

"I have," said Phil, shaking them in his half-open hand.

"Oh, great," said someone.

"You want to have a look at them?" said Phil. "You wouldn't know the difference anyway, but you can have a look. No? All right, I'm shooting a dollar. A dollar open."

"You're faded," said someone.

"Anybody else want a dollar?" said Phil.

"I'll take a dollar," said Billy Warden.

"A dollar to you, and a dollar to you. Anyone else? No? O.K. Here we go, and it's a nine. A niner, a niner, what could be finer. No drinks to a minor. And it's a five. Come on, dice, let's see that six-three for Phil. And it's a four? Come on, dice. Be nice. And it's a—a nine it is. Four dollars open. Billy, you want to bet the deuce?"

"You're covered," said Billy.

"You're covered," said the other bettor.

"Anybody else wish to participate? No? All right, eight dollars on the table, and—oh, what do I see there? A natural. The big six and the little one. Bet the four, Billy?"

"I'm with you," said Billy.

"I'm out," said the other bettor.

"I'm in," said a newcomer.

"Four dollars to you, four dollars to Mr. Warden. And here we go, and for little old Phil a—oh, my. The eyes of a snake. Back where you started from, Billy. House bets five dollars. Nobody wants the five? All right, any part of it."

"Two dollars," said Billy.

When it came his turn to take the dice, he passed it up and chose instead to make bets on the side. Thus he nursed his stake until at one time he had thirty-eight or nine dollars in his hands. The number of players was increasing, and all pretty much for the same reason: most of the boys had not yet got their Christmas money, and a crap game offered the best chance to add to the pre-Christmas bankroll.

"Why don't you drag?" said Andy Phillips. "Get out while you're ahead?"

"As soon as I have fifty dollars," said Billy.

The next time the shooter with the dice announced five dollars open, Billy covered it himself, won, and got the dice. In less than ten minutes he was cleaned—no paper money, nothing but the small change in his pocket. He looked around among the players, but there was no one whom he cared to borrow from. "Don't look at me," said Andy. "I have six bucks to last me till Christmas."

"Well, I have eighty-seven cents," said Billy. "Do you still want to spot me fifty to forty?"

"Sure. But not for a buck. You haven't got a buck," said Andy. "And I'm going to beat you."

They waited until a table was free, and played their fifty points, which Andy won, fifty to thirty-two. "I'll be bighearted," said Andy. "I'll pay for the table."

"No, no. Thirty cents won't break me," said Billy. "Or do you want to play another? Give me fifty to thirty-five."

"No, I don't like this table. It's too high," said Andy.

"Well, what shall we do?" said Billy.

"The movies ought to be letting out pretty soon. Shall we go down and see if we can pick anything up?"

"Me with fifty-seven cents? And you with six bucks?"

"Well, you have the Dodge, and we could get a couple of pints on credit," said Andy.

"All right, we can try," said Billy. They left the poolroom and went down to the street and reparked the Warden Dodge where they could observe the movie crowd on its way out. Attendance that night was slim, and passable girls in pairs nowhere to be seen. The movie-theatre lights went out. "Well, so much for that," said Billy. "Five after eleven."

"Let's get a pint," said Andy.

"I honestly don't feel like it, Andy," said Billy.

"I didn't mean you were to buy it. I'll split it with you."

"I understood that part," said Billy. "Just don't feel like drinking."

"Do you have to *feel* like drinking at Dartmouth? Up at State we just drink."

"Oh, sure. Big hell-raisers," said Billy. "Kappa Betes and T.N.E.s. 'Let's go over to Lock Haven and get slopped.' I heard all about State while I was at Mercersburg. That's why I didn't go there—one of the reasons."

"Is that so?" said Andy. "Well, if all you're gonna do is sit here and razz

State, I think I'll go down to Mulhearn's and have a couple beers. You should have had sense enough to quit when you were thirty-some bucks ahead."

"Darius L. Cooper didn't quit when he was thirty bucks ahead."

"Who? You mean the fellow with the cake-eater suit? His name wasn't Cooper. His name is Minzer or something like that. Well, the beers are a quarter at Mulhearn's. We could have six fours are twenty-four. We could have twelve beers apiece. I'll lend you three bucks."

"No thanks," said Billy. "I'll take you down to Mulhearn's and then I think I'll go home and get some shuteye. I didn't get any sleep on the train last night."

"That's what's the matter with you? All right, disagreeable. Safe at last in your trundle bed."

"How do you know that? That's a Dartmouth song," said Billy.

"I don't know, I guess I heard *you* sing it," said Andy. "Not tonight, though. I'll walk to Mulhearn's. I'll see you tomorrow."

"All right, Andy. See you tomorrow," said Billy. He watched his friend, with his felt hat turned up too much in front and back, his thick-soled Whitehouse & Hardys clicking on the sidewalk, his joe-college swagger, his older brother's leather coat. Life was simple for Andy and always would be. In two more years he would finish at State, a college graduate, and he would come home and take a job in Phillips Brothers Lumber Yard, marry a local girl, join the Lions or Rotary, and play volleyball at the Y.M.C.A. His older brother had already done all those things, and Andy was Fred Phillips all over again.

The Dodge, still warm, did not repeat the whining protest of a few hours earlier in the evening. He put it in gear and headed for home. He hoped his father and mother would have gone to bed. "What the hell's the matter with me?" he said. "Nothing's right tonight."

He put the car in the garage and entered the house by the kitchen door. He opened the refrigerator door, and heard his father's voice. "Is that you, Son?"

"Yes, it's me. I'm getting a glass of milk."

His father was in the sitting room and made no answer. Billy drank a glass of milk and turned out the kitchen lights. He went to the sitting room. His father, in shirtsleeves and smoking a pipe, was at the desk. "You doing your bookkeeping?" said Billy.

"No."

"What *are* you doing?"

"Well, if you must know, I was writing a poem. I was trying to express my appreciation to your mother."

"Can I see it?"

"Not in a hundred years," said Mr. Warden. "Nobody will ever see this but her—if she ever does."

"I never knew you wrote poetry."

"Once a year, for the past twenty-six years, starting with the first Christmas we were engaged. So far I haven't missed a year, but it doesn't get any easier. But by God, the first thing Christmas morning she'll say to me, 'Where's my poem?' Never speaks about it the rest of the year, but it's always the first thing she asks me the twenty-fifth of December."

"Has she kept them all?" said Billy.

"That I never asked her, but I suppose she has."

"Does she write you one?" said Billy.

"Nope. Well, what did you do tonight? You're home early, for you."

"Kind of tired. I didn't get much sleep last night. We got on the train at White River Junction and nobody could sleep."

"Well, get to bed and sleep till noon. That ought to restore your energy."

"O.K. Good night, Dad."

"Good night, Son," said his father. "Oh, say. You had a long-distance call. You're to call the Scranton operator, no matter what time you get in."

"Thanks," said Billy. "Good night."

"Well, aren't you going to put the call in? I'll wait in the kitchen."

"No, I know who it is. I'll phone them tomorrow."

"That's up to you," said Mr. Warden. "Well, good night again."

"Good night," said Billy. He went to his room and took off his clothes, to the bathroom and brushed his teeth. He put out the light beside his bed and lay there. He wondered if Henrietta Cooper's father had ever written a poem to her mother. But he knew the answer to that.

1964

1.

2.

3.

4.

5.

6.

7.

8.

9.

10.

11.

12.

MACDONALD

CHRISTMAS

VLADIMIR NABOKOV

After walking back from the village to his manor across the dimming snows, Sleptsov sat down in a corner, on a plush-covered chair he did not remember ever using before. It was the kind of thing that happens after some great calamity. Not your brother but a chance acquaintance, a vague country neighbor to whom you never paid much attention, with whom in normal times you exchange scarcely a word, is the one who comforts you wisely and gently, and hands you your dropped hat after the funeral service is over and you are reeling from grief, your teeth chattering, your eyes blinded by tears. The same can be said of inanimate objects. Any room, even the coziest and the most absurdly small, in the little-used wing of a great country house has an unlived-in corner. And it was such a corner in which Sleptsov sat.

The wing was connected by a wooden gallery, now encumbered with our huge north-Russian snowdrifts, to the main house, used only in summer. There was no need to awaken it, to heat it: the master had come from Petersburg for only a couple of days and had settled in the annex, where it was a simple matter to get the stoves of white Dutch tile going.

The master sat in his out-of-the-way corner, on that plush chair, as in a doctor's waiting room. The room floated in darkness; the dense blue of early evening filtered through the crystal feathers of frost on the windowpane. Ivan, the quiet, portly valet, who had recently shaved off his mustache and now looked like his late father, the family butler, brought in a kerosene lamp, all trimmed and brimming with light. He set it on a small table, and noiselessly caged it within its pink silk shade. For an instant a tilted mirror reflected his lit ear and cropped gray hair. Then he withdrew and the door gave a subdued creak.

Sleptsov raised his hand from his knee and slowly examined it. A drop of candle wax had stuck and hardened in the thin fold of skin between two fingers. He spread his fingers and the little white scale cracked.

~~~

The following morning, after a night spent in nonsensical, fragmentary dreams totally unrelated to his grief, as Sleptsov stepped out into the cold veranda, a floorboard emitted a merry pistol crack underfoot, and the reflections of the many-colored panes formed paradisal lozenges on the whitewashed cushionless window seats. The outer door resisted at first, then opened with a luscious crunch, and the dazzling frost hit his face. The reddish sand providently sprinkled on the ice coating the porch steps resembled cinnamon, and thick icicles shot with greenish blue hung from the eaves. The snowdrifts reached all the way to the windows of the annex, tightly gripping the snug little wooden structure in their frosty clutches. The creamy white mounds of what were flower beds in summer swelled slightly above the level snow in front of the porch, and farther off loomed the radiance of the park, where every black branch was rimmed with silver and the firs seemed to draw in their green paws under their bright, plump load.

Wearing high felt boots and a short fur-lined coat with a caracul collar, Sleptsov strode off slowly along a straight path, the only one cleared of snow, into that blinding distant landscape. He was amazed to be still alive, and able to perceive the brilliance of the snow and feel his front teeth ache from the cold. He even noticed that a snow-covered bush resembled a fountain and that a dog had left on the slope of a snowdrift a series of saffron marks, which had burned through its crust. A little farther, the supports of a footbridge stuck out of the snow, and there Sleptsov stopped. Bitterly, angrily, he pushed the thick, fluffy covering off the parapet. He vividly recalled how this bridge looked in summer. There was his son walking along the slippery planks, flecked with aments, and deftly plucking off with his net a butterfly that had settled on the railing. Now the boy sees his father. Forever lost laughter plays on the boy's face, under the turned-down brim of a straw hat burned dark by the sun; his hand toys with the chain of the leather purse attached to his belt; his dear smooth, sun-tanned legs in their serge shorts and soaked sandals assume their usual cheerful widespread stance. Just recently, in Petersburg, after having babbled in his delirium about school, about his bicycle, about some great Oriental moth, he died, and yesterday Sleptsov had taken the coffin—weighed down, it seemed, with an entire lifetime—to the country, into the family vault near the village church.

It was quiet as it can only be on a bright, frosty day. Sleptsov raised his leg high, stepped off the path, and, leaving blue pits behind him in the snow, made his way among the trunks of amazingly white trees to the spot where the park dropped off toward the river. Far below, ice blocks sparkled near a hole cut in the smooth expanse of white, and, on the opposite bank, very straight columns of pink smoke stood above the snowy roofs of log cabins. Sleptsov took off his caracul cap and leaned against a tree trunk. Somewhere far away, peasants were chopping wood—every blow bounced resonantly skyward—and beyond the light silver mist of trees, high above the squat log huts, the sun caught the equanimous radiance of the cross on the church.

At Christmas the Websters always had a tree spider-webbed with angel hair and ropes of tinsel. Underneath were figures of shepherds, wise men and a tiny manager that I looked for every year.

—*Washington Post*

They make themselves scarce around Christmas-time.

1969

~~~

That was where he headed after lunch, in an old sleigh with a high straight back. The cod of the black stallion clacked strongly in the frosty air, the white plumes of low branches glided overhead, and the ruts in front gave off a silvery blue sheen. When he arrived, he sat for an hour or so by the grave, resting a heavy, woollen-gloved hand on the iron of the railing, which burned his hand through the wool. He came home with a slight sense of disappointment, as if there in the burial vault he had been even further removed from his son than here where the countless summer tracks of his rapid sandals were preserved beneath the snow.

In the evening, overcome by a fit of intense sadness, he had the main house unlocked. When the door swung open with a weighty wail, and a whiff of special, unwintery coolness came from the sonorous iron-barred vestibule, Sleptsov took the lamp with its tin reflector from the watchman's hand and entered the house alone. The parquet floors crackled eerily under his step. Room after room filled with yellow light, and the shrouded furniture seemed unfamiliar; instead of a tinkling chandelier, a soundless bag hung from the ceiling, and Sleptsov's enormous shadow, slowly extending one arm, floated across the wall and over the gray squares of curtained paintings.

He went into the room which had been his son's study in summer, set the lamp on the window ledge, and, breaking his fingernails as he did so, opened the folding shutters, even though all was darkness outside. In the blue glass the yellow flame of the slightly smoky lamp appeared, and his large, bearded face showed momentarily.

He sat down at the bare desk and sternly, from under bent brows, examined the pale wallpaper with its garlands of bluish roses; a narrow office-like cabinet, with sliding drawers from top to bottom; the couch and armchairs under slipcovers; and suddenly, dropping his head onto the desk, he started to shake, passionately, noisily, pressing first his lips, then his wet cheek to the cold, dusty wood and clutching at its far corners.

In the desk he found a notebook, spreading boards, supplies of black pins, and an English biscuit tin that contained a large exotic cocoon which had cost three rubles. It was papery to the touch and seemed made of a brown folded leaf. His son had remembered it during his sickness, regretting that he had left it behind but consoling himself with the thought that the chrysalid inside was probably dead. Sleptsov also found a torn net: a tarlatan bag on a collapsible hoop (and the muslin still smelled of summer and sun-hot grass).

Then, bending lower and lower and sobbing with his whole body, he began pulling out one by one the glass-topped drawers of the cabinet. In the dim lamplight the even files of specimens shone silklike under the glass. Here, in this room, on that very desk, his son had spread the wings of his captures. He would first pin the carefully killed insect in the cork-bottomed groove of the setting board, between the adjustable strips of wood, and fasten down flat with pinned strips of paper the still fresh, soft wings. They had now dried long ago and been transferred to the cabinet—those spectacular Swallowtails, those dazzling Coppers and Blues, and the various Fritillaries, some mounted in a supine position to display the mother-of-pearl undersides. His son used to pronounce their Latin names with a moan of triumph or in an arch aside of disdain. And the moths, the moths, the first Aspen Hawk of five summers ago!

~~~

The night was smoke-blue and moonlit; thin clouds were scattered about the sky but did not touch the delicate, icy moon. The trees, masses of gray frost, cast dark shadows on the drifts, which scintillated here and there with metallic sparks. In that plush-upholstered, well-heated room of the annex, Ivan had placed a two-foot fir tree in a clay pot on the table, and was just attaching a candle to its cruciform tip when Sleptsov returned from the main house, chilled, red-eyed, with gray dust smears on his cheek, carrying a wooden case under his arm. Seeing the Christmas tree on the table, he asked absently, "What's that?"

Relieving him of the case, Ivan answered in a low, mellow voice, "There's a holiday coming up tomorrow."

"No, take it away," said Sleptsov with a frown, while thinking, Can this be Christmas Eve? How could I have forgotten?

Ivan gently insisted, "It's nice and green. Let it stand for a while."

"Please take it away," repeated Sleptsov, and bent over the case he had brought. In it he had gathered his son's belongings—the folding butterfly net, the biscuit tin with the pear-shaped cocoon, the spreading boards, the pins in their lacquered box, the blue notebook. Half of the first page had been torn out, and its remaining fragment contained part of a French dictation. There followed daily entries, names of captured butterflies, and other notes:

Walked across the bog as far as Borovichi . . .

Raining today. Played checkers with Father, then read Goncharov's "Frigate," a deadly bore.

Marvellous hot day. Rode my bike in the evening. A midge got in my eye. Deliberately rode by her dacha twice, but didn't see her. . . .

Sleptsov raised his head, swallowed something hot and huge. Of whom was his son writing?

Rode my bike as usual. Our eyes nearly met. My darling, my love . . .

"This is unthinkable," whispered Sleptsov. "I'll never know . . ."

He bent over again, avidly deciphering the childish handwriting that slanted up then curved down in the margin.

Saw a fresh specimen of the Camberwell Beauty today. That means autumn is here. Rain in the evening. She has probably left, and we didn't even get acquainted. Farewell, my darling. I feel terribly sad. . . .

"He never said anything to me . . ." Sleptsov tried to remember, rubbing his forehead with his palm.

On the last page there was an ink drawing: the hind view of an elephant—two thick pillars, the corners of two ears, and a tiny tail.

Sleptsov got up. He shook his head, restraining yet another onrush of hideous sobs.

"I-can't-bear-it-any-longer," he drawled between groans, repeating even more slowly, "I—can't—bear—it—any—longer . . ."

It's Christmas tomorrow, came the abrupt reminder, and I'm going to die. Of course. It's so simple. This very night . . .

He pulled out a handkerchief and dried his eyes, his beard, his cheeks. Dark streaks remained on the handkerchief.

". . . death," Sleptsov said softly, as if concluding a long sentence.

The clock ticked. Frost patterns overlapped on the blue glass of the window. The open notebook shone radiantly on the table; next to it the light went through the muslin of the butterfly net, and glistened on a corner of the open tin. Sleptsov pressed his eyes shut, and had a fleeting sensation that earthly life lay before him, totally bared and comprehensible—and ghastly in its sadness, humiliatingly pointless, sterile, devoid of miracles.

At that instant there was a sudden snap—a thin sound like that of an overstretched rubber band breaking. Sleptsov opened his eyes. The cocoon in the biscuit tin had burst at its tip, and a black, wrinkled creature the size of a mouse was crawling up the wall above the table. It stopped, holding on to the surface with six black furry feet and started palpitating strangely. It had emerged from the chrysalid because a man overcome with grief had transferred a tin box to his warm room and the warmth had penetrated its taut leaf-and-silk envelope; it had awaited this moment so long, had collected its strength so tensely, and now, having broken out, it was slowly and miraculously expanding. Gradually the wrinkled tissues, the velvety fringes unfurled; the fan-pleated veins grew firmer as they filled with air. It became a winged thing imperceptibly, as a maturing face imperceptibly becomes beautiful. And its wings—still feeble, still moist—kept growing and unfolding, and now they were developed to the limit set for them by God, and there, on the wall, instead of a little lump of life, instead of a dark mouse, was a great *Attacus* moth like those that fly, birdlike, around lamps in the Indian dusk.

And then those thick black wings, with a glazy eyespot on each and a purplish bloom dusting their hooked foretips, took a full breath under the impulse of tender, ravishing, almost human happiness.

(Translated, from the Russian text of 1925, by Dmitri Nabokov, in collaboration with the author)

1975

SOLACE

LINDA GRACE HOYER

Ada dropped a lighted match into the heap of Christmas paper at the edge of her woods and watched its flame consume the red tissue in which one of several gifts from her son, Christopher, had been wrapped. It was a clear day, with a stiff breeze from the northwest. She wore faded bluejeans with un-ravelling cuffs and a red mackinaw that had belonged to her husband, Marty. An inch of snow had fallen during the night and, against a cloudless sky, the balsam fir that Ada's mother had planted to add a touch of green to the gray woods in winter gently waved its wide branches. With snow on the ground and the wind coming the way it was, the risk of setting fire to the woods was minimal, Ada thought. But even while she prodded the pile of paper with a staff she sometimes used to steady her steps when walking outdoors, a green pickup truck turned in to her yard and Mr. Murdough, her nearest neighbor, jumped from the cab.

"I saw your fire," he said, "and thought it might be the woods."

"Oh, no, this is where I always burn the paper—very carefully," Ada said, and she turned to the youthful tricolored collie that earlier in the year she had bought from the custodian of the local animal shelter. "We love that woods, don't we, Peter Pup?"

"You know that woods has no fire lanes and there'd be no way for us to bring in a fire engine," Mr. Murdough said.

"I know that," Ada said. Mr. Murdough's unexpected arrival implied a need for his presence that Ada had not felt, and she did not smile.

"If you tell me where to find a bucket, I'll bring water from your spring, to douse the fire when you leave."

Though Ada previously had been unaware of Mr. Murdough's resemblance to her late husband, she noticed it now. Their straight blond hair, their deep-set hazel eyes and jutting jaws were similar. Especially like Marty was Mr. Murdough's determination to *help*.

The April that followed Marty's death, Mr. Murdough had driven his tractor into a field where Ada was hand-raking newly turned ground prior to

CHRISTMAS PAST

Oranges and peppermint candy, fruitcake long in the making but swift enough in the eating, with a little Bourbon whiskey poured over it. A chill in the air, if not the snow of dreams, and the dusty whiffs, at that woebegone time, of soft coal burning in the grate—this was Kentucky long ago, when we sat with our father at the upright piano and each night of Christmas week sang the hymns and the old songs of Christmas, many with their dog-trot rhymes of bed and head, night and bright.

Later, in New York, I collected Christmas records, and each year I play them. The most beautiful are the oldest: Caruso singing "Cantique de Noël" in 1916, before electrical recording, and reclaimed in early mono LPs. In spite of the great tenor's range and notable volume, what we know as "O Holy Night" seems to come from a distance, from the star in the East, a pastoral world in antiquity—or perhaps it's only the hum and scratch of the twenty-six-year-old album, "A Golden Age Christmas." Eliot's poem on the Magi begins, "A cold coming we had of it," and the senti-

planting peas in it and, above the roar of the engine, shouted, "That's not the kind of work you should be doing. It's too hard for you." There had been no time for Ada to explain that on account of a recent thunderstorm the soil was too wet to be worked any way but by hand. Looking as determined as Marty might have under the same circumstances, Mr. Murdough had sent the tractor careering back and forth, while she stood by and saw her garden ruined. Then, without speaking, Mr. Murdough had driven away, and Ada, rake in hand, had retired from the field. To this winter day, eight and a half years later, Ada had not returned to plant peas, though in summer she drove her own tractor-drawn mower into that field to cut a tangle of red clover and Queen Anne's lace that grew where peas might have grown.

In the face of Mr. Murdough's present determination, Ada managed a smile that felt dry, if not actually forced. "The spring is so close," she said. "I'll douse the fire, if necessary."

"Are you alone, Ada?"

"Yes, Mr. Murdough. I'm alone."

"I thought Christopher might've come. For Christmas."

"It's a long way for him to come, and I don't mind being alone on Christmas—or any day. In fact, I enjoy being alone. After all, we'll all be alone in our caskets."

ment is not alien to "Stille Nacht, Heilige Nacht" as sung by the matchless contralto Ernestine Schumann-Heink, in a tempo slower than that heard in the churches. She brings to the rather banal hymn a gravity and solemnity that might, if you like, foretell the strange future of the babe in the crib. My recordings of Christmas hymns sung by Elisabeth Schwarzkopf, Joan Sutherland, and others possess a jubilate accent indeed appropriate for a time of celebration, but not more fitting than the long-dead voices of a simpler, less opulent, and less spendthrift time.

In the notes to the old recording, I learned that during the twenties and thirties the tenor Giovanni Martinelli would rise up in the choir loft at St. Patrick's Cathedral during the Midnight Mass to sing, without previous announcement, "Gesù Bambino." What reciprocity can be imagined here? Perhaps the ring of a few coins tossed in the poor box.

—ELIZABETH HARDWICK, 1998

"I've never thought of that, Ada, and I'm not sure that you should have."

"I often attend my funeral in imagination. It can make Christmas alone seem happy."

"I'll suggest it as an exercise for my mother the next time she complains of being left alone. My father, as you know, was no saint."

"And now she thinks he was? A saint?"

"Yes."

"I know how that is."

"But Marty *was* a saint."

"Not quite," Ada said.

"I never heard him say an unkind word about anybody."

"I did."

"He was a great man."

"He was a singular man, with the ability to lead his students and acquaintances to accept their own singularity. That is a rare gift."

"Mother worries about you—all alone."

"Tell her not to worry. The Wertz sisters have invited me to share their Christmas dinner. And tell her to be glad that her son lives so close."

"Be careful when you drive today. There's ice under the snow."

"You take care, and have a merry Christmas."

"A merry Christmas to you, too." Briskly, Mr. Murdough returned to his truck and started in the direction of his mother's house with Peter Pup barking, leading the way.

~~~

A family of yellow jackets had nested during the summer in the ground not far from where Ada stood with her back to the fire, and the sharp stinging pain in her right ankle recalled summer's several clashes with its members; indeed, Ada would have been no more surprised to see a yellow jacket taking leave of her than she had been by Mr. Murdough's arrival a few minutes earlier. Widowhood, it seemed to her, was more surprising than her marriage had ever been.

What Ada saw when she looked down was not an angry yellow jacket but a fringe of flame where the right cuff of her bluejeans had been.

To Marty, an unexpectedly painful happening had been either "a new experience," and therefore a kind of "blessed event," or, as the blooming rhodora had been for Emerson, "its own excuse for being." Though disinclined to share Marty's stoical acceptance of surprises, Ada managed to bow from the waist and, with callused hands and a wry smile, stifle the flames. That done, she called the dog and went into the house with him. At this point, as she saw it, there was no need to douse the trash pile.

After her father's death, Ada had carried upstairs the cushioned maple chair she had given him for Christmas in 1934 and set it at the head of Christopher's bed. Abandoned, the bed and chair waited with an expectant air in the bedroom where Christopher had slept. Actually, they had the look Ada saw, on her way down the hall, reflected in her bathroom mirror. It was the look of a person who, although obviously of less use than she formerly was, continued to expect well of the future. Holding the medicine-cabinet door open, Ada was relieved to see that a magazine clipping Marty had pasted inside long ago was still there. She read it aloud while Peter Pup listened: " 'Whether caused by flame or chemicals, a burn should be flooded with water immediately for approximately fifteen minutes. A burn caused by chemicals should be examined by a doctor as soon as possible.'

"The treatment will be simple as taking a bath," she said, and, having closed the medicine-cabinet door, she opened both spigots of the bathtub. Much simpler, surely, than the application of apple butter and sliced raw potatoes, tied on with strips of an old sheet, that her mother had used when Ada had burned her arms in hot corn mush. How old had she been at the time? Three, perhaps? Ada remembered, as though it had happened today, the corn's color—pure gold—in an iron kettle on the arrowbacked chair. She remembered, too, how, after an awkward struggle with the bandages, her mother, who seldom had time to hold her, had taken her onto her lap and held her there until the pain was gone. Compared with that pain, the pricklings Ada felt while bathing her ankle were a discomfort, nothing more.

Ada was in the tub when the phone rang. "That's Lucy Wertz calling to say, 'Are you still alive?'" Ada told Peter Pup. And when, nude and waterlogged, she climbed from the tub and crossed the hall to answer the phone, she found that the caller was indeed Lucy Wertz.

"Were you at the barn?" said Lucy.

"No, I was taking a bath."

"In that case, you should have your breathing fixed, Ada."

"After the pulmonary lab tests, Dr. Hutchinson told me not to worry about my slight emphysema."

"Then perhaps you need an evaluation of your heart."

"Have you forgotten the Holter monitor I wore for one whole day last year, and the digitalis Dr. Razzano prescribed?"

"You may need another prescription."

"Right now what I need is a towel."

"You are coming to have dinner with us, aren't you?"

"Yes, after I'm dressed. If I'm not there by twelve, start dinner without me. Mr. Murdough was here and said there are patches of ice under the blowing snow."

"We've seen a car go by the house this morning. The road is open."

Ada didn't argue with her. Never having learned to drive, the Wertz sisters had sold their husbands' automobiles and forgotten the difficulties of driving in wintertime completely, so that nothing Ada might have said on that subject would have been useful.

"We'll pray that you have a safe trip," Lucy said, adding, "Jane's hungry."

"I'll try to be there by twelve," Ada said.

~~~

At ten minutes before twelve, Lucy Wertz, seeing Ada's blue compact in the snow-covered driveway beside the house, opened the back door and, with a delight so shrill that a stranger unaccustomed to Lucy's way of greeting visitors might have fled to the safety of the woods, said, "Merry Christmas, Ada. It's good to see you."

Familiar though Ada was with Lucy's greetings, they surprised her, so that without a word she followed Lucy into the kitchen, where Jane was turning the yams in a glaze of butter and sugar.

There, in the voice that a moment before had welcomed Ada, Lucy said, "Go on into the living room and wait until dinner is ready." To reinforce her command, Lucy led the way and, from the center of the room, said, "Sit down and *read* until I call you."

"In which one of the chairs would you like me to sit?" Ada asked, re-membering Marty's saying to her, "You can take the girl out of the country, but you can't take the country out of the girl." Lucy, Baltimore-born and for forty years a teacher in the public schools of that city, was trying to take the country out of the girl Ada no longer was.

Lucy said, "You may sit wherever you like."

But, of course, nothing could have been less true. If given her own choice of a place to sit, Ada would have stayed in the kitchen, where Jane was turn-ing the yams in their glaze of butter and sugar.

"The little dears! They still believe in Santa Claus."

"Then I'll sit here," Ada said, moving toward a very old Windsor chair with the patina of age and its frailty.

"That will be all right." The words came slowly, as though Lucy, knowing Ada's weight, would have preferred to have her sit on the davenport. But then, speaking crisply, she said, "*Read this,*" and left Ada on her own.

The magazine that Lucy handed to Ada was a monthly publication intended to advertise the virtues of that branch of Protestantism of which the Wertz sisters were members, and Ada dropped it, unopened, on the neat pile of magazines from which Lucy had taken it. That done, she sat down in the old Windsor chair and turned a critical eye on her surroundings.

The room was one she had known in childhood and remembered with great affection, because at that time a favorite aunt and uncle had owned the house and during her mother's illnesses had offered Ada the solace she needed. Later, when her mother had recovered, Ada went to visit Uncle Nathan and Aunt Elizabeth with her parents. On those festive occasions, she had been allowed to stay in the kitchen while meals were being prepared and, best of all, encouraged to feel that her being there was *helpful*. "Will you bring the balloon-backed chairs from the parlor?" Aunt Elizabeth would say if her sons were at home from the city and extra chairs were needed for the table. Or in warm weather, when milk and butter had to be refrigerated in the spring ditch, she would say, "Run for the butter and cream, Ada. The dinner is almost ready."

It seemed to Ada that all that was bright and warm in her memories of childhood had happened in this room. Now the room—with its newly plastered white walls and precious Persian rug—was bright without being warm. It was extraordinarily neat. But, remembering it as it had been seventy years ago, she resented this neatness. Both the piano and the bookcase were gone, along with Uncle Nathan's Boston rocker, where Aunt Elizabeth sat to mend his socks by the light of a huge kerosene lamp. Gone, too, was the horsehair sofa—that wonder of slippery elegance—where Ada herself sat while her cousin Mordecai played the piano. The room had held a round stove, with nickel-plated extensions to warm cold feet. And Ada had not wanted to be in the kitchen.

Her wait, happily, was not long, and when she joined Lucy and Jane in the dining room her plate had been filled.

"We prefer chicken to turkey," Jane said. "We hope you do, too."

"I like both. And this looks lovely," Ada said.

"Harvey liked ham," Lucy said. "What did Marty like?"

"Hamburger with cream sauce," Ada said.

"Bless his heart."

Seeing that the sisters had closed their eyes and bowed their heads in the silent blessing ordinarily asked by them, Ada inaudibly said, "Dear Lord, bless this house and help me to get home."

When their plates were as clean as good appetites could make them, Jane passed the fruitcake and Christmas cookies, while Lucy brought hot water to make instant coffee in their expectant cups. Meanwhile, Ada wondered who now alive in this world could bake mince pie the way her mother had.

Later, when the table had been cleared and Ada spoke of leaving, Lucy said, "Why, child? You've hardly said a word. You must tell us how Peter Pup is."

"Peter Pup is fine."

"And you?"

"I'm lucky to be here."

"Aren't we all?" Lucy said. "It's so *beautiful* here."

Jane, with a faraway look in her eyes, agreed, and said, "Yes, it is beautiful here. I was born in the middle class and expect to stay in it."

Taken by surprise, Ada laughed. "Middle class" was a term she seldom used, and if anyone had asked her where in America's complicated society she belonged, she almost certainly would have said, "I don't know."

Once, years ago, at a picnic on the church lawn, after telling Ada that both of her parents had migrated from Berlin to Baltimore, Lucy asked, with an anxious look, "You are *German,* aren't you?"

Ada said, "My father told me that we can't measure a snake while it's running." Remembering her rudeness on that occasion and hoping to make amends now, Ada said to Lucy, "I caught fire this morning."

"How, child?" Lucy and Jane said together.

"I was burning trash where I always do, and watching Peter Pup herding Mr. Murdough into his truck, when the fire took hold of my jeans."

"What did you do? Did you roll on the ground? Did you call Mr. Murdough?" They spoke as one person and that one Lucy.

"I smothered the flame with my hands."

"How could you?"

"Easily. It was a small flame, and I was lucky."

"Yes, you were lucky."

"And now I really must be going. I'm expecting Christopher to call."

"We'll call tonight to see how you are."

Ada wanted to tell Lucy that another interrogation on the subject of her health would be an invasion of privacy but found herself saying, "Thanks for the lovely dinner. It made a perfect day."

"Come back soon," Lucy said. "Be sure to drive carefully."

~~~

On the ice of the Wertz sisters' driveway the wheels of Ada's car spun for some time before she reached the sun-dried road. She was still ten miles from home and knew that snow had drifted into the road along the way. There was one small plain where, having had previous experiences with snowdrifts, Ada expected her car to stall, but when she got there, instead of a snowdrift she found two neat piles of snow, with the road, clear as could be, between them.

Seeing the green truck up the road, she knew that the man leaning on his shovel in the truck's shadow was Mr. Murdough. He was smiling in the complacent way that Marty smiled when, another day of teaching behind him, he walked from his parked car across the lawn toward their back porch.

Ada stopped her car. "What do I owe you, Mr. Murdough, for opening the road?" she asked.

"That's what neighbors are for."

"In that case, thank you *very* much. I want to be home by the time Christopher calls."

"You'll have no trouble from here on."

"You're a saint."

"Any time you need help—day or night—call me," Mr. Murdough said as Ada's car gathered speed.

Words like "That's what neighbors are for" were part of the local language and not to be taken without a grain of salt. They were, however, a comfort to hear. At home, Peter Pup would be waiting, and that, too, was a solacing thought.

When Christopher called, Ada was resting in the kitchen with the dog. When she told Christopher that on that very day both Mr. Murdough and a fire had visited her, he asked, "Was the fire Mr. Murdough's fault? Did he push you toward the trash pile?" Christopher's voice suggested a blend of genuine concern and amusement.

This was a form of banter she had used when Christopher was a child and he, out of a sense of loyalty—or was it fear?—still used.

"Have you seen a doctor?" Christopher wanted to know.

"On Christmas?"

"How *is* your health, Mother?"

"You know my heart is damaged?"

"I know. Dr. Hutchinson told me."

"And there is lung damage, too, and a considerable loss of memory."

"The way you describe it, it almost sounds like fun."

"But none of my doctors look amused when they see me. Have I lived too long?"

"Certainly not," Christopher said with conviction.

"That's *nice* to know."

"We'll talk again on New Year's Day, Mother. In the meantime, don't stand too close to the fire."

"Thanks for being a good boy, Christopher," Ada said, and settled the receiver back in its cradle.

Peter Pup, relieved of the obligation to eavesdrop, went to his nest and, with a deep sigh, curled up to sleep. Ada, after going to the window and making certain that it was the evening sun and not a brush fire burning among the gray trees beyond the old fir, turned on her radio and sat down to hear the last of the Christmas music. A shadow of the barn lay on the field, where fringes of dry buck grass moved like the gentle flame that had felt like the sting of a yellow jacket and, like the pain of a yellow jacket's sting, was soon gone.

1983

A CHRISTMAS STORY

GARRISON KEILLOR

It was Christmas Eve in Houston, and through the howling blizzard struggled the runaway nearsighted boy Jim, his T-shirt frozen to his back, his skinny arms limp from hauling his big golden retriever, Tony, who was wet and therefore much heavier than if the weather had been warm and sunny. Jim had left home that morning, because his folks were talking about flying to Aruba for the holidays and leaving him with the cleaning lady, and now big wet flakes were falling so thickly he couldn't see the nose on his own face—and Jim did have a pretty big beezer. "I'm done for, Tony," whimpered the myopic child sadly. Death was near. If only he had worn a coat or taken a limo! And then suddenly, with a loud *whump* and an *oof,* he walked into a small statue or something and fell down with Tony on top of him. It was a statue of a little black stableboy! This was his mom and dad's house! He had wandered through the blizzard in a full circle back to Hickey Avenue and the palatial home of his wealthy and irrepressible parents. He pounded weakly on the door with his small white hand.

~~~

Before the door opens, let's extend a big welcome to the folks at DioNate, which is making this story possible, and to the more than forty-six thousand partners in the DioNate work experience. A story can be pretty expensive to develop. And this one, conceptualized in 1983 by an editorial team from Winston-Price, was sold to a major fiction consortium, the Oso Company, which spun off its communications holdings in 1985 to Carver Pharmaceuticals, which was taken over in 1987 by Sun Dry, the electronics/airline-charter/pet-food conglomerate, which then became part of DioNate. At this point, the story was only a bare outline—Rich Boy Finds True Meaning of Christmas and Dies in Blizzard with Dog—but $21,600,000 had been invested in it already. If the readers of this magazine had to foot the whole bill, this issue would have cost you $53.87! Quite a savings, thanks to DioNate!

The door opened, and there was Alice, Jim's size-8 mom, in a beady blue silk gown from Italy or somewhere. "Jim! What?" she said. "You're outdoors! Sharon said you were in the solarium, using the tanning machine."

(Sharon! Why would she believe his sister Sharon, who was on drugs?)

"I ran away from home eleven hours ago, Mom!"

"Oh. Who's this?"

"It's my old dog, Tony. I've had him since he was a pup."

"Oh—I thought you had a pony."

The lobby twinkled with Christmas lights, pink and white and silver, and the rich, gloomy library was gaily festooned with pine boughs from the Hartz Mountains and red silk streamers and angels with spun-platinum hair. A sequoia wreath hung over the vast fireplace, where fragrant mesquite blazed away. In the glittering dining room, the table was decked with green linen, golden candlesticks, the rare Roi d'Alton china, with its handpainted gold filigree, and the good silver from his mom's side of the family, the wealthy Chesterfields. And through the great onyx arch he could see, standing thirty feet high in the Chinese rotunda, the Christmas tree, the most beautiful one anywhere in the world! It cost four thousand dollars to airlift it down from the High Sierras and truck it east to Texas.

"It looks nice. Marlon did a good job. I like it traditional," said Jim, though he was so nearsighted the tree looked like an upturned skiff. His mom always had the house professionally decorated at Christmas. Last year, Marlon had gone in for a Georgia O'Keeffe look, with sand, cactuses, stones, bleached bones, and Christmas bulbs inside cow skulls, and the year before it was lasers. Then Jim noticed the table was set for fifteen persons. But there are only four of us, he thought to himself.

~~~

As I mentioned, DioNate is picking up most of the tab for *publication* of "A Christmas Story," but, of course, corporate underwriting can't hope to cover all of the *writer's* costs. None of the $21,600,000 went to me, and I've had to spend a lot of time writing and rewriting and *re*writing to make sure the story is phenomenally good, and that's why I'm coming directly to you, my readers, and asking for your support. Only your generous gifts will insure that many more stories of this quality will keep coming your way. It only takes a minute to do this.

$10 (Contributor) _____

$25 (Patron) _____

$50 (Sustainer) _____

$100 (Good Neighbor) _____

$500 (Real Pal) _____

$1,000 (Racquetball Partner) _____

$5,000 (Best Friend, *limited to six*) _____

Visa ☐   Master ☐   Am Ex ☐   Other ☐

_____

Exp. Date _____

Signature _____

THANKS FOR YOUR SUPPORT!

~~~

"Why fifteen? Who's coming for dinner besides us?" asked Jim.

His mom shrugged. "Some people we met. I don't know. They seemed nice. A couple of fund-raisers from different colleges, our broker and his lover, some people from DioNate, and George Will, the ostrologist. He was on our cruise."

"Tony's cough is pretty bad," Jim said. "You don't suppose Dr. Will could give him a shot or something, do you? And I'm all pooped out. I gotta grab some shut-eye." He hauled the poor old pooch up the grand staircase and into Sharon's bedroom and boosted him up into her canopied bed. Tony groaned. How ironic to think that the dog might die on Christmas, here in this ornate bedroom the size of a gymnasium!

A moment later the door opened, and there was Sharon, his tall, willowy, successful (but dazed) older sister, in the arms of Vince, her vicious boyfriend, who was tugging on the shoulder strap of her blue jumper. "Beat it, scum," he snarled, and raised his fist to pound on Jim.

"Grrrrrrr," growled Tony, trying to leap up from under the covers, though he was much too weak.

Just as Jim was about to be pummelled by the loathsome Vince, Jim's dad, Jack, waltzed in. "Hi, kids," he said. "Hi, Tony. How's tricks?" He smelled of a cilantro after-shave, and he looked youthful and tanned and taut and extremely fit. In fact, he appeared to be several years younger than either of his children. He smiled effortlessly. "Look what just came from my kiln!" he cried.

"What is that?" asked Sharon.

Jack grinned at her. "It's a trivet," he said.

~~~

With literary costs rising each year, it becomes more and more difficult for writers to offer their stories to readers at a reasonable price. The 1989 Christmas Catalogue is one way you can help me keep on writing and not have to raise my rates. When you purchase one of these gifts, a portion of the price is earmarked for my writing program:

COLORFUL TILE TRIVETS. These handcrafted earth-tone tiles from Albuquerque are interesting additions to any kitchen counter. 6 × 6: $40 each.

OLD-TIME HOLLY WREATHS. A warm, traditional Christmas is yours with a supply of fragrant holly wreaths, sprays, and garlands from northern Wisconsin. One large crate: $164.

JUICY ORANGES. Put a little sunshine in Christmas with a selection of Florida's finest. One doz.: $15.

SHAKER LOVE SEAT. Handsomely fashioned from white birch. The classic simplicity of this heirloom piece will add distinctive charm to your home or office: $1,900.

~~~

"Tony's dying, I think, of pneumonia," said Jim.

"That's too bad. We'll get the best medical care available, regardless of cost," said Jack. "I think Dr. Will is coming for dinner. Maybe he can save him. We met him at the Woffats'. He seemed nice."

Downstairs, the bell rang—*bonggggg, bonggggg*. The door opened, and there were murmurs, and Alice yelled up the stairs, "Never mind. It's only the wine man."

Tony's eyes were small and red, his nose was dry and scaly. His tongue was white. Jim stayed near the bed, wondering if even the vast, ill-gotten fortune of his parents could make the dog well. Tears ran down his cheeks.

Dr. Will arrived at eight—a dapper little fellow in a yellow bow tie, who seemed to diminish as he approached. "Jim, what a pleasure," he said, easing onto the bed with a bland smile and surveying the old dog. "Alice asked me to check on Tony. How is he doing?"

"Near death."

"Here. We'll just have a look. Hmmmm. Let me just

check his eyeballs. Nnnhnnn. Sort of red. Corneal infection, I'm afraid. But no prob, Bob. We'll just do a corneal thing. Don't worry." He took out a pair of scissors and a hankie. "All we do is remove these old corneas and slip in a coupla new ones."

"No, please. No," Jim said, and looked away in pain.

"It'll bleed a lot for a while, but don't worry. As long as he doesn't blink, he won't feel a darned thing."

You're lying, just trying to reassure me, thought Jim, and then he heard two little snips as his dog's eyeballs were sliced. Tony moaned.

"That's him, Jim," said Dr. Will. "Now, where did I put the donor tissue? Did I leave it out in the car? Or—"

~~~

Have you ever thought you'd like to go on a winter cruise but not with thousands of owly seniors grumping around the tropics? Join us for a cruise on the S.S. Nordstrom. Ten days sailing through the sparkling blue, sun-drenched Caribbean with people just like yourself: young, humorous, quietly attractive. Thoughtful people. Readers. Not John Jakes' readers or Danielle Steele's or Stephen King's. *My* readers. Such as you, for example. *My* kind of people. Starts at $4,500, double occupancy.

~~~

"We'll have Tony put in a special place for blind dogs," Mom said. "He'll be happier there than with you, hard as that is to accept. You'll go away to Yale soon, honey, and life will be good for both of you."

"You're lying. You're going to have him killed in a gas chamber!"

"I promise you that Tony will be sent to a training center where he will learn to work with a seeing-eye bird and lead a life that is almost normal. They use canaries that sit on the dog's shoulder and hold in their beak long reins attached to the dewlaps."

Jim looked down at his poor old pal; a bandage covered Tony's head except for his dry, brown nose and big, floppy ears and friendly mouth. A bandage very poorly wrapped, he couldn't help but notice. Tape slapped on, the way a post-office clerk would do it. Downstairs, Dr. Will was hobnobbing with the other celebrities over drinks. "Dinner is Afghani this year. Why don't you join us?" his mom said. But Jim couldn't leave Tony.

Or could he? Dinner sure sounded good to him, and maybe Mom was right; you can't live a dog's life for him, can you? A blindy like this one, he'd have to learn how to depend on himself and not expect favors. Lots of blind dogs nowadays just lie around getting fat and lazy probably. That's a rather poor attitude. Maybe he ought to leave Tony and go downstairs and talk to Dr. Will and the other influential guests, in hopes of garnering recommendations for future employment, graduate school, etc. Maybe he ought to kick Tony so as to make him less emotionally dependent.

~~~

IRISH FISHERMAN'S SWEATER. Woven by elderly island women from 100% rough-cut wool with natural oils intact, in the centuries-old "herring net" style, this handsome garment, with traditional shawl neck, is guaranteed to be absolutely distinctive, unlike anything your friends have seen. Specify size. Black or navy blue: $215.

ANTIQUE COPPER BATHTUB. This finely crafted copy of a nineteenth-century French tub, with filigreed edging, turtle-claw feet, and inscription on base, can be used for bathing, or to store firewood, or simply as a work of art. 52 × 28 × 36: $2,800.

ENAMEL BRIEFCASE. Handcrafted porcelain with 23k. gold handles, blue velvet lining, this beauty is patterned after those used by lawyers in Renaissance Antwerp, and its investment value is well proven: $18,500.

~~~

I'd just like to close with a big thank you to DioNate and wish a Merry Christmas to their forty thousand employees and express my sincere thanks to those who gave so generously to support my writing program and wish bon voyage to the folks on the Nordstrom and thank the customers of the Christmas Catalogue. Allow eight weeks for delivery. Tony, by the way, got a new pair of eyes, and Jim's family was pulled together by the crisis and learned the true meaning of Christmas, which is not how *much* but how *well*. It's a time for quality of life. Jim is headed for college, and Sharon split up with Vince, who was an illiterate brute, and—how can I say this?—she is marrying me on Wednesday morning. It was a whirlwind romance, and after a honeymoon on St. Bart's we'll be home in the sixteen-room Romanesque stone mansion Alice and Jack presented us with, which stands on the banks of a ten-thousand-acre marsh and wildlife preserve. A person could disappear in there and never be found again. But that's another story.

1989

"*I know just what he's going to say. He's going to say, 'Look at this handsome attaché case my wife gave me for Christmas.'*"

CRÈCHE

RICHARD FORD

Faith is not driving them, her mother, Esther, is. In the car it's the five of them. The family. On their way to Snow Mountain Highlands—Sandusky, Ohio, to northern Michigan—to ski. It's Christmas, or nearly. No one wants to spend Christmas alone.

The five include Faith, who's the motion picture lawyer, arrived from California; her mother, who's sixty-four and who's thoughtfully volunteered to drive. Roger, Faith's sister's husband, a guidance counsellor at Sandusky J.F.K. And Roger's two girls: Jane and Marjorie, ages eight and six. Daisy, the girls' mom, Faith's younger sister, Roger's estranged wife, is a presence but not along. She is in rehab in a large Midwestern city that is not Chicago or Detroit.

Outside, beyond a long, treeless expanse of frozen white winterscape, Lake Michigan suddenly becomes visible. It is pale blue with a thin fog hovering just above its metallic surface. The girls are chatting chirpily in the back seat. Roger is beside them reading *Skier* magazine. No one is arguing.

Florida would've been a much nicer holiday alternative, Faith thinks. Epcot for the girls. The Space Center. Satellite Beach. Fresh fish. The ocean. She is paying for everything and does not even like to ski. But it has been a hard year for everyone, and someone has had to take charge. If they'd all gone to Florida, she'd have ended up broke.

Her basic character strength, Faith believes, watching what seems to be a nuclear power plant coming up on the left, is the feature that makes her a first-rate lawyer: an undeterrable willingness to see things as capable of being made better. If someone at the studio, a V.P. in marketing, for example, wishes a quick exit from a totally binding yet surprisingly uncomfortable obligation—say, a legal contract—then Faith's your girl. Faith the doer. Your very own optimist. Faith the blond beauty with smarts. A client's dream with great tits. Her own tits. Just give her a day on your problem.

Her sister is a perfect case in point. Daisy has been able to admit her serious methamphetamine problems, but only after her biker boyfriend, Vince, has been made a guest of the State of Ohio. And here Faith has had a role to play, beginning with phone calls, then attorneys, a restraining order, then later the state police and handcuffs. Going through Daisy's apartment with their mother, in search of clothes Daisy could wear with dignity into rehab, Faith found dildos; six, in all—one, for some reason, under the kitchen sink. These she put into a black plastic grocery bag and left in the neighbor's street garbage just so her mother wouldn't know. Her mother is up-to-date, she feels, but not necessarily interested in dildos. For Daisy's going-in outfit they decided on a dark jersey shift and some new white Adidas.

The downside on the character issue, Faith understands, is the fact that, at almost thirty-seven, nothing's particularly solid in her life. She is very patient (with assholes), very ready to forgive (assholes), very good to help behind the scenes (with assholes). Her glass is always half full. Stand and ameliorate, her motto. Anticipate change. The skills of the law once again only partly in synch with the requirements of life.

A tall silver smokestack with blinking silver lights on top and several gray megaphone-shaped cooling pots around it all come into view on the frozen lakefront. Dense chalky smoke drifts out the top of each.

"What's that big thing?" Jane or possibly Marjorie says, peering out the back-seat window. It is too warm in the cranberry-colored Suburban Faith rented at the Cleveland airport, plus the girls are chewing watermelon-smelling gum. Everyone could get carsick.

"This one's from you know who, so make a fuss and thank him."

"That's a rocket ship ready to blast off to outer space. Would you girls like to hitch a ride on it?" Roger says. Roger, the brother-in-law, is the friendly-funny neighbor in a family sitcom, although he isn't funny. He is small and blandly not-quite-handsome and wears a brush cut and black horn-rimmed glasses. And he is loathsome—though only in subtle ways, like TV actors Faith has known. He is also thirty-seven and likes pastel cardigans and suède shoes. Faith has noticed he is, oddly enough, quite tanned.

"It is not a rocket ship," Jane, the older child, says and puts her forehead to the foggy window then pulls back and considers the smudge mark she's left.

"It's a pickle," Marjorie says.

"And shut up," Jane says. "That's a nasty expression."

"It isn't," Marjorie says.

"Is that a new word your mother taught you?" Roger asks and smirks. "I bet it is. That'll be her legacy." On the cover of *Skier* is a photograph of Alberto Tomba wearing an electric-red outfit, running the giant slalom at Kitzbühel. The headline says, "GOING TO EXTREMES."

"It better not be," Faith's mother says from behind the wheel. Faith's mother is unusually thin. Over the years she has actually shrunk from a regular, plump size 12 to the point that she now swims inside her clothes, and,

"And don't forget—make it look like an accident."

on occasion, can resemble a species of testy bird. There are problems with her veins and her digestion. But nothing is medically wrong. She eats.

"It's an atom plant where they make electricity," Faith says, and smiles back approvingly at the nieces, who are staring out the car window, losing interest. "We use it to heat our houses."

"We don't like that kind of heat, though," Faith's mother says. Her seat is pushed up, seemingly to accommodate her diminished size. Even her seat belt hangs on her. Esther was once a science teacher and has been Green since before it was chic.

"Why not?" Jane says.

"Don't you girls learn anything in school?" Roger says, flipping pages in his *Skier*.

"Their father could always instruct them," Esther says. "He's in education."

"Guidance," Roger says. "But touché."

"What's 'touché'?" Jane says and wrinkles her nose.

"It's a term used in fencing," Faith says. She likes both little girls immensely, would like to punish Roger for ever speaking sarcastically to them.

"What's fencing?" Marjorie asks.

"It's a town in Michigan where they make fences," Roger says. "Fencing, Michigan. It's near Lansing."

"No, it's not," Faith says.

"Then, you tell them," Roger says. "You know everything. You're the lawyer."

"It's a game you play with swords," Faith says. "Only no one gets killed or hurt." In every way, she despises Roger and wishes he'd stayed in Sandusky. Though she couldn't bring the girls without him. Letting her pay for everything is Roger's way of saying thanks.

"Now, all your lives you'll remember where you heard fencing explained first and by whom," Roger says in a nice-nasty voice. "When you're at Harvard—"

"You didn't know," Jane says.

"That's wrong. I did know. I absolutely knew," Roger says. "I was just having some fun. Christmas is a fun time."

~~~

Faith's love life has not been going well. She has always wanted children-with-marriage, but neither of these things has quite happened. Either the men she's liked haven't liked children, or else the men who've loved her and wanted to give her all she longed for haven't seemed worth it. Practicing law for a movie studio has accordingly become extremely engrossing. Time has gone by. A series of mostly courteous men has entered but then departed, all for one reason or another unworkable: married, frightened, divorced, all three together. Lucky is how she has chiefly seen herself. She goes to the gym every day, leases an expensive car, lives alone at the beach in a rental owned by an ex-teen-age movie star who is a friend's brother and has H.I.V. A deal.

Late last spring she met a man. A stock-market hotsy-totsy with a house on Block Island. Jack. Jack flew to Block Island from the city in his own plane, had never been married at age roughly forty-six. She flew out a few times with him, met his stern-looking sisters, the pretty, social mom. There was a big blue rambling beach house facing the sea. Rose hedges, sandy pathways to secret dunes where you could swim naked—something she especially liked, though the sisters were astounded. The father was there, but was sick and would soon die, so that things were generally on hold. Jack did beaucoup business in London. Money was not a problem. Maybe when the father departed they could be married, Jack had almost suggested. But until then she could travel with him whenever she could get away. Scale back a little on the expectation side. He wanted children, would get to California often. It could work.

One night a woman called. Greta she said her name was. Greta was in love with Jack. She and Jack had had a fight, but Jack still loved her. It turned out Greta had pictures of Faith and Jack in New York together. Who knew who took them? A little bird. One was a picture of Faith and Jack exiting Jack's apartment building. Another was of Jack helping Faith out of a yellow taxi. One was of Faith, all alone, at the Park Avenue Café, eating seared swordfish. One was of Jack and Faith kissing in the front seat of an unrecognizable car—also in New York.

Jack liked particular kinds of sex in very particular kinds of ways, Greta said. She guessed Faith knew all about that by now. But "best not to make long-range plans" was somehow the message.

When asked, Jack conceded there was a problem. But he would solve it. Tout de suite (though he was preoccupied with his father's approaching death). Jack was a tall, smooth-faced, handsome man with a shock of lustrous, mahogany-colored hair. Like a clothing model. He smiled, and everyone felt better. He'd gone to Harvard, played squash, rowed, debated, looked good in a brown suit and oldish shoes. He was trustworthy. It still seemed workable.

But Greta called more times. She sent pictures of herself and Jack together. Recent pictures, since Faith had come on board. It was harder than he thought to get untangled, Jack admitted. Faith would need to be patient. Greta was someone he'd once "cared about very much." Might've even married. But she had problems, yes. And he wouldn't just throw her over. He wasn't that kind of man, something she, Faith, would be glad about in the long run. Meanwhile there was his sick father. The patriarch. And his mother. And the sisters.

That had been plenty.

~~~

Snow Mountain Highlands is a small ski resort, but nice. Family, not flash. Faith's mother found it as a "Holiday Getaway" in the Sandusky *Pennysaver*. The getaway involves a condo, weekend lift tickets, coupons for three days of Swedish smorgasbord in the Bavarian-style inn. Although the deal is for two people only. The rest have to pay. Faith will sleep with her mother in the "Master Suite." Roger can share the twin bedroom with the girls.

When Faith's sister Daisy began to be interested in Vince the biker, Roger had simply "receded." Her and Roger's sex life had lost its effervescence, Daisy confided. They had started life as a model couple in a suburb of Sandusky, but eventually—after some time and two kids—happiness ended and Daisy had been won over by Vince, who did amphetamines and, more significantly, sold them. That—Vince's arrival—was when sex had gotten really good, Daisy said. Faith silently believes Daisy envied her movie connections and movie life and her Jaguar convertible, and basically threw her life away (at least until rehab) as a way of simulating Faith's—only with a biker. Eventually Daisy left home and gained forty-five pounds on a body that was already voluptuous, if short. Last summer, at the beach at Middle Bass Island, Daisy in a rage actually punched Faith in the chest when she suggested that Daisy might lose some weight, ditch Vince, and consider coming home. "I'm not like you," Daisy screamed, right out on the sand. "I fuck for pleasure. Not for business." Then she'd waddled into the tepid surf of Lake Erie, wearing a pink one-piece that boasted a frilly skirtlet. By then, Roger had the girls, courtesy of a court order.

~~~

Faith has had a sauna and is now thinking about phoning Jack wherever Jack is. Block Island. New York. London. She has no particular message to leave.

Later she plans to go cross-country skiing under the moonlight. Just to be a full participant. Set a good example. For this she has brought her L.A. purchases: loden knickers, a green-brown-and-red sweater made in the Himalayas, and socks from Norway. No way does she plan to get cold.

In the living room her mother is having a glass of red wine and playing solitaire with two decks by the big picture window that looks down toward the crowded ski slope and ice rink. Roger is there on the bunny slope with Jane and Marjorie, but it's impossible to distinguish them. Red suits. Yellow suits. Lots of dads with kids. All of it soundless.

Her mother plays cards at high speed, flipping cards and snapping them down as if she hates the game and wants it to be over. Her eyes are intent. She has put on a cream-colored neck brace. (The tension of driving has aggravated an old work-related injury.) And she is now wearing a Hawaii-print orange muumuu, which engulfs her. How long, Faith wonders, has her mother been shrinking? Twenty years, at least. Since Faith's father kicked the bucket.

"Maybe I'll go to Europe," her mother says, flicking cards ferociously with bony fingers. "That'd be adventurous, wouldn't it?"

Faith is at the window observing the expert slope. Smooth, wide pastures of snow framed by copses of beautiful spruces. Several skiers are zigzagging their way down, doing their best to be stylish. Years ago she came here with her high-school boyfriend. Eddie, a.k.a. Fast Eddie, which in some ways he was. Neither of them liked to ski, nor did they get out of bed to try. Now skiing reminds her of golf—a golf course made of snow.

"Maybe I'd take the girls out of school and treat us all to Venice," Esther goes on. "I'm sure Roger would be relieved."

Faith has spotted Roger and the girls on the bunny slope. Blue, green, yellow suits, respectively. Roger is pointing, giving detailed instructions to his daughters about ski etiquette. Just like any dad. She thinks she sees him laughing. It is hard to think of Roger as an average parent.

"They're too young for Venice," Faith says. From outside, she hears the rasp of a snow shovel and muffled voices.

"I'll take you, then," her mother says. "When Daisy clears rehab we can all three take in Europe. I always planned that."

Faith likes her mother. Her mother is no fool, yet still seeks ways to be generous. But Faith cannot complete a picture that includes herself, her diminished mother, and Daisy on the Champs-Élysées or the Grand Canal.

"That's a nice idea," Faith says. She is standing beside her mother's chair, looking down at the top of her head. Her mother's head is small. Its hair is dark gray and not especially clean, but short and sparse. She has affected a very wide part straight down the middle. Her mother looks like a homeless woman, only with a neck brace.

"I was reading what it takes to get to a hundred," Esther says, neatening the cards on the glass tabletop in front of her. Faith has begun thinking of Jack again and what a peculiar species of creep he is. Jack Matthews still wears the Lobb cap-toe shoes he had made for him in college. Ugly, pretentious English shoes. "You have to be physically active," her mother continues. "You have to be an optimist, which I am. You have to stay interested in things, which I more or less do. And you have to handle loss well."

With all her concentration Faith tries not to wonder how she ranks on this scale. "Do you want to live to a hundred?" she asks her mother.

"Oh yes," Esther says. "Of course. You can't imagine it, that's all. You're too young. And beautiful. And talented." No irony. Irony is not her mother's specialty.

Outside, the men shovelling snow can be heard to say, "Hi, we're the Weather Channel." They are speaking to someone watching them out another window from another condo. "In winter the most innocent places can turn lethal," the same man says and laughs. "Colder'n a well-digger's dick, you bet," a second man's voice says. "That's today's forecast."

"The male appliance," her mother says pleasantly, fiddling with her cards. "That's it, isn't it? The whole mystery."

"So I'm told," Faith says.

"They were all women, though."

"Who was?"

"All the people who lived to be a hundred. You could do all the other things right. But you still needed to be a woman to survive."

"Lucky us," Faith says.

"Right. The lucky few."

~~~

This will be the girls' first Christmas without a tree or their mother. And Faith has attempted to improvise around this by arranging presents at the base of the large, plastic rubber-tree plant stationed against one of the empty white walls in the living room. She has brought a few red Christmas balls, a gold star, and a string of lights that promise to blink. "Christmas in Manila" could be a possible theme.

Outside, the day is growing dim. Faith's mother is napping. Roger has gone down to the Warming Shed for a mulled wine following his ski lesson. The girls are seated on the couch side by side, wearing their Lanz of Salzburg flannel nighties with matching smiling-bunny slippers. Green and yellow again, but with printed snowflakes. They have taken their baths together, with Faith present to supervise, then insisted on putting on their nighties early for their nap. To her, these two seem perfect angels and perfectly wasted on their parents.

"We know how to ski now," Jane says primly. They're watching Faith trim the rubber-tree plant. First the blinking lights (though there's no plug-in close enough), then the six red balls (one for each family member). Last will be the gold star. Possibly, Faith thinks, she is trying for too much. Though why not try for too much? It's Christmas.

"Would you two care to help me?" Faith smiles up at both of them from the floor where she is on her knees fiddling with the fragile green strand of tiny peaked bulbs she already knows will not light up.

"No," Jane says.

"I don't blame you," Faith says.

"Is Mommy coming here?" Marjorie says and blinks, crosses her tiny, pale ankles. She is sleepy and might possibly cry, Faith realizes.

"No, sweet," Faith says. "This Christmas Mommy is doing herself a big favor. So she can't do us one."

"What about Vince?" Jane says authoritatively. Vince is a subject that's been gone over before. Mrs. Argenbright, the girls' therapist, has taken special pains with the Vince issue. The girls have the skinny on Mr. Vince but wish to be given it again, since they like him more than their father.

"Vince is a guest of the State of Ohio right now," Faith says. "You remember that? It's like he's in college."

"He's not in college," Jane says.

"Does he have a tree where he is?" Marjorie asks.

"Not *in* his house, like you do," Faith says. "Let's talk about happier things than Mr. Vince, O.K.?"

What furniture the room contains conforms to the Danish style. A raised, metal-hooded, red-enamel-painted fireplace has a paper message from the condo owners taped to it, advising that smoke damage will cause renters to lose their security deposit. The owners are residents of Grosse Pointe Farms, and are people of Russian extraction. Of course, there's no fireplace wood except for what the furniture could offer.

"I think you two should guess what you're getting for Christmas," Faith says, carefully draping lightless lights on the stiff plastic branches. Taking pains.

"In-lines. I already know," Jane says and crosses her ankles like her sister. They are a jury disguised as an audience. "I don't have to wear a helmet, though."

"But are you sure of that?" Faith glances over her shoulder and gives them a smile she has seen movie stars give to strangers. "You could always be wrong."

"I'd better be right," Jane says unpleasantly, with a frown very much like one her mom uses.

"Santa's bringing me a disk player," Marjorie says. "It'll come in a small box. I won't even recognize it."

"You two're too smart for your britches," Faith says. She is quickly finished stringing Christmas lights. "But you don't know what *I* brought you." Among other things, she, too, has brought a disk player and an expensive pair of in-line skates. They are in the Suburban and will be returned in L.A. She has also brought movie videos. Twenty in all, including "Star Wars" and "Sleeping Beauty." Daisy has sent them each fifty dollars.

"You know," Faith says, "I remember once a long, long time ago, my dad and I and your mom went out in the woods and cut a tree for Christmas. We didn't buy a tree, we cut it down with an axe."

Jane and Marjorie stare at her as if they already know this story. The TV is not turned on in the room. Perhaps, Faith thinks, they don't understand someone actually talking to them—live action presenting its own unique problems.

"Do you want to hear the story?"

"Yes," Marjorie, the younger sister, says. Jane sits watchful and silent on the orange Danish sofa. Behind her on the white wall is a framed print of Brueghel's "Return of the Hunters," which after all is Christmassy.

"Well," Faith says. "Your mother and I—we were only nine and ten—we picked out the tree we desperately wanted to be our tree, but our dad said no, that that tree was too tall to fit inside our house. We should choose another one. But we both said, 'No, this one's perfect. This is the best one.' It was green and pretty and had a perfect shape. So our dad cut it down with his axe, and we dragged it through the woods and tied it on top of our car and brought it back to Sandusky." Both girls have now become sleepy. There has been too much excitement, or else not enough. Their mother is in rehab. Their dad is an asshole. They're in Michigan. Who wouldn't be sleepy? "Do you want to know what happened after that?" Faith asks. "When we got the tree inside?"

"Yes," Marjorie says politely.

"It was too big," Faith says. "It was much, much too tall. It couldn't even stand up in our living room. And it was too wide. And our dad got really mad at us because we'd killed a beautiful living tree for a bad reason, and because we hadn't listened to him and thought we knew everything just because we knew what we wanted."

Faith suddenly doesn't know why she's telling this particular story to these innocent sweeties who do not particularly need an object lesson. So she simply stops. In the real story, of course, her father took the tree and threw it out the door into the back yard, where it stayed for weeks and turned brown. There was crying and accusations. Her father went straight to a bar and got drunk. And later their mother went to the Safeway and bought a small tree that fit and which the three of them trimmed without the aid of their father. It was waiting, trimmed, when he came home smashed. The story had usually been one others found humor in. This time all the humor seemed lacking.

"Do you want to know how the story turned out?" Faith says, smiling brightly for the girls' benefit, but feeling completely defeated.

"I do," Marjorie says.

"We put it outside in the yard and put lights on it so our neighbors could share our big tree with us. And we bought a smaller tree for the house at the Safeway. It was a sad story that turned out good."

"I don't believe it," Jane says.

"Well, you should believe it," Faith says, "because it's true. Christmases are special. They always turn out wonderfully if you give them a chance and use your imagination."

Jane shakes her head as Marjorie nods hers. Marjorie wants to believe. Jane, Faith thinks, is a classic older child. Like herself.

~~~

"Did you know"—this was one of Greta the girlfriend's cute messages left for her on her voice mail in Los Angeles—"did you know that Jack hates—hates—to have his dick sucked? Hates it with a passion. Of course you didn't. How could you? He always lies about it. Oh, well. But if you're wondering why he never comes, that's why. It's a big turnoff for him. I personally think it's his mother's fault, not that she ever did it to him, of course. I don't mean that. By the way, that was a nice dress last Friday. You're very pretty. And really great tits. I can see why Jack likes you. Take care."

~~~

At seven, the girls wake up from their naps and everyone is hungry at once. Faith's mother offers to take the two hostile Indians for a pizza, then on to the skating rink, while Roger and Faith share the smorgasbord coupons.

At seven-thirty, few diners have chosen the long, harshly lit, sour-smelling Tyrol Room. Most guests are outside awaiting the nightly Pageant of the Lights, in which members of the ski patrol ski down the expert slope holding lighted torches. It is a thing of beauty but takes time getting started. At the very top of the hill, a great Norway spruce has been lighted in the Yuletide tradition just as in the untrue version of Faith's story. All is viewable from the Tyrol Room through a big picture window.

Faith does not want to eat with Roger, who is slightly hung over from his gluhwein and a nap. Conversation that she would find offensive could easily occur; something on the subject of her sister, the girls' mother—Roger's (still) wife. But she is trying to keep up a Christmas spirit. Do for others, etc.

Roger, she knows, dislikes her, possibly envies her, and is also attracted to her. Once, several years ago, he confided to her that he'd very much like to fuck her ears flat. He was drunk, and Daisy had not long before had Jane. Faith found a way not to acknowledge this offer. Later he told her he thought she was a lesbian. Having her know that just must've seemed like a good idea. A class act is the Roger.

The long, wide, echoing dining hall has crisscrossed ceiling beams painted pink and light green and purple—something apparently appropriate to Bavaria. There are long green tables with pink plastic folding chairs meant to promote good times and family fun. Somewhere else in the inn, Faith is certain, there is a better place to eat, where you don't pay with coupons and nothing's pink or purple.

Faith is wearing a shiny black Lycra bodysuit, over which she has put on her loden knickers and Norway socks. She looks superb, she thinks. With anyone but Roger this would be fun, or at least a hoot.

Roger sits across the long table, too far away to talk easily. In a room that can conveniently hold five hundred souls, there are perhaps ten scattered diners. No one is eating family style. Only solos and twos. Youthful inn employees in paper caps wait dismally behind the long smorgasbord steam table. Metal heat lamps with orange lights are overcooking the prime rib, of which Roger has taken a goodly portion. Faith has chosen only a few green lettuce leaves, a beet round, and two tiny ears of yellow corn. The sour smell makes eating unappealing.

"Do you know what I worry about?" Roger says, sawing around a triangle of glaucal gray roast-beef fat, using a comically small knife. His tone implies he and Faith lunch together daily and are picking up right where they've left off; as if they didn't hold each other in complete contempt.

"No," Faith says, "what?" Roger, she notices, has managed to hang on to his red smorgasbord coupon. The rule is you leave your coupon in the basket by the breadsticks. Clever Roger. Why, she wonders, is he tanned?

Roger smiles as though there's a lewd aspect to whatever it is that worries him. "I worry that Daisy's going to get so fixed up in rehab that she'll forget everything that's happened and want to be married again. To me, I mean. You know?" Roger chews as he talks. He wishes to seem earnest, his smile a serious, imploring, vacuous smile. Roger levelling. Roger owning up.

"Probably that won't happen," Faith says. "I just have a feeling." She no longer wishes to look at her salad. She does not have an eating disorder, she thinks, and could never have one.

"Maybe not." Roger nods. "I'd like to get out of guidance pretty soon, though. Start something new. Turn the page."

In truth, Roger is not bad-looking, only oppressively regular: small chin, small nose, small hands, small straight teeth—nothing unusual except his brown eyes, which are slightly too narrow, as if he had Finnish blood. Daisy married him, she said, because of his alarmingly big dick. That or, more important, lack of that, in her view, was why other marriages failed. When all else gave way, that would be there. Vince's, she'd observed, was even bigger. Ergo. It was to this quest Daisy had dedicated her life. This, instead of college.

"What exactly would you like to do next?" Faith says. She is thinking how satisfying it would be if Daisy came out of rehab and had forgotten everything, and that returning to how things were when they still sort of worked can often be the best solution.

"Well, it probably sounds crazy," Roger says, chewing, "but there's a company down in Tennessee that takes apart jetliners. For scrap. And there's big money in it. I imagine it's how the movie business got started. Just some harebrained scheme." Roger pokes macaroni salad with his fork. A single Swedish meatball remains on his plate.

"It doesn't sound crazy," Faith lies, then looks longingly at the smorgasbord table. Maybe she is hungry. Is the table full of food the smorgasbord, she wonders, or is eating it the smorgasbord? Roger has slipped his meal coupon back into a pocket. "Do you think you're going to do that?" she asks with reference to the genius plan of dismantling jet airplanes.

"With the girls in school, it'd be hard," Roger says, ignoring what would seem to be the obvious—that it is not a genius plan. Faith gazes around distractedly. She realizes no one else in the big room is dressed the way she is, which reminds her of who she is. She is not Snow Mountain Highlands. She is not even Sandusky. She is Hollywood. A fortress.

"I could take the girls for a while," she suddenly says. "I really wouldn't mind." She thinks of sweet Marjorie and sweet but unhappy Jane sitting on the Danish modern couch in their sweet nighties, watching her trim the rubber-tree plant. Just as instantly she thinks of Roger and Daisy being killed in an automobile crash. You can't help what you think.

> She has so revolted against the overornate, complicated and expensive Christmas wrapping jobs, says a pal, that she's seriously considering doing up her parents in old newspapers and string.
>
> —*Cleveland Plain Dealer*
>
> A thought that has flashed through many a mind.
>
> 1961

"Where would they go to school?" Roger says, alert to something unexpected. Something he likes.

"I'm sorry?" Faith says, and flashes Roger, big-dick Roger, a second movie star's smile. She has let herself be distracted by the thought of his timely death.

"I mean where would they go to school?" Roger blinks. He is that alert.

"I don't know. Hollywood High, I guess. They have schools in California. I guess I could find one."

"I'd have to think about this," Roger lies decisively.

"O.K.," Faith says. Now that she has said this without any previous thought of ever saying anything like it, it immediately becomes part of everyday reality. She will soon become the girls' parent. Easy as that. "When you get settled in Tennessee you could have them back," she says without conviction.

"They probably wouldn't want to come back," Roger says. "Tennessee'd seem pretty dull after Hollywood."

"Ohio's dull. They like that."

"True," Roger says.

No one, of course, has thought to mention Daisy in preparing this new arrangement. Daisy, the mother. Though Daisy is committed elsewhere for the next little patch. And Roger needs to put "guidance" in the rearview mirror.

The Pageant of the Lights is just now under way—a ribbon of swaying torches swooshing down the expert course like an overflow of lava. All is preternaturally visible through the panoramic window. A large, bundled crowd has assembled at the hill's bottom, many members holding candles in scraps of paper like at a Grateful Dead concert. All other artificial light is extinguished, except for the big Christmas spruce at the top. The young smorgasbord attendants have gathered at the window to witness the pageant yet again. Some are snickering. Someone remembers to turn the lights off inside the Tyrol Room. Dinner is suspended.

"Do you downhill?" Roger asks, manning his empty plate in the half darkness. Things could really turn out great, Faith understands he's thinking. Eighty-six the girls. Dismantle plenty jets. Just be friendly.

"No, never," Faith says, dreamily watching the torchbearers schuss from side to side, a gradual sinuous dramaless tour down. "It scares me."

"You get used to it." Roger suddenly reaches across the table where her hands rest on either side of her uneaten salad. He actually touches then pats one of these hands. Roger is her friend now. "And by the way," he says creepily, "thanks."

~~~

Back in the condo, all is serene. Esther is still at the skating rink. Roger has wandered back to the Warming Shed. He has a girlfriend in Port Clinton. A former high-school counsellee, now divorced. He will be calling her, telling her about the new plans, telling her he wishes she were with him at Snow Mountain Highlands and that his family could be in Rwanda. Bobbie, her name is.

A call to Jack is definitely in order. But first Faith decides to slide the newly trimmed plastic rubber-tree plant nearer the window, where there's an outlet. When she plugs in, most of the little white lights pop cheerily on. Only a few do not, and in the box are replacements. Later, tomorrow, they can fix the star on top—her father's favorite ritual. "Now it's time for the star," he'd say. "The star of the wise men." Her father had been a musician, a woodwind specialist. A man of talents, and a drunk. A specialist also in women who were not his wife. He had taught committedly at a junior college to make all their ends meet. He had wanted her to become a lawyer, so naturally she became one. Daisy he had no specific plans for, so she became a drunk, and, sometime later, an energetic nymphomaniac. Eventually he had died, at home. The paterfamilias. After that her mother began to shrink. "I won't actually die, I intend just to evaporate" was how she put it when the subject arose. It made her laugh. She considered her decrease a natural consequence of loss.

Whether to call Jack in London or New York or Block Island is the question. Where is Jack? In London it was after midnight. In New York and Block Island it was the same as here. Half past eight. Though a message was still the problem. She could just say she was lonely; or had chest pains; or worrisome test results. (The last two of which would later need to clear up mysteriously.)

London, first. The flat in Sloane Terrace, a half block from the tube. They'd eaten breakfast at Oriel, then Jack had gone off to work in the City while she did the Tate, the Bacons her specialty. So far from Snow Mountain Highlands—this is the sensation of dialling—a call going a great distance.

Ring-jing, ring-jing, ring-jing, ring-jing, ring-jing. Nothing.

There was a second number, for messages only, but she'd forgotten it. Call again to allow for a misdial. *Ring-jing, ring-jing, ring-jing.* . . .

New York, then. East Forty-ninth. Far, far east. The nice, small slice of river view. A bolt-hole he'd had since college. His freshman numerals framed on the wall. 1971. She'd gone to the trouble to have the bedroom redone. White everything. A smiling picture of her from the boat, framed in red leather. Another of them together at Cabo, on the beach. All similarly long distances from Snow Mountain Highlands.

Ring, ring, ring, ring. Then *click,* "Hi, this is Jack"—she almost speaks to his voice—"I'm not" etc., etc., etc., then a beep.

"Hi, Jack, it's me. Ummm, Faith. . . ." She's stuck, but not at all flustered. She could just as well tell everything. This happened today: the atomic-energy smokestacks, the rubber-tree plant, the Pageant of the Lights, the smorgasbord, the girls' planned move to California. All things Christmassy. "Ummm, I just wanted to say that I'm . . . fine, and that I trust—make that hope—that I hope you are, too. I'll be back home—in Malibu, that is—after Christmas. I'd love—make that, enjoy—hearing from you. I'm at Snow Mountain Highlands. In Michigan." She pauses, discussing with herself if there'd be further news to relate. There isn't. Then she realizes (too late) she's treating this message machine like her Dictaphone. And there's no revising.

Too bad. Her mistake. "Well, goodbye," she says, realizing this sounds a bit stiff, but doesn't revise. There's Block Island still. Though it's all over anyway. Who cares? She called.

~~~

Out on the Nordic Trail, lights, soft yellow ones not unlike the Christmas-tree lights, have been strung to selected fir boughs—bright enough so you'd never get lost in the dark, dim enough not to spoil the spooky/romantic effect.

She does not really enjoy this kind of skiing either—height or no height—but wants to be a sport. Though there's the tiresome waxing, the stiff rented shoes, the long, inconvenient skis, the sweaty underneath, the chance that all this could eventuate in catching cold and missing work. The gym is better. Major heat, but then quick you're clean and back in the car. Back in the office. Back on the phone. She is a sport but not a sports nut. Still, this is not terrifying.

No one is with her on nighttime Nordic Trail 1, the Pageant of the Lights having lured away other skiers. Two Japanese men were at the trailhead. Small beige men in bright chartreuse Lycras—little serious faces, giant thighs, blunt no-nonsense arms—commencing the rigorous course, "the Beast," Nordic Trail 3. On their small, stocking-capped heads they'd worn lights like coal miners to shine their way. They have disappeared.

Here the snow virtually hums to the sound of her sliding strokes. A full moon rides behind filigree clouds as she strides forward in the near-darkness of crusted woods. There is wind she can hear high up in the tall pines and spruces, but at ground level there's no wind—just cold radiating off the metallic snow. Only her ears actually feel cold, they and the sweat line of her hair. Her heartbeat is hardly elevated. She is in shape.

For an instant then she hears distant music, a singing voice with orchestral accompaniment. She pauses in her tracks. The music's pulses travel through the trees. Strange. Possibly, she thinks between deep breaths, it's Roger—in the karaoke bar, Roger onstage, singing his greatest hits to other lonelies in the dark. "Blue Bayou," "Layla," "Tommy," "Try to Remember." Roger at a safe distance. Her pale hair, she realizes, is shining in the pure moonlight. If she were being watched, she would look good.

And wouldn't it be romantic, she thinks, to peer down through the dark woods and spy some great, ornate, and festive lodge lying below, windows ablaze, some exotic casino from a movie. Graceful skaters on a lighted rink. A garlanded lift still in motion, a few, last alpinists taking their silken, torchless float before lights-out. Only there's nothing to see—dark trunks and deadfalls, swags of snow hung in the spruce boughs.

And she is stiffening. Just this quickly. New muscles visited. No reason to go much farther.

Daisy, her sister, comes to mind. Daisy, who will very soon exit the hospital with a whole new view of life. Inside, there's of course a twelve-step ritual to accompany the normal curriculum of deprivation and regret. And someone, somewhere, at some time possibly long ago, *someone* will definitely turn out to have touched Daisy in some way detrimental to her well-being, and at an all too tender age. Once, but perhaps many times, over a series of terrible, silent years. Possibly an older, suspicious neighborhood youth—a loner—or a far too avuncular school librarian. Even the paterfamilias will come under posthumous scrutiny (the historical perspective as always unprovable, yet undisprovable, and therefore indisputable).

And certain sacrifices of dignity will then be requested of everyone, due

"I'm afraid a wallet would only make him say something sarcastic."

to this rich new news from the past; a world so much more lethal than anyone believed; nothing the way we thought it was; if they had only known, could've spoken out, had opened up the lines of communication, could've trusted, confided, blah, blah, blah. Their mother will, necessarily, have suspected nothing, but unquestionably should've. Perhaps Daisy herself will have suggested that Faith is a lesbian. The snowball effect. No one safe, no one innocent.

Up ahead in the shadows, Ski Shelter 1 sits to the right of Nordic Trail 1—a darkened clump in a small clearing, a place to wait for the others to catch up (if there were others). And a perfect place to turn back.

Shelter 1 is open on one side like a lean-to, a murky school-bus enclosure hewn from logs. Out on the snow beside it lie crusts of dinner rolls, a wedge of pizza, some wadded tissue papers, three beer cans—treats for the forest creatures—each casting its tiny shadow upon the white surface.

Though seated in the gloomy inside on a plank bench are not schoolkids but Roger. The brother-in-law, in his powder-blue ski suit and hiking boots. He is not singing karaoke at all. She has noticed no boot tracks up the trail. Roger is more resourceful than first he seems.

"It's effing cold up here." Roger speaks from inside the shadows of Shelter 1. He is not wearing his black-frame glasses now, and is hardly visible, although she senses he is smiling—his narrow eyes even narrower.

"What are you doing up here, Roger?"

"Oh," Roger says from out of the gloom, "I just thought I'd come up." He crosses his arms, extends his hiking boots into the snow-light like a high-school toughie.

"What for?" Her knees feel knotty and weak from exertion. Her heart has begun thumping. Perspiration is cold on her lip, though. Temperatures are in the low twenties. In winter the most innocent places turn lethal. This is not good.

"Nothing ventured," Roger says.

"I was just about to turn around," Faith says.

"I see," Roger says.

"Would you like to go back down the hill with me?" What she wishes for is more light. Much more light. A bulb in the shelter would be very good. Bad things happen in the dark which would prove unthinkable in the light.

"Life leads you to some pretty interesting places, doesn't it, Faith?"

She would like to smile. Not feel menaced by Roger, who should be with his daughters.

"I guess," she says. She can smell alcohol in the dry air. He is drunk, and he is winging all of this. A bad mixture.

"You're very pretty. Very pretty. The big lawyer," Roger says. "Why don't you come in here."

"Oh, no thank you," Faith says. Roger is loathsome but he is also family. And she feels paralyzed by not knowing what to do. She wishes she could just leap upward, turn around, glide away.

"I always thought that in the right circumstances, we could have some big-time fun," Roger goes on.

"Roger, this isn't a good thing to be doing," whatever he's doing. She wants to glare at him, not smile, then realizes her knees are shaking. She feels very, very tall on her skis, unusually accessible.

"It *is* a good thing to be doing," Roger says. "It's what I came up here for. Some fun."

"I don't want us to do anything up here, Roger," Faith says. "Is that all right?" This, she realizes, is what fear feels like—the way you'd feel in a late-night parking structure, or jogging alone in an isolated area, or entering your house in the wee hours, fumbling for a key. Accessible. And then suddenly there would be someone. A man with oppressively ordinary looks who lacks a plan.

"Nope. Nope. That's not all right," Roger says. He stands up, but stays in the sheltered darkness. "The lawyer," Roger says again, still grinning.

"I'm just going to turn around," Faith says, and very unsteadily begins to shift her long left ski up out of its track, and then, leaning on her poles, her right ski up out of its track. It is unexpectedly dizzying, and her calves ache, and it is complicated not to cross her ski tips. But it is essential to remain standing. To fall would mean surrender. Roger would see it that way. What is the skiing expression? Tele . . . Tele-something. She wishes she could Tele-something. Tele-something the hell away from here. Her thighs burn. In California, she thinks, she is an officer of the court. A public official, sworn to uphold the law, though regrettably not to enforce it. She is a force for good.

"You look stupid," Roger says.

She intends to say nothing more. Talk is not cheap now. For a moment she thinks she hears music again, music far away. But it can't be.

"When you get all the way around," Roger says, "then I want to show you something." He does not say what. In her mind—moving her skis inches each time, her ankles stiff and heavy—in her mind she says "Then what?" but doesn't say that.

"I really hate your whole effing family," Roger says. His boots go crunch on the snow. She glances over her shoulder, but to look at him is too much. He is approaching. She will fall and then dramatic, regrettable things will happen. In a gesture he himself possibly deems dramatic, Roger—though she cannot see it—unzips his blue ski suit front. He intends her to hear this noise. She is three-quarters turned. She could see him over her left shoulder if she chose to. Have a look at what the excitement is about. She is sweating. Underneath she is drenched.

"Yep. Life leads you to some pretty interesting situations." There is another zipping noise. It is his best trick. Zip. This is big-time fun in Roger's world view.

"Yes," she says, "it does." She has come fully around now.

She hears Roger laugh, a little chuckle, an unhumorous "hunh." Then he says, "Almost." She hears his boots squeeze. She feels his actual self close beside her.

Then there are voices—saving voices—behind her. She now cannot help looking over her left shoulder and up the trail toward where it climbs into the darker trees. There is a light, followed by another light, little stars coming down from a height. Voices, words, language she does not quite understand. Japanese. She does not look at Roger, the girls' father, but simply slides one ski, her left one, forward into its track, lets her right one follow and find its way, pushes on her poles. And in just that amount of time and with that amount of effort she is away. She thinks she hears Roger say something, another "hunh," a kind of grunting sound, but can't be sure.

～～

In the condo everyone is sleeping. The rubber-tree lights are twinkling. They reflect in the window that faces the ski hill, which is now dark. Someone, Faith notices (her mother), has devoted much time to replacing the spent bulbs so the tree can twinkle. The gold star, the star that led the wise men, lies on the coffee table like a starfish, waiting to be properly affixed.

Marjorie, the younger, sweeter sister, is asleep on the orange couch under the Brueghel scene. She has left her bed to sleep near the tree, brought her quilted pink coverlet with her.

Naturally Faith has locked Roger out. Roger can now die alone and cold in the snow. Or he can sleep in a doorway or by a steam vent somewhere in the Snow Mountain Highlands complex and explain his situation to the security staff. Roger will not sleep with his pretty daughters this night. She is taking a hand in things. These girls are hers. Though how strange not to know that her offer to take them would be translated by Roger into an invitation to fuck. She has been in California too long, has fallen out of touch with things middle-American. How strange that Roger would say "effing." He would also probably say "X-mas."

Outside on the ice rink two teams are playing hockey under high white lights. A red team opposes a black team. Net cages have been brought on, the larger rink walled off to regulation size and shape. A few spectators stand watching. Wives and girlfriends. Boyne City versus Petoskey; Cadillac versus Cheboygan or some such. The little girls' white skates lie piled by the door she has now safely locked with a dead bolt.

It would be good to put the star up, she thinks. Who knows what tomorrow will bring. The arrival of wise men couldn't hurt. So, with the flimsy star, which is made of slick aluminum paper and is large and gold and weightless and five-pointed, Faith stands on the Danish dining-table chair and fits the slotted fastener onto the topmost leaf of the rubber-tree plant. It is not an elegant fit by any means, there being no sprig at the pinnacle, so that the star doesn't stand as much as it leans off the top in a sad, comic, but also victorious way. (This use was never envisioned by tree-makers in Seoul.) Tomorrow they can all add to the tree together, invent ornaments from absurd and inspirational raw materials. Tomorrow Roger will be rehabilitated and become everyone's best friend. Except hers.

Marjorie's eyes have opened, though she has not stirred. For a moment, on the couch, she appears dead.

"I went to sleep," she says softly and blinks her brown eyes.

"Oh, I saw you," Faith smiles. "I thought you were just another Christmas present. I thought Santa had been here early and left you for me." She takes a careful seat on the spindly coffee table, close beside Marjorie—in case there would be some worry to express, a gloomy dream to relate. A fear. She smooths her hand through Marjorie's warm hair.

Marjorie takes a deep breath and lets air go smoothly through her nostrils. "Jane's asleep," she says.

"And how would you like to go back to bed?" Faith says in a whisper.

Possibly she hears a soft tap on the door. The door she will not open. The door beyond which the world and trouble wait. Marjorie's eyes wander toward the sound, then swim with sleep. She is safe.

"Leave the tree on," Marjorie instructs, though asleep.

"Sure, sure," Faith says. "The tree stays on forever."

She eases her hand under Marjorie, who by old habit reaches outward, caresses her neck. In an instant she has Marjorie in her arms, pink covers and all, carrying her altogether lightly to the darkened bedroom where her sister sleeps on one of the twin beds. Gently she lowers Marjorie onto the empty bed and re-covers her. Again she hears soft tapping, although it stops. She believes it will not come again this night.

Jane is sleeping with her face to the wall, her breathing deep and audible. Jane is the good sleeper, Marjorie the less reliable one. Faith stands in the middle of the dark, windowless room, between the twin beds, the blinking Christmas lights haunting the stillness that has come at such expense. The room smells musty and dank, as if it has been closed for months and opened just for this night, these children. If only briefly she is reminded of Christmases she might've once called her own. "O.K.," she whispers. "O.K., O.K., O.K."

~~~

She undresses in the master suite, too tired to shower. Her mother sleeps on one side of their shared bed. She is an unexpectedly distinguishable presence there, visibly breathing beneath the covers. A glass of red wine half-drunk sits on the bed table beside her curved neck brace. The very same Brueghel print as in the living room hangs over their bed. She will wear pajamas, for her mother's sake. New ones. White, pure silk, smooth as water. Blue silk piping.

She half closes the bedroom door, the blinking Christmas lights shielded. And here is the unexpected sight of herself in the cheap, dark door mirror. All still good. Intact. Just the small scar where a cyst has been removed between two ribs. A meaningless scar no one would see. Thin, hard thighs. A small nice belly. Boy's hips. Two good breasts. The whole package, nothing to complain about.

Then the need of a glass of water. Always a glass of water at night, never a glass of red wine. When she passes the living-room window, her destination the kitchen, she sees that the hockey game is now over. It is after midnight. The players are shaking hands in a line on the ice, others skating in wide circles. On the ski slope above the rink, lights have been turned on again. Machines with headlights groom the snow at treacherous angles.

And she sees Roger. He is halfway between the ice rink and the condos, walking back in his powder-blue suit. He has watched the game, no doubt. He stops and looks up at her where she stands in the window in her white p.j.s, the Christmas lights blinking as a background. He stands and stares up. He has found his black-frame glasses. Possibly his mouth is moving, but he makes no gesture to her. There is no room in this inn for Roger.

In bed her mother seems larger. An impressive heat source, slightly damp when Faith touches her back. Her mother is wearing blue gingham, a night-dress not so different from the muumuu she wears in daylight. She smells unexpectedly good. Rich.

How long, she wonders, since she has slept with her mother? A hundred years? Twenty? Odd that it would be so normal now. And good.

She has left the door open in case the girls should call, in case they wake and are afraid, in case they miss their father. She can hear snow slide off the roof, an automobile with chains jingling softly somewhere out of sight. The Christmas lights blink merrily. She had intended to check her messages but let it slip.

Marriage. Yes, naturally she would think of that now. Maybe marriage, though, is only a long plain of self-revelation at the end of which there's someone else who doesn't know you very well. That is the message she could've left for Jack. "Dear Jack, I now know marriage is a long plain at the end of which there's" etc., etc., etc. You always think of these things too late. Somewhere, Faith hears faint music, "Away in a Manger," played prettily on chimes. It is music to sleep to.

And how would they deal with tomorrow? Not the eternal tomorrow, but the promised, practical one. Her thighs feel stiff, though she is slowly relax-ing. Her mother, beside her, is facing away. How, indeed? Roger will be re-habilitated, tomorrow, yes, yes. There will be board games. Songs. Changes of outfits. Phone calls placed. Possibly she will find the time to ask her mother if anyone had ever been abused, and find out, happily, not. Looks will be passed between and among everyone tomorrow. Certain names, words will be in short supply for the sake of all. The girls will learn to ski and enjoy it. Jokes will be told. They will feel better. A family again. Christmas, as al-ways, takes care of its own.

1998

holiday SPIRITS

COMMENTS

E. B. WHITE

At this season of the year, merry to some, not merry to others, we should like to send greetings abroad through town and country. We particularly greet people on benches, and others who wait, motionless, for something to happen. We send Christmas wishes to little auks, and to hunger marchers. To tree surgeons' mothers, and to men in change booths in the Eighth Avenue subway. To candlemakers and all manufacturers of tops that whir. To people whom clams poison. To people who can't remember names, and to the persons whose names they can't remember. To Schrafft's hostesses. To conditioners of dogs everywhere. We greet all makers of the coffee that beggars want a dime for a cup of. Greetings to the wives of retired army officers. We greet all minor poets, and men who started a mustache Wednesday. To the prisoners in the Yonkers jail, and to little boys whose birthday is December 21. To the fattest woman in the world save three. To receptionists and to the young graduates of universities who fill out cards marked "To see—About—." To people whose food doesn't agree with them. To the hatters of Danbury, Conn. To judges of pigeon races, and to manufacturers of gum labels. We greet retouchers of photographs of all sorts, and people who wrestle with bears. Most particularly, though, we send greetings to people on benches, and others who wait, motionless, for something to happen.

1932

They are not wrapped as gifts (there was no time to wrap them), but you will find them under the lighted tree with the other presents. They are the extra gifts, the ones with the hard names. Certain towns and villages. Certain docks and installations. Atolls in a sea. Assorted airstrips, beachheads, supply dumps, rail junctions. Here is a gift to hold in your hand—Hill 660. Vital from a strategic standpoint. "From the Marines," the card says. Here is a small strip of the Italian coast. Merry Christmas from the members of the American Fifth (who waded ashore). This is Kwajalein, Maloelap, Wotje. This is Eniwetok. Place them with your other atolls, over by the knitted scarf from Aunt Lucy. Here is Gea. If the size isn't right, remember it was selected at night, in darkness. Roi, Mellu, Boggerlapp, Ennugarret, Ennumennet, Ennubirr. Amphibious forces send season's greetings. How pretty! A little reef-fringed islet in a coral sea. Kwajalein! A remembrance at Christmas from the Seventh Division. Los Negros Island. Put it with the others of the Admiralty Group. Elements of the First Cavalry Division (dismounted) have sent Momote airfield, a very useful present. Manus, largest of the Admiralties. Lorengau, taken from the Japanese garrison in the underground bunkers. Talasea airdrome. Wotho Atoll (a gift from the 22nd Marine Regiment). Emirau Island, and ten more atolls in the Marshalls to make your Christmas bright in 1944: Ujae, Lae, Lib, Namu, Ailinglapalap (never mind the names), together with a hundred-and-fifty-mile strip of the northern New Guinea coast, Tanahmera Bay and Humboldt Bay, together with Hollandia. "From some American troops covered with red mud."

Here is a novel gift—a monastery on a hill. It seems to have been damaged. A bridge on Highway 6. A mountain stronghold, Castelforte (Little Cassino, they used to call it). And over here the roads—Via Casilina and the Appian Way. Valleys, plains, hills, roads, and the towns and villages. Santa Maria Infante, San Pietro, Monte Cerri, and Monte Bracchi. One reads the

names on the cards with affection. Best wishes from the Fifth. Gaeta, Cisterna, Terracina, the heights behind Velletri, the Alban Hills, Mount Peschio, and the fortress of Lazio. Velletri and Valmontone. Best wishes from the Fifth. The suburbs of Rome, and Rome. The Eternal City! Holiday greetings from the American Fifth.

Who wouldn't love the Norman coast for Christmas? Who hasn't hoped for the Atlantic Wall, the impregnable? Here is the whole thing under the lighted tree. First the beaches (greetings from the Navy and the Coast Guard), then the cliffs, the fields behind the cliffs, the inland villages and towns, the key places, the hedgerows, the lanes, the houses, and the barns. Ste. Mère Eglise (with greetings from Omar Bradley and foot soldiers). This Norman cliff (best from the Rangers). St. Jacques de Nehou (from the 82nd Airborne Division, with its best). Cherbourg—street by street, and house by house. St. Remy des Landes, La Broquière, Baudreville, Neufmesnil, La Poterie, the railroad station at La Haye du Puits. And then St. Lô, and the whole vista of France. When have we received such presents? Saipan in the Marianas—only they forgot to take the price tag off. Saipan cost 9,752 in dead, wounded, and missing, but that includes a mountain called Tapotchau. Guam. "Merry Christmas from Conolly, Geiger, and the boys." Tinian, across the way. Avranches, Gavray, Torigny-sur-Vire, a German army in full retreat under your tree. A bridge at Pontorson, a bridge at Ducey, with regards from those who take bridges. Rennes, capital of Brittany (our columns fan out). Merry Christmas, all! Brest, Nantes, St. Malo, a strategic fortress defended for two weeks by a madman. Toulon, Nice, St. Tropez, Cannes (it is very gay, the Riviera, very fashionable). And now (but you must close your eyes for this one) . . . Paris.

Still the gifts come. You haven't even noticed the gift of the rivers Marne and Aisne. Château-Thierry, Soissons (this is where you came in). Verdun, Sedan (greetings from the American First Army, greetings from the sons of the fathers). Here is a most unusual gift, a bit of German soil. Priceless. A German village, Roetgen. A forest south of Aachen. Liége, the Belfort Gap, Geilenkirchen, Crucifix Hill, Uebach. Morotai Island in the Halmaheras. An airport on Peleliu. Angaur (from the Wildcats). Nijmegen Bridge, across the Rhine. Cecina, Monteverdi, more towns, more villages on the Tyrrhenian coast. Leghorn. And, as a special remembrance, sixty-two ships of the Japanese Navy, all yours. Tacloban, Dulag, San Pablo . . . Ormoc. Valleys and villages in the Burmese jungle. Gifts in incredible profusion and all unwrapped, from old and new friends: gifts with a made-in-China label, gifts from Russians, Poles, British, French, gifts from Eisenhower, de Gaulle, Montgomery, Malinovsky, an umbrella from the Air Forces, gifts from engineers, rear gunners, privates first class . . . there isn't time to look at them all. It will take years. This is a Christmas you will never forget, people have been so generous.

1944

❄

To perceive Christmas through its wrapping becomes more difficult with every year. There was a little device we noticed in one of the sporting-goods stores—a trumpet that hunters hold to their ears so that they can hear the distant music of the hounds. Something of the sort is needed now to hear the incredibly distant sound of Christmas in these times, through the dark, material woods that surround it. "Silent Night," canned and distributed in thundering repetition in the department stores, has become one of the greatest of all noisemakers, almost like the rattles and whistles of Election Night. We rode down on an escalator the other morning through the silent-nighting of the loudspeakers, and the man just in front of us was singing, "I'm gonna wash this store right outa my hair, I'm gonna wash this store . . ."

The miracle of Christmas is that, like the distant and very musical voice of the hound, it penetrates finally and becomes heard in the heart—over so many years, through so many cheap curtain-raisers. It is not destroyed even by all the arts and craftiness of the destroyers, having an essential simplicity that is everlasting and triumphant, at the end of confusion. We once went out at night with coon-hunters and we were aware that it was not so much the promise of the kill that took the men away from their warm homes and sent them through the cold shadowy woods, it was something more human, more mystical—something even simpler. It was the night, and the excitement of the note of the hound, first heard, then not heard. It was the natural world, seen at its best and most haunting, unlit except by stars, impenetrable except to the knowing and the sympathetic.

Christmas in 1949 must compete as never before with the dazzling complexity of man, whose tangential desires and ingenuities have created a world that gives any simple thing the look of obsolescence—as though there were something inherently foolish in what is simple, or natural. The human brain is about to turn certain functions over to an efficient substitute, and we hear of a robot that is now capable of handling the tedious details of psycho-analysis, so that the patient no longer need confide in a living doctor but can take his problems to a machine, which sifts everything and whose "brain" has selective power and the power of imagination. One thing leads to another. The machine that is imaginative will, we don't doubt, be heir to the ills of the imagination; one can already predict that the machine itself may become sick emotionally, from strain and tension, and be compelled at last to consult a medical man, whether of flesh or of steel. We have tended to assume that the machine and the human brain are in conflict. Now the fear is that they are indistinguishable. Man not only is notably busy himself but insists that the other animals follow his example. A new bee has been bred artificially, busier than the old bee.

So this day and this century proceed toward the absolutes of convenience, of complexity, and of speed, only occasionally holding up the little trumpet (as at Christmastime) to be reminded of the simplicities, and to hear the distant music of the hound. Man's inventions, directed always onward and upward, have an odd way of leading back to man himself, as a rabbit track in snow leads eventually to the rabbit. It is one of his more endearing qualities that man should think his tracks lead outward, toward something else, instead of back around the hill to where he has already been; and it is one of his persistent ambitions to leave earth entirely and travel by rocket into space, beyond the pull of gravity, and perhaps try another planet, as a pleasant change. He knows that the atomic age is capable of delivering a new

"Oh dear! And we didn't send them a card!"

package of energy; what he doesn't know is whether it will prove to be a blessing. This week, many will be reminded that no explosion of atoms generates so hopeful a light as the reflection of a star, seen appreciatively in a pasture pond. It is there we perceive Christmas—and the sheep quiet, and the world waiting.

1949

❄

From this high midtown hall, undecked with boughs, unfortified with mistletoe, we send forth our tinselled greetings as of old, to friends, to readers, to strangers of many conditions in many places. Merry Christmas to uncertified accountants, to tellers who have made a mistake in addition, to girls who have made a mistake in judgment, to grounded airline passengers, and to all those who can't eat clams! We greet with particular warmth people who wake and smell smoke. To captains of river boats on snowy mornings we send an answering toot at this holiday time. Merry Christmas to intellectuals and other despised minorities! Merry Christmas to the musicians of Muzak and men whose shoes don't fit! Greetings of the season to unemployed actors and the blacklisted everywhere who suffer for sins uncommitted; a holly thorn in the thumb of compilers of lists! Greetings to wives who can't find their glasses and to poets who can't find their rhymes! Merry Christmas to the unloved, the misunderstood, the overweight. Joy to the authors of books whose titles begin with the word "How" (as though they knew)! Greetings to people with a ringing in their ears; greetings to growers of gourds, to shearers of sheep, and to makers of change in the lonely underground booths! Merry Christmas to old men asleep in libraries! Merry Christmas to people who can't stay in the same room with a cat! We greet, too, the boarders in boarding houses on 25 December, the duennas in Central Park in fair weather and foul, and young lovers who got nothing in the mail. Merry Christmas to people who plant trees in city streets; Merry Christmas to people who save prairie chickens from extinction! Greetings of a purely mechanical sort to machines that think—plus a sprig of artificial holly. Joyous Yule to Cadillac owners whose conduct is unworthy of their car! Merry Christmas to the defeated, the forgotten, the inept; joy to all dandiprats and bunglers! We send, most particularly and most hopefully, our greetings and our prayers to soldiers and guardsmen on land and sea and in the air—the young men doing the hardest things at the hardest time of life. To all such, Merry Christmas, blessings, and good luck! We greet the Secretaries-designate, the President-elect: Merry Christmas to our new leaders, peace on earth, good will, and good management! Merry Christmas to couples unhappy in doorways! Merry Christmas to all who think they're in love but aren't sure! Greetings to people waiting for trains that will take them in the wrong direction, to people doing up a bundle and the string is too short, to children with sleds and no snow! We greet ministers who can't think of a moral, gagmen who can't think of a joke. Greetings, too, to the inhabitants of other planets; see you soon! And last, we greet all skaters on small natural ponds at the edge of woods toward the end of afternoon. Merry Christmas, skaters! Ring, steel! Grow red, sky! Die down, wind! Merry Christmas to all and to all a good morrow!

1952

❄

As Christmas draws near, there seems to be less peace on the earth of the Holy Land than practically anywhere else, and we therefore wish an extra portion of good will to all who live beneath the Star of Bethlehem. We wish a surcease of rancor to the angry, a sackful of restraint to the hotheaded, and to everybody a moratorium on political debts. Our merriest Christmas wishes go to those whose lives have been harried by holiday preliminaries: to the novice skaters at Rockefeller Center, forced to take their lessons before so unusually many challenging eyes; to Salvation Army tuba players on Fifth Avenue, manfully making their music despite the double jeopardy of cold lip and jostled elbow; to a temporary saleswoman we saw at Saks with tears in her eyes and the book "Creatures of Circumstance" tucked under her arm; to a bulky, mink-clad lady we bumped into on Madison Avenue, who (a prep-school mother?) was trying to look as if she habitually walked around carrying a brace of hockey sticks; to the girl in the Barton's candy ad, nibbling self-consciously on a chocolate Christmas card; and to a young man we watched directing pedestrian traffic in front of the Lord & Taylor show windows (he was wearing a crash helmet, and we hope he survived). Our especially sympathetic regards go to those anonymous bulwarks of industry, the people who clean up offices after office parties. May they all find a bottle of Christmas cheer cached behind a filing cabinet!

We wish a Merry Christmas to the man in the moon, and also to an enterprising Long Island man who has been selling earth dwellers lots on the moon. (A Happy Light-Year to his customers.) Merry Christmas and congratulations to the ninety-two-year-old doctor to whom the Army—which now has forty-one generals of a rank equal to or higher than the loftiest attained by George Washington—has just given a reserve promotion from captain to major. Merry Christmas to Captain Eddie Rickenbacker, who has turned sixty-five, and may he, too, make the grade ere long. Merry Christmas, when it comes to that, to the Army, which has indulgently permitted a pfc. in Korea to retain ownership of some land he impulsively bought there, for the establishment of an orphanage.

Merry Christmas to all orphans and strays everywhere, including our dog, who vanished last week. May somebody throw her a bone. Merry Christmas to all the defenders of lost and little causes, among them an animal-loving outfit beguilingly called Defenders of Furbearers. (Merry Christmas to furriers, too.) Merry Christmas to all the institutions endowed by the Ford Foundation, and a particularly rollicking Noël to one beneficiary—the hard-pressed hospital that reluctantly closed its doors on December 1st, never dreaming that succor was imminent. (What delightful evidence that Santa comes only when your eyes are shut!) Merry Christmas to the Foundation's controversial offspring, the Fund for the Republic, which is under considerable political attack at the moment and has just diplomatically added two offspring of literary men to a panel of judges for a TV-program contest it is sponsoring—Robert A. Taft, Jr., whose father wrote "A Foreign Policy for Americans," and Philip Willkie, whose father wrote "One World." Merry Christmas to one world, including all Germanys, all Koreas, all Vietnams, all Chinas, and both Inner and Outer Mongolia.

1955

THAT'S TOO BAD DEPARTMENT

[Headline in the Saratogian]

CHRISTMAS CALLED NOEL IN PARIS, SARATOGIAN WHO RESIDED THERE SAYS.

1938

Tree

Deadly Weapon

The Unsigned Card

Warning re Santa Claus

Office Wit

Pre-Christmas Smirk

SPIRIT OF CHRISTMAS

SALLY BENSON

Margaret Cummings lifted the large copper bowl, filled with unopened Christmas cards, from the living-room table and carried it over to a bridge table that stood in front of the couch. "Now, then," she said, setting the bowl down.

Mr. Cummings, who was sitting on the couch, put aside a copy of the *Saturday Evening Post* and sighed. "Are you going to check them with your list?" he asked.

"Certainly I'm going to check them with my list. I always do. At least, you can check them as I read them to you. There's no sense in keeping people on your list when they don't remember you. And if we find *we've* forgotten someone, we can still get a card in the mail tonight. The list is on my desk."

Mr. Cummings got up and went over to the desk. He was a small, slender man who was untouched by the gaiety of the season. And although, after dinner, he had helped his wife trim their tree, he had done so with a sort of mathematical precision, interested only in the technical details of the business. He had fastened the tree firmly in its stand, tested the lights, straightened the wires on the ornaments, and unwound the tinsel. The twenty Christmases he had lived through since his marriage had left him with a mild distaste for red and green ribbons, tissue paper, Christmas seals, and the smell of spruce trees.

"It's under the blotter," Mrs. Cummings said. She pulled a straight chair up to the bridge table and sat down. "You might bring that letter-opener, too."

Mr. Cummings brought the letter-opener and the list and sank back on the couch again. "All set?"

"This looks like an ad," Mrs. Cummings said, holding up a square white envelope. She slit it open and her face fell. "It's from Chris. Chris Panagakos. Why, I feel *terribly* about it. I haven't bought a thing there for months, not since I decided to pay cash and go to the A. & P." She ran her finger lightly over the card. "It's engraved, too. And in very good taste. Really, in *very* good taste. It just says 'Compliments of the Season' and 'Panagakos Brothers.' "

"Well," Mr. Cummings said, fingering the list, "do you want to send them a card or don't you?"

"Of course not. I'll just stop in and buy some little thing. Here's one from the Archer girls. You know, Bobby Archer's sisters. I suppose that's intended to be Mattie Archer carrying that boar's head. Any of the Archers would drop dead on a mouthful of boar's head with *their* stomachs. Why, Mattie Archer is ridden with ulcers. Ridden with them."

"O.K.," Mr. Cummings said. "They check."

"Goodness!" Mrs. Cummings exclaimed. "This one's written all over, like a letter. It says, 'Angus is in high school and Barbara is continuing her studies at St. Mary's. We all hope to go

East next summer.' Why, it's from this girl I went to college with. This girl was a girl—I hate to say this, but—well, she was crazy. Not exactly crazy, but *odd.* And why she would ever think I would give a hoot about what her children are doing I'm sure I *can't* say. Helen Smosely was her name. Did you ever hear of anything like it? And it's a good thing she signed it 'Helen Smosely Martin,' because if she'd signed it 'Helen Martin,' I wouldn't have known who she was from a hole in the ground. Put her down for next year, Bill, because she's in Detroit and if I send her a card tonight, she'll know I just did it because I got one from her."

Mr. Cummings took the card and copied the name and address from it carefully.

"I can't get over it," Mrs. Cummings said. "Helen Smosely. She probably got my address from the *Alumni Quarterly.* Here's a card from those friends of yours in New Mexico—the Ryans. I sent them one on your account. Look, their card has a swastika on it. Not very appropriate, considering. You'd think they'd realize how people might feel about swastikas, although I suppose, living in New Mexico, they still think of them in the old way." She shook her head. "Helen Smosely. Here's one from the Burchells. It ends, 'There is laughter everywhere, And the shouts of little children fill the wintry air.' Although I don't see how they would know when they haven't any little children and never did have. I don't believe people can read the verses on the cards they buy or they'd never buy them. I thought ours looked nice this year, didn't you, Bill?"

Mr. Cummings put one hand to his forehead and frowned. "Let's see—"

"Oh, Bill!" Margaret Cummings laughed. "You've forgotten. If that isn't *too* funny! Wait until I tell Frannie. You just about slay her anyway. It was the photograph of our fireplace that we took last Christmas. Remember how pretty the fireplace looked last Christmas? And I must say I think it was smart of me to have it photographed and plan so far ahead."

"Oh, sure."

"Well, I never told you, but after the cards were all done I had a better idea. Next year, I think it would be cute to have my stocking and your sock hanging from the fireplace and to have my head coming out of my stocking and your head coming out of your sock." She put her head to one side and looked at him speculatively.

"Might be hard to do," he said.

"Nonsense! They do all sorts of things nowadays with photography."

"You'd better step on it," he said. "It's getting late."

"I'm going to plan on it for next year." She fumbled in the bowl and opened another envelope. "Here's one addressed to you. Signed 'Frances Swett.'"

"Swett?" Mr. Cummings repeated. "Never heard of him."

"Never heard of *her*," Mrs. Cummings corrected. "It's spelled with an 'e.'"

"Well, never heard of her, then."

"It's a nice little card," Mrs. Cummings said sweetly. "A five-cent card, but very neat and in good taste. Just a holly wreath, and it says, 'A Merry

Christmas and a Happy New Year.' The signature is in a woman's handwriting."

"Let's see it." Mr. Cummings held out his hand.

"You must have heard of her," Mrs. Cummings insisted, and handed him the card. "There it is. S-w-e-t-t. Could it be somebody in your office?"

"Nope," he answered. "There's nobody in our office named Swett."

"Someone who *was* in your office, then?"

"If she was, I don't remember her."

"Well, she remembered *you*," Mrs. Cummings said. "Not that it matters. We'd better hurry."

She began to open the envelopes, calling off the names to Mr. Cummings, who checked them with the list. Soon the table was covered with cards and the bowl was empty.

"All through?" Mr. Cummings asked.

"Yes, that was the last," she said. She got up and, going over to the tree, switched on the lights. "That is, everybody is accounted for except for the

"No 'Ho-ho-ho' at all, Mr. Reynolds, is better than a 'Ho-ho-ho' that doesn't come from the heart."

girl who sent you that little card." She reached up and began draping the tinsel more loosely on the branches.

Mr. Cummings watched her as she stood with her back to him. Even in the soft-colored light from the tree he could see that her hair was very gray. And, although her dress was a becoming color, it pulled slightly across her hips and shoulders. Underneath the tree lay the packages that she had arranged so they would give the best effect. She was really very young, he thought. He looked through the cards on the table until he found the one addressed to himself. He opened it and looked at the name Frances Swett. Suddenly he had a vague and pleasant recollection of a girl who had come to his office with a letter of introduction. He remembered that he had been helpful and almost courtly. He tore the card in half and, getting up, he walked to the fireplace and threw the pieces in.

"Probably a mistake of some kind," he said. "Must be more than one William Cummings in the telephone book." He went over to Margaret and put his arm carelessly around her shoulders. She stopped arranging the tinsel and turned her head toward him so that she could look into his eyes.

He kissed her lightly on the cheek and looked up at the tree. "Smells good," he said.

1940

"Do we have any anti-Christmas cards?"

TWO PEOPLE HE NEVER SAW

JOHN McNULTY

Eddie Casavan and Harry Marnix were walking up Fifth Avenue, around Fiftieth Street, when Christmas suddenly closed in on them. It got a tighter hold on Casavan, but the feel of Christmas clamped down on both of them. The store windows, the sharp air, the lights coming on in the late afternoon, and the couple of drinks they had on their walk must have done it.

They were turning off the Avenue when Eddie said, "I don't seem to want anything for Christmas any more."

"It's for the kids," Harry said. "It's a time for the kids, Christmas."

"Long after I was a kid I still wanted something for Christmas," Eddie said. "I'm forty-nine and it must have been only a couple of years ago that it came to me I didn't want anything for Christmas any more. I don't this year. The stuff in the windows looks nice, but I don't want any of it."

"It's mostly kids' stuff—things for kids for Christmas," Harry said.

"I know about that, but it's not what I mean," Eddie answered. "Let's go in this place. I got an hour. You going anyplace?"

"All right," said Harry. "No, I'm not. Not right away."

They weren't high. A little talky, maybe—nothing like tight. Eddie ordered two drinks. "Two Scotch highballs," he said, the more old-fashioned way of saying what practically everybody in New York now means by saying "Scotch-and-soda."

"I don't even want to go anyplace for Christmas, that's what I mean," Eddie went on as the bartender made up the drinks and left the bottle on the bar.

"I used to like to go to the six-day bike races," said Harry.

"They didn't have them at Christmas," Eddie said.

"I know it, but I used to like to go to them in winter and I don't seem to want to any more," Harry explained. "They don't have them, anyway, come to think of it."

"For Christmas I used to plan ahead," Eddie said. "Even up to a couple of years ago. And I always figured someplace to go or something to do special for Christmas. Now there's nothing I want and nothing I want to do."

"They used to yell 'B-r-r-rocco!' at the bike races," Harry said.

That got nowhere, and Eddie and Harry fiddled with the long glass sticks in their glasses.

~~~

"There *is* something I'd like to do at Christmas at that," Eddie said after a while. "But it's impossible, maybe nuts."

"Christmas is nuts, a little," Harry said.

"Only way it could happen'd be an Aladdin's lamp. You rub it, you get what you want," Eddie continued. "Or if one of those kind-hearted demons or something would hop out of that Scotch bottle there and grant a wish. That's kid stuff, I guess."

Fragment of conversation overheard on the Congressional Limited: "What I miss most, I miss that prewar Christmas spirit—you know, getting fried at lunch the day before and deciding to go up to Bonwit Teller's and get the wife a present."

—C. E. NOYES AND RUSSELL MALONEY, 1944

"Christmas is a kids' gag," Harry said. "As childish as six-day bike races, come to think of it. It felt like Christmas walking up the Avenue, didn't it? What if the gink should hop out of the bottle? What about it?"

"I was thinking that, too," Eddie said. "He could cook it up for me."

"What?"

"I'd like to take two people to Christmas dinner, a couple a people I never saw."

"Yuh?"

"One of them would be maybe forty now, a woman," Eddie said. "Oh, I don't know how old, tell the truth. Don't know how old she was when I first met her. No, wait a minute. The point is, I never met her."

"Movie star? Some notion like that?"

"No, no. Hell, no. Do you think I'm a kid?"

"No, what I mean is, Christmas is for kids. I didn't have you in mind."

"I often thought of her since. This was when I was having it tough one time, maybe fifteen years ago. Living in a furnished room on East Thirty-ninth Street—"

"And are they something, furnished rooms!" Harry put in.

"Furnished rooms are something if you've lived through and pull out of it you never forget them," Eddie said.

"I been in 'em." Harry nodded.

"God, I was sunk then!" Eddie said. "I was drinking too much and I lost one job after another. This time I was looking for a job and coming back every afternoon to the furnished room about four o'clock. That's how I never saw this girl."

"What girl?" Harry asked.

"The one I want to take to dinner at Christmas."

"If the gink comes out of the bottle," Harry said.

"Yeh, if he does. I remember I'd have a few beers after getting half promises of jobs, and I'd plank myself down on the bed in this little bit of a room when I came home four o'clock in the afternoon. It was the smallest room I was ever in. And the lonesomest."

"They get lonesome," Harry said.

"The walls are thin, too. The wall next to my bed was thin. Must have been like cardboard. This girl lived in the next room, the one I never met."

"Oh, yeh, yeh?" Harry said.

"I could hear her moving around. Sometimes she'd be humming and I could hear that. I could hear her open the window, or shut it if it was raining."

"Never see her?" Harry asked.

"No, that's the point of it. I almost thought I knew her, the way I could

" 'Season's Greetings' looks O.K. to me. Let's run it by the legal department.

hear her. I could hear her leave every afternoon, about quarter past four. She had a kind of a lively step. I figured she was a waitress somewhere. Some job like that, don't you think?"

"I don't know, maybe a waitress, but *why,* though?" Harry said, and took a drink.

"Why *was* she a waitress, or why did I figure it out she's a waitress?" Eddie asked.

"Yeh, I mean why?" Harry answered in such a way that it meant how was it figured out.

"Oh, I could have been wrong. She had some steady job like waitress. She used to come home almost on the dot, quarter past one in the morning. You

"Oh, no! There goes our Christmas bonus."

could set your clock on it. I used to look at my clock when she came in. Gee, her steps sounded tired when she was coming up the hall. She must have worked hard. She'd put the key in the lock and I'd hear that. I didn't sleep very good then. Worrying about a job, one thing and another. It'd be quarter past one by my clock. I hung on to that clock. I got it yet."

"Some people hate clocks in their room while they're sleeping," Harry said.

"They haven't lived in furnished rooms," Eddie said. "A clock is a great thing in a furnished room. This was a green one, ninety-eight cents. In a furnished room a clock is somebody there with you, anyway. The ticking sounds as if you're not altogether alone, for God's sake, if it's only the clock that's there with you."

"Never saw this girl—that's what you said?"

"Never saw her. Maybe she wasn't exactly a girl. I couldn't prove she wasn't a woman, older than a girl. When she hummed, though, I figured it sounded like a girl. Funny I never bumped into her in the hallway. Just didn't happen to. But I spoke to her once."

"Spoke to her?" Harry asked.

"Yeh. It was a gag. I told you I could hear everything. Well, her bunk was right next to mine—with only this wall there. And one afternoon she was getting up and she sneezed. It sounded funny from the next room. So I said very loud, '*Gesundheit!*' I remember she laughed. Her laugh sounded twenty-five."

"But you don't know, do you?"

"No, I don't and I won't. But if she was that age then, she'd be forty, around that, now, wouldn't she?"

"When was this?"

"I said about fifteen, could be sixteen years ago."

"Twenty-five and fifteen is forty, yes. She could be forty now," Harry said. "She could have been a bum. Did you ever think of that?"

"Harry, Harry, Harry, you don't get it at all! She couldn't have been a bum.

NO FOOLING

Early this month, a man whose garage delivers and picks up his car daily found on the front seat a card reading, "Merry Christmas from the boys at the garage." He had every intention of sending the garage a Yuletide check for his well-wishers, but he had taken no action as of last week, when he was favored with another card; to wit: "Merry Christmas from the boys at the garage. Second notice."

—J. SOANS AND GEOFFREY HELLMAN, 1951

A bum wouldn't have to live in such a bad room. I wanted to know her only because we were two people both having it tough together, and still and all we weren't together except when I said '*Gesundheit.*' "

Harry finished his drink and said pleasantly, "No, I don't mean it. I don't think she could have been a bum. Anyway, she would be about forty now, all right."

~~~

Eddie finished his drink and beckoned to the barkeep, who came and poured soda into the glasses. Eddie put in the whiskey, and when he put down the bottle he looked expectantly at it for a minute or two.

"And the guy would be about my own age now, about forty-nine or so, wouldn't he?" Eddie asked.

"Excuse me, but what guy?" Harry asked. "Oh, yeh, yeh, the guy."

"The one I'd like to take to Christmas dinner with her to the best place in town. Take the two of them. I've got a few bucks these days. I pulled through the furnished rooms all right, didn't I? I was thinking that, coming up the Avenue when the lights were going on."

"You're rambling, chum. Who is this feller, or maybe who was he?" Harry asked.

"It's 'who was he?' I don't know where he is, or is he dead or alive. I never saw his face. He was the soldier who picked me up in France. He picked me up off the ground, in the pitch dark, and he didn't have to."

"In the war?"

"Sure, in the war. Not this one, the other. But I bet it's happening too in this one."

"When you got hit, you mean?" Harry asked.

"That's the time, of course. You know how I hate professional ex-soldiers, guys always talking the other war. I don't want to be one of those."

"Oh, I know that, Eddie, I know it. But I know you were in the other one and got hit."

"It wasn't getting hit. That wasn't so much. It's this feller I often thought about at odd times all these years. Just to boil it down, it certainly was dark as hell, and there was no shooting going on at all. The first sergeant, guy named Baker, was with me. He got killed, I found out later. He stopped the big pieces of this shell. I only got the little pieces. We were going back through this town, going to find a place to sleep."

"A little French town?" Harry asked.

"What else? This was in France, for God's sake, so it was a little French town. Anyway, they suddenly threw one over and it hit right where we were, because the next thing I was pawing the wall of the house we were walking alongside of. I was trying to get up and my legs felt like ropes under me. When I went to stand up, they coiled."

"You were hit, all right," Harry said. "I saw your legs in swimming many a time, the marks on them."

"Oh, I don't care about that. The point is, this feller. I come to, there in the pitch dark, and somebody was prodding me with his foot. And whoever it was, he was saying, 'What's the matter, what's the matter?' I answered him. I said, 'My goddam legs.'"

"It was this guy, you mean?"

"Yes, him," Eddie said. "And then I passed out again. Well, I never saw the guy. I never saw his face. He could be black or white. He could be an angel, for all I know to this day. Anyway, he's who carried me through that pitch dark, and he didn't have to. He could have left me there. And I must have been bleeding like hell. Next thing, I came to, and I was lying on a table. It was an aid station in a cellar someplace. A doc was pouring ether by the canful over holes in my leg. That ether turns cold as hell if you pour it on anything. The guy wasn't around. Anyway, I didn't think of him then. Who the hell was he? I don't know. If it wasn't for that feller I never saw, I wouldn't be here today."

"It's a pretty good day to be here," Harry said.

Eddie took a drink and so did Harry. "That's the two of them—the ones I'd like to take to dinner when it comes to be Christmas night. But I won't."

"No, you won't," said Harry. "There's nothing coming out of the bottle but Scotch."

1944

The New Yorker

Dec. 19, 1977

One Dollar

THE NEW YORKER

FLESH AND THE DEVIL

PETER DE VRIES

The office where Frisbie worked as vice-president in charge of purchases had its Christmas party a week early, because the head of the corporation was leaving for Miami, but otherwise it was like any other Christmas party. Everyone stood around self-consciously at first, drinking whiskey from paper cups, then bandied intramural jokes as the liquor thawed them, and ended up by slinging arms around one another in general camaraderie. Frisbie found himself dancing (to music from a radio that had been left in the office since the World Series) with a Mrs. Diblanda, hired temporarily for the Christmas rush. He left with Mrs. Diblanda when the party broke up, and they stopped at a neighboring bar for another drink. Frisbie had told his wife not to figure on him for dinner, as there was no way of knowing how long the party would last or how substantial the refreshments would be. There had been loads of canapés, so little edge was left on his appetite, but when, calling a cab, he offered to drop Mrs. Diblanda off at her apartment and she invited him up for a last drink and maybe a bite of supper, he accepted. They had a couple of drinks, and then—quite naturally, it seemed—Frisbie kissed her. Mrs. Diblanda, a divorced woman of about thirty who lived alone, transmitted a clear sense of readiness for anything, but just at that moment the image of Mrs. Frisbie interposed itself between him and Mrs. Diblanda, and he rose, got his hat and coat, excused himself, and left.

Now, this forbearance struck Frisbie as a fine thing. How many men he knew—fellows at the office, say—tempted by an isolated pleasure that could have been enjoyed and forgotten with no complications whatever, would have denied themselves? Damn few, probably. The more he thought of it, the more gratifying his conduct seemed, and, presently, the more his satisfaction struck him as worth sharing with his wife, not for the light the incident put him in but as a certification of their bond. Superimposed upon the good spirits in which his drinks had left him, his moral exhilaration mounted. There were no cabs outside Mrs. Diblanda's apartment house, and, hurrying on foot through a cool, needling drizzle that he found ravishing to his face,

Frisbie tried to put himself in a woman's place, and couldn't imagine a wife not grateful for the knowledge of her husband's loyalty. By the time he reached home, he had decided to tell Mrs. Frisbie of his.

~~~

It was twenty minutes to ten when Frisbie entered the house. He greeted his wife with a jovial hoot from the hall when she called from upstairs to ask if it was he. He hung up his coat and hat and went on up to the bedroom, where Mrs. Frisbie was sitting in bed, filing her fingernails with an emery board. He answered a few questions about what the party had been like, and then took off his coat and vest and carried them into his closet. "Guess what," he said from there. "I had a chance to have an affair."

The sound of the emery board, which he could hear behind him, stopped, then resumed more slowly. "I say I had a chance to sleep with someone. A woman," he said. He reached for a wire hanger and knocked two or three to the floor in a tangle. He stooped to retrieve one, slipped his coat and vest onto it, and hung them up. "But I declined," he said, attempting to strike a humorous note.

The sound of the emery board stopped altogether. "Who's the woman?" Mrs. Frisbie asked in a tone slightly lower than normal.

"I don't see what difference that makes," Frisbie said. "All I'm saying is there was this woman I didn't sleep with. I just have an idea lots of men would have."

"Anyone I know?" she persisted.

"Watch who you're calling irrelevant."

k her home and went up to her
emporaneity of all this galled
ésumé continued. "You were
have slept with her, which
ding up to it. What?"
well above his ordinary
nching her cigarette
sing gown from a
les. Frisbie stood
go any further,"
e on dow

be of his
dit?" he
e car-
"The
er his
et the legs
it," he said, slip-
sers on a hanger and
He took off his shoes and
e the closet door, finished
and got into a pair of pajamas.
it the emery board on the night-

de her and thoughtfully shook a cigarette out of a pack. Frisbie
hile in the closet, smoothing down the sleeves of hanging coats and
a check of the garments suspended there. "Two of these suits need
g," he said, emerging.

is wife struck a match and lit the cigarette. "How did you find out you
ld sleep with her?" she asked.

A filament of anger began to glow inside Frisbie. "Just a while ago," he
said.

"Not when—*how*. How did you find out you could?"

"What's the difference?" he said, kicking his shoes into a corner.

"You were up in a woman's apartment with her," Mrs. Frisbie said. "It was

probably somebody from the office. You to
flat." Her hopeless failure to see the gay ex
Frisbie, filling him with resentment. The cold
drinking. You reached a point where you could
couldn't come out of a clear sky but had things lea

"If you must know, I kissed her!" Frisbie said,
tone.

His wife threw back the covers and got out of bed, p
out in an ashtray on her night table. She picked up a dr
chair, slipped into it, and thrust her feet into a pair of mu
watching these movements as though mesmerized. "It didn't
he said.

She knotted the cord of her robe and drew it tight. "Co
stairs," she said. "We'll talk about it there."

~~~

Frisbie followed his wife down the stairs, drawing on a warm ro
own, for the house seemed suddenly chilly. "Don't I get any cre
protested. She marched on, her mules making a scuffing thud on t
peted steps. "I mean there in my mind's eye was your face," he said.
minute I kissed her, I knew I couldn't go whole hog."

"Fix a drink," his wife said, turning into the living room.

"Right."

Frisbie went to the cellarette. He had the illusion that it was the dead
night. The ice cubes clacked idiotically into the glasses. He mixed Scotch

"No, this is crazy. We mustn't."

and-sodas for both of them. Behind him, he knew, his wife was sitting erect in the middle of the sofa, her knees together and her hands in her lap, looking across the room. "Isn't there a French proverb 'A stumble may prevent a fall'?" he asked, and a moment later, "Who said, 'Women are not seduced, men are elected'? Somebody."

These remarks were made with no great thought of carrying weight, but were pasted flat on the silence like decalcomania. Frisbie handed his wife a Scotch-and-soda, and she took several swallows and set the glass down on an end table.

"Now, then," she said, "how did it all get started? What has there been between you?"

"Nothing, really," he said, picking up his drink from the cellarette. He had meant the "really" as an emphasis, but he realized that it came out as a kind of qualification. He walked to the mantel and stood there. "You're not looking at this thing right," he said. "Think of it just as the tail end of an office party—and you know what they're like. People kissing one another you'd never dream of." He gave a little reminiscent laugh. "Funny—I mean, to stand off and watch all that, which has *no* connection with their daily lives. Clarke, there, with his arm around his secretary, kissing her. Old H. Denim smacking everybody in sight."

"Smacking everybody is different."

"I kissed others."

It made no sense. They had simply floated off on a cake of ice, Frisbie thought, into a sea of absurdity. That they would at last fetch up on a farther shore he took for granted, though he couldn't at the moment see how.

"How can a woman ever be sure of her husband again?" his wife asked rhetorically, and then talked on.

Frisbie could recall a hundred plays of marital stress in which husbands and wives spatted brightly or tumbled adroitly through colorful arcs of emotion, but he could think of nothing to say now. He frowned into his glass and ran the tip of his finger around the rim. Once, he grinned and looked at his feet. After taking him to task from various points of view, suggesting particularly that he put himself in his wife's place and imagine what *he* might think of *her* in another man's arms, Mrs. Frisbie broke off and looked into her own glass. "How did you feel?" she asked. "When you—did it."

Frisbie spread his free hand in a gesture preparatory to replying, but she interrupted him before he could speak. "No, don't tell me," she said. "I don't want to know about it." She looked at him squarely. "Tell me you'll never do a cheap thing like that again."

With that, Frisbie's resistance, till now smoldering and tentative, flared up. He took a drink, planked his glass on the mantel, faced his wife deliberately, and answered in words that surprised him as much as they did her, "A man can't guarantee his emotions for the rest of his life."

His wife rose and strode to the window. "Well!" she said. "What have we here?"

"Somebody trying to make a mountain out of a molehill," Frisbie said, warming now that he had found his tongue. "It's time we went at these things in a grown-up way. Why shouldn't there be sexual freedom as well as political? Let's look at it from a civilized point of view."

"You must be mad," Mrs. Frisbie said.

"Plenty!" he said. "I was reading an article in a magazine—that one right there on the table—some sex facts about the American male, based on statistics. Well, it seems that before marriage the average man has three point five affairs. *After* marriage—aside from his wife, of course—the average man has point seven affairs."

Mrs. Frisbie dug a package of cigarettes out of the pocket of her robe. "Let's hope you've had yours," she said.

He calculated a moment. "I'd say that's the grossest possible exaggeration

"Of course, I wouldn't want a card that says <u>too</u> much."

of what occurred this evening," he said. "And that so far you've got very little to complain of."

That way lay anything but reconciliation. Mrs. Frisbie wheeled around. "Surely you don't mean any of this. You *can't!*" she cried. "Or you wouldn't have brought the whole business up the way you did. You couldn't get it off your chest soon enough." The reflection seemed to give her pause. "I suppose I should have appreciated that more, except that you caught me so by surprise." She assessed this new idea, and Frisbie with it. "You *had* to tell me before you could lay your head on your pillow. Wasn't that it?"

Like a man who, trying to trim his sails to contrary winds, finds a breeze springing up from an unexpected quarter, Frisbie prudently tacked for harbor on those lines. He sighed voluminously and flapped his arms at his sides. "I told you what I did because I thought it was something you ought to know," he said.

"You thought you owed it to me."

"Something like that," said Frisbie.

"Don't think I don't appreciate that part of it," Mrs. Frisbie said.

"Then let's leave it that way," he said, snapping on a table lighter, and, walking over to her, extended the flame to her unlighted cigarette. He lit one himself.

Still, she seemed to withhold something from the promise of eventual good graces, as though wanting yet a gesture from him to complete the ritual. She prompted him, at length. "You *are* sorry, aren't you?" she said.

Frisbie was reviewing to himself the hour's events, tracing their origins in that misguided impulse he had had when homebound. "I did a damn foolish thing tonight," he reflected, thinking aloud.

"One you'll not do again if the chance arises," Mrs. Frisbie said.

"You can say that again!" Frisbie said, walking back to the mantel and reaching for his drink. "You can certainly say that again."

1950

> To the many parishioners who sent us holiday greetings we send thanks and greetings. Two odd little incidents occurred. A lady in Toledo sent us a typewritten greeting which we mistook for a manuscript and rejected with our usual promptness and severity. With amazing amiability she mailed it right back; for when a woman wishes us well, nothing can stop her. Another reader, of the opposite temper, submitted for publication a greeting which he had sent to his friends. Everybody had told him it was good enough to print in *The New Yorker*. He said we could publish it provided we used his name. All in all a flighty season, holier and more larkish than we have known in some time.
>
> —E. B. WHITE, 1935

At bottom it's a woman's affair, a chance in the darkest of months to put on some gaudy clothes and get out of the house. Those old holidays weren't scattered around the calendar by chance. Harvest and seedtime, seedtime and harvest, the elbows of the year. The women do enjoy it; they enjoy jostle of most any kind, in my limited experience. The widow Covode as full of rouge and purple as an old-time Scollay Square tart, when her best hope is burial on a sunny day, with no frost in the ground. Mrs. Hortense broad as a barn door, yet her hands putting on a duchess's airs. Mamie Nevins sporting a sprig of mistletoe in her neck brace. They miss Mr. Burley. He never married and was everybody's gallant for this occasion. He was the one to spike the punch and this year they let young Covode do it, maybe that's why Little Polka Dots can't keep a straight face and giggles across the music like a pruning saw.

Adeste, fideles,
Laeti triumphantes;
Venite, venite
In Bethlehem.

"As soon as you finish up with those new twenties, Louie, I wish
you'd get to work on my wife's Christmas cards."

Still that old tussle, "v" versus "wenite," the "th" as hard or soft. Education is what divides us. People used to actually resent it, the way Burley, with his education, didn't go to some city, didn't get out. Exeter, Dartmouth, a year at the Sorbonne, then thirty years of Tarbox. By the time he hit fifty he was fat and fussy. Arrogant, too. Last sing, he two or three times told Hester to pick up her tempo. "Presto, Hester, not andante!" Never married, and never really worked. Burley Hosiery, that his grandfather had founded, was shut down and the machines sold South before Burley got his manhood. He built himself a laboratory instead and was always about to come up with something perfect: the perfect synthetic substitute for leather, the harmless insecticide, the beer can that

turned itself into mulch. Some said at the end he was looking for a way to turn lead into gold. That was just malice. Anything high attracts lightning, anybody with a name attracts malice. When it happened, the papers in Boston gave him six inches and a photograph ten years old. "After a long illness." It wasn't a long illness, it was cyanide, the Friday after Thanksgiving.

The holly bears a prickle,
As sharp as any thorn,
And Mary bore sweet Jesus Christ
On Christmas day in the morn.

They said the cyanide ate out his throat worse than a blowtorch. Such a detail is satisfying but doesn't clear up the mystery. Why? Health, money, hobbies, that voice. Not having that voice makes a big hole here. Without his lead, no man dares take the lower parts; we just wheeze away at the melody with the women. It's as if the floor they put in has been taken away and we're standing in air, halfway up that old sanctuary. We peek around guiltily, missing Burley's voice. The absent seem to outnumber the present. We feel insulted, slighted. The dead flee us. The older you get, the more of them snub you. He was rude enough last year, Burley, correcting Hester's tempo. At one point, he even reached over, his face black with impatience, and slapped her hands that were still trying to make sense of the keys.

> *Rise, and bake your Christmas bread:*
> *Christians, rise! The world is bare,*
> *And blank, and dark with want and care,*
> *Yet Christmas comes in the morning.*

Well, why anything? Why do *we?* Come every year sure as the solstice to carol these antiquities that if you listened to the words would break your heart. Silence, darkness, Jesus, angels. Better, I suppose, to sing than to listen.   1970

"That will be ninety cents, cash on the counter, and never mind
what I'll find under my tree on Christmas morning!"

O tannenbaum

HOMECOMING

WILLIAM MAXWELL

It was nearly dark, and Jordan Smith, walking along with his eyes on the ground, came to a stretch of sidewalk where the snow had not been scraped off but was packed hard and icy. He looked up and, a trifle surprised, saw that he had come to the Farrels'. There were lights in the downstairs windows and the house was just as he had remembered it. Yet there was something wrong, something that made him stand doubtfully at the edge of the walk that had not been tended to.

He had come back to Watertown to spend Christmas with his family—with his father and mother, and his two brothers, who were both younger than he was and not quite grown. But they were not entirely the reason for his wanting to come home. Before he went away, he used to be with Tom and Ann Farrel a great deal of the time. So much, in fact, that it used to annoy his mother, and she would ask him occasionally why he didn't pack his things and go move in with the Farrels. And there was nothing that he could say; no way that he could explain to his mother that Farrel and Ann had somehow filled out his life for him and balanced it. They were the first friends that he had ever had. And the best, really. For that reason it would not do for him to go back to New York without seeing Farrel. He had never even meant to do that. But he had hoped to run into Farrel somewhere about town, coming or going. He had hoped that he wouldn't have to face Farrel in his own house now that Ann was not here. Now that Ann was dead, Jordan said to himself as he turned in and made his way up to the porch. He rang the bell twice. After a time the door opened slowly and a rather small boy looked out at him.

"Hello," Jordan said. "I've come to see your father, Timothy. Is he home?"

The boy shook his head. With a feeling which he was ashamed to recognize as relief, Jordan stepped across the sill into the front hall and the door closed behind him.

"How soon do you expect your father?" he said.

"Pretty soon."

"How soon is that?"

"I don't know." The boy seemed to be waiting stolidly until Jordan had proved himself friend or enemy.

"I expect you don't remember me. It's been three years since I left Watertown. You weren't so very old then."

Jordan had not meant to stay, but he found himself taking off his overcoat and his muffler and laying them across the newel post. The last time he had come here, Ann had met him at the door and her face had lighted up with pleasure. "It's Jordan," she had said. Even now, after three years, he could hear her voice and her pleasure at the sight of him. "Here's Jordan, Tom. He's come to say goodbye."

The front hall and the living room were both strangely still. Forgetting that he was not alone, Jordan listened a moment until the oil furnace rumbling away to itself in the basement reassured him.

"I can't stay," he said aloud to Timothy. On the hall tree was an old battered gray hat of Farrel's. Jordan started to hang his new brown one beside it, and then he changed his mind. With the hat still in his hand, he followed Timothy into the living room. There was a Christmas tree in the front window, with red balls and silver balls and tinsel and tin foil in strips hanging from it, and strand upon strand of colored lights that were not lighted. Under the tree Timothy's presents were still laid out, two days after Christmas, in the boxes they had come in: a cowboy hat, a toy revolver, a necktie and handkerchiefs, a giant flashlight, a book on scouting.

"Santa Claus must have been here," Jordan said.

Timothy did not consider, apparently, that this remark called for any answer. He waited a moment and then announced, "You're Jordan."

"That's right—Jordan Smith. But I didn't think you'd remember me."

He looked at the boy hopefully, but Timothy's face remained grave and a little pale, just as before. Jordan went over to the square, heavy, comfortable chair which was Farrel's favorite and sat down in it, and Timothy settled himself on the sofa opposite. For lack of anything better to do, Jordan took his hat and began to spin it, so that the hat went around wildly on his finger.

"You've grown, Timothy. You must have grown at least five or six inches since I saw you last."

Timothy crossed one foot over the other in embarrassment, and dug at the sofa with his heels.

"If this keeps up, we'll have to put weights in your pockets," Jordan said, and his eyes wandered past Timothy to the china greyhounds, one on either side of the mantel. "They're Staffordshire," Ann used to tell him proudly. "And if anything happened to them, I wouldn't want to go on living." Well, Jordan thought to himself—well, there they are. Nothing has happened to them. And the hat spun off the end of his finger and landed on the rug at his feet.

"Now look what I've done!" he exclaimed as he picked the hat up and placed it on Timothy's head. The hat came down well over Timothy's ears, and under the brim of it Timothy's eyes looked out at him without any eyebrows. This time Timothy was amused.

"It's too big for me," he said, smiling, and placed the hat on the sofa beside him.

"Now that it's dark outside," Jordan suggested, "why don't we light the tree?"

"Can't," Timothy said.

"Won't it light?"

Timothy shook his head.

"Get me the screwdriver, then."

A change came over Timothy. For the first time his face took on life and interest. "What do you want the screwdriver for?" he asked.

"Get me one," Jordan said confidently, "and I'll show you."

As soon as Timothy was out of the room, Jordan got up and went over to the fireplace. The greyhounds needed dusting, but there was nothing the mat-

We have to report that last week we encountered a man who owns a house with a small front yard on the upper East Side. He put up a small Christmas tree in the small yard and a large policeman came around and told him to take it down until he got a permit for it. He duly got the permit, and at the same time, in a how-far-is-this-regimentation-going spirit, inquired about other regulations pertaining to the observance of Christmas in the old-fashioned manner, having a suspicion that all the merriment had been legislated or regulated out. He found that on the whole Christmas fun is still possible but you must get permission from the proper authorities. He was told, he reported to us, that carol-singing is permissible without a permit of any kind, coming, in the police viewpoint, under the right of free assemblage. Carollers must not solicit alms, however, or exhibit evidence of having dipped too freely into wassail, and they mustn't sing within five hundred feet of a hospital, a church while a service is going on, or a court in session. Christmas trees anywhere outdoors in New York City are lumped in with

ter with them. Not a crack or a chip anywhere. Jordan put them down again carefully and turned, hearing a slight disturbance outside. The *Evening Herald* struck the side of the house. It was a sound that he had never heard anywhere but in Watertown. He remembered it so perfectly that he couldn't believe that he had been away. Except for Ann, he said to himself as he made his way around the Christmas tree to the front window—except for her, everything was exactly the same. He had come home. He was here in this house that he had thought so much about. And, strangely, it was no satisfaction to him whatever.

Outside, the snow had begun again. Watching the paper boy wheel his bicycle down the icy walk, Jordan wondered why he had not stayed in New York over the holidays; why it was that he had wanted so much to come home. For weeks he had been restless, uneasy, and unable to keep from thinking of home. At night he could not sleep for walking up and down these streets, meeting people that he had known, and talking to them earnestly in his mind. Now that he was here, he didn't feel the way he had expected to feel. People were awfully nice, of course, and they were pleased to see him, but it was no kind of a homecoming. Not without Farrel and Ann. Wherever he went he found himself mentioning her, without meaning to especially. And it shocked him to see that people did not care about her any more. They had grown used to her not being here. Some of them—one or two, at least—complained to him about Farrel. They liked Farrel, they said. You couldn't help liking Tom Farrel. They still enjoyed having a drink with street fairs by the police; you have to ask them for a permit. A permit from the Department of Water Supply, Gas and Electricity is necessary if you want to put electric lights on the tree, and if you're going to light a tree, you have to use electricity, because all other forms of illumination are forbidden. A permit from the Parks Department is required for putting up a tree in a public park or square. People planning to venture outdoors in Santa Claus costume are reminded of Section 887, Subdivision 7, of the Code of Criminal Procedure, which forbids wearing any sort of mask or false face in public, except by guests invited to a masquerade. You're perfectly safe wearing a false face to a masquerade, provided that your host has obtained from the police a licence to stage such an affair. Santa Claus costumes without beards are O.K., and the cops may even wink at a beard which doesn't conceal much of your face. Merry Christmas, and be sure to keep in touch with your mouthpiece.

—RUSSELL MALONEY AND HAROLD ROSS, 1940

him every now and then. And there was no question but that Ann's death was a terrible loss to him. But if she had lived, the doctor said, she would never have been well, probably. And it was a year and a half since she had been rushed to the hospital in the middle of the night, to be operated on. Tom ought to begin now to get over it. He was nursing his grief, people said.

Jordan broke off a strip of tinsel from the Christmas tree, for no particular reason, and started with it for the kitchen. At the door of the dining room he met Timothy with the screwdriver. There was a woman with him also— a tired, tall woman with gray hair that was parted in the middle, and an uncompromising look about the corners of her mouth. Jordan nodded to her.

"I'm Mrs. Ives," the woman said. "What do you want with the screwdriver?"

"I want to fix the tree," Jordan explained, realizing suddenly why it was that Farrel had taken her for a housekeeper. If Farrel had got a younger woman and a more sympathetic one, there would have been talk. "Timothy says the lights don't work, and if we have a screwdriver we can tell which one is burnt out."

"Oh," the woman said. "In that case, I guess it's all right. You come to see Mr. Farrel, didn't you?"

"Yes." Jordan could see that she was trying to make up her mind whether or not she ought to ask who he was; whether it would be polite.

"Will Mr. Farrel be home soon?" he asked.

"Sometimes he comes right home from the office, and sometimes he doesn't." She answered Jordan's question patiently, as if it had already been asked a great many times. As if it were a foolish question, and one that nobody knew the answer to. "Mostly he doesn't come home till later."

"I see." Jordan turned to Timothy, who was tugging at his sleeve. Together they dragged a straight chair across the room from the desk to the Christmas tree. Jordan balanced himself on the chair and unscrewed the first bulb. Then he looked around for the housekeeper. She was not there any longer. She had gone back to the kitchen. "I may not be able to wait," he said, and handed the little red bulb to Timothy, who was standing below him. When Jordan applied the screwdriver to the socket, nothing happened. The lights did not go on. "It wasn't that one," he said.

Timothy handed the light back to him.

"No, sir," Jordan said, looking down at him thoughtfully. "It certainly wasn't."

Nor was it the second bulb, or the third, or the fourth. All of the lights on the first strand were good, apparently. As Jordan started on the second strand, he asked in what he hoped was a casual way, "Do you like Mrs. Ives?"

"She's all right," Timothy said. And he looked down then, as if Jordan had made a mistake and would after a second realize it. They did not speak for a time, but Jordan went on handing the bulbs to Timothy and testing the sockets with his screwdriver. When Timothy had no bulb to hold, he untwisted the wires with his hands. Quite suddenly, when Jordan came to the third bulb from the end, the whole tree blazed into light.

"It was that one!" he exclaimed, and took the new yellow bulb which Timothy held up to him. There was a moment when the lights went off again, but Jordan screwed the yellow bulb into the socket; then the lights came on and stayed on.

"How's that?" he asked.

"Fine," Timothy said, with the lights shining red and blue on his face.

Jordan stepped down from the chair and surveyed the tree from top to bottom. He could go now. There was no reason for him to stay any longer.

"When you grow up, Timothy," he said, "we'll go into the business." Then he picked his hat up from the arm of the sofa where Timothy had been sitting. "O.K.?"

"O.K.," Timothy said.

"Don't forget, then."

Jordan went out into the front hall and took his scarf from the newel post. He listened for the whir and rumble of the furnace, but this time it was not enough. Now that the Christmas tree was lighted, the house was even more unnaturally quiet. Up and down the street, in other houses, people would be sitting down to dinner, but Mrs. Ives had not yet turned the dining-room light on, and the dining-room table was not even set. It seemed wrong to go away and leave a child alone here, in this soundless house. Timothy was standing in the living room, watching him, and did not appear to be upset. But when he left, Jordan thought—what would happen to Timothy *then?*

He wound the scarf round his throat and held it in place with his chin until he had worked himself into his overcoat. When he had finished and was drawing on his gloves, he said brightly, "Smith and Farrel, Fixers of Plain and Fancy Christmas Trees."

Timothy was looking right at him, but there was no telling whether the boy had heard what he said. It seemed rather as if he hadn't. "Do you have to go?" Timothy said.

"I'm afraid I do." Jordan was about to make up a long, elaborate, and convincing excuse, but there were footsteps outside on the porch, and both of them turned in time to see the door thrown open. A man stood in the doorway, with snow on his shoulders and the evening paper clasped tightly under one arm.

"Jordan," he said, "for Christ's sake!"

"Sure," Jordan said, nodding.

"But I've been looking for you all over town!"

Jordan braced himself as the man caught at him slowly with his eyes, and with his voice, and with his two hands.

"And I've been right here," Jordan said helplessly, "all the time."

1938

OCCURRENCE ON THE SIX-SEVENTEEN

GEORGE SHEPHARD

The six-seventeen for Springwood was waiting in the station last Christmas
Eve. It was longer than usual by several cars, the authorities having foreseen
that a number of men who habitually caught earlier trains would linger this
afternoon at office parties. The car in which I sat was in its usual condition,
though. The spread of evening papers was normal and there were the same
rows of those patient, characteristic commuters' necks that know exactly how
long they must remain pressed against the seat back and are grimly set to endure it.

A number of these necks, mine among them, turned suddenly when a
commotion began at the back of the car. A gentleman was in difficulties
there, attempting to drag a Christmas tree through the door. He appeared
prosperous enough in his gray homburg and chesterfield, but the tree was
obviously a very shoddy specimen. It looked as a tree should look not on
Christmas Eve but a week after New Year's. Very likely it was a relic of an office party—raffled off, perhaps, or just swiped in a moment of bravado by its
present possessor.

The gentleman's efforts caused little excitement in the car. People smiled
knowingly at one another and resumed the reading of their papers. After
considerable tugging, the gentleman managed to get his tree past the door.
As he floundered down the aisle with it, the conductor advanced from the
other end of the car to meet him. "I'm sorry," said the conductor, polite but
brisk, "you can't bring that tree in here."

The gentleman adjusted his hat, which had been pushed over one eye
during his struggles. "This tree is my own property," he said. "You mean to
say I can't carry my own property on this railroad?"

"We can't allow trees. You'll have to leave it behind."

People in the seats nearby were taking an interest and there were some
protests. "Say, wait a minute, there." "What the hell you mean, leave it behind?" "Can't carry a tree on Christmas Eve?"

"I'm sorry, friends," said the conductor. "It's against the rules. We can't have that tree in here."

"Damn the rules," someone said. The protests sounded angrier and the conductor might have found himself in a difficult situation if the gentleman, refusing to take advantage of his support, had not said mildly, "Very well," picked up the tree, and started out with it.

The tree was deposited on the station platform, the conductor vanished toward the rear of the train, and the gentleman came back into the coach, dropped into a seat next to a window, and began to stare moodily at the hat of the man in front of him. It seemed that the incident was closed. But no. In a moment the owner of the tree raised his voice. "I've got a Christmas tree out there they won't let me ride in the train. Anybody want to buy a Christmas tree you can't bring in a train?"

"What do you want for it?" called a brown felt.

"Wha'm I bid?"

"Ten cents."

"Fifteen," offered a derby.

"Twenty."

"Twenty-five."

"I'll give you fifty," cried the brown felt.

"Yours for fifty cents, f.o.b. Hoboken."

"Bring it aboard."

"Can't do that. Not allowed," said the tree's late owner.

"Oh, it's not allowed, eh?" said the new owner. "That certainly is just too bad." He left the car and returned with the tree as the train started. He had two or three assistants—those who had spoken loudest against the conductor. Between them they set the tree up in the aisle directly beneath one of the lights, which it was not quite tall enough to touch.

Under the glare its forlornness was fully evident. The purchaser seemed not very proud of his bargain; he stood looking at it in a discouraged sort of way. "What about this tree, anyway?" he said. "What do you call it? Has it got a name?"

The vendor made no answer. He had gone to sleep.

"No, I suppose it hasn't got a name. What good would a name do it anyway? What this tree needs is tinsel," said the new owner. He looked at the bundles in the baggage racks up and down the car. "Must be some tinsel in all those bundles. Who'll give some tinsel for our little tree?"

There was no doubt that he had the attention and sympathy of the car; everybody was listening, but no one made a move to produce tinsel. However, the man in the derby, who had bid for the tree, began to tear his newspaper into strips lengthwise. He passed a handful of these strips to the owner of the tree. "Here's tinsel," he said. The pair of them set about strewing the scrawny branches with tatters of newsprint. The notion caught on. Half the papers in the car were being torn up and trimmers began to crowd around the tree.

In the midst of this ceremony, the conductor came back through the car. He hesitated by the tree as if uncertain about interfering again. The man in the derby touched his elbow. "It's all right, conductor," he said. "Look here." He pulled out a wallet and showed the conductor something inside the flap.

The conductor grinned. "Oh, certainly it's all right, sir," he said. "Go right ahead." It mattered little to him, I imagine, whether the man in the derby really identified himself as someone of authority or merely showed a driving licence, so long as his own face was saved. He passed on through the car.

The laxness (if it *was* laxness) of the conductor allowed him to escape antagonism, but the performance of the brakeman won positive applause. The brakeman appeared when the tree was already overloaded; he carried a bunch of those colored slips which, if you're not careful, they stick in your hatband. These he had strung together on a bit of twine. Advancing down the aisle, he placed his offering upon the tree and without saying a word retired. At the door he paused and bowed. "Merry Christmas from the Lackawanna Railroad," he said.

It was tacitly admitted that the brakeman's offering completed the trimming of the tree. Nothing more could be added. But the conviviality which the tree had fostered was at flood tide. "How about us giving a Merry Christmas to the Lackawanna?" someone shouted. "No hard feelings toward anyone on Christmas Eve. Come on, boys, let's sing." And they sang, one or two at first, raggedly, but soon a full chorus:

> *Merry Christmas to* you,
> *Merry Christmas to* you,
> *Merry Christmas, Lackawanna,*
> *Merry* Christ*mas to you.*

After that it was only a question of choosing other songs. Some wag started "We Won't Get Home Until Morning" and was hushed. Another hit the popular fancy with "Jingle Bells." Thereafter they worked at the standard Christmas repertoire, whether or not they knew the words—"O Come, All Ye Faithful, la-la la-la laaa-la," "Silent Night," and the rest.

The tree dominated the car. Fully half the passengers were gathered about it and most of the rest had folded their papers and sat leaning over seat backs, singing or at least attending to what went on. Only three or four rockbound spirits continued determinedly to read the day's news.

The party was in full swing when the conductor made his last appearance. "Springwood!" he called this time. "Springwood!" The cry set a long chain of reflexes in motion. One, two, ten, twenty dropped away from the tree; there was a wild flapping of overcoats being donned and bundles descending from the baggage racks. Hatted, coated, and laden, they were lined up at the doors long before the train stopped, as the commuter's custom is.

Last to leave the car, I glanced back and saw the tree abandoned in a loneliness of green plush and glaring light and torn newspapers.

Outside, the travellers by the six-seventeen were marching along the platform and up the stairs to the street level, each, as usual, wrapped tight in his own habit, unseeing and unaware of any mortal in the crowd around.

1939

TREE

For some years, we have been among the many thousands of people who have gone to the Metropolitan Museum at the Christmas season to see a dazzling tree ornamented with eighteenth-century Neapolitan baroque angels, cherubs, and Nativity figures. This year, we decided to get there early to watch the tree being decorated, in the Medieval Sculpture Hall, and to talk with the person who gave the handsome ornaments to the Museum—Loretta Hines Howard. When we arrived, we found that ten large screens had been set up around the tree to conceal the work area from the public. Only the upper half of the tree was visible, and it was covered with angels, stars, and electric candles. Near the very top, about eighteen feet above the floor, Mrs. Howard was perched on an aluminum ladder, finagling a candle into its proper position on a bough. We slipped through a space between the screens and went inside.

All was chaos. Pieces of papier-mâché desert scenery, for the crèche, were lying here and there on sawhorses, cherubs were resting at random on cartons and tables, and electric cables lay in coils and loops on the floor. We looked at the tree—an artificial one, which stands twenty feet high on a red platform three feet high. To our surprise, the bottom half of the tree was utterly nude, consisting merely of a square green trunk. Around the trunk, angels danced in midair, suspended from vertical wires fastened to the platform. Mrs. Howard descended the ladder and greeted us. "Three-ring circus," she said, gazing about at

the disarray. "We've been working for five weeks—two electricians; my assistant, Enrique Espinoza, over there; and myself. We use an artificial tree because of fire regulations. The whole process of ornamenting it is extremely complicated. I'm trying to simplify it, because I don't expect to live forever. I'm sixty-five, and when I'm gone the Metropolitan staff will have to do it *all*." Mrs. Howard, who has fluffy white hair and a peppery, no-nonsense demeanor, was wearing a rumpled blue denim smock, rumpled bluejeans, black moccasins, and bifocals with light-blue frames. Removing the bifocals, she held them about fifteen inches away and examined them. "Dirty," she said. "Can't see a thing."

As she polished them, we asked her where the limbs of the lower half of the tree were. "Over here," she said, leaping around several stacked cartons and digging into a large box in a corner. We followed her, and she handed us a long green bough with a metal hook at one end. "That end goes into the trunk," she said. "The boughs are made of wire and dyed bristles. They look like an explosion of green baby-bottle brushes, don't they?"

We asked Mrs. Howard if she had any favorites among the collection of a hundred and forty Neapolitan figures that she gave to the Metropolitan in 1964.

"I love them all," she said. "I could no more have a favorite than I could have a favorite child. I have, incidentally, four children, nineteen grandchildren, one great-grandchild, and another on the way. My husband, Howell H. Howard, died playing polo at Meadow

Brook in 1937. He was a paper manufacturer. His father had a famous horse called Stagehand, who once beat Seabiscuit in the Santa Anita Handicap. That was interesting, not only because Seabiscuit was hard to beat but because Seabiscuit was owned by a man who was also named Howard—C. S. Howard. No relation to us."

Mrs. Howard dashed away to help Mr. Espinoza untangle a nest of electric cords, and we picked up a book lying nearby—a recently published picture book about Mrs. Howard's collection, with a commentary written by Olga Raggio, a Metropolitan curator of Western European Arts. Leafing through it, we learned that the collection combines two Christmas traditions of ancient origin: the crèche and the German custom of the adorned tree. Both date from the sixteenth century in the forms in which we see them throughout the world today, but their origins are much older. In the Middle Ages, trees were hung with red apples as a symbol of the story of Adam and Eve and the tree in the Garden of Eden. The crèche, as a visual representation of the birth of Christ, can be traced to Nativity scenes on sarcophagi as early as the fourth century. Most of Mrs. Howard's figures came from a famous collection that belonged to the Catello family of Naples. Ranging in height from twelve to fifteen inches, they are quite flexible and can be bent into a variety of positions. Their bodies are made of fibre and wire, their limbs are of excellently carved wood, and their heads and shoulders are sculptured in terra-cotta. Their faces have a variety of exceedingly lifelike ex-

pressions, from serene half smiles on the angels' faces to startled gapes on the shepherds'. Most of them are still wearing their eighteenth-century cloth costumes.

Mrs. Howard whizzed by, and we asked her how she had become a collector. "In 1925, the year I was married, my mother gave me a Christmas present of three figures—Mary, Joseph, and the Infant—which she found in Marshall Field's, the Chicago department store. I'm originally from Chicago; my father was in lumber. Over the years, I collected more and more. One day, Henry Francis Taylor, who used to be the director of the Metropolitan, told me about the great Catello collection, and I began to correspond with the Catello family. It took me three years of correspondence to buy the pieces I wanted; I had to get them to bring down the price. Still I had never met the Catellos, so one day, during a visit to Italy, I went to call on Mr. Catello. Everybody was in mourning. He had died. I asked them what he had died of. They said of joy. They were quite serious. It seems that he had gone to Paris because he had heard that José María Sert, the painter, had a marvellous collection of crèche figures there. But Sert had died, and his widow had died, and Mr. Catello had to search everywhere for the collection. He finally found it in a warehouse. He looked at it, bought it, and expired of joy."

—CONSTANCE FEELEY, 1969

TOKIO CHRISTMAS

MAX HILL

The day of Pearl Harbor, I was given a number, No. 867, and put away in a five-and-a-half-by-nine-foot cell in Sugamo Prison, which the Japanese blandly describe as the Tokio Kochisho, or Tokio Retaining Place. In May, at which time I was still in Sugamo, I was tried and found guilty of sending to the Associated Press, in my capacity as correspondent, stories which, according to the very flattering judge, were "detrimental to Japan's diplomacy." I was sentenced to serve eighteen months, but the sentence was suspended when the United States government insisted that all correspondents be included in the first exchange of nationals, and actually I got out of Sugamo in June, when I was removed to the comparative freedom of an internment camp and then shipped off to New York on the Gripsholm, so my total stay there was six months. Six months in a Tokio retaining place can be tedious.

My cell had cement walls and one tiny barred window. The furnishings were a bed, a washbowl, a toilet, a broom, and two *tatami*, or rice-straw mats. I wasn't permitted to sit or lie on the bed until bedtime, and if I wanted to sit down, I had to sit on the floor or on the toilet. Mostly, I chose the latter. Each day I was awakened at five o'clock. Then I had to sweep my cell and make my bed. At six-thirty a guard brought in breakfast, at eleven o'clock lunch, and at three o'clock supper, all three meals invariably consisting of a bowl of warm water, a bowl of seaweed or turnip-top soup, and a cup of cold boiled rice and barley, mixed. At four o'clock the door of the cell was double-locked for the night, and a little later a bell rang, the signal for prisoners to go to bed. The electric light in the cell was turned on and left on throughout the night, shining down on my face. The temperature in the cell was almost always below freezing; I was sure of that because the water in the basin placed under the defective drain of my washbowl almost always had a coating of ice. It was only in bed that I had any chance of thawing out, if not precisely of getting warm. I spent a good part of my day, therefore, looking forward to four o'clock.

I had been in Sugamo just a few days when I made the unJapanese mistake of trying to keep my feet warm. The Japanese always slip off their shoes before stepping on their *tatami*, and they expect others to do the same. I was more interested in not freezing my feet than in observing this picturesque custom, and often, in crossing my cell, I walked over my *tatami* without removing my shoes. Once, as I was committing this desecration, a gold-toothed guard, padding through the corridor on an inspection tour, caught me. "*Damé*," he growled as he entered the cell. That means "bad." Obviously pleased with the result of his expedition down the drafty corridor, he ordered me to take off my shoes, grabbed them, and departed. I didn't get them back until four months later. In the meantime I had to walk around in my socks. The only advantage of this was that it gave me one more thing to do to occupy my time. In an effort to warm my feet, I could spend many hours sitting on the toilet wiggling my toes.

Otherwise, I had two principal ways of killing time. One was to count the branches on a pine tree that I could see from my window. My count varied between a hundred and fifty and two hundred and was never the same twice in succession. To see the tree at all, however, I had first to kneel on the toilet in an especially awkward position, then push open one side of a frosted-glass panel at the bottom of the window, twist my neck, and peer out with my head way on one side. I was able to frame the entire tree in the small triangle formed by the opening in the window. My other principal occupation was trying to recite the names of the forty-eight states. I kept track of my progress by means of nine counters I had made by breaking up a straw pulled from my broom. For three solid months my total was always forty-seven states, no matter what part of the continent I started with. In my mind I could see the Atlantic coast plainly, so I usually started with the Atlantic states, then moved west by tiers of states, tracing an imaginary map on the wall with my finger. But sometimes I would try a name-by-name cruise through the Great Lakes, or take off from the Pacific Northwest. Whichever gambit I used, the total remained forty-seven. The missing state became an obsession. It disturbed me more than the gold-toothed guard, who always smelled of tobacco and made me long for a cigarette—even a Japanese cigarette, which tastes like the stale hay I smoked as a boy. At the end of the three months the forty-eighth state emerged from the back of my head. It was Mississippi. I felt that remembering it called for some celebration, and drank a toast to Mississippi in cold water.

The acoustics in Sugamo were uncanny. I couldn't even whisper to myself without bringing the guard all the way down from his station at the far end of the corridor to investigate. My counting the branches on the pine tree or naming the states never did get much of a rise out of him, but on one occasion, early in my stay, I did something that really seemed to worry him. It was when I first happened to think of the fact that Christmas was coming. It was the fifteenth of December. Why, I thought, there are only seven more shopping days till Christmas, and I started to laugh. The guard came trotting down to my cell and walked in to see what was up. He found me still laugh-

"Any discount to the trade?"

ing. It was no use trying to explain to him what was so funny, and I didn't say anything. He stood for a while, looking at me with a puzzled expression, then glumly walked away.

My seventeenth day in prison was the day before Christmas. It was particularly cold and particularly gloomy. My household chores were finished early and I couldn't even amuse myself by counting the branches of the tree, for it had snowed the night before and the fluffy flakes obscured their outlines. I spent most of the day sitting on the toilet, wiggling my toes. As usual, I was in bed shortly after four P.M., long before it was technically Christmas Eve. After I had been asleep for about two hours, I heard the clanking of a key in my lock. I sat up. The door creaked open and the gold-toothed guard walked in. He was grinning and carrying a cardboard box about the size of a hatbox. He took the lid off and peeked inside. Coming over to my bed, he bowed low, said, "*Dozo*" ("Please"), and shoved the box into my hands. Inside was an oddly shaped object wrapped in tissue paper. Mighty nice of them, I thought, and I said, "*Dom-arigato*" ("Thank you very much"). I pulled off the tissue paper. Underneath was an artificial Christmas tree about a foot high and set in a little white tub; its stiff green branches were flecked with artificial snow, which glittered in the electric light. Scattered through the package were bits of tinsel and a number of ornaments—a small silver heart, a miniature Santa Claus, a star.

"*Ano-ne*" ("By the way"), the guard said hesitantly. Then, handing me a small slip of white paper, he explained that the tree had been sent to me by the prison officials and that he needed my chop, or mark, on the slip to make it proper for them to take the money for the tree from the cash of mine they had in safekeeping. The tree would cost me, I learned, two yen, or about fifty cents. I put my chop on the slip. I felt sure that the guard had no idea what Christmas was. Where, I nevertheless asked him, did the officials get the tree? It was one of hundreds, he answered, that had been made long ago by prisoners to sell in the United States. I assumed that the war had put an end to that business, and evidently I was the best prospect they had left, maybe the only one.

The guard left me, slamming the door. I got out of bed and knelt down on one of the mats. I set the tree in a corner of the cell and took the ornaments and tinsel out of the box. "Merry Christmas," I said to myself, and began to hang the ornaments and drape the tinsel on the tree.

1942

A COUPLE OF NIGHTS BEFORE CHRISTMAS

J. F. POWERS

In Father Urban's days of glory on the road, it had been his custom when he arrived at a place to attend to the details of billeting first. Early in his career, this had been a matter of self-preservation; in recent years there had been less to worry about. Pastors had put themselves out for Father Urban, not because he represented the Order of St. Clement—which, as a minor-league outfit near the bottom of the standings, didn't open many doors—but because he was famous in his own right, as a preacher. Accidents would happen, though, and if Father Urban chanced to draw a bad bed in a rectory where better ones were to be had, he might mention—his manner was laconic—that he was going to a hotel to sleep. Or if he struck a rectory where the food was *too* bad, he might arrange to eat most of his meals out, sometimes taking the pastor with him—if the fault lay there, rather than with a woman in the kitchen—and thus heaping coals of fire on the man's head. It wasn't that Father Urban had "exaggerated ideas of the material side of life," as one old desert rat of a pastor had tried to tell him. Father Urban could rough it as well as the next one if that was called for, but he saw no merit in encouraging poor hospitality. In a small way, Father Urban had done for the rectories of America what Duncan Hines did for restaurants and motels.

But Father Urban had become too successful for his own good—or so he sized it up—and had aroused jealousies in the Order. This, he believed, was why he had been taken off the road and assigned to St. Clement's Hill, as they were now calling the Order's retreat house near Duesterhaus, Minnesota—and there he had done little. His will, it seemed, had been affected by his transfer and immobilization; he was being made to stand in the corner. His old shock tactics were just not suited to his situation. His mood was strange to him. He didn't like his narrow iron bed at Duesterhaus, and he knew that better beds were to be had even there, but he wasn't doing anything about it, or about the almost total absence of heat in his room.

Father Wilfrid, the rector, was pursuing a strategy that Father Urban understood the reason for—economy—but didn't comprehend in detail. Some rooms were heated not at all, and some only part of the time, depending on the sun and changes in the weather and wind. The dining room was the one place in the big old house where you could really be out of the weather. In the evening, there was a brief interval when the room wasn't occupied. This was after Brother Harold, who did all the dirty work, had retired to the kitchen with the dishes, and the three resident priests had gone their separate ways. (In outer Minnesota, the winters—and the summers, too, with their mosquitoes, deer flies, and no-see-ums—play hell with that traditional feature of life in a religious community, the after-supper stroll.)

One evening late in December, Father Urban had gone up as usual to his cold room to get cigars; Father Wilfrid to his cold office to get cigars; and Father John to the chapel, which was also cold, for a visit to the Blessed Sacrament. (Jack had been assigned to Duesterhaus at the same time as Father Urban, but probably for the opposite reason: lack of success.) Soon the three priests would be together again in the dining room, the heart of the little community at St. Clement's Hill.

The dining room lay directly over the furnace, and was warmed by the kitchen fires and, sometimes, by the afternoon sun. In view of these facts, Father Wilfrid had had the thermostat controlling the furnace moved there. Father Urban had got the impression that Wilf expected to be remembered for this as another man might be remembered for his converts or his work among the poor. "Sure—I could've left it in the office, where it was, and I'd have kept warm," Wilf would say. "But why heat the whole house just to keep one man warm? I'm not the only one."

To this, Father Urban, on his arrival at Duesterhaus, had responded "Good idea," or something like that, but he had since become aware of a serious flaw in Wilf's argument, and, hearing Wilf on the subject nowadays,

Father Urban would say to himself, "Yes, and if he'd left it where it was, *we* might've kept warm, too—in our rooms and in chapel."

Visitors were sure to hear about the moving of the thermostat, and even when the four Clementines were sitting around by themselves, Wilf would work it into the conversation. He might break the silence of the evening with it, as if he had intuitive knowledge that one of those under him was about to entertain a doubt as to his fitness for the rector's job. Father John seldom complained, and was not the kind of man, anyway, that Wilf had to trouble himself about, and Brother Harold, whatever he might think—and he wasn't so dumb—was loyal to the rector, so it was probably for Father Urban's benefit that Wilf alluded to the moving of the thermostat. Father Urban reflected that he might indeed lack the virtues of Brother Harold and Jack, but what were virtues in them would be something else again in a man of more vision. Weakness, he thought. He regarded cheeseparing and ineptitude as the special vices of the Clementine Order, and did not suffer them gladly.

Father Urban was thinking along these familiar lines when he entered the dining room for the evening. He went over to the Christmas tree and plugged in the cord, which Wilf, doubtless, had been the one to pull out a few minutes earlier. The tree bloomed—red, green, blue, and yellow—in only eight places. Father Urban plugged in the electrified crib that stood under the tree, and slowly oxen, sheep, and shepherds appeared and disappeared, going around and around the Holy Family and the Three Kings. Maybe the animals and shepherds were, as Jack said, a little like ducks in a shooting gallery, but Father Urban had never before seen a crib like this one, nor had any of the others. The crib had been sent by Billy Cosgrove, one of Father Urban's hottest "connections" back in Chicago. In the short time they'd known each other, Billy, who was in real estate, had provided the Order with an excellent address (offices and living quarters) on the Near North Side, and had shown signs of being just what the Clementines needed—a really big benefactor. He had taken Father Urban's transfer badly, calling it "one hell of a way to run a railroad," and what could perhaps have been a mighty river flowing to the whole Order's benefit had been reduced to a trickle of small gifts. Billy was responsible for the large hamper of food and liquor that was also under the tree.

There were many presents there, most of them sent by Father Urban's admirers all over the country, and from among them he had selected his gifts to Jack, Wilf, and Brother Harold. In other years, at the Novitiate of the Order, near Chicago, where he had usually spent Christmas, Father Urban had always received gifts enough to go around, and much appreciated they were by those to whom he passed them on. Christmas just wouldn't be the same at the Novitiate with Father Urban gone. At Duesterhaus, with only the four of them there, Father Urban was being lavish; most of what he got was junk, of course, but Jack, Wilf, and Brother Harold would all be wearing, eating, smoking, or otherwise using it in the months ahead.

Nearly all the packages had been forwarded from the Novitiate, for few of Father Urban's admirers knew his present whereabouts. In his Christmas cards, he had made no mention of his new assignment; it would just seem that he had mailed his cards from some stopping-off place, as he often had in the past. There was no point in going into the details of his life with everybody who sent him a card or a gift, and maybe in another year he'd be back on the road, where he belonged. And, anyway, he was trying not to think about his hard luck during the Christmas season.

Father Urban liked Christmas—receiving and giving, and having a tree. Until that morning, however, there had been no tree, though the woods were full of them. There would not have been one then, either—a real one—if Father Urban hadn't acted. Father Urban, when he saw Wilf removing a little wire-and-paper one (apparently the traditional tree at Duesterhaus) from a box, had taken to the woods with an axe. He had operated on the old seminary principle of don't-ask-unless-you-can-take-no-for-an-answer. Once the deed was done, what could Wilf say? When Father Urban came into the dining room with his tree, a seven-footer, Wilf had said "Well!" but he hadn't gone on. Maybe he'd recognized only that it was too late to do anything about the tree, and maybe he'd recognized more. "Makes mine look sick," he had said eventually, surrendering the single cord of lights. The question was, of course, whether Wilf had disposed of the artificial tree or had stored it away for another year. But to Father Urban, who had expected real trouble, the incident was hopeful.

"Balsam," Wilf said now, entering the dining room. "You wouldn't get that nice clean smell with spruce. Cigar?"

"I've got one here somewhere," Father Urban said. He wasn't so hard up yet that he had to accept one of Wilf's cigars, but he had been at Duesterhaus long enough to know that it was a mistake to offer one of his to Wilf. There was a box of cigars waiting under the tree for Wilf, from Father Urban—not the kind Father Urban could use but several cuts above what Wilf ordinarily smoked and was in the act of touching off.

"Nice," Wilf said through the smoke.

Father Urban looked sharply at Wilf, but he was referring to the electrified crib. "Yes," Father Urban said. "I wonder where Billy got it."

"I wonder if it shouldn't be in the chapel," Wilf said. "It and the tree."

Father Urban moved around to the other side of the tree, controlling himself. He wanted the tree to be where he could enjoy it.

"I guess one tree wouldn't be enough in the chapel," Wilf said.

Father Urban said, "That's right." Wilf had anticipated what would have been his first argument—that they ought to have a number of trees in the chapel if they were going to have any at all.

"Of course, if we had retreatants here now we'd need trees there," Wilf said.

"Oh, yes," said Father Urban. Who ever heard of retreatants at Christmas? The trees were safe in the woods, and Wilf knew it.

"I guess the good Lord will understand," Wilf said, and went to his chair.

"Who better?" said Father Urban. The good Lord knew what it was like at Duesterhaus. And there were others who knew. When Father Urban had been at Duesterhaus a week or so, he had received a bogus CARE package.

"Very funny," Wilf had said at the time. "You know who did it, don't you?"

"No." Apparently Wilf regarded the package itself as legitimate, so Father Urban had said nothing to spoil the illusion.

"Well, if you don't know, I won't tell you," Wilf had said.

Father Urban, going by things that had been said before, guessed that Father Louis had sent the package. Father Louis had done time under Wilf at Duesterhaus, was one of Father Urban's few friends in the Order, and—knowing Father Urban and knowing Duesterhaus—had probably thought such a joke would be worth the trouble.

Jack, usually the last of the three priests to arrive for the long evening in the dining room, came in and stood by the tree. Father Urban toyed with the idea of waiting him out, making him ask for what he wanted. Jack wouldn't ask, though, and he wouldn't use his eyes on you, like a dog, though that was what he was like—a dog that always wanted you to go for a walk. In Jack's case, it was checkers.

Father Urban decided to get it over with. Since he had to play, he would seem to do so willingly. "Care for a game?" he inquired. "Or don't you?" He was being cruel to Jack, in a mild sort of way, making it harder for him just when the end was in view. Father Urban felt justified because Jack didn't realize he was being teased, and he ought to have to pay in some way for being such a nuisance about checkers.

"Whatever you say, Urban."

"Well, frankly, I'd like to play."

"Good," Jack said.

When they had first got out the board, several weeks back, Wilf had played, but either he didn't like the game or he didn't think it looked good for him to be beaten, as he was by Jack, and he no longer played. He sat in his chair, with his breviary on the table beside him, and read the paper. If asked to play, he'd answer, "I have some office to say." Later, asked again and still reading the paper, he'd say, "Maybe after a while." You understood by now that he had some office to say.

For Father Urban, the really annoying thing about this ruse was that it apparently went down with Jack. Or maybe it didn't, and Jack just preferred playing with Father Urban. This was a pleasing thought to Father Urban, but

"It just seems ridiculous to get rid of it now, with Christmas only a couple of months away."

ROOSEVELT SPRUCE

There was such a to-do last week about Elliott Roosevelt's Christmas trees that we thought we ought to get in on it, so we marched down to the nearest of the vacant lots he rented briefly as sales places in this city. The trees, as perhaps everyone knows, were planted ten years ago by Elliott's father, are selling at a top price of $1.95, and have been maligned by several competitors as being early needle-droppers and not really Christmas trees anyhow but, to employ a term heretofore unused in local conifer circles, skunk spruce. Luckily, we found Mr. Roosevelt himself at the lot. We asked him first about the skunk-spruce allegation. "Look," he said, "our trees are Norway spruce and white spruce, mostly Norway. The original Christmas trees in Germany, where Christmas trees originated, were Norway spruce. All over Europe today, Norway spruce is still the traditional Christmas tree. That hundred-foot tree at Rockefeller Center is a Norway. What's happened in the New York market is this: Most of the dealers here get their trees from Canada, Maine, Vermont, and New Hampshire. They used to get spruce that had been cut in September or October and then tightly bundled. Well, if a Norway's packed like that, it will dry out in thirty days. So the local dealers switched mostly to balsam, which holds its sap longer. But *our* spruce, at Hyde Park, aren't cut before December 1st and aren't jammed together, and we've had tests made showing that you can keep one of them in a house for a month and a half without any appreciable loss of needles. As for our trees having a skunklike odor—well, smell one." We did. Smelled like a Christmas tree.

This is Mr. Roosevelt's second year in the Christmas-tree business. (His mother is a silent but enthusiastic partner in the tree venture.) Last season, he told us, he sold nearly twenty thousand trees, in Poughkeepsie and Hyde Park. This year, he expects to sell sixty-five thousand spruce—fifty thousand here and the remainder upstate, in Hyde Park, Poughkeepsie, Buffalo, Syracuse, Schenectady, and Tonawanda. His local lots, which he leased for two weeks, are open twenty-four hours a day, are kept stocked by trucks that leave Hyde Park at two-hour intervals, and are

only up to a point. Even if he didn't discover something better to do in the long evenings, he could just get tired of checkers, couldn't he? The only light in the dining room came from the chandelier, by which he and Jack played checkers at the card table and Wilf read the paper hour after hour. Father Urban wished that it were possible to spend more time in his room—awake, that is. It was cold there—cold beyond endurance, to say nothing of comfort—and Father Urban didn't want to fall into the practice of going to bed directly after supper. It just wouldn't look right, and he might ruin his health—or if not that, exactly, so habituate his body and mind to sleep that manned by twenty-five young men and women, more than half of whom are actors recruited for the occasion by a theatrical friend of Faye Emerson, who is, of course, Mrs. Elliott Roosevelt. Members of the cast of salesmen have appeared in "Command Decision," "Dream Girl," the Michael Redgrave "Macbeth," and "Hope Is the Thing with Feathers." We spoke to one of the actors, who said that his present job, entailing, as it does, a good deal of exposure to fresh air, is not only remunerative but astonishingly bracing. Another salesman, or saleswoman, is a young lady who was Miss Emerson's backstage maid during the recent Broadway run of "The Play's the Thing."

Some of the sales staff are on the lookout for people who buy a lot of trees, since there is a rumor that some competitors have been purchasing them and reselling them at around a dollar a foot. Elliott doubts that there is anything to the report, because trees sell wholesale for less than he is charging retail. He has himself bought five carloads wholesale, or around twelve thousand trees. "The average dealer," he told us in explanation of this trans-action, "figures he's lucky if he can sell ten per cent of his trees up to the last week before Christmas. He counts on doing ninety per cent of his business the final week. Now, I sold thirty per cent of all my spruce by the sixteenth, and on that basis I figured I might run out of trees by the twenty-second, so I went in the open market and picked up some balsam. I'll let them go at my regular prices and still make a good profit on them. I've had some pretty nasty letters from other dealers," he continued. "They claim it's unfair for me to undersell them. Well, this Christmas-tree business has always been a bonanza, a racket, and, the way I look at it, I'm being fair to the customers, who, after all, vastly outnumber the dealers. Why, I'll bet I've spoken to five hundred people who've told me they never could afford a tree before. By the way, I have a hunch that there's going to be a last-minute shortage of trees around town this year and that by Christmas Eve there'll be a tremendous jump in prices—except for mine, that is. Care to look at a nice six-footer for only a dollar seventy-five?"

—ROBERT A. SIMON AND
E. J. KAHN, JR., 1948

he'd *never* be any good after supper. This could seriously impair his usefulness if he ever left Duesterhaus.

"Hey, take it easy!" said Father Urban. Jack's right leg, which had a tendency to vibrate during play, had suddenly swung out of control, jarring the card table. And now, with his leg still going, Jack was inching forward, advancing in his chair as his checkers advanced on the board. When he moved, his fingers flew off his men as if he were a virtuoso of the piano. He made one more move and sat back. Sometimes Father Urban could tell more about the game from Jack's position in the chair than from the checkers on the board. Usually, when Jack retreated in his chair, it meant that the turning point had been reached. This time, though, it seemed to Father Urban that Jack was a little premature. Father Urban made one of his unorthodox moves. It then became clear to him that the decisive action had already taken place on another part of the board and that the game was all but over. They played it out, of course, and Father Urban took his defeat gracefully. It was just a game, wasn't it? And he didn't blame Jack for getting excited over checkers. What else, when you got right down to it, could Jack do well? "Yes, I think this is your game," Father Urban said.

He watched Jack setting up for the next one. Poor Jack! He had once had something of a reputation as a writer, but there hadn't been a new pamphlet from him in twenty years. In that time, the Order had employed him first as a teacher and then as a preacher, like Father Urban, on the road. Jack had just got by, even by Clementine standards. It really came down to checkers for Jack. Of course, his spiritual life was good.

"What do you know about this game chess?" Jack asked.

"I doubt that you'd do so well at chess," Father Urban said, thinking *he* would be better at that.

"Chess is a very old game," Wilf informed them, from his chair.

Father Urban looked over at Wilf in annoyance. A remark like that was actually meant to be instructive.

"Ever play it?" Jack asked.

"No, and I don't intend to," said Father Urban.

"Well, we don't have a board," Jack said, as if to reassure him.

From the other side of the newspaper, which cloistered him from them but did nothing of the sort for them, Wilf said, "Your board's the same, but your counters are different."

"Is that *so?*" said Father Urban.

"Oh, yes. Altogether different. It's a different game," said Wilf.

That was the kind of thing that made Father Urban want to *fight*. "I'd say the principle is the same," he said.

There was a slight delay before Wilf's reply was transmitted over the paper wall. "*I'd* say the principle is the same in all games."

Father Urban couldn't think of an exception to this rule. He moved a checker—into danger, he saw too late. He turned again to Wilf, as to a lesser tormentor, and noted the full-page "Season's Greetings" advertisement by the merchants of Minneapolis. It had candles and reindeer in it; no camels, no crib. Even about Christmas, Father Urban and Wilf had differed. Fire and water. Father Urban ordinarily thought of himself as the fire, but in the matter of Christmas observances he had been the water.

Wilf had been active locally in a crusade to decommercialize Christmas. This Wilf and his collaborators hoped to do by getting people to go to church more and by having merchants emphasize the true meaning of Christmas in their store windows and advertising. Signs and slogans played a big part in the crusade, as they did in Wilf's own life.

For Wilf to associate with a lot of screwballs was one thing, Father Urban believed, but it was something else again for Wilf to associate the poor Order of St. Clement and the struggling retreat foundation near Duesterhaus with a dubious cause. Father Urban believed that the avowed ideals behind the crusade were best left to the proper authorities; if these ideals deserved dissemination, the hierarchy would know it, and whatever was done, or not done, should be done under their auspices. If Wilf had expected Father Urban and Jack to follow in his steps, he must be badly disappointed. They had taken no part in the crusade. For this reason, perhaps, it had never been discussed at Duesterhaus. Father Urban had stayed clear of the whole business until the very last.

But he had recently gone to Olympe, a town of fifteen thousand, to address the Lions Club on another subject, and there, during the question period, he had been asked about the crusade. In reply, he had said that he found Christmas as it was celebrated nowadays still pretty much to his liking. He felt that merchants, to mention only one group, were doing honor in the way best suited to them and their talents. He cited the example, from literature, of the mute tumbler whose prayer took the form of acrobatics before the altar of Our Lady.

This had gone over very well with Father Urban's commercial audience.

MAKE YOUR OWN

CHRISTMAS TREE
You'll need:
· An old broom
· Lots of imagination

ORNAMENTS
You'll need:
· Shredded wheat
· Plenty of nerve

GIFT WRAP
You'll need:
· Newspaper
· Excellent gifts

R. Chast

He had been asked, however, if his position wasn't the opposite of that held by the man in charge of St. Clement's Hill—and if so, how come? Father Urban had got out of this rather nicely by saying that what the questioner referred to as his position was hardly a position; it was simply an *opinion*, as, indeed, was the contrary view. There had always been differences of opinion in the Church, and, indeed, such could occur in any organization, and perhaps even in the best-run families, between husband and wife—so he had been told.

This had got him a laugh. Then, with the audience on his side, he had become serious. He was not saying that differences of opinion were a good thing in themselves, but he did think there was much to be said for taking them for what they were—healthy manifestations of the democratic process. If his audience thought the difference of opinion in question was bad, they should hear of some of the others that arose between "the man in charge" and himself. For example, the foundation had been known as the Retreathouse of the Order of St. Clement, and when they were renaming the place—which he hoped his audience, Catholic or not, would find time to visit—the man in charge had been in favor of calling it Mount St. Clement, whereas Father Urban had wanted it to be St. Clement's Hill, and they had called it the latter. Here Father Urban did a double take and said, "I wonder how *that* happened!"

They had loved him in Olympe. He had sunk his teeth into a real audience again, and it had tasted good to him after more than a month of confinement at Duesterhaus. This was the sort of thing that had kept him going in the past. At Duesterhaus, without it, he would waste away, he feared. But oh, he had checked Wilf's fire, and, what was more important, he had taken the heat off the Order—off St. Clement's Hill. In fact, he had put the place on the map for a lot of people who mattered in the area. Unfortunately, although his remarks about Christmas were fully reported in the Olympe daily paper and reprinted in the Duesterhaus weekly, Father Urban hadn't been picked up by the Twin Cities papers, in one of which Wilf had been described as a purist about Christmas, the scourge of Santa Claus and all his works. Father Urban sent Billy Cosgrove the accounts from the Olympe and Duesterhaus papers—just for the laughs, he said—but in truth he was rather pleased with his remarks and imagined that Billy would be.

Jack was setting up the board for another game.

"Say," said Father Urban, and, having said that much, didn't know how to go on. Luckily, Brother Harold entered the dining room, his kitchen chores completed. "Say, maybe Brother, here, would like to take my place," Father Urban said.

"No, Brother's got his work to do," Wilf said.

"I thought so," said Father Urban.

He watched Brother Harold, who was studying showcard painting by mail, go over to the sideboard and get out his equipment. His work hung over every door—literally every door—in the house: "CLOSET," "TOILET," "ATTIC," "ROOT CELLAR," and so on. He had labored all through the autumn on signs for Wilf's crusade, and he was now working on a commission from Wilf's brother, who ran a variety store in Berwyn, Illinois. Brother Harold hoped to break into the sacred-art field later on. Wilf had promised him the chapel when he was ready for it.

"If you'd rather not play," Jack said to Father Urban.

"Not at all. I just thought I'd give somebody else a chance. Go ahead."

"Go first?"

"Why should I go first? You won the last game, didn't you? The one who wins goes first. Let's play the game." Father Urban was sore. It was getting pretty bad when Jack, of all people, could condescend to him, and when it was assumed by everyone that he had nothing better to do with his time than play checkers—unlike Wilf, with his paper, and Brother Harold, with his work. It was only out of consideration for Jack that Father Urban played checkers at all. He didn't like the game, and he wasn't much good at it—

though this was maybe the fault of the game itself. He was suspicious of checkers as a game. He wondered if its complexity might not be an illusion, if, in fact, there was much more to checkers than there was to ticktacktoe, and if Jack (because he got to move first each time, and made no mistakes) could ever be beaten again.

A few minutes later, Jack suddenly sat back in his chair, abandoning the game. He said that a long-distance call for Wilf had come in that afternoon. The caller had been a reporter. For Father Urban, this was the absolute limit; he couldn't recall anything like this—Jack talking to someone else in the room while a game was in progress.

"From the Twin Cities?" Wilf asked. He had let down the wall, the better to talk to Jack.

"Yes, but I don't remember which paper," Jack said.

"Did he say he'd call again?" Wilf asked.

"No, he didn't."

"And probably won't now," Wilf said. "Too late. Probably had to make his deadline."

"I'm sorry," Jack said.

"Not your fault," Wilf said, and to Father Urban he didn't seem as disappointed as he should have been at missing a call from a reporter.

Jack was worried. "I told the operator you weren't here, but this fellow told her he'd speak to anybody."

"Sounds like a deadline to me," Wilf said. He either was or thought he was familiar with newspaper parlance and practice. "What'd the fellow want—another statement on the campaign?"

"Yes," Jack said. "I didn't have anything to say. I realize now the call was simply a waste of the paper's money."

Wilf nodded gravely. "I only hope the fellow didn't take it amiss."

"He didn't seem to," Jack said.

"I hope not," said Wilf. He put up the wall again. "You never know when we'll need those fellows in our work."

Here Father Urban—who felt Wilf had implied that if Jack had seen fit to make a statement it would have been in support of Wilf's cause—intervened. "In my opinion, Jack did the right thing," he said. "He didn't have anything to say, so he didn't say anything. *I'd* say you can do a lot worse than that."

Wilf made no reply. And Father Urban believed he knew why. He believed that Wilf wanted out of the crusade but had seen no honorable way out until Father Urban spoke to the Lions. Wilf, he thought, now realized that by accepting Father Urban's view (the essence of which was charity, rather than holier-than-thou singularity) he would not be going back on his cause but going beyond it, and so, in a larger sense, on with it. Wilf, whether he liked it or not, had had a lesson from Father Urban in what the Episcopalians called churchmanship.

"Take your time," Father Urban said to Jack, who was meditating his next move, and stood up to stretch. He looked at the tree and then went over to it and squatted down. There was something wrong. The inside of the stable was rather dim, because Father Urban had chosen to illuminate it with a dim blue bulb, but he could see that the bambino wasn't in its place. It hadn't fallen out of bed from the vibration of the turntable. It wasn't lying on the floor of the stable. The bambino was gone.

Hearing the paper crackle in Wilf's hands, Father Urban turned around—just too late, he thought, to catch Wilf observing him. Father Urban stood up. "I don't think that's funny," he said. Jack looked up from the checkers. Brother Harold, at the dining-room table, glanced up from his work. "The bambino isn't in the crib," Father Urban explained.

Jack came over to the tree and got down on all fours. He started to put his hand inside the crib.

"Look out!" Father Urban said—barely in time, for Jack had his hand in the way of the moving animals and shepherds. "You can see he's not there. You don't have to go poking around. He's just not *there*—and I want to know why."

Brother Harold bent to his work. Wilf rattled his paper, taking a fresh grip on it, and settled deeper in his chair. He sent a message over the wall to them: "*He's not born yet!*"

Father Urban had anticipated this answer, and was not amused. Nor, apparently, was Jack. Stiff in his joints, he was slowly rising from the floor, rearing up the last few inches to more than his full height, then settling down to

Dec. 14, 1981   THE   Price $1.25
NEW YORKER

it. He made his way back to his chair and checkers. He looked worried, as well he might; Jack hated trouble.

Father Urban stood his ground, by the tree. "All right, Father," he said. "You've made your point." His tone was threatening—the undisguised, true voice of his feelings.

Wilf was silent and invisible. Father Urban wavered. Should he make a stand? "It's my crib," he could say. Or should he go off to bed? He glanced at Jack, who was staring down at the checkers. Why didn't Jack say something? Jack was chicken. Father Urban glanced over at Brother Harold. He felt that Brother Harold was against him.

He went to his chair and sat down. He now knew what he had to do—*nothing*. It wasn't necessary to make a stand or to go off in a huff. He had Wilf where he wanted him. As long as the situation remained unchanged, each passing moment would redound to Father Urban's credit and to Wilf's shame. It was Wilf's move.

But it was Father Urban's move in the other game—the one he was playing with Jack—and he made it: a bad one. Jack, of course, showed him no mercy. Father Urban sniffed. He wondered if Jack's whole personality might not have been different—aggressive—if checkers had not become his only accomplishment. Jack certainly got back at the world in checkers.

Something was coming over the wall: "Hospital nun I once knew in Omaha, she used to take all the baby Jesuses out of the cribs. You know—every floor had its tree and crib. She put them all back on Christmas morning."

Not good enough, Wilf, thought Father Urban, holding to his strategy of silence. He had Jack guessing, too. Jack still expected him to fly off the handle. Jack's right leg had stopped vibrating.

More was coming over the wall: "It focussed people's attention on the real significance of Christmas. The idea of *waiting,* if you know what I mean."

Jack dutifully faced the wall while Wilf spoke, but he didn't comment. Father Urban's eyes were on the checkers.

"It's still Advent," Wilf murmured, turning a page.

Father Urban sensed that Wilf, turning the page, had stolen a look at him. Jack cleared his throat and, in a tone even more timid than was customary with him, said, "I see what you mean, Father, and I grant there's a lot in what you say. But I've been wondering if the shepherds themselves should be present yet. Or even Mary and Joseph. In the attitudes we see them in, I mean. And the Three Kings. The animals—yes, they would be there, of course. Not running around in circles, though, as they are in this particular crib."

"He's right!" Wilf cried.

He had thrown down the paper and was on his feet; he was confessing the error as his, but not *all* his. He offered no apology to Father Urban, and thereby indicted him—made it appear that, on the authority of Jack's sound doctrine, they had both been wrong, and that he, at least, was ready to admit it. That was the impression Wilf was giving, and it infuriated Father Urban. He had come a long, long way. He who had preached to the world, and, you might say, won, now contended with fools in the wilderness, and lost. What star had led him to this?

He watched Wilf go over to the crib, not sure what the man would do next but determined to stop him if he laid a finger on the other figures. When this happened, Father Urban would make the stand he should have made earlier. Wilf, however, was taking the bambino out of his pocket. He disconnected the crib, knelt, and extended his hand to put the bambino back in the simulated straw.

This was the moment, the move, that Father Urban had been waiting for. "*Thanks*" was all he'd say. "*Thanks*" said as Father Urban could say it would be enough to show that he considered that Wilf had bowed to him. Doubtless Jack expected Father Urban to do something of the sort.

But then Father Urban didn't take the opportunity, after all. He let it pass. He decided that if Wilf would just leave it at that, so would he. He would have taken great pleasure in asserting himself, in demanding and getting simple justice, but he was gaining more this way. And wasn't that what it all came down to? Christmas meant peace—not to men but to men of good will. It was hard, though—very hard—to see someone like Wilf having it both ways, and at Father Urban's expense.

Wilf, having restored the bambino to the straw, plugged in the circuit that lit the blue bulb and started up the animals and shepherds, and then he went back to his chair. He picked up the paper, and, boldly meeting Father Urban's gaze, he said, "Just shows how wrong we can be sometimes."

We! This was too much for Father Urban's good will. There were worse things than war. He glared at Jack—the peacemaker, who looked at him now—staring Jack down, his eyes following Jack's back to the checkerboard. There he saw a surprising opportunity, and he decided to deal with Jack first. With his only king, Father Urban jumped this way and that, taking a dreadful toll. He had won the game.

"Why didn't I see that!" From the way Jack said it, Father Urban knew that Jack had seen it all, had offered himself and his checkers for sacrifice. Thereupon the desire to deal with Wilf died in Father Urban.

Father Urban, and perhaps Wilf, too, sensed the rare peace now reigning among them, but Jack rejoiced in it visibly. Still, a moment later, it was Jack who broke the spell. "You know, Urban, I don't feel right about those animals," he said—not, Father Urban knew, to be critical but just to be saying something. For a moment, they had all been lifted up, and this was Jack's way of letting them down lightly to earth. "I've always understood that what heat there was at Bethlehem came from the animals. By rights, they should be closer to the Holy Family. Of course, I realize that's impossible in this particular case."

Father Urban looked over at the tree, at the hamper of food and liquor. "Let's open one of Billy's bottles," he said.

1957

christmas
CAROLS

CHRISTMAS WEEK

PARKE CUMMINGS

When saplings pass for Christmas trees,
   And glowing bulbs of red and green
Bedeck the Strands and Rivolis,
   And here and there a wreath is seen,

When everywhere Salvation Nells
   To passers-by their carols sing,
And rub their hands and toll their bells,
   While castanets with quarters ring,

When theatres proffer matinées
   Throughout the week, and actors groan,
And reminisce of better days,
   And weaklings dread to shop alone,

When markets teem with greens and meat,
   Their floors bestrewn with sawdust clean,
And office-boys are swift and neat,
   And messengers alert and keen,

When bankers quote the Golden Rule,
   And visitors enjoyment seek,
And lads and maids are home from school,
   New York's engulfed in Christmas week.

                  1926

CHRISTMAS EVE
(AUSTRALIA, 1943)

KARL J. SHAPIRO

The wind blows hot. English and foreign birds
And insects different as their fish excite
The would-be calm. The usual flocks and herds
Parade in permanent quiet out of sight,
And there one crystal like a grain of light
Sticks in the crucible of day and cools.
A cloud burnt to a crisp at some great height
Sips at the dark condensing in deep pools.

I smoke and read my Bible and chew gum,
Thinking of Christ and Christmas of last year,
And what those quizzical soldiers standing near
Ask of the war and Christmases to come,
And, sick of causes and the tremendous blame,
Curse lightly and pronounce Your serious name.

1943

"Fifty-ninth Street, Columbus Circle. Change for the B, D, and uptown
express. Step lively, watch the closing doors, and once the train is in motion
start singing 'Good King Wenceslas.'"

A CHRISTMAS CAROL

JOHN CIARDI

The stores wore Christmas perfectly
With little bells to ring for sales.
In neon, the Nativity
Proclaimed the spirit never fails.
Accessory to Monsieur's paunch,
Madame's embezzled look
Harassed the velvet screen where Punch
(Watched by wide-eyed kids) forsook
Judy. Forced to abdicate,
She did a wonderful children's trick
And disappeared in billingsgate
Like a chattering monkey-on-a-stick,
And reappeared (gift-wrapped) to be
The nephew on the itemized list.
Monsieur, impatient, turned to flee,
But Madame had him by the wrist:
"Three more, my dear, and we are done.
Now, please be patient." Box by box,
The puppets waited one by one:
Judy next to Goldilocks,
Pluto by Pinocchio,
Mickey next to Jack-Be-Quick.
Neon, pink upon the snow,
Made of every flake a wick
Till the last item itemized
By Madame, and the little bells,
Collateral to the surprised
Morning look of boys and girls,
Made carols on the children's air
And brought a smile to Tiny Tim
And to Madame and to Monsieur,
Making a sudden light in her,

Ten years' difference in him,
And so much difference in me
I'm ready to forgive you all
For what you'll turn around and be,
Starting at nine the usual
Morning after memory.

1946

CHRISTMAS EVE

JOHN CIARDI

Salvation's angel in a tree
Stared out at Blake, and stares at me
From zodiacs of colored bells,
And colored lights, and lighted shells,
A cherub's face above a sheet:
No arms, no torso, and no feet,
But winged and wired against the Fall,
And a paper halo over all—
A nineteen-hundred-year-old doll
In a drying tree. What does it see?
The house is sleeping; there's only me
In the cellophane snow by the lethal toys
That wait all night for the eager boys:
Metal soldiers, an Indian suit,
Raider's tools, and gunner's loot.
I mash my cigarette, and good night,
Turn off the angel and the light
On a single switch. The children toss
In excited sleep. Alone in the house,
I feel the old, confusing wind
Shake the dark tree and shake my mind,
Hearing tomorrow rattle and bang

Louder than all the angels sang.
By feel, I lower the thermostat
And pick my way through a creaking flat.
The demon children, the angel doll,
Sleep in two darks off one dark hall.
I move through darkness memorized,
Feeling for doors. One half-surprised
Wish stays lit inside my head.
I leave it on and go to bed.

1947

WHAT EVERY WOMAN KNOWS

PHYLLIS McGINLEY

When little boys are able
    To comprehend the flaws
In their December fable
    And part with Santa Claus,
Although I do not think they grieve,
How burningly they disbelieve!

They cannot wait, they cannot rest
For knowledge nibbling at the breast.
They cannot rest, they cannot wait
To set conniving parents straight.

Branding that comrade as a dunce
Who trusts the Saint they trusted once,
With rude guffaw and facial spasm
They publish their iconoclasm,
And find particularly shocking
The thought of hanging up a stocking.

But little girls (no blinder
   When faced by mortal fact)
Are cleverer and kinder
   And brimming full of tact.
The knowingness of little girls
Is hidden underneath their curls.

Obligingly, since parents fancy
The season's tinsel necromancy,
They take some pains to make pretense
Of duped and eager Innocence.

Agnostics born but Bernhardts bred,
They hang the stocking by the bed,
Listen for bells, and please their bette
By writing Kringle lengthy letters,
Only too well aware the fruit
Is shinier plunder, richer loot.

For little boys are rancorous
   When robbed of any myth,
And spiteful and cantankerous
   To all their kin and kith.
But little girls who draw conclusions
Make profit of their lost illusions.

1948

CHRISTMAS FAMILY REUNION

PETER DE VRIES

Since last the tutelary hearth
Has seen this bursting pod of kin,

I've thought how good the family mold,
How solid and how genuine.

Now once again the aunts are here,
The uncles, sisters, brothers,
With candy in the children's hair,
The grownups in each other's.

There's talk of saving room for pie;
Grandma discusses her neuralgia.
I long for time to pass so I
Can think of all this with nostalgia.

1949

LANDSCAPE OF THE STAR

ADRIENNE RICH

The silence of the year. This hour the streets
Lie empty, and the clash of bells is scattered
Out to the edge of stars. I heard them tell
Morning's first change and clang the people home
From crèche and scented aisle. Come home, come home,
I heard the bells of Christmas call and die.

This Christmas morning in the stony streets
Of an unaccustomed city, where the gas
Quivers against the darkly shuttered walls,
I walk, my breath a veil upon the cold,
No longer sick for home or hunted down
By faces loved, by gate or sill or tree
That once I used to wreathe in red and silver
Under the splintered incense of the fir.

I think of those inscrutables who toiled,
Heavy and brooding in their camel train,
Across the blue-wrapped stretches: home behind,
Kingdoms departed from, the solemn journey
Their only residence; the starlit hour,
The landscape of the star, their time and place.

O to be one of them, and feel the sway
Of rocking camel through the Judaean sand—
Ride, wrapped in swathes of damask and of silk,
Hear the faint ring of jewel in silver mesh
Starring the silence of the plain, and hold
With rigid fingers curved as in oblation
The golden jar of myrrh against the knees.

To ride thus, bearing gifts to a strange land,
To a strange king, nor think of fear and envy,
Being so bemused by starlight of one star,
The long unbroken journey, that all questions
Sink like the lesser lights behind the hills;
Think neither of the end in sight nor all
That lies behind, but dreamlessly to ride,
Traveller at one with travelled countryside.

How else, since for those Magi and their train
The palaces behind have ceased to be
Home, and the home they travel toward is still
But rumor stoking fear in Herod's brain?
What else for them but this, since nevermore
Can courts and states receive them as they were,
Nor have the trampled earth, the roof of straw
Received the kings as they are yet to be?

The bells are silent, silenced in my mind
As on the dark. I walk, a foreigner,
Upon this night that calls all travellers home,

The prodigal forgiven, and the breach
Mended for this one feast. Yet all are strange
To their own ends, and their beginnings now
Cannot contain them. Once-familiar speech
Babbles in wayward dialect of a dream.

Our gifts shall bring us home—not to beginnings
Nor always to the destination named
Upon our setting forth. Our gifts compel,
Master our ways, and lead us in the end
Where we are most ourselves, whether at last
To Solomon's gaze or Sheba's silken knees
Or winter pastures underneath a star,
Where angels spring like starlight in the trees.

1953

THE PASSING OF ALPHEUS W. HALLIDAY
(A DECEMBER TALE)

E. B. WHITE

Old Mr. Halliday, year upon year,
Showed small zest for the season of cheer.
At Santa's name, at holly's mention,
He sank in coils of apprehension.
A selfish man in his way of living,
He had no talent for gifts and giving;
The Yule, with its jumble of thistles and figs,
Was a lonely time in his bachelor digs.
Shopping for mistletoe, tinsel, and tree,
Alpheus Halliday still could foresee
Sitting in solitude, feet by the fire,
Opening things that he didn't desire.

(He determines to correct this and give himself a walloping present.)

One grim noon, on his way to Saks,
Halliday halted, wheeled in his tracks,
Returned to the office, went up in the lift,
And ordered Miss Forbush wrapped as a gift.
Little Miss Forbush, out of Accounting,
Wrapped and sent (with his spirits mounting),
Sweet little Forbush, tidy and teeming,
Wreathed in the light of an old man's dreaming.

(She is delivered to his home by United Parcel Service and placed under the tree.)

When Halliday wakened on Christmas morn,
He felt at peace and as though reborn.
The window was frosted, the gray clouds drifting,
A heavenly light, and the soft snow sifting.
He shaved and dressed and descended the stair
To see if old Santa had really been there.
Joyous and eager, he knelt at the tree,
Untied the red ribbon, and set his gift free.
He smoothened Miss Forbush and straightened her hair,
Then settled himself in his favorite chair.
Breathless with happiness, Halliday saw
That his gift to himself was a gift without flaw,
And though it was patently fraught with symbols,
It wasn't a thing you could buy at Gimbel's.

(She was something, all right.)

All the long morning, under the tree,
She lay there as quiet as quiet could be,
And there was a quality quite serene
About this relaxed and irregular scene.
There was never a hint of play or tussle;
Neither one of them moved a muscle.

The room had a clarity, cool and nice,
As though the two figures were sculptured in ice.

(I wish I had a photograph of it.)

All the long morning, in grateful surmise,
Alpheus Halliday studied his prize.
He seemed to be tracing, in Forbush's trance,
Patterns of loveliness, strains of the dance;
He seemed to be dreaming and tending the fires
Of old and, I trust, imprecise desires.
He seemed to be seeking to capture again
Certain lost fragrances, woods after rain.

(Miss Forbush very sensibly turns into barley sugar.)

At noon, ere either one had stirred,
A timely miracle occurred:
In silence and with gentle grace
She shed her mortal carapace;
Her form, her face, her eyes, her hair
Were barley sugar now for fair,
And though it seem to you incredible,
Miss Forbush . . . well, was fully edible.

(Halliday is well known for his sweet tooth.)

Stiffly but hungrily, Halliday rose,
Picked up Miss Forbush, and sampled her toes.
Here was the answer to all his vague wishes:
Little Miss Forbush was simply delicious.
Anxious to linger, yet hot to devour,
He ate his way onward, hour after hour.
The window was frosted, the gray clouds drifting,
A heavenly light, and the soft snow sifting.
Just as he finished her brow and her hair,

Old Mr. Halliday died in his chair.
Too much free sugar and time that's been spended—
Halliday's life was most tranquilly ended.
Perfect his passing as sweet was his tooth,
He died from an overindulgence in youth.

(Let us not judge him too harshly in this season of mercy and forgiveness.)

1955

ALL'S NOËL THAT ENDS NOËL,

OR, INCOMPATIBILITY IS THE SPICE OF CHRISTMAS

OGDEN NASH

Do you know Mrs. Millard Fillmore Revere?
On her calendar, Christmas comes three hundred and sixty-five times a year.
Consider Mrs. Revere's Christmas spirit; no one can match it—
No, not Tiny Tim or big Bob Cratchit.
Even on December 26th it reveals no rifts;
She is already compiling her list of next year's gifts.
Her actions during the winter are conscientious and methodical,
Now snipping an advertisement from a newspaper, now clipping a coupon
    from a periodical.
In the spring she is occupied with mail-order catalogues from Racine and
    Provincetown and Richmond and Walla Walla,
Which offer a gallimaufry of gewgaws, gadgets, widgets, jiggers, trinkets,
    and baubles, postpaid for a dollar.
Midsummer evenings find her trudging home from clearance sales, balanc-
    ing parcel upon parcel,
With blithe heart and weary metatarsal.
Soon appear the rolls of garish paper and the spools of gaudy ribbon,
And to describe the decline and fall of Mr. Revere it would take the pen of
    a Gibbon.
Poor Mr. Revere—such harbingers of Christmas do not brighten him,

They simply frighten him.

He cringes like a timid hobo when a fierce dog raises its hackles at him;

Wherever he steps, ribbons wind around his ankles and paper crackles at him.

He feels himself threatened by Christmas on all fronts;

Shakespeare had Mr. Revere in mind when he wrote, "Cowards die many times before their deaths; The valiant never taste of death but once."

These are the progressively ominous hints of impending doom:

First, he is forbidden to open a certain drawer, then a certain closet, and, finally, a certain room.

If Mr. Revere looks slightly seedy as he goes his daily rounds

It's because his clean shirts and socks are now out of bounds.

Indeed, the only reason he gets by,

He remembers previous years and has provided himself with haberdashery he can drip and dry.

The days of September, October, November are like globules of water on the forehead of a tortured prisoner dropping;

Each is another day on which he has done no Christmas shopping.

At this point the Devil whispers that if he puts it off until Christmas Eve the shops will be emptier,

A thought than which nothing could be temptier,

But Christmas Eve finds him bedridden with a fever of nearly ninety-nine degrees, and swaddled in blankets up to his neck,

So on Christmas morn he has nothing for Mrs. Revere but a kiss and a check,

Which somehow works out fine, because she enjoys being kissed

And the check is a great comfort when she sits down on December 26th to compile her next year's list.   1957

"Miss Harwood, please see to it that the halls are decked."

SAINT NICHOLAS,

MARIANNE MOORE

might I, if you can find it, be given
a chameleon with tail
that curls like a watch spring; and vertical
on the body—including the face—pale
  tiger-stripes, about seven
    (the melanin in the skin
  having been shaded from the sun by thin
    bars; the spinal dome
      beaded along the ridge
    as if it were platinum)?*

If you can find no striped chameleon,
might I have a dress or suit—
I guess you have heard of it—of *qiviut?*
And, to wear with it, a taslon shirt, the drip-dry fruit
  of research second to none,
    sewn, I hope, by Excello,
    as for buttons to keep down the collar-points, no.
      The shirt could be white—
        and be "worn before six,"
      either in daylight or at night.

But don't give me, if I can't have the dress,
a trip to Greenland, or grim
trip to the moon. The moon should come here. Let him
make the trip down, spread on my dark floor some dim
  marvel, and if a success
    that I stoop to pick up and wear,
    I could ask nothing more. A thing yet more rare,

*Pictured in *Life,* September 15, 1958, with a letter from Dr. Doris M. Cochran, Curator of Reptiles and Amphibians, National Museum, Washington, D.C.

though, and different,
        would be this: Hans von Marées'
St. Hubert, kneeling with head bent,

    form erect—in velvet, tense with restraint—
hand hanging down; the horse, free.
Not the original, of course. Give me
a postcard of the scene—huntsman and divinity—
    hunt-mad Hubert startled into a saint
        by a stag with a Figure entined.
        But why tell you what you must have divined?
        Saint Nicholas, O Santa Claus,
            would it not be the most
        prized gift that ever was!

1958

THE MAGUS

JAMES DICKEY

It is time for the others to come.
This child is no more than a god.

No cars are moving this night.
The lights in the houses go out.

I put these out with the rest.
From his crib, the child begins

To shine, letting forth one ray
Through the twelve simple bars of his bed

Down into the trees, where two
Long-lost other men shall be drawn

Slowly up to the brink of the house,
Slowly in through the breath on the window.

But how did I get in this room?
Is this my son, or another's?

Where is the woman to tell me
How my face is lit up by his body?

It is time for the others to come.
An event more miraculous yet

Is the thing I am shining to tell you.
This child is no more than a child.

1960

THE CHRISTMAS CACTUS

L. M. ROSENBERG

All during the Christmas rush
I waited for the thing to come alive.
Eyed it while I gift-wrapped scarves,
withered it with scorn as I threw
the green and silver bundles under the tree.
By New Year's
I vowed to be happy
living with just stems.

Then one day in February,
the worst month of the year—
making up in misery what it lacks in length—
the blooms shot out,
three ragged cerise bells that rang

their tardy hallelujahs on the sill.
Late bloomers,
like the girls that shine
and shine at long last
at the spring dance
from their corner of the gym.

1981

ICICLES

ROBERT PINSKY

A brilliant beard of ice
Hangs from the edge of the roof
Harsh and heavy as glass.
The spikes a child breaks off

Taste of wool and the sun.
In the house, some straw for a bed,
Circled by a little train,
Is the tiny image of God.

The sky is fiery blue,
And a fiery morning light
Burns on the fresh deep snow:
Not one track in the street.

Just as the carols tell
Everything is calm and bright:
The town lying still,
The street cold and white.

Is only one child awake,
Breaking the crystal chimes?—
Knocking them down with a stick,
Leaving the broken stems.

1983

CHRISTMAS IN QATAR

CALVIN TRILLIN

(A new holiday classic, for those tiring of "White Christmas" and "Jingle Bells")

VERSE:
The shopping starts, and every store's a zoo.
I'm frantic, too: I haven't got a clue
Of what to get for Dad, who's got no hobby,
Or why Aunt Jane, who's shaped like a kohlrabi,
Wants frilly sweater sets, or where I'll find
A tie my loudmouthed Uncle Jack won't mind.
A shopper's told it's vital he prevails:
Prosperity depends on Christmas sales.
"Can't stop to talk," I say. "No time. Can't halt.
Economy could fail. Would be my fault."

CHORUS:
I'd like to spend next Christmas in Qatar,
Or someplace else that Santa won't find handy.
Qatar will do, although, Lord knows, it's sandy.
I need to get to someplace pretty far.
I'd like to spend next Christmas in Qatar.

VERSE:
Young Cousin Ned, his presents on his knees,
Says Christmas wrappings are a waste of trees.
Dad's staring, vaguely puzzled, at his gift.
And Uncle Jack, to give us all a lift,
Now tells a Polish joke he heard at work.
So Ned calls Jack a bigot and a jerk.
Aunt Jane, who knows that's true, breaks down and cries.
Then Mom comes out to help, and burns the pies.
Of course, Jack hates the tie. He'll take it back.
That's fair, because I hate my Uncle Jack.

CHORUS:

I'd like to spend next Christmas in Tibet,
Or any place where folks cannot remember
That there is something special in December.
Tibet's about as far as you can get.
I'd like to spend next Christmas in Tibet.

VERSE:

Mom's turkey is a patriotic riddle:
It's red and white, plus bluish in the middle.
The blue's because the oven heat's not stable.
The red's from ketchup Dad snuck to the table.
Dad says he loves the eyeglass stand from me—
Unless a sock rack's what it's meant to be.
"A free-range turkey's best," Ned says. "It's pure."
"This hippie stuff," Jack says, "I can't endure."
They say goodbye, thank God. It's been a strain.
At least Jack's tie has got a ketchup stain.

CHORUS:

I'd like to spend next Christmas in Rangoon,
Or any place where Christmas is as noisy
As Buddhist holidays might be in Boise.
I long to hear Der Bingle smoothly croon,
"I'm dreaming of a Christmas in Rangoon"—
Or someplace you won't hear the Christmas story,
And reindeer's something eaten cacciatore.
I know things can't go on the way they are.
I'd like to spend next Christmas in Qatar.

1994

TREE WITH ORNAMENTS BY MY MOTHER

ELIZABETH MACKLIN

It could be a wintering bear this year,
long furred & yet unclassified fat fir, rearing
uncrouched by the couch, a bear cub, my first—
a Douglas?—first ever long-needle pine & name unknown.

So thickly fern-broom-, borzoi- or yak-feathered,
whisks under eaves, that ornaments disappear:
the forest of branches has made an interior,
all of her ornaments inside in, and not shown.

But let them try to remain hidden: glass-bird
light paint glows like a house in the woods at four,
snowbound-warm and excited given. It hides this year
but desires to be seen—makes no grief—to be spoken.

This year's tree makes its scent felt across the yards
in between; the past at last has remade the present. *Hark
not to the shining idols* but to their singular deity, inward
invisible bird fir fragrance, who says they could even be broken.

1999

25.XII.1993

JOSEPH BRODSKY

For a miracle, take one shepherd's sheepskin, throw
In a pinch of now, a grain of long ago,
And a handful of tomorrow. Add by eye
A little bit of ground, a piece of sky,

And it will happen. For miracles, gravitating
To earth, know just where people will be waiting,
And eagerly will find the right address
And tenant, even in a wilderness.

Or, if you're leaving home, switch on a new
Four-pointed star in Heaven as you do,
To light a vacant world with steady blaze
And follow you forever with its gaze.

(Translated, from the Russian, by Richard Wilbur)

1999

NATIVITY POEM

JOSEPH BRODSKY

Imagine striking a match that night in the cave:
Imagine crockery, try to make use of its glaze
To feel cold cracks in the floor, the blankness of hunger.
Imagine the desert—but the desert is everywhere.

Imagine striking a match in that midnight cave,
The fire, the farm beasts in outline, the farm tools and stuff;
And imagine, as you towel your face in enveloping folds,
Mary, Joseph, and the Infant in swaddling clothes.

·alphonse normandia

Imagine the kings, the caravans' stilted procession
As they make for the cave, or, rather, three beams closing in
And in on the star; the creaking of loads, the clink of a cowbell;
(No thronging of Heaven as yet, no peal of the bell

That will ring in the end for the Infant once he has earned it).
Imagine the Lord, for the first time, from darkness, and stranded
Immensely in distance, recognizing Himself in the Son
Of Man: His homelessness plain to him now in a homeless one.

(Translated, from the Russian, by Seamus Heaney)
2000

FLIGHT TO EGYPT

JOSEPH BRODSKY

Inside the cave (an off-plumb dugout,
But a roof above their heads, for all that),
Inside the cave the three felt close
In the fug of fodder and old clothes.

Straw for bedding. Beyond the door,
Blizzard, sandstorm, howling air.
Mule rubbed ox; they stirred and groaned
Like sand and snowflake scourged in wind.

Mary prays; the fire soughs;
Joseph frowns into the blaze.
Too small to be fit to do a thing
But sleep, the Infant is just sleeping.

Relief for now. They've gained a day:
Herod off his head, his army
Outwitted but still closing in,
And the centuries also, one by one.

That night, as three, they were at peace.
Smoke like a shy retiring guest
Slipped out the door. There was one far-off
Heavy sigh from the mule. Or the ox.

The star looked in across the threshold.
The only one of them who could
Know what its fervent staring meant
Was the Infant. But He was *infans*, silent.

(Translated, from the Russian, by Seamus Heaney)

2000

GREETINGS, FRIENDS!

FRANK SULLIVAN

It may be argued, and with some reason,
That we could skip this Christmas season,
There being no great cause for mirth
And precious little peace on earth.
Not me. I'm sorry, but I'll keep Yule
With any kindred spirit who'll
Accompany me in a Christmas caper,
So how's about it, Muriel Draper?

I'll keep Christmas until hell freezes
With Joan Blondell and Royal Cortissoz,
Franchot Tone and Justice Stone,
And Mr. and Mrs. Joseph Cohn;
With Howard, Ruth, and Peter Moody,
Surrogate George O. Tuck and Trudy,
Morris Bishop, Sam Byrd,
Donald Duck and Mortimer Snerd.
Though Bethlehem's star's eclipsed by Mars,
My glass is clinking with Bert Lahr's;
Though good old Civ is on the brink,
I'll take a chance and lift a drink
To General Gamelin of France,
To Justice Hughes and Vivian Vance,
Ed Wynn, Billy Conn,
Caesar Bozzo, Thomas Mann,
The Ward Cheneys, Irene Dunne,
And all the boys at Twenty-One,
The Bradfords, Mary Rose and Roark,
And the friendly Ganymedes at the Stork,
June Walker, Joe Kerrigan,
George Ritchie, Tom Berrigan,
Bob Davidson and Marietta,
The Carl Van Dorens and Papa Moneta.
I drink a wassail to Dave Cort,
To Lida Thomas and Viscount Gort,
Raymond Parker, Winston Churchill,
Charlie Merz and Freddie Birchall,
Senator Hattie Caraway,
Premier Ed Daladier,
Lester Cuddihy, Zorina,
Leopold and Wilhelmina.
Pardon the proud alumnal beam
I cast upon the Big Red Team,
The rootin', tootin' mass Blitzkrieg
That flattened out the Ivy League;
Oh, far above Cayuga's waters,

With its waves of H_2O,
Cornell's sons and Cornell's daughters
Have a perfect right to crow!
Here's to Tony Canzoneri,
Tom Chalmers, Daise Terry,
Sam Forrest, Georges Enesco,
Mario Castelnuovo-Tedesco!
The world's a vast Pandora's box,
But I still have faith in Fontaine Fox,
In Sophie Kerr and David Niven,
The *New Republic* and Bruce Bliven,
Edward Johnson and the Met,
The Gibbses, Arthur and Jeannette,
Mrs. Caroline O'Day,
Ruth Gordon, Alice Faye,
Frank Buck and M. K. Gandhi,
Dan Parker, Baby Sandy,
Louis Sobol, Grantland Rice,
Father Cashin and Garrett Price,
Don Stewart, Harriette Finch,
Parker Merrow and Walter the Winch,
Ernest Lindley, Gertrude Macy,
Leggett Brown and Spencer Tracy.
Give out some Christmas propaganda
For Veloz and his pal Yolanda,
For Johnny Cheever and Wickham Steed,
McKinlay Kantor, Senator Mead,
The John Roys, Don Beddoe,
The McIntoshes, Blanche and Neddo,
Dorothy Stickney, Miriam Doyle,
Rebecca West, Selena Royle,
John Hadfield of J. M. Dent,
Paul Robeson and Silas Bent.
God rest the G. O. Pachyderm,
But give us Frank for another term!
Thus having disposed of politics,
I clasp to my arms the Sheldon Dicks.

~~~

Assuming a more surly vein,
Let's wish a whacking Yule chilblain
To Father Coughlin, the clerical wowser,
And every other rabble-rouser.
And then, in doggerel-cum-verse,
Let's launch a hearty Christmas curse
On the Nazi-minded everywhere,
Whether here or over there;
In our midst or oversea,
All Kuhns look alike to me.
So raise your mugs and drink distress
To Rosenberg and Rudolf Hess;
Dismay to Comrade Molotoff—
For Czar: Prince Michael Romanoff!
Here's hoping something dire may happen
To Goebbels, Himmler, and von Papen,
To Göring and von Dribblepuss,
And their whilom sidekick, Benny the Muss!
Wise Men who are really wise
Will keep one eye upon the skies,
For the Holy Night is rent by bomb
As Ouija reads the Führer's palm.
Lebensraum he wants? So! Well,
Let's hope he gets it soon, in hell.
And his Kremlin crony, Joe the Tricky—
Give him a Finn, but make it a Mickey!
Of all these knaves we crave surcease;
What this world needs is a good Blitzpeace.

1939

GREETINGS, FRIENDS!

FRANK SULLIVAN

The début of this Christmas stanza,
This annual Yule extravaganza,
Took place in 1932,
So silver greetings, friends, to you,
And frankincense and myrrh and nard
From your aging but still frisky bard.

For Ike, three rousing Christmas cheers
And vigor through the coming years.
A New Year bow to Borden Deal,
Edith McCarty, and Howard Keel.
We'll roar out a couple of gladsome staves
To whoop it up for the doughty Braves,
And hymn the glory of Fortune's Pet—
Who else but Selva Lewis Burdette?
Charge your glasses and drink to the health
Of Good Queen Bess and her Commonwealth!
Nab the nearest Christmas mummer;
Get him to mum for Christopher Plummer,
And do his stuff for Dick Surrette,
Romney Brent, Carol Burnett,
Ruth Anderson, Niels Bohr,
Ted Atkinson, and Senator Gore.
Minnesingers, sound your A!
Launch a paean for Dorothy Day,
For Ed Wynn, Carmel Quinn,
Ellin Berlin, and all their kin;
And add a toast to all the kith
Of Master Joseph Michael Smith.
Noël, Noël to Coco Chanel,
Hunt Bradley, Maria Schell,
And a bend of the knee from this genuflector
To Captain and Mrs. William Waechter.
Peace to thee, O Matt McDade!
Joy to Banker Katie McQuade!
Minstrels, raise a stout hosanna
For Herbert Erb and Charlie Manna;
Sing noisily, yet civilly,
For Saul Bellow of Tivoli;
And belt out a carol for Buff Donelli,
For George Hemstead and his consort, Ellie,
For Polly Hanson, Frank Lary,
And the *Atlantic*, on its centenary.
Buon Natale, Carmen Basilio!

Long may you champ it, *mio figlio!*
Nancy Walker! Jane Morgan!
Love from me and Paul Horgan!
Peace to tycoon Cyrus Eaton,
Cantinflas, and Cecil Beaton!
Wassail to Borough President Cashmore,
Arkansas Editor Harry Ashmore,
And a genial, cozy, cricket-on-the-hearthy
Kind of Yule for Kevin McCarthy.
Tootle an anthem for Conrad Janis,
Edmund Gilligan, and Marya Mannes;
Trill a Christmas obbligato
To serenade Jockey Frank Lovato;
And sound the rebeck and the hautboy
For that old reliable rider No Boy.
Sing tooraloo for Shirley MacLaine;
Sing hi-de-ho for John Ruane,
Terry Brennan, Eddie De Hass,
Lester Pearson, and Peggy Cass.
Vintner, spike the Christmas brew
For Stork Sanford and the Cornell crew;
Pass the port to Ezra Benson,
Harold Craig, and May Swenson.
We'll dance the lancers with Jo Van Fleet,
Gargle a brandy with Cabell Greet,
And with seasonal zeal we'll ululate
For Pauline Sadlon, Sam Slate,
Percy Waram, Jane Greer,
And Altrincham, the Prickly Peer.
We'll sing in praise of Nigel Dennis;
We'll ascertain where Leo Penn is,
And crack a bottle of rare champagne
For Leo, and for Eddie Lane.
Thomas Chalmers, of Firenze—
Love from me and Gisele MacKenzie!
Gerald, Constance, and Archie Moore—
Love to you from Charlie Poore!

Bake a Christmas cake for Quincy Porter;
Send a Christmas tie to Enos Slaughter;
Send opulent gifts to Anthony Quayle
And a Broun by the name of Heywood Hale.
Choir, please warble a New Year glee
For André Laguerre and Nathalie,
And lift your voices in sweet accord
To gladden the spirits of Benson Ford.
A Merry Christmas to Dorothy Quick,
To Connie B. Gay, of Lizard Lick,
And the dolciest kind of *far niente*
To Bambi Linn and Tony Parenti.
Now let us sit with Rudolf Bing
And tell glad stories of Nicholas King,
And raise a glass of vintage hock
To the *Herald Trib* and Ambassador Jock.
We'll paint the town with Frank Lloyd Wright
From New Year's Eve until Twelfth Night;
We'll go on a high old Yule carouse
With Kathy Crosby and her spouse,
With Sterling North and Anthony West
And Gerald Green and Denzil Best.

~~~

The year is going. Let it go.
It hasn't brought us much but woe—
Khrushchev, Faubus, flu, and frights,
Inflation, Nasser, satellites,
And other plagues from Pandora's box.
But are we therefore on the rocks?
Not so, my hearties! With cautious tread
We'll enter the year that lies ahead,
Not elated, not downcast,
Glad to be rid of the year that's past,
Hoping the coming year of grace
Will bring Peace on Earth and Peace in Space.

1957

GREETINGS, FRIENDS!

ROGER ANGELL

Rap, rap! To order! May we dispense
With last year's minutes, whose trifling sense
Proposed immediate end to woe
And a party neath the mistletoe—
A plan I trust will bear repeating
At this, our latest Yuletide meeting?
Faithful readers, God rest you well
And give you each a sweet Noël.
Who knows? Perhaps the muse will send a
Hug to *you* in our agenda;
Would there were rhymes enough for all
Within this dogged caterwaul!
Karol Wojtyla! Well, that's a rhyme
We won't hunt up this Christmastime,
Now that there is hardly call to—
Happy Christmas, Pope John Paul II!
And happy hols, dear Claudia Weill,
Cornell MacNeil, and Kitty Carlisle.
Season's greetings, Allegra Kent!
Hail to Jimmy, our President!
Wassail to Rosalynn, the President's spouse,
And Fred Astaire and Timothy Crouse!
Ring out, carillons, for the sake
Of Carmine Peppe and Eubie Blake,
Then chime in a more dulcet strain
For lovely Queen Noor al-Hussein;
Now let some joyous bongs be heard
For Justice Rose Elizabeth Bird,
And next a brassy triple bob
For Alydar and Rusty Staub,
And then tack on a cheerful coda
For Cyrus Vance and Ron Swoboda!

I wish a Yule right out of Boz
For Henny Youngman and Amos Oz;
Let Fezziwigian bliss befall
Tito Gaona and Tom T. Hall.
May Christmas Eve be brisk and snowy
For Heinrich Böll and David Bowie,
And the morn break all crisp and tingly
For Swoosie Kurtz and Darryl Stingley;
And may the Day itself go gladly
For Sen.-elect and Ms. Bill Bradley!
Hello, Santa? Hold that sleigh!
I have some toys for Nora Kaye,
Valerie Harper, Jerry Rafshoon,
And our man in Moscow, Malcolm Toon.
Hello, Bekins? Will you cart in
Crates of presents for Ned Martin,
Zubin Mehta, Sissela Bok,
Samuel Beckett, and Pete LaCock?
I'm here to state that naught can alter
My deep esteem for Stephanie Salter;
I want it known that what I harbor
Are friendly thoughts for Myron Farber,
Ellsworth Kelly, Nick Nolte,
George Balanchine, and Sir Georg Solti.
Adeste, shoppers! Let costs go hang!
Let's do up Christmas with a bang!
To arms against Old Man Inflation!
We'll spend with more imagination
And seek out true epiphanies
At Bloomingdale's and Tiffany's
With lavish gifts for Crystal Gayle,
Günter Grass, and Clamma Dale.
Come, seed a storm of Christmas bills
With things to cheer up Garry Wills,
Walter Matthau, Kathleen Raine,
Viktor Korchnoi, and Frank MacShane!
With friends like these, there's no tomorrow;

Twixt shop and bank we'll spend and borrow,
Get stocking toys by Fabergé
For Cheryl Tiegs and Jack Macrae,
Find diamonds like the Koh-i-noor
For Gemma Jones and Melba Moore,
And a nice blue Maserati
For Yale's A. Bartlett Giamatti.
Then quickly we'll snap up a set
Of Lalique bowls at Parke Bernet
For Andrew Young, Paloma Picasso,
Hildegard Behrens, and Ella Grasso,
And a golden trinket by Cellini
To please Maurizio Pollini;
Then cases of some modest wine
(Like Château Margaux '29)
For John Belushi, Seymour Krim,
Laz Barrera, Barbara Pym,
Governor Carey, Claiborne Pell,
Nancy Teeters, and Tom Carvel!
On New Year's Eve, we'll share a schnapps
With the Martin Mulls and the Joseph Papps,
Then sip a delicious *crème de moka*
With Meat Loaf and Lee Iacocca;
We'll crack a bottle of muscatel
With Wolfman Jack and Quentin Bell,
And clink a glass of *vin du pays*
With D. D. Lewis and I. M. Pei;
We'll quaff some cups of antifreeze
With Janet Guthrie and Parton Keese,
And toss off a brandy smash
With Louise Bourgeois and Johnny Cash.
Nancy Kassebaum, Bernadine Morris,
Will ye nae sup a wee doch-an-dorris?
Well supped, ladies! Now gie us a glee
For Anwar Sadat and Muhammad Ali!
A toast to Tsenator Paul E. Tsongas!
A toast to the whole damn U.S. Congras!

To Truth and Beauty! To Helen Reddy!
To the next Prime Rate and Crazy Eddie!

~~~

Good friends, we've come to our envoi,
Which bids you each a year of joy,
And invokes, to close these greetings,
The spirit of Camp David's meetings—
Peace to us all, that is to say,
Upon this ancient holiday!

1978

GREETINGS, FRIENDS!

ROGER ANGELL

Good reader, ho, it's me once more,
Your careworn super at the door,
With mop in hand and heated face:
The *work* I do around this place—
Sweep out the bygone Christmastimes,
Unkink the twisted lights and rhymes,
Dig out the trusty metaphors,
Re-Fezziwig the chimes and floors,
And make this joint look nearly new
For partyings (though déjà vu)
With friends and neighbors we wish well
On the occasion of Noël.
No tip! My pleasure! Let's begin
With hugs for Ursula K. Le Guin.
Fellow-creatures, near or far,
We hail you each, and Caleb Carr.
How neat it is to be the bearer
Of greetings for our friend Jim Lehrer;
Happy days, Hideo Nomo,

Sheryl Crow, and Andrew Cuomo.
Ah, there, Dr. Rudy Crew,
David Hare, Elisabeth Shue—
Peace, you chaps, and also pax on
Miranda Weese, Samuel L. Jackson,
Ivan Klíma, and (though sadly)
Departing Senators Nunn and Bradley.
Warm wishes from this august bureau
To Kazuo Ishiguro;
The same to you, Tegla Loroupe,
Joanna Trollope, and Quincy Troupe.
Let blessings rain, all touchy-feely,
To cheer up Hurricane McNeeley,
And laurel leaves in heaps or layers
Around Cal Ripken, prince of stayers;
And with him Tim Biakabutuka,
Young Marzoratis (Guy and Luca),
Jon Bon Jovi, Susan Lucci,
Jenny Jones, and Leo Nucci.
Descend, bright angels, in a band,
Upon Viswanathan Anand,
With Christmas music just for him
And Jane Smiley and Mary Grimm.
Tweet the flute and sound the oboe
For Dr. Ruth, Rebecca Lobo,
Joseph Volpe, Jose Mesa,
Joan Chen, and Mother Teresa,
All whilst some higher heralds—hark!—
Let drop their chords on Marcia Clark.
And carols (or enhanced CDs)
For Jeanne Calment and Morris Dees,
Daw Aung San Suu Kyi, the brave Nobelist,
And Yo Yo Ma, cherubic cellist.
Come Christmas, gang, it's understood,
We rollerblade the neighborhood—
Arm-in-arming, happy campers

Bearing toys or laden hampers.
Here a wreath and there a parcel,
Now a fractured metatarsal!
Backward! Sidewise! What can match it?
Each of us a flying Cratchit
Spreading gifts and some dismay
Among our friends this special day.
Bill Gates (*Wie geht's?*), strap on your skates
And we'll go sweep up Kathy Bates,
Julie Just, Andie MacDowell,
David Bouley, and Alma Powell.
Without ado, without a care,
We'll grab the hand of Deirdre Bair
And chain along in cheerful flow
To drop a toy on Coolio,
A negligee for (yay) Fay Wray,
Some tricks from Schwarz for Ricky Jay,
Plus geese to grace the groaning board
Of Geoffrey Becne or Geoffrey Ward,
Unless, by luscious scents beguiled,
We press a call on Julia Child—
Though pausing first to just say hi
To B. B. King, R. B. Kitaj,
Isaac Mizrahi, Sharon Stone,
Fiona Shaw, and John Malone.
Home from these amusing labors,
We'll bask in asked-in Labs and neighbors
And, circled round by lights and kith,
Toss down a warming noggin with
Lauren Holly, Beverly Cleary,
Christopher Reeve, and Timothy Leary.
Then party on in larger units
Around the tree with Stanley Kunitz,
Mo Vaughn and Mira Sorvino,
Daniel Okrent, Dan Marino,
Jimmy Smits, Lois Smith Brady,
Ridley Scott, and Scott O'Grady.

To fling the old year's glooms away,
We'll bring in Penny Hardaway,
King Hussein, and Suzanne Farrell,
Cigar, Pixar, and Crate & Barrel,
Each Met and Jet, Rockette, et cet.,
And da Guarneri String Quartet!

~~~

The clock's run down, our verse is done:
A happy New Year, everyone!
Rhymees, readers (gentle allsome!)—
Pals, we pine for you and balsam
At Christmastide and through the fleeting
Hours until our next year's meeting.
Till then, old friends, what we beseech
Is peace and blessings, all and each.

1995